THE CHAMPA FLOWERS

Ivorson in Laos

A Novel

By

Alan Melton

ISBN: 1453802215
ISBN-13: 9781453802212

Dedicated to the Sterns,
The Virginias, and the
Flying Squad.

Linguistic Note

Vietnamese family names come first, given names last. The middle names are simply sex indicators, "van" for men, "thi" (pronounced "tea") for women. There are only a handful of family names in Vietnam, of which the most common is Nguyen (pronounced "Ngwen"). Given names are therefore used for purposes of identification, e.g. Nguyen van Huu would be simply called Huu (pronounced "who"). Nga, Ly and Cao are all pronounced roughly as they would be in English.

Historical Note

In early 1968, the United States was at war in Southeast Asia. In South Viet Nam, American soldiers and Marines, supported by Air Force and Navy air power, were locked in combat with the Viet Cong, who had staged a massive surprise offensive. No war in history had ever been conducted more in the public view. Each day's battles were reported by a horde of reporters and TV cameramen from every corner of the earth.

In the neighboring Kingdom of Laos, despite the neutrality officially guaranteed to it by the 1954 Geneva Accords, the same war was being waged. There were, however, two big differences between the battle fields. The first was, in Laos here were only a handful of Americans involved, and they weren't in uniform. The North Vietnamese and their puppets, the Pathet Lao, in spite of their easy victories over the Royal Lao Army, were harried, ambushed, and denied access to the fertile rice fields and cities of the Mekong River valley by an army composed of assorted hill tribesmen, raised, trained, and led by paramilitary officers of the American CIA.

The second difference was that, albeit just as vicious and bloody as the war in Vietnam, no one outside Laos knew it was going on. There were no reporters or TV crews. By tacit mutual consent of the parties, it was a war conducted in the shadows.

The war in Laos was not confined to the mountains up-country. It was waged as well in the sleepy Lao capital of Vientiane, where the North Vietnamese and U.S. embassies were separated by less than two miles of ramshackle French colonial architecture.

This city war was fought more with cunning and subversion than with overt bloodshed, and only occasionally did the smell of burnt gunpowder blend with the reek of the open sewers and the delicious aroma of the champa flowers.

Prologue

Vientiane, Laos, 4 February 1968

It had been an hour since Huu killed the traitor, after shoving a rag in his mouth to muffle his screams. The traitor's American master, however, did not yet know that his spy was dead, and soon would arrive for a meeting with him. When the Yankee came, he would die, as well.

It was dark on the dirt road and even darker in the copse of vegetation where the road bent sharply to the south. Huu cupped his cigarette in his hands so that it wouldn't give away his position under the branches of the wild mango trees, and he squinted through its glow toward the distant lights of the bars and brothels of Dong Palan quarter. Nothing was moving on the road yet.

He felt along the branch of the tree beside him until he found the thin steel cable he had looped over it. The cable snaked away down the trunk of the mango tree, through the undergrowth and across the dusty road to the tree on the other side where it was secured.

Huu shivered in the night air. The cool season had lasted long this year. The frogs in the ditches and ponds were silent, and even the mosquitoes were torpid. Only one or two had buzzed in his ear since he took his position.

He scolded himself for letting the cold affect him. A little cold was nothing to a soldier awaiting battle. Even as Huu waited here, his country's soldiers were killing other Americans across the length and breadth of South Vietnam. The great Tet offensive was under way. Many cities had been taken. The Saigon puppet regime was on the brink of collapse.

Huu felt that he, also, was contributing to that great offensive tonight, here in feudal, backward Laos, five hundred miles from Saigon. The CIA officer he was waiting for had recruited a trusted local cadre—the traitor whose throat Huu had just cut—to plant a listening device in the electrical system of Huu's embassy. That was an act of war against his homeland.

As senior intelligence officer of the North Vietnamese Embassy in Vientiane, it was Huu's duty to defend it against such aggression, and tonight he was doing do just that.

Further, killing this American would not only fulfill Huu's duty, but be a source of profound personal satisfaction as well. If he lived to be a hundred, he would never forget the humiliation of having to admit to the Ambassador that one of his hand-picked cadre had been corrupted by the dollars of the neo-colonialists. The memory produced a sour taste in his mouth.

A slender beam of light appeared at the edge of the built-up area, a kilometer away. Huu stiffened in anticipation. He checked his watch in the light of the cigarette's glow. The timing was right, and it was the headlight of a motorcycle. Was it the American? He would know soon. He threw down the cigarette and stubbed it out under his sandal.

The headlight approached, moving at a brisk pace, its beam bouncing up and down over the hard, lateritic surface of the road. It was less than five hundred meters away now. In a moment, it would pass the observation post where his deputy, Phuong, was hiding. Huu felt his breathing quicken.

He felt excitement rise within himself and sternly repressed it. An experienced soldier of the Revolution should have more self-control. He was not a schoolboy. He had killed before.

He could hear the engine of the motorcycle now. He listened to it intently. There was a sharp bend in the road just before it reached Huu's position, and it was just on Huu's side of the bend that he had stationed Phuong, to make sure it was indeed the American. He reached out for the dangling end of the steel cable, found it, and wound it around his right hand. He balanced himself on his feet. He was ready.

The sound of the engine grew louder. The loom of the headlight appeared, casting long shadows on the vegetation across the road. The light grew brighter. Huu's muscles tensed.

Ah! There was the signal. Two short flashes from Phuong's flashlight. It was the American. Phuong had recognized him as he passed by. Huu hauled down on his end of the cable. It rose up out of the dust of the road, as taut as a bow-string. He looped his end of it quickly around the stub of the branch he had broken off, pulled it tight, and hung on with all his might.

The headlight of the motorcycle began turning back in Huu's direction. Would the Yankee see the cable? Huu held his breath. The machine came around the bend and began accelerating again. It roared toward Huu, the light of its headlamp dancing on the dusty road.

As it drew abreast of him, the cable bucked in Huu's hands. He heard a twang, and a grunt. The driver flew backward off his seat. The front end of the motorcycle reared into the air like a bee-stung horse, then crashed to the ground.

Huu hastily disengaged his hand from the cable. Keeping his eyes focused on the motionless figure on the road, he felt around the base of the tree for the large stone he had placed there. He picked it up, ran out on to the road, and knelt beside the prostrate westerner.

He raised the stone to strike, then slowly lowered it again. The American's head sagged from his shoulders at a grotesque angle. The wire had broken his neck. The rock would not be needed. Huu left the dead man and hastened exultantly across the road to unfasten the other end of the cable.

He felt good. The Embassy was secure again. His dishonor was avenged, and if the Americans were foolish enough to send a replacement for this dead serpent, Huu would kill him, too.

Chapter One

Ivorson took one last look up and down the dusty lane. He saw no one, so, suitcase in hand, he climbed the steps to the front porch of the yellow stuccoed bungalow and knocked on the door. The shade of the porch was welcome after his long walk from the main road where he'd left the taxi.

He heard steps inside the house. The door opened a crack, and a cool gray eye examined him for a moment before the door opened wide. The owner of the gray eyes held out a hand. "Welcome to Laos, Ivorson. Glad you're here."

Ivorson assessed the Chief of Station, Ventiane. Terence Riley was a slender, sandy-haired man in his late forties. Ivorson knew him only by his reputation, which was that of an ambitious sonofabitch. That didn't bother Ivorson. He'd worked for tough Station chiefs before.

Riley locked the door behind them and led the way to the chairs. The safe house, on a side street off Wattay Road, was virtually unfurnished; there were just the three straight–backed chairs, a card table in the living room, and a refrigerator and some glasses in the kitchen. A window air conditioner, set in the wall, groaned inefficiently at the task of cooling them.

Riley sat down, shoved a bottle of Coke across the card table at Ivorson and said, "Pardon the lack of amenities." His gray eyes never strayed from Ivorson's face. Ivorson wondered if that was something he did to impress newcomers. If so, it didn't work on Ivorson.

"Have you checked in with USAID?" Riley asked him. The reference was to the United States Agency for International Development, which had a large presence in Laos, and which was Ivorson's cover organization.

"No," Ivorson answered, "I wanted to talk with you first. My USAID/Vietnam orders say I'm assigned to USAID/Laos/supply. I can't live that cover. I don't know a damn thing about supply."

"No problem," Riley assured him. "The supply assignment lets you office with our technical officer in the compound warehouse, where there's a secure phone link to me at the Embassy, and it'll keep you away from our other officers. You won't have any actual cover duties to perform, so you don't have to worry about fooling the genuine USAID types and local-hires.

"The USAID Director didn't like the idea," Riley added, "but I had to assume that our normal USAID cover is compromised, so I got the Ambassador to overrule him. I hope he doesn't take it out on you."

An uneasy feeling began crawling along Ivorson's gut. Why did Riley have to assume that the normal USAID cover was comprised, and why did Ivorson have to keep away from the other Station officers in the compound?

When COS/Saigon asked him if he'd take a transfer to Laos, the reason given was that a Vientiane Station officer had been killed in a traffic accident and he needed an experienced Vietnam operations officer, fast. Ivorson had jumped at it, grateful for the chance to leave Vietnam with his reputation intact.

"Has something happened to our USAID cover?" he asked warily.

"I need to fill you in on that," said Riley. He fished out a cigarette and seemed to be deliberating his next words. When they came, however, there was nothing equivocal about them.

"The wreck that killed Jim Reagan—-your predecessor--was not an accident," he said flatly. "Jim was snatched off his motorcycle on his way to an agent meeting, by a wire stretched across the road."

An ugly copper taste leaped into Ivorson's mouth. He swallowed to get rid of it and then asked, "Who did it?"

COS looked grim. "The agent Jim was going to meet was a local Vietnamese electrician, ostensibly a northern sympathizer, who had finally got access to do some re-wiring at the North Vietnamese Embassy. They must have caught on."

God damn, thought Ivorson viciously. Why hadn't he been briefed on this before he accepted the job? "Was the agent a double?"

"Maybe," Riley answered bleakly, "but maybe not. He's vanished. They could have tortured Jim's identity out of him, or maybe Jim's cover was blown some other way. That's why I went to war with the USAID Director to get you into a cover slot we'd never used before. I didn't want you contaminated."

Ivorson's stomach twisted into a solid lump. Someone at the North Vietnamese Embassy had murdered his predecessor, and now Ivorson was expected to pick up his cases, in isolation from the Station, in an unfamiliar town, and without the local language or knowledge of the operational situation.

He wasn't at all sure he could handle that. The memory of what happened to him during Tet was still as fresh as if it had been last night: the crash of the apartment door breaking in, him confused, fearful, awakening and groping for the gun beside the bed; the shadowy shapes of the intruders; his frantic pumping of the action of the riot gun until the hammer clicked on empty, with the door, the wall and his attackers all disintegrating as the heavy buckshot loads tore through them.

Ever since that night, the Fear had been inside him. It was a palpable, spreading cancer, whose tentacles displaced reason and courage and made every minute on the street a nightmare. It had robbed Ivorson of his ability to function.

COS/Saigon knew he had It. He'd alluded to It when he offered Ivorson the Vientiane assignment, saying that Ivorson needed to spend some time in a safer environment. Safer environment! That description was laughable in the circumstances Riley had just described to him, only Ivorson didn't feel like laughing.

Riley must have seen at least some of his feelings. "Wondering why I didn't let you into this picture before you came here?" he asked.

Ivorson nodded emphatically. He damn sure was.

"Simple," said Riley. "I didn't want to give you an excuse to refuse the assignment."

Red anger bubbled up through Ivorson's funk. Riley had Shanghai'd him. He could see how the man had acquired his reputation. "That was dishonest," he said flatly.

"I couldn't afford the luxury of honesty," Riley answered calmly. "The war in Vietnam's created a huge shortage of experienced case officers in Asia. Headquarters couldn't offer me anyone who even began to match your qualifications."

He leaned toward Ivorson and lowered his voice. "The job you're inheriting," he said intensely, "is the highest-priority requirement the Agency has today. It has to have a first class officer. I had headquarters review every file in Vietnam Operations for me, Ivorson. You were the obvious choice. You've got the languages, you're a proven recruiter, and you have a reputation for producing results under pressure."

Ivorson wasn't appeased. The "highest-priority requirement" label was too transparent, a bait for a seasoned campaigner like him to bite on. "And what exactly is this super-mission?" he inquired.

Riley frowned at the irony. "Are you on board? Only four people in this country are briefed on this operation. I'm not going to satisfy idle curiosity."

"No, sir," Ivorson snapped, further angered by the attempt to manipulate him. "I'm not on board. You've brought me into a killing ground without warning me of the danger, and USAID can't be relied on to protect my cover. You tell me what I'm here for, or I won't play."

Displeasure glinted at him from Riley's eyes. Ivorson didn't care. The more he thought about this situation, the less he wanted anything to do with it. He might even be better off to go back to Headquarters and pull himself together there. His reputation wouldn't suffer too much. Probably.

"All right." Riley's voice was hard. He obviously didn't like being balked. "It's simple. I want you to get the key to the North Vietnamese diplomatic code."

The words were so unexpected and the idea was so far-fetched, that Ivorson snorted aloud. What had Riley been smoking? That code key had to be one of the most tightly guarded documents on earth. Every CIA Station, world-wide, had been targeted to obtain it for years. NSA had spent millions trying to break it.

"You find that amusing?" COS asked him acidly. "Let me tell you something, Ivorson. I receive messages regularly from both Headquarters and the White House on the subject. They don't think it's funny at all. Especially since Tet."

"I don't think it's funny either," said Ivorson unrepentantly. "Just impossible."

Riley's eyes turned glacial. "I don't waste my time on impossibilities," he snapped. "Jim's asset was going to re-wire the North Vietnamese Embassy for them. He'd agreed to implant a device to monitor the emanations from the code machine. That's really what we're after. It apparently builds some Vietnamese cultural bias into the encryption process that NSA hasn't been able to handle."

Jim's agent may have agreed to bug the code room, thought Ivorson, but Jim's agent was dead. And so was Jim, and so was the operation.

Riley might have been reading his mind. He leaned toward Ivorson confidentially. "Jim had another operation going. It could be as good as the electrician. The Embassy chauffeur is an ethnic Black Thai. He's unhappy, and the Wright brother's little sister has got her hooks in him. That's what I want you to take over." brothers' - possessive plural

An Embassy official--non-Vietnamese--in a honey trap? In spite of himself, Ivorson was interested. "Who are the Wright brothers?" he asked.

Something that might have been a smile flickered on Riley's lips. "That comes from their code names," he said. "Wilbur and Orville.

They're Black Thais, too. Wilbur is a local cop. He runs our surveillance team. You'll meet them tomorrow night. If you take the job, that is."

He looked at Ivorson with obvious irritation. "For Christ's sake, Ivorson, I'm offering you the chance of a lifetime. If you pull it off, your next assignment is a Station of your own. I had to wait years to get a shot half as good as this."

The last statement was undoubtedly true, Ivorson silently conceded. Many officers spent a full career in the Directorate of Operations and never received an assignment with as much promotion potential.

And Ivorson wanted promotion. Not for the salary and prestige. Those were only symbols. He wanted what they stood for: proof of competence, indisputable evidence that the inept, frightened kid who could never please his West Point father had become one of the best of them, in the toughest game on earth.

He knew that he had a need to prove himself which often drove him beyond the point where prudent men stopped. That drive had rewarded him with his present rank and reputation in the Agency. It had also come very close to getting him killed.

That drive was pushing him to accept, in spite of Riley's high-handed tactics, but could he handle the Fear? It had followed him from Saigon like his shadow. It was screaming in his ear right now, urging him to tell Riley to shove his job and scurry home to the safety of a desk at Langley.

Yet the thing was so big, so incredibly important. The White House was following it, for God's sake. If Ivorson could pull it off, he would never again have to prove anything to anyone at all. Maybe not even to himself.

He simply couldn't allow the Fear to keep him from a prize like that. And after all, he told himself, Vientiane was a hundred times safer than Saigon. This was not the hot war but the secret war, and he would have a brand-new, unused cover.

Besides, for all its present virulence, the Fear had to be just a passing phenomenon. Ivorson had proven his bravery on many occasions in the past. He'd get it back again. He was Ivorson, for God's sake, the biggest tiger in the jungle!

Actually, he realized grimly, he really didn't have a choice. Riley had asked for him, by name, out of all the officers in Vietnam Operations. If he flinched, not only would his reputation be shattered, but worse yet, he wouldn't be able to look at himself in the mirror. To cut and run would be self-betrayal. He had to say yes, no matter how frightened he was.

✲ ✲ ✲

An hour later, he carried his suitcase from the safe house back up to Wattay Road, hailed a cab, and finally made the driver understand where he wanted to go. That was different from Saigon. Even before Ivorson's hard-earned Vietnamese became fluent, he'd been able to get around here quite well in French. He hoped he didn't have to learn Lao. The strange lettering he'd seen on the front of the airport terminal looked utterly alien to him.

He studied his map of the city as they drove into town. They were travelling toward town on Wattay Road, which ran parallel to the Mekong River. If he went the other way, past the airport, the street turned into RN 13 and would take him to Luang Prabang, the royal capitol. Or, more likely, into a Pathet Lao ambush. Ivorson didn't intend to try it. He'd had enough ambushes.

He put away his map and looked out the window at the city. It was a tiny little place compared to Saigon, of course, but there were some similarities: there was the same concrete block construction of commercial buildings and the same bilious yellow paint common to all of French Indochina. In the residential areas, however, he saw houses built up in the air on pillars.

The sight reminded him of what a Special Forces sergeant had told him one night in a bar in Saigon: "When the houses go up in the air, you know you've hit the border. Of course, it don't make a shit. They shoot at you over there, too."

But the most obvious difference from Saigon that Ivorson could see was that scarcely anyone here could shoot at him. There were no weapons in sight on the streets. That was reassuring except that Ivorson wasn't armed anymore, either. He'd turned in his Walther PPK before he left Saigon. The absence of its weight on his belt made him feel defenseless. He'd draw a new one here first thing tomorrow.

The cab took him through the center of the downtown area, which didn't look to be much more than ten blocks by four or five. Half of that seemed to be taken up by Buddhist temples. Another difference from Saigon: the monks here wore bright orange robes instead of brown. Traffic was light and included carts with enormous wheels, drawn by water buffaloes.

The sounds of the city were familiar: honking horns, buzzing motorcycles, and the blaring of cacophonous Asian music from a multitude of transistor radios. The smell of burning charcoal and cooking garlic reached his nostrils through the open windows. No culture shock there.

They turned north on a broad, sun-blasted boulevard, past a large marketplace and up a long slope toward some sort of monument still under construction.

They turned left on the traffic circle around the monument and entered a residential neighborhood of old French colonial residences. Brilliant purple and orange-colored bougainvillea vines poured over the walls of the compounds.

The word "peaceful" popped into Ivorson's mind for the first time in years. He began to feel better about his situation. The Fear couldn't last long in an Eden like this.

They reached the USAID guesthouse, a whitewashed concrete block motel, and Ivorson paid the fare of five hundred kip, using the local money he'd bought at the change counter in the airport.

The five hundred kip note, worth a dollar, was a big, gaudy, French-printed thing that you had to fold in two to get in your billfold. It had a picture of the king on one side and a pretty girl in front of a Buddhist temple on the other. So far, she was the best-looking girl he'd seen in Laos and not because he hadn't been looking. It had been over a month since he'd had a woman.

The clerk at the guesthouse gave Ivorson the key to an apartment and directed him to the entrance of the USAID/Laos compound. He left the suitcase in the apartment and walked the hundred yards to the gate. The guard, armed only with a nightstick, took his white face as sufficient identification and waved him through.

A Boy Scout troop could take this place, Ivorson thought. Nonetheless, it had been here for years, untouched by the Communists. That was reassuring.

The USAID compound was a big place, a rough triangle two blocks long by a block or so wide, all behind its high concrete wall.

Dominating one side of the street that ran from gate to gate through the center of the compound was a large, windowless masonry building, with sign "Administration" over the door.

He entered it and made his way to the Personnel Office. In the outer office were a number of local-hire personnel. At the desk closest to the inner office door sat a plump young oriental woman wearing an *ao dai,* the Vietnamese national women's costume.

Shit. A Vietnamese, working in the personnel office that was going to have charge of his file. That was two strikes against his new cover before he even got started. She wasn't the only one, either. The name "Nguyen thi Nga" leaped to his eye from a nameplate on an unoccupied desk. That made at least two of them.

The plump girl's nameplate declared her name to be Ly. "May I help you?" she asked him, in moderately-accented English.

"My name is Peter Ivorson," he told her. "I just arrived from Saigon. I'd like to see Miss Odom, the assistant Personnel Officer." Riley had told him to ask for her. She was cleared for handling the files of Agency officers.

Ly got up and knocked on the door of the inner office.

"Come in," said a muffled female voice.

Ly opened the door and announced, "Mr. Ivorson is here."

"He is?" the voice in the office was soft and pleasant, but it sounded surprised, and not altogether pleased. "Ask him to come in."

The girl opened the door wide and motioned for Ivorson to enter. He thanked her, making a conscious effort not to speak in Vietnamese. He'd be a lot safer in Vientiane if none of the local Viets knew he could understand them.

Ivorson looked at Lisa Odom, sitting behind her desk, and liked what he saw. He judged her to be a few years less than his own thirty-one, with wide-set light blue eyes, a pert nose and short, sun-streaked brown hair. A quick look showed him no rings. There were no pictures of males in the office, either, except for a framed photo of a smiling older man with a model airplane in his hands. Almost certainly her father. Vientiane was looking better by the minute.

"Why didn't you let us know you were coming?" she asked him rather sharply, folding the letter she held in her hands and putting it in the drawer of her desk. "I would have sent a driver for you."

It wasn't exactly a warm welcome. "I got a seat on the plane at the last minute," he answered mildly. "It wasn't any problem to take a taxi."

"Oh. Well, now that you're here, we'll start your processing. We can't do it all this afternoon, but maybe we'll have time to get you some ID and put you on the payroll."

Her tone gave him to understand that it was inconsiderate of him not to have reported at eight in the morning. He made a downward revision of his hopes for her contribution to his enjoyment of Vientiane but held onto his conciliatory manner. "Whatever you can do will be fine. I do need to ask you for a car until I can get some transportation of my own."

She frowned at the request. "A car? Well, all right. I'll have one of the drivers take you where you need to go."

Hmm. She was not only snappish, she was a little slow-witted, too. "I'm afraid that wouldn't be secure." He said. "I need to drive myself."

Her frown deepened. "I can't let you have a car without a local license."

Ivorson felt his neck getting warm. "I was advised that an international license would be acceptable," he told her. "I have one."

For some reason, that seemed to irritate her. "May I see it?" Ivorson handed it over. What was this woman's problem?

She studied the international license. "I'm not sure I can do this," she said.

Ivorson had had enough. "Mr. Riley assured me that you would provide me with a car," he said tartly. "If you have a problem with that, perhaps you should call him and tell him what it is."

She colored, and thrust the license back across the desk at him. "All right, then. You Agency people always expect special treatment."

For an instant, Ivorson just stared. He couldn't believe what he'd heard. This was a cleared personnel officer? Then an awful thought crossed his mind. Had he closed the door behind him? Ly's desk was not three feet on the other side of it. The Fear rose up, grimacing, out of his belly. He twisted in his seat to look. Thank God. The door was closed. As he turned back to face Lisa Odom, anger brought him up out of his chair.

"Listen to me, lady," he grated. "Less than a month ago, a gang of VC broke down my door in Saigon. They came to kill me."

Lisa Odom shrank away from him as he leaned over her desk, her china blue eyes large with fright. "The only reason they didn't succeed," he snarled at her, "is because I blew them all over the apartment."

She now looked as if she might throw up.

"They knew who I was," he ranted on, "because some smart-ass like you had made a crack like you made just now where a VC sympathizer could hear it."

She was as far back in her chair as she could get, her face as white as ash. "For goodness' sake, Mr. Ivorson," she stammered, "there's nothing to be so angry about."

"Bullshit there's not," he replied. "For your information, that's a Vietnamese sitting outside your door. Suppose Ly had heard that comment? Who would she think that 'you Agency people' referred to? New USAID officers? Not on your life! They'd love to know about me over at the North Vietnamese Embassy, Miss Odom. How do you know she's not on their team?"

That idea made his voice crack. He heard it, and that made him even angrier.

"That's crazy," Lisa stammered. "Ly is a loyal employee."

The naiveté of the statement was unbelievable. "She's a Viet, lady." He almost shouted the words. "Not even God knows which side she's on! And who gave you the right to bet my life on her politics, anyway?"

He leaned even further over her desk. "You get this straight, Miss Odom: no Vietnamese employee is to handle my personnel file, nor are they to know that I speak their language."

Her face flushed. "Local employees are not allowed to handle US employees' files, Mr. Ivorson, and I'll thank you to let me handle my own office."

Ivorson became aware that the noise level in the outer office had dropped. He struggled to keep his voice down. "You don't have to like me or my agency," he hissed, "but you God damn well do have to protect me because that's part of your job. I'm here, in this cover, with the approval of the Ambassador, and if you blow it for me, you'll explain why to him." He emphasized the threat by slapping his hand on her desk top.

She held her hands up in front of her face defensively, as if she thought he might hit her. Well, let her think so, the holier-than-thou bitch! Who was she, to be playing games with his life?

They stood like that for a moment longer, then Ivorson dropped heavily into the chair. *Jesus!* He had a long way to go to recover his nerve.

Ever since the attempt on his life in Saigon, he'd spent a lot of time trying to analyze the source of the Fear. He'd realized that a large part of it came from what he'd just told Lisa Odom: someone--who the hell knew who--had made an ill-advised comment like hers and had been overheard by a VC penetration of the Embassy there, and the result had been that Ivorson's name got put on a kill list. The sheer, random, uncontrollable nature of it was terrifying, and he damn sure didn't want to go through it again.

She slowly lowered her hands and, avoiding his eyes, rolled her chair back up to the desk. "There was so need for such a violent reaction, Mr. Ivorson," she said in a quavering voice. "I meant no harm by my comment. It just slipped out. I'm-" she stumbled over the word, "—I'm sorry. I'm sure Ly didn't overhear it. And anyway," she added earnestly, "you really don't have to worry about her. She's been with USAID since long before I came here."

His threat to take her to the Ambassador had obviously struck home. Fine. Let her sweat. He looked at her balefully. "I'll check out Miss Ly through my own sources, Miss Odom," he told her. "In the meantime, let's go on with our business."

Still avoiding his eyes and keeping as far away from him as she could, she led him down the hall to an adjacent office. Ivorson could feel Ly's curious eyes on his back as they went. He didn't like the feeling.

✡ ✡ ✡

Trying to control the tremor in her voice, Lisa assigned the task of Ivorson's in-processing to one of her American subordinates, then returned to her own office. Peter Ivorson didn't say either good-bye or thank you. She sat back down at her desk. Her hands were still trembling.

She had never had so much hostility directed at her in her life. At one point, she had really thought that he was going to hit her. It had been terrifying.

And it was sad, too, if you thought about it. Imagine a big, strong man like him being afraid of sweet, chubby little Ly!

Of course, if the story he had told her was true, he certainly had reasons to be afraid of Vietnamese in general. Could that really have happened? Had he really killed those men? The idea made her shudder.

She didn't approve of the CIA or the sneaky, underhanded things she'd heard it did, but she certainly didn't want to get any of its employees killed. He had been right about that: it *was* her duty to protect the cover of the CIA men in USAID, even if the Director didn't like having them there, and it *had* been thoughtless of her to parrot one of the Director's comments about the Agency. If only he hadn't arrived just when he had. She had just been reading Dad's letter, telling her about his illness, when Ly knocked. She hadn't wanted to see Peter Ivorson or anyone else. That was what had made her so short with him.

His threat to tell the Ambassador preyed on her mind. Suppose he actually did it? The Director said that Ambassador Buckley was infamous for being the only pro-CIA ambassador in the Foreign Service. Might he send her home?

She didn't want to go home. She loved being in Vientiane. It was a hot, dusty, backward place, but there was so much to be done here for the people of Laos. They were the innocent bystanders of the war in Indochina. They needed everything, and USAID was really helping. Her job made her feel that she was making a difference in the world she lived in.

Perhaps she ought to apologize again. Grovel, even. But, darn it, it hadn't been entirely her fault. He had over-reacted terribly. The memory of some of the things he'd said to her made her cheeks warm.

And to think that she had actually been looking forward to his arrival. There were so few interesting single men in town, and his file had intrigued her. He had an M.A. in International Relations. He had studied in Mexico and been in Germany with the Air Force. He knew a number of languages, including the Vietnamese he expected her to keep secret.

And he was good-looking, too. Not tall—five-ten, perhaps--but well built, with light brown hair and hazel-green eyes under dark, peaked brows.

Well, she was certainly not interested in him now. He had threatened her, impugned her professionalism, and frightened her to death. She made up her mind that she was going to be absolutely proper in all her dealings with both him and his file, but she was going to keep as far away from Peter Ivorson as she could.

Chapter Two

Ivorson followed Riley through the safe house door and saw the smile. He couldn't possibly have missed it. It was radiant, irresistible, a smile that lit up the dark corners of the room and conveyed to him the certainty that the smiler was about to tell Ivorson the funniest story he had ever heard. Attached to the back of the smile was Wilbur.

Ivorson hadn't see many Asian men he'd thought were handsome, but looking at the one before him now, he had to concede that any woman, be she white, brown or black, would think Wilbur was a damned good looking man. His fine features were set harmoniously on his face, and his black eyes shone with intelligence and good humor.

His fraternal twin, Orville, resembled him, but was shorter, darker and much more reserved. Wilbur had recruited Orville, and a number of his other sibling and cousins, to man the Station's surveillance team, after his own recruitment by Jim Reagan.

Riley, speaking French, made the introductions. "Wilbur, Orville, this is Mr. Peter. He is replacing Mr. Jim."

Orville smiled and nodded. Wilbur drew himself up to his full five foot six, snapped his heels together, and said formally, "je suis enchanté de faire votre connaissance, Mistair Peetair." Then, by way of confirmation, added in English, "No shit."

Ivorson just barely kept his laugh inside. "I'm delighted to meet you, too, Wilbur," he answered. "Our chief has told me a lot of good things about you. I'm sure we're going to work well together."

"Ah, oui, bien sur," said Wilbur. "No shit."

They shook hands on it. Ivorson had the absurd feeling that he'd known Wilbur all his life. He was going to have to watch himself. It would be easy to lose his objectivity around this charmer.

Wilbur and Orville had both Black Thai and Lao names, too, of course. Their family had taken refuge in Laos after their father's death—on the French side—at Dien Bien Phu.

The homeland of the Black Thai was the high country of North Vietnam, where they had been driven, centuries before, by the Vietnamese, whom they loathed. Consequently, they had welcomed the French colonialists. A lot of the French colonial army at Dien Bien Phu had been Black Thai. After the French lost Vietnam, they re-settled as many Black Thai as they could, mostly in Laos, which was still under French control, and where the language was similar.

Having made the introductions, Riley departed for another meeting, and left Ivorson and his agents to break out some scotch and celebrate the new working relationship.

"Tell me about Hoang Bac Cam, the North Vietnamese chauffeur," Ivorson invited them, after the second drink. "I understand that your sister is friendly with him."

Wilbur looked at him sternly and wagged a correcting finger. "No, Mistair Peetair. HE is friendly. She only pretends. No decent Black Thai girl could truly like a boot-licker of the Viets. No shit!"

Orville nodded in emphatic agreement.

"I read about your family's background today," Ivorson said to Wilbur. "You do have ample reason to dislike the Vietnamese."

Wilbur's face congealed into an expression that made Ivorson forget he'd ever seen the man smile. "The Vietnamese killed my father," Wilbur said in low-pitched, intense French. "For centuries they have enslaved my people. Now, because of them, we have to leave our homeland and live in a foreign country. Whatever I can do to hurt them, I will do."

Orville nodded his agreement. The hatred Ivorson felt emanating from the brothers was as tangible and inexhaustible as the Mekong. He didn't have to worry about the motivation of these agents. On the contrary, he'd have to be careful that they didn't let their hatred run away with them and try to turn Ivorson into THEIR agent in a private war against all things Vietnamese.

"I want to hurt the Vietnamese, too," he told them, "starting with the recruitment of Hoang Bac Cam. I've been reading Mister Jim's files on the case. Now I'd like for you to tell me about it yourselves, right from the beginning."

For the next two hours, they did just that.

At seven-thirty the next morning, he got out of Orville's old taxi, which doubled as a control vehicle for the surveillance team and made his way toward the fresh vegetable vendors in the open-air portion of the Vientiane morning market. In spite of the early hour, it was already warm. Yesterday, the thermommeter had climbed to over ninety degrees.

The market buildings formed a square a hundred yards on each side at the southeast corner of the market ground. Around their exterior on the north, west, and south was a great open field of hard-packed dirt. There, individual merchants stood behind tables or squatted on the ground behind the bamboo trays or sheets of plastic on which they displayed their wares. From noon on, the area was a deserted jumble of tables, folded umbrellas, and trash, but now, early on a Friday morning, it was jammed with merchants and shoppers.

Ivorson passed in front of the tailors' shops, and was besieged by a horde of Indians, each urging him to come inside, have coffee or a cold drink, and examine the merchandise.

He waded through them and began prowling the rows of merchants squatting on the ground at the east end of the marketplace, looking at and occasionally buying some vegetables or fruit to cover his presence there, while keeping his eye on the area across Mahosot Road, where Wilbur had told him the North Vietnamese usually parked.

He had come to the market to see for himself the personae in the human drama he was directing. He knew their faces, names, and official assignments from Station files, but that was no substitute for seeing them in the flesh, and now was the time to do it, since he was fresh off the plane and not yet known to the Opposition. Besides, he hadn't built the reputation that had made Riley ask for him by letting other people do his work.

Wilbur's little sister, Sengdara–the name meant starlight, Wilbur said—had come by the safe house last night to be presented to him. A pert, saucy girl with flirting eyes, she was the bait in the honey trap. He could see why Cam found her attractive. Ivorson did, too. What he wanted to see this morning was the body language between her and Cam.

At seven-fifty, an elderly Mercedes with diplomatic plates approached from the direction of Khoun Boulom Road. It backed into the curb near the entrance to the lane that led to Khouadine, the most populous Vietnamese quarter in the city.

Ivorson squinted into the morning sun. Was that Haong Bac Cam at the wheel? He had studied the photographs of the chauffeur that Orville had taken surreptitiously from his taxi, but Ivorson wanted to look at the man in the flesh.

He realized that he was staring, and made himself examine the cucumber that was being held up for his inspection by a wizened old woman with thin streams of red betel nut juice running from the corners of her mouth.

After a few seconds, he risked another peek at the parked car. The driver was indeed Cam. He and the two passengers, shopping bags in hand, were just crossing Mahosot Road toward the market buildings.

The chauffeur was shorter, darker, and more solidly built than his Vietnamese compatriots. He was reasonably presentable, which was a relief. A homely man, no matter how lonely, might wonder how a girl as pretty as Sengdara had happened to fall for him.

Ivorson turned around and walked rapidly back to the west, toward an opening between the closely-packed merchants through which he could move further away from the building and observe without being noticed.

It took him almost two minutes to reposition himself. The Vietnamese were still inside the market. All right. Now then, where was Sengdara?

He finally found her, two rows south and forty yards east of his position, squatting under a large, bamboo-ribbed, wax-paper umbrella. Her vegetables were displayed before her on a sheet of plastic. Ivorson hunkered down in front of a pile of rambutans, and waited for Cam to appear.

✡ ✡ ✡

Dong, the head cook walked in front. Cam came next, and Phuong, Huu's deputy was in back. Their route took them through the north side of the market building, where they visited a tobacconist and a seller of rubber sandals. Both were trusted local cadre. Cam's job at each of these stops was to position himself just inside the door of the shop, looking back in the direction from which they had come for possible surveillance.

Nguyen van Huu had left the Embassy ahead of them this morning. He had walked down to Khoualouang Road and caught a cab to town, where he was now wandering idly from shop to shop. The idea was that Huu would draw the hostile surveillance, leaving Phuong's contacts in the market unobserved. It had always worked in the past, and Cam could see no one following them today, either.

He nodded the all-clear to Phuong as they left the second shop, and at the next exterior exit, they went outside. After the relative cool of the shady interior, the brilliant sun and heat struck Cam like a physical blow. The hot season was beginning early this year.

In front of them was a sea of vendors, arranged in ragged east-west rows with an open space in front of them for the customers to stand in. The more affluent merchants rented large umbrellas from the market. Others brought their own. The poor, of whom there were many, sat in the sun.

The three worked their way slowly through the crowd, trying to look around them without seeming to be on the lookout. When they reached the second row of merchants north of the building, they split up. Phuong went west, Cam and Dong east. If, despite their efforts, they had failed to notice surveillance, this maneuver would split it.

The split-up was also necessary in order to find the mother of Papaya, the code name for one of Huu's most important agents who worked for the Americans at USAID. Messages between her and Huu were passed back and forth through her mother. Cam knew who Papaya really was. When he first arrived in Vientiane, she had visited the Embassy once or twice in the company of her mother. He was, of course, not privileged to know the contents of the notes, and he hadn't told anyone else in the Embassy that he knew her on sight.

Papaya's mother came to the market daily, to sell vegetables. A widow, with neither funds to rent a regular space nor male relatives to bully competitors for her, she had to take whatever room she could find available from day to day.

She usually located herself to the west of the exit aisle, so Phuong would probably find her. Cam didn't even bother to look for her. He was trying to locate Sengdara.

He saw her now, twenty meters farther down the row he and Dong were in, sitting in the shade of her umbrella, the sharpened bamboo shaft of which had been driven into the ground beside her.

The sight of her almost took his breath away. She usually wore a Lao skirt, but today she had on an ankle-length black silk skirt and a bright green blouse with frogged buttons up the front: the traditional Black Thai women's costume. It was a signal of solidarity, meant for his eyes only!

She was bargaining with a customer over some scallions from the pile on the low, round bamboo table in front of her. The customer and she were obviously well acquainted. They joked and laughed as they haggled. Sengdara's shining hair danced and bobbed around her shoulders as she shook her head to refuse an offer from the buyer. Cam's heart yearned for her.

She concluded her sale, waved good-bye to her customer, and turned her head in Cam's direction. For an instant, her eyes met his and locked there, with an intensity that left him shaken. It still amazed him that their relationship could have reached this point. They had met right here, in the market, when he heard her speaking Black Thai as he passed. Struck by her looks, he had stopped and chatted with her, very casually and briefly, so that the Viets wouldn't notice. The acquaintance had ripened in the same way: a day at a time, a minute a day.

It galled him that it had to be like that, but the "uncles" didn't allow any fraternization with local girls. Once a month, the embassy staff went together to a whorehouse off Wattay Road to relieve their needs. For socialization, there was the weekly Sunday open house for local sympathizers, but, of course, they were all Vietnamese. The most Cam ever got from any of the girls was a nod of recognition.

Amazingly, his flirtation with Sengdara had not only escaped detection, but even born fruit to the point that her fingers lingered on his as she passed him the vegetables he bought from her. And then, a month ago, it had all changed.

She had become sulky, demanding that he come to call on her older brother and ask for permission to court her properly. His explanations of his situation made no difference. "You are not a man," she taunted him under her breath. "You are a slave. Don't bother me anymore. Go home to Hanoi and marry a Viet girl." She'd used the impolite word for Vietnamese.

For two weeks, she had refused to even speak to him. Finally, in desperation, he had promised to meet with her at night, the next time he was out of the embassy alone. It was madness on his part, he knew. The only times he was allowed out by himself were the occasions when Nguyen van Huu made him carry or retrieve secret messages for his other prize agent, code-named Mango. Cam had no idea who Mango was, but he had to be very important. The messages were disguised and hidden, to be picked up later. If Huu caught Cam meeting a local girl during one of those missions, he would be sent directly to the front in South Vietnam. The idea made him shudder.

Nonetheless, deprived of his reason by his longing for the young woman, he had committed himself. Only later had he realized how it could be safely done. Huu insisted that Cam walk, rather than drive, to and from the message sites, no matter how far they were from the embassy. If he took a taxi instead, he could easily save an hour and spend it with Sengdara.

Yesterday, he had asked her for her telephone number so he could alert her to meet him, but one of the uncles had called him away before she could write it down. "I'll pass it to you the next time you come," she had whispered.

Today was the day. Dong, still looking for Papaya's mother, was several paces ahead of Cam as he approached Sengdara's stall. Cam couldn't see Phuong at all. It was safe.

He came abreast of Sengdara. Dong was still plodding ahead. Cam squatted down on his haunches in front of her. "Sa bye dee?" he murmured. "Is your health good?" He picked up a bunch of scallions from her tray and examined it, in case Dong should turn around. "Do you have the number for me?" he whispered.

"I will pass it to you with your change," she murmured, then asked out loud, "What will you buy?"

He shot a glance after Dong. Oh-oh! He had turned around and was looking for Cam. "Give me a kilo of these scallions," he told her, dipping in his pocket for some money. He came out with a five hundred kip note and handed it to her.

Dong had spotted him and was gesturing for him to come on. She dug in her purse for his change. He saw her slip a piece of paper between the two one-hundred kip notes before she handed them to him.

She filled a plastic sack with scallions. He took it from her, stuffed it in his shopping bag as he stood up. Dong had an irate look on his face. It was time to go.

"I will be waiting," she whispered, her eyes speaking volumes to him from under long, downcast lashes.

"Cam!" Dong shouted at him. "Come on. You always make me wait for you."

Cam hastened to join him. Dong sniffed at the quality of the scallions, but didn't ask any questions about Sengdara. He didn't seem to have noticed the Black Thai dress, either.

Phuong rejoined them. He had found Papaya's mother and given her a note from Huu. They continued their shopping. Dong and Phuong did the buying and made Cam carry the shopping bags.

As they returned to the market buildings to buy meat, the three of them walked near Sengdara again. Cam lagged a step behind the others and glanced at her as he passed. She gave him a quick smile.

"Hurry up, Cam," Phuong snapped at him over his shoulder. "Don't be so slow!"

Cam mentally called him the ultimate insulting Black Thai word for a Vietnamese and walked just a fraction slower.

He was about to take an irretrievable step. He was both excited and terrified by the idea, but at least he wasn't going to risk his freedom for mere seconds of her company. The next time they met, it would be for an hour. A whole hour! Compared to what they had had up to now, it was like an eternity. That was worth taking chances for.

✲ ✲ ✲

Ivorson watched with elation as the three North Vietnamese got into the Mercedes and drove away. There was definitely an operational possibility here! Cam had quivered like a male dog around a bitch in heat while he was talking to Sengdara.

Ivorson caught the girl's eye as he walked back to the taxi rank. He had given Wilbur a picture of himself to show her. She gave him the barest hint of a nod. All right! She had passed Cam the telephone number. Now all they could do was wait for Cam to call her and arrange the tryst.

Once that happened, of course, things would get complicated. Ivorson wanted to tape the conversation between Sengdara and the chauffeur when they met. Assuming, of course, that the meeting place chosen by Cam was suitable for that, and also assuming that Cam didn't beat Wilbur and Ivorson to the site. He'd told Sengdara that he needed at least half an hour's notice, but that was damn little time for Wilbur to notify Ivorson and get themselves moving. It would take split-second timing and a lot of luck.

And how the hell did Cam expect to get out alone at night? Ivorson couldn't figure it out. The only Embassy officer the surveillance team had ever spotted out by himself was Nguyen van Huu, who was nominally Counselor of Embassy, but whom the Station believed was the Rezident, the intel chief.

Jim Reagan's now-vanished agent had been hired by Huu to rewire the Embassy. That, plus the fact that he roamed around the city on foot by himself, almost certainly confirmed the Station's belief about him. However, he had never been observed by surveillance making any contacts that might have been clandestine. Ivorson made a mental note to review the team's surveillance technique. The Viets seemed to be doing some things that his boys weren't seeing.

That had to change. Ivorson didn't want a fly going through that embassy gate, day or night, without his knowing about it. He couldn't afford to put all his money on the Cam/Sengdara relationship, either, no matter how good it looked. Honey traps were notoriously tricky. There had to be something else he could do to get a look at that code machine, and he intended to find out what it was, and then do it.

Still and all, he reflected, as he got back in Orville's cab, things were looking pretty good. And the best part was that he hadn't been goosey at all this morning, even though he'd been the only white face in the midst of thousands of brown ones. That realization made him feel good. He was getting his nerve back already!

Chapter Three

"If you want a non-intrusive technical penetration, you're shit out of luck. You'd better stick with the Cam operation—we need an agent who can get inside that Embassy."

The advice was coming from Jack Lawrence, the Station's technical officer, and Ivorson didn't like it at all. The tech might or might not be right about the technical aspects, but Ivorson wasn't about to accept operational judgments from a solder-iron jockey.

The tech had been TDY in Pakse during Ivorson's initial week in Vientiane, so this was their first conversation. Lawrence was several years older than Ivorson, blond, and pudgy. Both his expression and tone of voice conveyed some doubt that Ivorson had sufficient mental capacity to understand what he was saying.

"I've looked at that place out there for months, from every angle I could think of, "Lawrence continued, "trying to figure some way he could get inside it technically without intruding physically on the premises. There isn't any."

Ivorson felt his neck getting warm. From his review of the files during the past few days, he knew that his dead predecessor, Jim Reagan, had been the initiator of the efforts that Lawrence was now taking sole credit for.

Not bothering to keep the dislike out of his voice, he asked, "Do you know anything about an aerial survey I've been reading about? I can't find any pictures."

Lawrence went over to a map filing cabinet, unlocked it, and pulled out a large sheet of photographic paper. He brought it back and spread it out on the top of the work bench in front of Ivorson.

"There it is," he said. "I had the Air Force fly a U-2 mission out of U-Tapao, down in Thailand, to get this for me."

That was bullshit, too, thought Ivorson. Yesterday, he had seen the file copy of the cable in which Jim Reagan had made that request of the Air Force.

The photograph itself was magnificent. Ivorson could see every detail of the North Vietnamese Embassy compound. A man was standing in front of the double garage, washing an older model black Mercedes with a sponge and a plastic bucket. It had to be Hoang Bac Cam.

There were several buildings within the walled compound. The garage, with servants' quarters behind it, was on the west side. The chancery, also with servants' quarters in back, was in the middle. East of the chancery was another building, almost as wide as the chancery, but less than half as deep.

"There's no nearby location from which any of our non-intrusive systems will work," Lawrence said pedantically. "The only place near enough is this house here, in this little Lao village just across the west wall of the Viet compound, but it's not placed right for our purposes, and a Lao house wouldn't work even if it were. The gear takes up a lot space, it's got to be concealed, and it uses a lot of electrical power, none of which this Lao village offers. On the east side of the compound, there's nothing useable at all."

Ivorson swallowed his disappointment at that news and returned to his study of the photo. Where was the damned radio room, anyway? In the chancery or the other building? Reagan's reports from the now-vanished electrician described it as a dormitory. According to him, its first floor consisted of four separate rooms housing two people each. He hadn't been allowed upstairs, so he wasn't sure about that area.

The aerial view showed Ivorson the fibro-asbestos tiled roofs of the chancery and dormitory, with antenna towers mounted on each of them. He got a magnifying glass from Lawrence's workbench and studied the antennas.

He could see the long wire running between the towers and the down-wire running from the center of it back to the side wall of the dormitory. From there, it presumably ran under the eaves to the radio room. Progress! He now knew which building the radio was in. But which room was it? Probably upstairs.

The roof of the dormitory was asymmetrical, running out farther from the ridgepole on the front than it did on the back, presumably to cover a balcony or walkway which gave access to the rooms on the second floor. A narrow roofed walkway connected the dormitory with the second floor of the chancery.

Someone had inked in the dimensions of the buildings in the photographs, as well as the distances from each of them to the nearest wall. "Where did we get these measurements?" Ivorson asked.

"I sneaked down there one night and measured the wall of this house down the road," Lawrence told him, pointing to a nearby compound on the photograph. Ivorson could hear the pride in his voice. "Then I extrapolated everything from that known figure."

Ivorson had read Reagan's memo about the measuring operation, too. He had initiated it, not the tech, and been there along with him, taking the measurements. Ivorson's opinion of Lawrence hit rock bottom.

The rear of the dormitory stood one and a half meters inside the back wall of the compound. The narrow space between the dormitory and the wall seemed to be packed dirt, save at the west end, where an open concrete drain ran back to the wall, and presumably, through it into the swamp behind the compound.

Several palms overshadowed the servants' quarters behind the chancery and garage, but there were no trees along the wall behind the dormitory, nor in the swamp behind it. The wall itself, however, had shards of glass set in concrete along its top, to discourage intruders.

There was an open space of twelve meters between the dormitory's east end and the wall of the compound, which had been turned into a vegetable garden. Ivorson could clearly see the tilled rows of soil and planting stakes. On the other side of that wall, a small Lao house stood in the middle of a treeless lot. No help on that side.

The swamp behind the rear wall extended unbroken to the border of the photograph. "How far back does this marsh go?" Ivorson asked Lawrence. "Are there any houses back there, off the picture?"

"It goes on for hundreds of yards," Lawrence answered promptly. "The nearest house in that direction is a quarter-mile away, and it's in a Lao village. There's no high ground back there at all."

"How deep is the swamp?"

Lawrence frowned at the question. "I don't know," he said reluctantly. It was obvious that he disliked having to make the admission.

Ivorson decided then and there to keep Lawrence as far away from his operations as he possibly could. Taking credit for Reagan's operations just made the tech an asshole, but a man whose ego kept him from admitting ignorance was deadly dangerous.

"Anyway," said Lawrence, "ankle deep or ass deep, you can't do anything out there. You'd stand out like a beacon light."

That did it. Ivorson had had all he could take. "Let's get something straight, Jack," he told the tech coldly. "I'll defer to your knowledge on technical matters, but what I can or cannot do in that swamp is an operational decision, and that's my business, not yours. Jim Reagan was in charge of this case before his death, and I'm in charge of it now. Is that clear?"

Lawrence flushed. For a moment, his eyes locked belligerently with Ivorson's. Then he looked away. "Okay, chief," he said, sarcasm dripping from the last word. "Any other 'technical' questions?"

Ivorson ignored the tone of voice. He'd made his point. "Yes," he said, "there are. Suppose you had been thinking about non-intrusive penetration of the radio room instead of having Jim's agent plant a device. Is there any other technical gear you might have thought of using?"

Lawrence's face was sulky, but he seemed to be seriously considering the question. "No," he said finally. "If you're after the code machine, you want to read the emanations from it, and to do that, you have to be real close. A bug in the wall near it or on its electrical system is ideal. The next best thing would be to see the thing in action. Failing that, just hearing it operate, even without reading its electronic output, might be helpful."

A querulous tone crept into Lawrence's voice. "You may not like taking my advice," he said, "but you're going to get it anyway. What you need is an agent who can get in there and get to that target. With Jim's guy gone, it's the chauffeur, or nothing." He turned his back on Ivorson, and began examining a tape recorder.

"Thanks for the tip," Ivorson said shortly. He choked back the other things he wanted to say, appropriated the aerial photograph and took it back into his own office for more study.

Aside from having Lawrence for an office-mate, he was pretty well pleased with his set-up. The end of the warehouse where they were located had been bricked off from the rest of the building.

Their end had its own entrances, both for people and vehicles, since it also served as the garage for the Station's operational cars: two small, non-descript Japanese cars, with a variety of quick-mount license tags in their trunks.

The area around Ivorson's desk and safe had been partitioned off from the tech's shop, with its workbench and stock of cameras, recorders, microphones and key blanks.

Thinking over Lawrence's final speech, Ivorson hoped the tech was wrong about the impossibility of a technical operation. The Cam case looked good right now, but it could go to hell in a minute, and if it did, Ivorson had to have something else to fall back on. He'd been dragooned into this assignment, but now that he was in it, he damn well intended to succeed.

Lawrence was right about one thing, though: Ivorson needed a source of information about the physical layout of the Embassy; someone who could give him an accurate picture of what lay underneath the tantalizing roofs on the photograph in front of him.

What about Tran van Cao? Ivorson had read his file. He was the Lao Special Branch's authority on the North Vietnamese Embassy and its local sympathizers. A Viet himself, he was a former French colonial policeman who had gotten out of North Vietnam after a year in a Viet Minh underground prison, an experience that left him with a permanent limp.

Cao had been in liaison with the Station for years, but within the past six months, he had been recruited unilaterally by none other than Riley himself, with whom he shared attendance at early morning Mass at the Vientiane Cathedral. Riley had recruited Cao to provide the Station with a window on the internal workings of the Lao police, but he could be valuable to Ivorson, as well.

Cao ran a string of low-level assets recruited from the local Vietnamese community. Surely he'd had them do a survey of the interior of the Viet Embassy buildings: who worked and slept where, and so on.

COS met Cao on Monday nights. Today was Monday. Why not ask Riley to let Ivorson tag along tonight, in a phony mustache and with an introduction in alias, so he could debrief the policeman?

He went back out to the tech shop and called COS's office on the secure telephone. Riley agreed to his request. Cheered by his progress (and also by Lawrence's obvious annoyance as he overheard what Ivorson was up to), Ivorson returned to the aerial photograph. In preparation for tonight's meeting with Cao, he intended to study the photograph until he had memorized every inch of the Embassy compound.

When a twinge of hunger caused him to look at his watch, he was startled to see that it was almost one o'clock. If he wanted to get any lunch, he'd better get moving. He locked the photo again in the map file, left the warehouse, and hurried across the sun-smitten asphalt street to the American Community Association, or ACA. It was a dark brown mishmash of a wooden structure across from the Administration building, which boasted a bar, a dining room, a swimming pool, and very old movies twice a week.

Ivorson was mentally reviewing the interior of the Vietnamese Embassy compound in his mind's eye as he trotted up the ACA steps. He didn't see the girl on the porch until they collided. She staggered from the impact. The fist-full of money she was carrying flew in all directions.

Ivorson caught her arm and kept her from falling. "I'm sorry, miss!" he said. "Are you all right? Let me help you pick up your money."

She looked up at him with startled eyes. She was wearing a bright pink *ao dai,* so she had to be a Vietnamese, but her eyes weren't Asian. They were very large and round and the irises were light brown, with flecks of green in them.

Her body wasn't Vietnamese, either. Her full breasts strained at the form-fitting silk bodice, and the swell of her hips did wonderful things for the black silk pants she wore under the *ao dai.* She must be Eurasian.

Noticing the direction of his glance, she blushed and pulled her arm out of his hand. He couldn't remember having seen a Viet girl blush before. The effect was lovely. Her honey-gold cheeks turned peach, and the contrast between her glowing skin and the anthracite black of her long, gleaming hair was striking. It struck him that he was looking at one of the most beautiful women he had ever seen.

He knelt beside her and helped her pick up the dropped bills and coins. "I really am sorry," he repeated. "Are you sure you're all right?"

She glanced at him neutrally for an instant then dropped her eyes again. "I am not hurt," she said in low-voiced, precise English. "I was just startled. I didn't see you coming."

They got all the money picked up. "Let's put it here on the rail of the porch," he suggested, "and count it to be sure we've got it all." He wanted an excuse to keep talking to her.

"I can do it alone," said the girl. "You were in such a hurry; you must have important work to do inside."

"What I'm doing right now is the most important thing I have to do today," he assured her with a smile.

She looked up sharply at the flirtatious tone in his voice. Her lovely lips compressed. He didn't seem to be making a very good impression. He tried again to get conversation going. "Do you work here?"

"Yes, in Personnel." She kept her eyes down.

Personnel? Ah! This must be the other Vietnamese girl in Ly's office, the one whose name he'd seen on the empty desk as he went to his meeting with Lisa Odom. "Let me see if I can guess your name," he told her teasingly. "I think you must be Nguyen thi Nga."

That finally got her to look at him. "How do you know my name?" she asked.

"I have been told that the most beautiful girl in Laos is Nguyen thi Nga," he told her solemnly, "so it was easy to guess."

She looked back at the floor, and the peach color returned to her cheeks. "You pronounce my name so well," she said in Vietnamese. "Do you speak my language?"

Pleased that he was making some progress, he came within a millisecond of responding in the same language. Damn! That was close! He'd been so wrapped up in the woman that he'd forgotten to pronounce her name American style. He feigned puzzlement. "I'm sorry, I didn't understand what you jut said."

She flicked a glance up at him through long black lashes. "You pronounced my name so well; I thought you might speak Vietnamese. Yes, I am Nguyen thi Nga. May I know your name, too?"

"I'm Peter Ivorson. I just arrived in Laos last week." He put out his hand.

She shook it very briefly. "Are you new here, Peter Ivorson? I have not seen you before." The question was friendly, her voice was less so.

"I'm in Supply," he told her. "I just got here."

"Oh, in the warehouse. Did you come from the United States?"

"No, I was transferred directly from Saigon."

"Ah." She dropped her eyes again. "I have to go back to my office now," she said. "I am late." She moved around him to the steps.

"Goodbye, Nga. I'm glad to meet you."

"Goodbye." She didn't look back. She didn't say she was glad to meet him, either.

Ivorson stared hungrily after her. The movement of her hips set the back panel of the *ao dai* swaying as she walked. He felt himself stir. She sure wasn't friendly, but my God, she was beautiful! She would have been remarkable in Saigon. Here, among the dark-skinned, broad-featured Lao girls, she was in a class all by herself.

He had been out to visit the bars and brothels in Dong Palan, the local red-light district, a couple of times since his arrival and had wound up bedding a Thai whore in the Morocco Bar. She was the best looking woman out there, but he wasn't interested in sharing a woman with other men. Aside from the danger of disease, the idea offended his ego.

He wanted a woman of his own. As a matter of fact, he decided, he wanted that woman right there—Nguyen thi Nga. It would be an interesting challenge; something to while away the evenings while he waited for Hoang Bac Cam to call Wilbur's sister. If he ever did.

✲ ✲ ✲

Nga could feel the American's eyes on her back as she walked across the street. He was so big and bold, so sure of himself, this Ivorson, like all the western men. His green eyes had undressed her right on the steps of the ACA! He was a *ba muoi lam.* The words meant "thirty-five," but the reference was to the animal image accompanying number 35 on the Vietnamese national lottery: a billy goat, sexually insatiable and utterly shameless.

She felt less flustered when the door of the administration building closed behind her. He said he was newly arrived from Saigon. It was curious that she hadn't heard about anyone new coming to the warehouse. She didn't handle the Americans' files, of course, but there was always gossip in the office, especially a new single man.

She supposed this one was single. He acted single and wore no rings. Of course, some of the married men here without their wives were the worst *ba muoi lams* of all.

Might this Ivorson be the man Uncle Huu was watching for? Huu had told her that the people in USAID/Plans were really CIA agents. Mr. Reagan, who was killed last month in the traffic accident, had been a CIA spy, Uncle Huu said. He had assigned Nga to be alert for his replacement. So far, one hadn't arrived.

Huu hadn't said anything about CIA people in Supply, but it wouldn't surprise Nga if this Ivorson were up to no good. He was very sure of himself, as if he knew something no one else knew.

She went to Miss Odom's office and rapped gently on the open door. The American woman looked up at her from behind her desk. She was pretty, Nga supposed, if you liked that pale white skin, and she was undoubtedly intelligent, but as naïve and as trusting as a twelve-year old.

"I'm sorry to be late," Nga said. "I got run over in the door of the ACA by the new man in Supply. He knocked all my change on the ground and then wanted to talk to me."

Miss Odom's initial reaction was a puzzled frown. "What new man from–oh, yes, Mr. Ivorson. What did he want to talk to you about?"

Nga shrugged. "Trying to flirt." Miss Odom's expression became distinctly irritated. "It's not my fault," Nga said defensively.

Miss Odom looked apologetic. "Of course it isn't, Nga. I'm not upset with you at all. Go on back to work."

"Yes, Ma'am. Who is Mr. Ivorson replacing?"

"Hmm? Oh, no one. He's an additional employee. We've been trying to fill that slot for quite some time." There was something almost artificially casual in the American woman's answer.

Nga nodded, smiled, and went to her own desk. It struck her as strange that Miss Odom didn't seem to know who Nga was talking about at first, especially when he had just filled a long–vacant slot.

She decided to mention the new man to Uncle Huu, even if he wasn't in the Plans section. Then a second thought struck her. Suppose he did turn out to be a spy? Would Huu want her to "befriend" him, by which he meant that Nga was to become his girlfriend?

No! She wouldn't do that again, no matter how important it was to Uncle Huu, and no matter how nice he had always been to her and her mother! The thought of another hairy, bad-smelling white man fondling her made her want to retch. Especially not that *ba muoi lam,* Peter Ivorson, with his lascivious eyes.

Perhaps she should not mention this Ivorson. But if she didn't, and it turned out that he was the one Huu was looking out for, she would never be able to face Uncle Huu again. No, she'd better do her duty and just hope that Peter Ivorson turned out to be just another arrogant, unpleasant American.

Chapter Four

Wilbur daubed a last streak of dark brown pancake makeup on Ivorson's face and stood back to admire the effect. "You brown, same Lao, now," he announced with amusement, "but no Lao have nose like that." The observation sent him off into a fit of laughter.

Ivorson took a look at himself in the mirror he'd brought to the safesite. He might not look like a Lao to Wilbur, but with his hair dyed black and his brown face, he didn't look like an American either, and that was the idea.

Jack Lawrence had been reluctant to hand over the disguise material and then visibly miffed when Ivorson declined his offer to apply it. Ivorson had enjoyed the tech's pique.

Still chuckling, Wilbur dug into a paper sack and came out with two items which he presented to Ivorson with a flourish: the first was a suppository, made of some sort of hard wax. The second was a condom. Ivorson stared at them uncomprehendingly. "What's this for? We're going to the swamp, not a whore house."

"Swamp have plenty sangsue—leech," Wilbur said. He was trying out his English this evening, of which he was undeservedly proud. Ivorson didn't have the heart to ask him to stick with French.

"You no want have leech inside," said Wilbur, "you put wax in cul, cover sexe with preventatif." Suiting the action to the words, he demonstrated.

Ivorson was embarrassed as hell, but followed his example. He'd suffer more than embarrassment to keep a leech from crawling up either of the orifices in question.

He was wearing a too—small outfit of black cotton shirt and trousers, bought in the morning market. Wilbur had on a similar black shirt and a *paa salong*, the long, gray-and-black checkered cotton skirt that Lao men wore at home. Wilbur now sprayed himself and Ivorson's disguise one last time with insect repellant and gave a thumbs-up of approval. "Numba one," he pronounced. "We go."

Orville drove the battered old taxi, with Wilbur and Ivorson in the back. They approached the Vietnamese Embassy from the east, but a quarter-mile short of reaching it, they turned off to the north on a shockingly bad dirt track that ran out into the countryside along the top of a dike. Orville turned off the headlights.

Three hundred yards out on the dike, they stopped. The interior light bulb of the cab had been removed. Ivorson and Wilbur scrambled out in the dark, the taxi banged and thumped away over the potholes, and they were left alone on the road. The swamp was on their left, dry rice paddies on their right.

Wilbur rolled up the skirt of his sarong in front, reached through his legs, pulled the back of the skirt up tight between his thighs, and tucked it in at the waist. Ivorson, who had gone to Lutheran Sunday schools as a kid, had heard the Old Testament phrase, "girding up his loins," many times. Now, at last, he knew what it meant.

Wilbur swung a broad leather belt over his head and left shoulder. From it, a two-foot scabbard hung down his back. The handle of the knife it contained stuck up over his left shoulder.

"Swamp have plenty snake," he whispered. "If we meet, they try bite, I cut head."

Ivorson concealed a shudder. He had a deep-seated aversion to snakes and had been resolutely avoiding the thought that the fetid black swamp might contain some. He forced himself to step gingerly off the road and into the water. His leg promptly sank calf-deep into ooze, which sucked at his sneaker and tried to pull it off as he moved.

He cursed silently and struggled along behind Wilbur, who was already wading off into the dark. The odor of the foul-smelling gas churned up by his passage made Ivorson want to retch. He clenched his teeth and kept going, bulling his way through the mass of tightly packed lotus, water hyacinth and marsh grass.

After a few dozen yards, the water got shallower and the going was easier. According to the measurements Ivorson had taken from the aerial photograph, they had to travel four hundred yards west in order to arrive behind the Embassy. They were now, perhaps, a hundred and fifty yards north of its wall. The night was quite dark, but they were able to maintain their course by the lights of the houses ahead of them, to the west.

The swamp got deeper again, almost up to Ivorson's waist. He tried not to think about leeches, but failed. The water stayed waist deep. He wondered how deep it got during the rainy season. Probably over his head. While he was thinking about that, he bumped into Wilbur, who had come to a stop.

"Embassy there," whispered Wilbur, pointing into the darkness. Ivorson looked along his arm. He could just see the outline of the building against the background light of the city beyond them. They needed to move closer. He motioned Wilbur forward again.

Ten minutes later, they were directly in back of the dormitory and fifty yards behind the compound wall. Wilbur squatted down until only his head showed above the water and vegetation. Ivorson reluctantly imitated him, and hoped to Christ that his suppository hadn't melted.

The smell of rotting vegetation was overwhelming. Mosquitoes and gnats hummed viciously in Ivorson's ears, and he had to keep blowing them out of his eyes. If the insect repellent didn't work, he'd look like a raw hamburger tomorrow.

He wiped off the luminous dial of his watch and squinted at it. Sixteen minutes before ten. It was Monday night, March 4th. The weekly scheduled radio traffic from Hanoi was at ten o'clock. Not long now.

The ground floor rooms of the dormitory were apparently all occupied. Over the top of the wall, he counted four windows with light shining out of the glass panes set above the wooden shutters. On two of the windows, the shutters themselves were open. He could hear an amplified voice coming through one of them. Wilbur nudged him and hissed, "Radio Hanoi."

There were four windows on the top floor, as well, but all of them were dark. Hmmm. Could Tran van Cao have been wrong?

When he had asked Cao about the Embassy last night, the crippled little man, in his bird-like, chirping French, had said the radio room was located in the center of the upper floor of the dormitory. That had seemed right to Ivorson, based on the general area where the antenna wire came down, but if it was so, why were the rooms dark? He looked at his watch again. Twelve minutes to ten.

There was no breeze at all, but Ivorson could hear rustling movement in the lily pads around him. He wondered what was causing the sound, and then decided that he really didn't want to think about it. The insects whined. An occasional frog croaked. Then, at nine fifty-four, a light came on in the second room from the east end of the top floor.

Cao had been right, after all! That had to be the radio room, warming up for the transmission from Hanoi. He pulled out the small notebook he had in his shirt pocket and noted the time.

The wooden shutters of the room were thrown open. Ivorson could see the figure of the man inside quite clearly. He must be letting the room cool off. That was good. Ivorson made a mental note to look for air conditioners on the building wall. If there weren't any, chances were that the windows were always open during radio traffic.

The man refastened the screen behind the shutters and disappeared from view. Now nothing was visible inside the room but an ochre-colored wall. Minutes ticked by. Ivorson and Wilbur waited, insects crawling on their faces and necks.

The Station communications people were also monitoring the broadcast. Ivorson had synchronized his watch with their time and asked them to keep a careful log of the start and end time of the transmission from Hanoi.

He reasoned that shortly after the end of the radio schedule, the Embassy code clerk would decipher the message. If the code machine were not in the radio room, a light should come on elsewhere in the compound soon after the transmission ended.

If that didn't happen, but the light in the radio room stayed on for a protracted time after the transmission stopped, the hypothesis would be that the code machine was in the same room with the radio.

There was, of course, a third possibility: the radio room could go dark shortly after the end of the broadcast schedule, but no other lights would be turned on anywhere else. If that happened, Ivorson was out of luck.

He looked at his watch again. Five minutes after ten. According to the Station, the encoded traffic from Hanoi to the Embassy varied wildly in length from one week to the next. All Ivorson could do was time the light and compare notes with the communications people later.

They waited. Ivorson's thigh muscles were screaming from the unaccustomed squatting position. He tried shifting his weight from one side to another. It occurred to him that the last time he'd watched a lighted window this intently, it had been a college dormitory, and a girl had been undressing behind it. That was a long time ago.

At ten fourteen, the man re-appeared in the window and closed the shutters. A few seconds later, the light in the room went out. Ivorson blinked his eyes, trying to re-adjust them to the dark. He made a note of the time. What would happen now?

The light came on in the room immediately west of the one where it had just gone out. A moment later, the shutters opened. It looked to Ivorson like the same man who had been in the first room. "Same," Wilbur confirmed in a whisper.

The man disappeared, and the window remained open. Ivorson and Wilbur squatted in the swamp. Ivorson's thighs were torturing him now. He slowly moved to a kneeling position on one knee to relieve his cramped muscles. As he did so, the water around him began to swirl and hiss with movement. Startled, he almost leapt to his feet.

Wilbur's hand on his arm restrained him. "Baw pen yang," he hissed, using the first Lao expression that every foreigner learned. "Is nothing. Only leech."

Only leech! Jesus Christ! It took an enormous effort for Ivorson to remain kneeling. The water around him gradually grew calm again. What were they doing down there? He thought he could feel a thousand little mouths gnawing at his body. Were they real, or was it just in his mind?

The agony continued another twenty-three minutes. Then the man appeared again and closed the shutter. An instant later, the light went out. Ivorson checked his watch, noted the time in his notebook, and stood up. His overstressed leg muscles were so relieved that they almost gave way under him.

"Let's go," he whispered to Wilbur, turned toward the distant dike, and began wading.

A long, thick shape in the vegetation just in front of him began to wriggle. Ivorson's stomach clenched into a fist of fear. He tried to jump backward and lost his balance. He fell with a splash. The snake's head and his own were less than a yard apart. Its mouth was opening. He felt a shout forming in his throat.

His back collided with something solid, there was a metallic whispering sound, and Wilbur bent forward over him, his arm whipping down in an arc. There was a splashy chopping sound. The snake went into a frenzy of uncoordinated writhing and looping, then abruptly uncoiled and lay still.

"Ne bougez pas! Don't move," whispered Wilbur in his ear. They stayed there, motionless, for what seemed to Ivorson like an eternity. There was no reaction from either the Embassy or any other of the houses along the road. No lights came on. No voices were raised.

Finally, Wilbur stood and pulled on his sleeve. "Good," he murmured, "No one heard. Allons." Ivorson heard the knife slithering back into it scabbard, and Wilbur pushed by him. "I walk first." That suited Ivorson just fine.

Wilbur scooped up the still form of the snake and draped it around his neck. The tail and severed neck of the serpent hung down into the water on either side of him. It must be eight or nine feet long, and at least four inches in diameter.

"You lucky," Wilbur hissed over his shoulder. His English, abandoned in the stress of the snake's attack, had returned. "This snake skin pretty to hang on wall. I do for you."

Fuck the skin, Ivorson thought. Just let me get out of this swamp!

Only minutes after they reached the dike, a car engine sounded to their north. It was Orville, right on time. Ivorson got in the back seat. Wilbur threw the body of the snake into the trunk along with the knife, and scrambled in after him.

Ivorson sagged against the door. His nostrils full of the stench of the swamp mud on his legs and sneakers. He felt the empty, almost nauseating letdown of adrenaline withdrawal, but he also felt as if he'd just won the Irish Sweepstakes.

First, and most importantly, the Fear hadn't disabled him.

Even when snake and he were face to face, he hadn't felt the total paralysis he'd suffered in Saigon.

Secondly, it was a ninety percent probability that he'd just located the Viet code room, and the sonofabitch was on an outside wall with an open window! If he could just figure out a way to get a look through that window at the code machine, it might save years of bloody warfare. Not to mention making Ivorson's name a household word in the Directorate of Operations.

While they rattled along toward the small wooden house in Nongbon district which was their safesite, Wilbur continued practicing his English while he burned off the dozen or so white leeches attached to his legs with a cigarette. Thin streams of blood from their bites flowed down his heavily muscled calves. Ivorson didn't even want to think about what his own legs looked like.

"That snake no dangerous for you, Mistair Petair," Wilbur assured him. "He squeeze snake, no poison. He too small kill man. He only bite."

"I'm glad to hear that, Wilbur." Ivorson hoped his voice sounded normal. It was great to have an agent with balls the size of cantaloupes, until you had to get out there in the dark with him and find out how big your own were. That issue, at least, was settled. Wilbur's were bigger.

"You happy what we do tonight, Mistair Petair?" Wilbur asked him.

Ivorson punched him lightly on the shoulder. "You bet your ass I'm happy, Wilbur," he said, "and just as soon as I get my hands on my billfold, I'm going to make you happy, too. You were terrific out there tonight."

Wilbur beamed. "I like you too much, Mistair Petair. You go wade in swamp, you no scared leech, no scream when snake come, you give Wilbur kip like drunk man. You numba one."

Ivorson grinned back at the Asian. "Wilbur," he said, "this is the beginning of a beautiful friendship. You and I are going to rip those Viet bastards a new asshole."

Wilbur's smile grew positively beatific. "No shit," he agreed.

On Friday afternoon, Ivorson bought a motorcycle and rented a house, both of them from the wife of an Air America pilot who was going back to the States after her husband had crashed up-country.

The woman, whose face bore the traces of protracted crying, struggled to control her two small children as she showed Ivorson the place. That was another difference between Vientiane and Saigon: there were no dependents in Viet Nam, but the serenity of Vientiane permitted wives and children to accompany their husbands.

The casualties of the secret war didn't make headlines like the ones in Vietnam, he reflected, but the men were just as dead, and the widows just as devastated. Maybe this gal's situation would have been better now had she been back in the States. It was bad, either way.

The motorcycle was a 150cc Honda road bike. It didn't have much guts, but it would be basic transportation, at least until the rains started.

The house was small: only two bedrooms, modest living and dining rooms, an outdoor kitchen and an indoor bath, complete with bidet–a vestige of la culture francaise.

The small front yard was enclosed by a high wall, festooned with purple and peach bougainvillea. Behind the substantial metal gate was a short drive that led to a carport, more than large enough for his motorcycle.

The backyard was marvelous. Completely enclosed by the same wall, it was an oasis of watered green grass and bright tropical flowers in the sun-seared surroundings of hot-season Vientiane. Near the house stood a large frangipani tree–champa, the Lao called them. Its gnarled limbs were bare now, but when the rains came, it would leaf out and perfume the entire compound with its sweet, creamy-white flowers.

The location was almost ideal. There were no other houses immediately next to his. Nothing but a rice paddy was behind him, and best of all, there were four possible exit routes via neighboring roads. He agreed to assume the woman's lease, paid for the motorcycle, stumbled awkwardly through an expressions of condolences, and drove the bike back to the USAID compound.

As he parked the motorcycle, Ivorson saw Nguyen thi Nga and Ly crossing the compound street toward the ACA. Both of them were wearing *ao dais*.

Ivorson had always considered the *ao dai* the ideal woman's costume. It covered the body completely, from the top of the neck down to the ankles, and it could not possibly be sexier.

The silk top, with its high mandarin collar, was form- fitting. The long skirt, worn over black or white silk pants was slit up to the waist on both sides, and the resulting panels of cloth in front and back floated in the breeze as the woman walked. The effect was of a bright-colored butterfly.

Ivorson caught up with the two of them at the front door. "Good afternoon, Miss Nga."

She turned around. He saw recognition in her eyes. She frowned for just a split second, then leaped away from the door and grasped one of the posts that supported the porch roof. "Don't run over me," she cried in mock terror. "I will get out of your way." Ly stared at her in astonishment.

So did Ivorson. It was the last reaction he had expected. People nearby were staring at them, but in spite of the embarrassment that caused him, he had to laugh. "It's all right," he assured her. "I'm not in a hurry today. You're quite safe."

"Thank heaven," she said, her eyes teasing him. "I have been afraid to go outside all day."

She turned to Ly and said, "He's the one," in Vietnamese. Ly clapped a hand to her mouth and giggled. Her expression said very clearly that she had been fully briefed on Ivorson's first meeting with Nga.

"Do you know my friend, Ly?" Nga asked him. She works in Personnel, too.

"I remember Miss Ly very well," said Ivorson. "How are you, Ly?"

Ly giggled.

Nga said to her, "I'm sure you remember my telling you about Mr. Ivorson, Ly. He made a big impression on me the other day."

Ivorson's ears were definitely warm now. Both girls laughed.

Ivorson began to be irritated at being the object of such prolonged public amusement. Nga must have seen it in his face. She took a step forward and laid a hand on his bare arm. "I'm sorry," she said. "I won't tease anymore."

Ivorson felt as if he'd just been touched by a live electrical wire. "All right," he answered. "I'll forgive you, if you'll let me buy you a drink." He didn't have any idea what had caused the radical change in Nga's attitude toward him, but he certainly intended to make the most of it.

They went to the snack bar by the pool, which at this time of the day was filled with splashing USAID children and their mothers—a far cry from Saigon, indeed.

The two girls decided on lemonade. Ivorson ordered them from the Lao waitress, along with a beer for himself. The drinks came, and they toasted each other ceremoniously. "To our friendship," proposed Ivorson, clinking glasses with each of them. "I promise I won't run over either of you, ever again."

Nga said something to Ly in Vietnamese. She spoke in Northern dialect, and Ivorson didn't get it all, but he grasped that it had to do with studying English. He tried to project the bland politeness of one who understands nothing of what he is hearing.

Nga turned back to him. "Mister Ivorson, we would like to ask you a favor."

"If it is too much trouble, please say so. Don't agree just to be polite."

Now what was this about? "All right, what can I do for you?"

"Could you give us English lessons? Perhaps at noon or right after work? Only an hour a week would help us. We both have to help our mothers at home, and can't take the time to go downtown to the Lao-American Association. USAID doesn't offer classes here anymore."

Ivorson could hardly believe his luck. He had been wracking his brain for some way to see Nga again, and she was handing it to him on a silver platter! Her homely friend Ly went along with the deal as a chaperone, of course, but where there was a will, there was a way.

Immediately after his encounter with Lisa Odom, he had had Station files checked on both Ly and Nguyen thi Nga and had found no derogatory information on either of them.

Both had been born in Laos, of Tonkinese mothers who had themselves been babes in arms when their parents left Vietnam. When the French took Laos as a Protectorate, they had quickly discovered that the country had no artisan class, so they had brought such people from Tonkin China—North Vietnam–which was a full-blown French colony. Ly's grandfather was one such artisan.

Nga's father, on the other hand, had been one Phillipe Martin, a sergeant in the French Army. All in all, they both had biographies about as innocuous as a Vietnamese could have.

The chubby girl was gazing at him with transparent hopefulness. Ivorson could see why Lisa Odom had thought he was paranoid about Ly. It really was very hard to imagine her being deceitful.

He couldn't read Nga's expression. She too looked hopeful, but something else was there, as well. Maybe it was repressed sexual desire. He sure hoped so.

"I'd be delighted to give you girls English lessons," he assured them. "When and where shall we do it?"

"We can use the classroom behind the APO," Nga answered promptly. "The classes that were there have been moved to the Lao American Association, downtown. What is best for you?" she asked him. "Noon or after work?"

They decided to start on Monday after work. The girls declined Ivorson's offer of another drink, claiming that they had to walk to town and buy some cloth. Ivorson regretted his lack of a car. He couldn't take them both on the Honda.

They left him on the porch of the ACA. He watched them walking away toward the compound gate, Nga's long black hair and pink *ao dai* floating in the light breeze. She turned and called to him over her shoulder, "Goodbye, Peter."

A warning bell sounded in Ivorson's brain. Why was she publicly encouraging him? He was no doubt considered an eligible bachelor, but with her face and body, she could have her pick. And why the sudden friendliness today after her coldness at their first meeting? Would her desire for English lessons account for that?

Maybe he ought to mention her name to Wilbur, who had laid almost every layable female in town, unmarried or otherwise. Wilbur drew the line at Vietnamese, but he certainly couldn't have failed to notice a woman as gorgeous as Nga.

On the other hand, if Wilbur found out that Ivorson was lusting after a Viet, he'd probably quit on the spot and take the whole team with him.

No, better not check with Wilbur. But, after all, Ivorson was no babe in arms. He was going into this with his eyes wide open, and, on the face of it, Nga had no connection with North Vietnam other than the accident of her grandparents' birth there, and the influence of her European father had diluted even that.

Besides, she was the most exotic, most beautiful female he had ever met in his life.

He sensed someone beside him and at the same time smelled a hint of apple blossom. He turned and saw Lisa Odom, looking up at him with an expression that could not by any stretch of the imagination be described as admiring.

"I see you've gotten over your fear of Vietnamese women, Mr. Ivorson," she said, in a saccharine sweet tone. "I'm so glad."

Ivorson felt his neck getting warm. Damn the woman! She would have seen him with Nga and Ly. He cast about for something to say then decided that no matter what he came up with, it would only make him a bigger target. He clamped his mouth shut and nodded noncommittally.

"Nothing to say on the subject today?" Lisa asked. "Well that's not really surprising. Nga has left a lot of men around here speechless." She gave him a smile that would have frozen alcohol and marched off down the steps.

Ivorson felt like kicking her. The bitch! She had really driven the needle home. The realization that he had had it coming, at least in part, added to his embarrassment. Furious with both her and himself, he wheeled around and went back into the ACA for another beer.

✲ ✲ ✲

By the time Nga reached home, it was quite dark. She felt her way over the rough stones through the archway in the wall that surrounded the Chinese cemetery. The light coming through the window of the two-room caretaker's house was faint.

The smells of charcoal, garlic, and cooking rice greeted her as she entered the tiny house. "Good evening, mother," she called.

"Hurry up and wash," was the answer. "The food is almost ready." Her mother's sunken eyes looked at her accusingly from under a lined brow and thinning gray hair. It was hard for Nga to see, in the face looking at her now, the beautiful, smiling young woman in the faded photograph which hung on the living room wall. Time, and Nga's father, had done that.

Nga flicked a glance at the photo. She was in it, too, at the age of ten years. Her father had still been with them, then. There were no pictures of him in the house, now. Once it had become clear that he was neither coming back to Laos nor going to have them join him in France, her mother had thrown the pictures out.

His abandonment left them in desperate poverty. Nga's mother's youth and beauty had been casualties in their struggle to survive. Nga herself had had to barter her body when she was thirteen, in the days of their greatest need, for food to eat. That was how her mother got the caretaker's job at the cemetery, too, and how Nga got her own job at USAID.

Her French heritage had given her the right to attend the Cathedral school and Lycee, but that was the only advantage it conferred on her. She grew up to be a beauty, but, even so, the marriageable males of the Vietnamese community had not been able to overcome their families' distaste for her mixed blood. None had proposed marriage. And now she was twenty-six, an old maid.

Oh, she had had western suitors, both French and Americans, but how could she even consider marrying one of them? Not after the desperate struggle for survival that her father's abandonment had forced on her and her mother! She saw him in every white face that smiled at her.

When she met Nguyen van Huu, at one of the Embassy open-houses for the local community, she was already working at USAID, and the Americans had just intervened in South Vietnam.

Huu was kind and gentle. He treated her with respect, and she admired him enormously for his dedication and rectitude. When he offered her a chance to participate in the struggle against the new despoilers of her ancestral homeland, she accepted willingly. After all, who had more reason than she, among the local Vietnamese, to struggle against the Caucasians?

She often regretted that decision. It had cost her dearly. Her cultivated "friendship" with John Reagan, at Huu's direction had made other Vietnamese women, her childhood friends, think of her as a prostitute, or even a traitor. Except for Ly, they all shunned her now.

Uncle Huu forbade her to explain to them. He said she must bear it, that it was her patriotic duty. After the Americans had been beaten, the others would be told and would respect her for what she had done, as he did.

It was his respect, not theirs, that she coveted, and that made her continue, but she was frightened all the time. Suppose she was caught working for Uncle Huu? Not only would she lose her job at USAID, so precious to her and her mother, but the Lao puppet government would certainly put her in jail. The idea was horrifying.

And now, just as she had feared, Huu wanted her to become "friendly" with Peter Ivorson. He had insisted, over Nga's violent objections, that she ask the American for English lessons.

She wished Ivorson had not accepted. Right from their first meeting, he had disturbed her. She hated his face, with those bold eyes and goats-horn eyebrows, so much like her memories of her father's. She wished she had never mentioned his name to Huu. She wished she were fat and plain, like Ly. She was afraid!

Chapter Five

The Pilatus Porter rolled out onto final approach for a landing at the USAF/RTAF airbase at Udon Thani, Thailand, thirty miles away from Vientiane. It was early on Wednesday morning and Ivorson was in the right-hand front seat.

He'd become fascinated with flying during his Air Force years in Germany. He had won a private pilot's license in both powered planes and gliders at the local aeroclub and had even logged several dozen hours of bootlegged flying time in a T-33 jet trainer, but this was his first exposure to the Swiss-built Short Takeoff and Landing (STOL) aircraft.

The pilot pulled off power. With full flaps down, the Porter descended toward the field at a very steep angle. They passed over the runway threshold. Then, while they were still some thirty feet in the air, the pilot pushed the propeller pitch control lever to full reverse position.

The turboprop engine responded with an awful howl. The fuselage shuddered at the braking effect of the big propeller's radical change in pitch. Aghast, his stomach an iron ball of fear, Ivorson clutched at the door handle.

The plane seemed to stop in mid-air. Ivorson tensed himself for the impending impact. But the aircraft settled gently down onto the runway and waddled forward at idle to the departure taxiway, its turbine engine yodeling triumphantly as it turned in front of a flight of four bomb-laden F-4s waiting for take-off.

The American pilot leaned over toward Ivorson. "I love to show these fighter jocks that shit," he shouted in a west Oklahoma accent. "It makes their eyes bug right out of their fuckin' heads."

Indeed, Ivorson could see the startled eyes of the first F-4 pilot staring at them over the top of his oxygen mask. He understood why. The maneuver had done some pretty dramatic things to his eye pressure, too.

He was met on the transient ramp by an Air Force captain, of about his own age. "Hi, Mr. Ivorson, I'm Captain Ken Stein, Air Force Intelligence. Welcome to Udorn."

They drove in a jeep to Base Operations, picked up another captain—this one from the local weather squadron—and, with the tower's blessing, crossed the taxiway and bumped across the infield to a metal shed located about halfway down the length of the runway. All the while, flights of F-4s and propeller driven A-1Es, loaded with bombs and rockets, were taking off.

The weather captain unlocked the shed. "I did the morning launch a couple of hours ago," he told Ivorson, "but the combat missions will all be out of here in a little while, and then we'll let another one fly for you. In the meantime, you can see how they work."

The shed was about twelve feet long. It contained only a long table, two large, upright metal cabinets and half a dozen gray metal industrial gas bottles. One of the bottles was strapped to a dolly, and a valve with a gauge and a rubber hose was screwed into its top.

The weather captain unlocked the metal storage cabinet and pulled out a cardboard box, about six by four by four inches in size. He took the box over to the long table, opened both it and its inner plastic container, and pulled out a tan-colored package of rubber, which he unfolded on the table.

It proved to be a large balloon. The weather captain wheeled the gray bottle on its dolly over to the table, pushed the hose into the mouth of the balloon, and turned on the valve. There was a hiss, and the balloon began to fill.

"How do you measure the amount of helium?" Ivorson asked him. "Pounds of pressure, or what?"

"We don't bother," was the answer. "We just tie on what we're going to lift, and when it comes off the deck, we know we've got enough gas. Of course, in our case, we're sending the sonde up to altitude. The higher it goes, the more the helium expands and the bigger the balloon gets. If we over-fill it on the ground, it's likely to explode before it reaches the height we want."

"Ah." That wasn't going to be Ivorson's problem. "How much does your instrument package weigh?"

The weather captain squinted in recollection. "Not over six pounds at the most." He looked at Ivorson with frank curiosity. "How much weight do you need to lift?"

"About twenty pounds, I think," said Ivorson. "But I'm not concerned with over-filling. Mine will be a very low level flight. Tethered, actually."

The weather captain and Captain Stein exchanged glances. They were obviously consumed with curiosity. Ivorson didn't enlighten them.

The balloon began to lift off of the table. The weather captain closed the valve on the gas bottle. "We'd better finish this outside if we're going to use that much gas," he said. "Otherwise, we won't be able to get the balloon out the door."

He pulled a length of binder-twine from a roll hanging on the wall, cut it off with his pocket knife, and whipped half a dozen turns around the throat of the balloon. With the balloon in one fist, he pulled the filler hose loose. "One of you guys wheel the dolly outside," he said, and started for the door. The half-inflated balloon trailed along behind him like a clumsy air-borne puppy.

Ivorson beat Captain Stein to the handles of the dolly. They set it up outside the shed and continued the inflation process. Ivorson opened his briefcase and pulled out the metal scale disks he had brought with him. Wilbur had obtained them on loan from a rice merchant in Vientiane who owed him a favor.

They were in kilos, of course, but that wasn't too tough. 2.2 pounds for each kilo; ten kilos equals 22 pounds. Better to have too much lift than not enough. He put ten kilos worth of the weights back in the briefcase, which probably weighed two pounds itself, say twenty-four pounds total. He was just guessing at this point. There would be a TV camera, a battery, motors, maybe even a coaxial cable to get the images to a recorder on the ground.

By now the balloon was fully inflated, a globe six feet across, tugging frantically at the weather captain's arm. "Okay," he said. "That'll do it, for sure. Shut 'er off. I need you to go back in the shed and bring me some more twine. Come to think of it, better bring the whole roll. We'll have to beef it up when we make a tether, or our civilian friend here is likely to lose his briefcase."

Captain Stein brought the twine and, while the weather captain held the balloon, he and Ivorson wove a five-strand rope of the twine a couple of feet long. They tied one end to the balloon's throat and the other to the handle of Ivorson's briefcase. Then they made another rope of twine forty feet long by twisting eight strands of twine together.

Ivorson tied one end to the briefcase handle and knotted the other end around his wrist. The weather captain checked the runway and taxiways. "Okay," he said. "This morning's airstrikes are all out-bound. Let's see what happens."

Ivorson let go of the balloon. It immediately lifted off into the sky, angling slightly to the east in the now-hot breeze. Ivorson hung on to the twine tightly, not knowing how much pull to expect when it came up short at the end of the tether. It was a hard jerk, but the twine ropes held. His briefcase looked silly as hell, suspended almost forty feet in the air.

Fully inflated, the balloon looked immense to Ivorson. How could he keep something that big from being seen? He'd have to spraypaint it black, for openers.

He began walking around, pulling the balloon behind him, trying to get a feel for its controllability. It followed him reasonably well. As long as the wind was light, one man could probably handle it. That was good news. He couldn't take a parade out into the swamp.

The bad news was the question of direction. No matter which way he walked, the balloon always moved away from him in the same direction–down the wind. How in the hell was he going to resolve that problem?

Being careful not to get his tether hung up on the roof of the shed, Ivorson walked back to join the other men. By the time he got there, his arm ached from the effort it took to hold the balloon. They had definitely over-filled it. All he needed was just enough lift to get it moving upward. Some experimentation was in order.

When he reached the captains, he began to pull the balloon downward. That took a lot more energy. The balloon wanted to fly. Ivorson began to fear that the twine would break. Captain Stein got on the rope with him and began pulling hand over hand. "Easy, easy," cautioned Ivorson. "I don't want to lose that briefcase!"

The words had scarcely left his mouth when the rope went slack in his hands. Oh, shit! The tether had broken. Where was he going to get replacement scale weights for Wilbur's friend in Udorn, Thailand?

He looked up and caught sight of his briefcase plummeting downward, directly toward the jeep. Thank God! It was the thinner rope, connecting the balloon to the briefcase that had broken. The balloon, freed of its burden, was sailing off skyward in the direction of Vietnam.

The briefcase landed square in the middle of the jeep's hood with an impressive bang. It put a deep dent in the hood, but the briefcase remained in one piece.

The weather captain, who had been standing about five feet from the jeep, insisted that they get a nylon rope before the experiment continued.

By the time Ivorson got back to Vientiane, sunburned and carrying his own supply of four balloons and a small tank of helium, he had learned how much of the gas it took to lift a twenty-four pound payload to forty feet without breaking the tether or pulling his arms out of their sockets.

He had also learned, when the breeze freshened during the afternoon, that at any windspeed over ten knots, the balloon bucked at the end of the tether to such an extent that he probably couldn't get a picture of the goddamn Embassy building, let alone of anything the size of a code machine.

Even if the wind were calm, he was still a long way from being able to look at the code machine. First, he was going to have to figure out how to: (a) get that enormous damned balloon close enough to the target so the television lens could see anything without the entire Embassy staff spotting it; and (b) get the balloon to hold still. It turned and twisted on the end of its tether at random. How was he going to control that rotation so that he could hold the lens on what he wanted to see?

At the moment, he could see no solution to either problem. He needed some technical advice. As distasteful as the idea was, he might have to bring Jack Lawrence into the picture.

He did it the following morning, and he didn't enjoy it any more than he'd thought he would. Still, Lawrence didn't make more than one or two supercilious remarks before the technical challenge caught his imagination. Challenged or not, however, the tech couldn't come up with any better ideas than Ivorson for controlling the balloon. "We've got to get some Headquarters expertise for this job," he told Ivorson. "I'll send a cable today to Hawaii and ask the Regional Technical Officer to come out here TDY and talk to us."

Ivorson didn't like the idea of the request coming from the Tech rather than himself, but he couldn't see any alternative and agreed with as much good grace as he could muster. The RTO arrived five days later and, to Ivorson's relief, proved to be a former Saigon tech whom Ivorson both liked and trusted. Furthermore, he turned out to be a gold mine of information on the subject of low-light television.

It turned out that Tech/Headquarters could supply a small video camera with a special long lens capable of providing high-resolution pictures through the code room window from a range of up to fifty feet. What it saw could be transmitted via a coaxial cable to a video recorder small enough to fit into a backpack.

Ivorson's guess about the weight of the camera had been on the low side. The camera, together with its battery and the recorder, would weigh right at thirty pounds. Even so, it was still well within the lifting capability of the weather balloon. Ivorson sent a cable to Technical Support at headquarters and ordered two each of the camera, battery and cable.

That, unfortunately, was the last good news he got. The RTO was as unable as he and Lawrence to cope with the need to aim the camera in the right direction and keep it trained on its target while filming.

The two techs naturally wanted to do some experimentation, and since Ivorson refused to allow any testing in Laos, on security grounds, the three of them made another trip to Udorn Air Base. They flew four more balloons and had a lot of fun, but at the end of the day, they didn't have any more ideas than they'd had when they arrived.

The RTO (and Jack Lawrence too, to give the devil his due) were fascinated with the technical challenge the problem presented. Ivorson was of two minds about their enthusiasm. He needed their help, but the more deeply the techs became involved, the more tenuous his own control over the operation was going to be.

His worst fears were realized when he came into the office on Monday and discovered that, over the weekend, without bothering to consult him, Lawrence and the RTO had sent off a lengthy eye-only message to Tech Support/ Headquarters. A reply had already been received. Ivorson seethed. The damned techs had taken over the balloon operation.

"It's going to be terrific," the RTO enthused, waving the cable from Headquarters under Ivorson's nose. "They've made it a crash project, money and manpower no object. They're going to build a mini-blimp of black neoprene-coated fabric, ten feet long by four feet in diameter." He was so excited at the prospect that he was practically jumping up and down. Lawrence smiled smugly.

You bastard, though Ivorson. You blind-sided me.

"The TV camera and recorder will both be inside the gas bag," the RTO continued, "along with a transmitter. That'll do away with the weight and awkwardness of the coaxial cable." Despite his anger at being out-maneuvered, Ivorson had to admit the advantages of that.

"The blimp will be powered with two silent, battery-powered, electrical fans, which will not only propel it, but blow enough air over its control surfaces to assure positive directional response in all three axes: pitch, yaw, and roll."

"The thing will be remotely controlled by radio, of course, and, best of all, because of the size and sophistication of its control systems, altitude can be handled, as well as direction. That does away with the need for a tether."

Ivorson could get enthusiastic about that, too. It meant there was no need to risk any personnel behind the Vietnamese Embassy, including—and in particular–himself. The blimp could be launched from the back of a truck parked on the dike that he and Wilbur had used as the rendezvous point for the reconnaissance in the swamp.

"Those Headquarters guys are really hot for this," the RTO assured Ivorson. Ivorson didn't doubt it a bit. The techs he had worked with in the past had loved their gadgets, sometimes to the point that their ultimate operational use got lost sight of. He had visions of a massive technical task force from Headquarters arriving in Vientiane with their plaything. They'd probably want to parade it down Setthatthirath Avenue.

"Now we're going to really get somewhere with this operation," Jack Lawrence assured him. Ivorson could hear the double-entendre in his voice. What he meant was that Lawrence was going to get somewhere. Since it was officially labeled a technical operation, he would have, at least, equal say with Ivorson in its deployment.

Ivorson didn't look forward to that one bit. This was his idea, his operation. Left to his own devices, Lawrence wouldn't have come up with it in a hundred years. Now, however, just because a particular technical device was required, Lawrence would claim the operation as his own and try to relegate Ivorson to the role of an interested, but impotent (Ivorson would see about that!) spectator.

The prospect put him in a black state of mind. He found himself hoping that the blimp would blow up on its maiden voyage, like the Hindenburg (hardly likely, since helium didn't burn), and then be became disgusted at himself for thinking that way. What mattered, he kept telling himself, was the mission, not who got to carry it out. He found it a difficult thought to keep in focus.

The RTO departed for Hawaii. The rest of March passed with no further word on the project from Tech/Hqs. The weather got hotter; a lot hotter. The thermometer went through the hundred-degree mark every day. Electricite du Laos, utterly incapable of generating enough power to handle the demand of the air-conditioners, was off more often than it was on, which meant the water didn't run, either.

Ivorson learned some Lao from Oum, Wilbur's diminutive aunt, whom he had hired as a combination cook and maid. She was four feet, ten inches tall, weighted eighty three pounds and looked like an oriental version of Mary Poppins, with her hair pulled up in a tight bun right on top of her head. She was cheerful, clean, a good cook and hated Vietnamese as much as Wilbur. Her husband had died at Dien Bien Phu, too.

"Baw mee fie," she would greet him when he came home from work. "There's no electricity." Also, "Gaw baw mee nam"—no water either. He'd as soon not have needed the new vocabulary. It didn't help his state of mind a bit that the Hoang van Cam operation was still on high-center. Wilbur kept the telephone absolutely free from six o'clock on every night, but Cam didn't call Sengdara.

Ivorson had Sengdara put pressure on him when she saw him in the market, but his response, according to her, was always the same: "I'll call when I can. Believe me. Trust me."

As April arrived, Ivorson reluctantly directed her to limit her contact with the chauffeur to one conversation every other week. It was just too dangerous to continue at the present pace. Some sharp-eyed NVN sympathizer was going to spot her talking to the chauffeur and get suspicious.

He had Sengdara tell Cam that it was for his safety; that she couldn't bear it if he got in trouble because of her. She reported that Cam actually wept when she told him they had to limit their contact. That, at least, was good news. The hook was set, but when was the fish going to bite?

Ivorson had a rather sharp disagreement with COS over that decision. "I've got the White House shoved up my ass on his operation, Ivorson," Riley told him over the secure telephone. "They want to see progress, not a slow-down."

"If Cam gets spotted with Sengdara," Ivorson retorted, "the White House won't have any operation to bother you about. We can't recruit him in the goddamn marketplace. Tell them to keep their shirts on."

Riley said he didn't like being talked to that way by a subordinate. Ivorson didn't apologize.

In spite of that friction, however, Riley let Ivorson have two more meetings with Tran van Cao, his personally recruited agent, the North Vietnamese expert of the Lao National Police. Ivorson used them to systematically debrief Cao on all of the local Vietnamese who visited the Embassy, in the hope that some vulnerability or susceptibility might emerge on which an approach could be made to one of them.

The effort proved fruitless, but Ivorson enjoyed it more than most of the things he had done lately, despite the fact that he was allergic to the smoke of Cao's chain-smoked Gitane cigarettes.

Cao was a tiny, bird-like little man with nicotine-stained claws for fingers. His French sounded like a bird, too. It used every tone of northern dialect Vietnamese. In fact, he was so diminutively engaging that Ivorson had no trouble understanding why Riley believed so strongly in him. He was a sort of Vietnamese version of Wilbur.

On the other Vietnamese front, Ivorson's campaign to get inside the fair body of Nguyen thi Nga made no more progress than the operation against

Cam. He saw her regularly, two hours a week—along with Ly, of course—in the classroom behind the Army Post Office in the USAID compound. He lusted for her more every time he saw her. Sometimes she appeared receptive. She flirted with him often during class, and when they shook hand at the end of the lesson, she left her hand in his too long for it to be anything but an invitation.

Outside the classroom, however, she was formal, even distant, and despite his best efforts, she gave him absolutely no opportunity to see her alone, not even in the USAID compound, much less outside. Ivorson was beginning to feel a real kinship with the North Vietnamese chauffeur, and he resented the hell out of it. He wasn't used to being thwarted by women.

On top of all of it, he was getting out of shape. The heat made it torture to run, no matter how early in the morning he went out. At noon on a particularly hot day in mid-April, he decided to begin making use of the pool at the ACA. Swimming some laps would be good exercise.

He did a moderately successful swan dive off the low board and came to the surface a foot from Lisa Odom's nose.

"Sorry," he said stiffly. "I didn't mean to come so close to you."

"It wasn't your fault," she said. "I pushed off from the side without looking." She was wearing a skimpy two-piece bathing suit, in which she looked—as nearly as Ivorson could see without obviously staring—very nice.

"I understand that you're giving English lessons to Ly and Nguyen thi Nga," she went on. "I guess I ought to apologize for calling you paranoid." Having planted that dart, she stroked swiftly toward the ladder on the other side of the pool.

Resentful, Ivorson tried to think of some reason why that wasn't a fair thing for her to say, and realized that there really wasn't any. He HAD been paranoid when he arrived in Laos, he supposed. Under the calming effect of the dusty little city, the Fear had retreated so far into the back of his mind that he was hardly aware of its presence. He had drawn a weapon from the Station—another Walther PPK—but after a few weeks he had stopped carrying it. It was in the bedside table, at home.

Lisa climbed up the ladder out of the pool. She had a lovely figure, with slender, tanned legs that went all the way from her pear-shaped fanny to the center of the earth. The sight of them made him wonder if he ought to try to make peace with her, but he dismissed the idea. She might be good-looking, but she was anti-CIA and a spiteful bitch into the bargain. He had enough frustration on his hands with Nga. Why open himself up for more?

He'd just have to keep spending his pay on occasional visits to the Morocco Bar.

Chapter Six

Nga hadn't budged from her desk since Miss Odom went to eat. The other girls in the office had all left the compound for someone's birthday lunch. Nga had volunteered to cover the office. She wasn't wanted at the party anyway, and it gave her the opportunity she had been waiting for. Now that she was alone, however, she was paralyzed with indecision.

This was the time to do it. The key to the separate file closet in which the Americans' 201 files were kept was in Miss Odom's desk. All she had to do was go in there, take the key, and open the door. She could find and skim through Peter Ivorson's file in a matter of minutes.

But, God, she was so frightened. She wished with all her heart she had never agreed to help uncle Huu do this. Suppose that Miss Odom, or someone else, came in and caught her? What could she say? No excuse would work. She would lose her job at USAID, and then how would she and her mother live?

She might even be arrested, or deported. Although born in Laos, she was still a "resortissante vietnamienne," allowed to live here on tolerance. The Americans had enough influence with the Lao government to have her sent away, perhaps to Saigon. She shuddered at the idea.

Nguyen van Huu had insisted that she look at Ivorson's file. He said it would be easy for her. And it would be. All she had to do was get up and go do it. But then, if she did it, and found proof that Peter really was a CIA spy, Huu would insist that she become "very friendly" with him.

She shrank from the idea. Things were tolerable the way they were now. She had to admit Peter was a good teacher, and as long as Ly was there with her, Nga could tolerate his bold eyes on her body, and an occasional touch of his hands.

She could tell Huu that she wasn't able to get to the files—that she couldn't get the keys. But he was relying on her. And he was a good man. A patriot, not a *ba muoi lam* lecher like Peter Ivorson. She owed it to Uncle Huu and her mother's homeland to overcome her fear and do her duty.

She rose from her chair, and then sat back down again. She looked at her watch. She only had a little time left before Miss Odom came back. Abruptly, before she could change her mind again, she sprang from the chair, lunged across the room and into Miss Odom's office, and pulled open the desk drawer.

The key was there, on a silver ring. She looked around. The office was empty. She left Miss Odom's office and crossed to the inner room where the files were kept. No one was in the hall outside either. She had the whole area to herself.

She let herself into the unlocked room where the local personnel files were stored in rows of gray metal filing cabinets and closed the door behind her. At the other end of the room was another door. She ran to it, fit the key into the lock and turned, half-hoping that it wouldn't open.

It turned without resistance. She pushed the door open. It was dark inside. She felt on the wall for the light switch, found it, and turned it on.

The area was scarcely more than a large closet in which there were three—drawer filing cabinets, just like the ones used for the local-hire personnel files. On each drawer was a metal frame that held a rectangle of cardboard, and on the cardboard were letters indicating the first letter of the last names of the people whose files were in that drawer.

She quickly scanned the drawer fronts. A-D. E-H. I-L. There is was! She pulled open the file drawer and began thumbing through the thick cardboard file jackets insides. She found the one she wanted almost immediately, pulled it out of the file drawer and opened it.

Ivorson, Peter Henry. Born March 26, 1937. For goodness sake! He'd had a birthday less than three weeks ago, and he hadn't said a word about it. Place of birth: Ames, Iowa. She wasn't exactly sure where that was. Somewhere in the middle of the United States.

She read through the file, cursing her stupidity for not having brought a pencil and paper with her. She'd been too frightened and excited to think of it. Well, she'd just have to remember as much as she could.

She looked for any mention of the CIA, but there was none at all. According to the file, he had joined USAID in 1965 and been assigned to USAID/Vietnam in the supply section in Saigon. From there, he had been transferred to Vientiane. Perhaps uncle Huu was wrong about him.

My, he spoke a lot of languages: Spanish, and French and German. And Vietnamese! He'd told her he didn't understand what she said, but the file said he had been tested at 3/3. That was better than her English! Why had he lied to her? And look at this! In parentheses after the test score was the word "protect." That made no sense. You didn't protect a language. Or could it be the fact that he spoke Vietnamese that was to be protected? That was strange.

But that was all she found. It was a very thin file, compared to the files of the local-hire employees she worked with. Why? On impulse, she pulled the next file in the drawer. It belonged to Tom Jackson. She knew him. He worked in Agriculture. His file was much thicker. She opened it and leafed quickly through it. Jackson had worked for USAID only a year longer than Peter. Why was the file so much thicker?

Of course! Fitness reports. There were no fitness reports in Peter's file. That was odd. But no, it wasn't either. Peter had just arrived from Saigon. His files from USAID/Vietnam hadn't arrived yet, that was all. It was a normal file. The conclusion cheered her immensely. She was finished with Peter Ivorson!

She put Jackson's file back and looked through Peter's one more time. She really had to hurry! Miss Odom would be back soon.

There was a crease across the bottom of the last page in the file, as if the page had been folded up. She lifted the bottom of the page at the crease. On the back side, in Miss Odom's handwriting, was a penciled notation. "Separate file maintained in Dir.'s safe."

Oh, no. A separate file, kept in the Director's safe! There was something about Peter Ivorson that not even the American file clerks were allowed to know! That was very suspicious, especially in combination with his hiding his ability to speak Vietnamese. Uncle Huu must be right. Peter Ivorson was the enemy. Her stomach lurched at the thought of what that meant for her.

She looked at her watch. God, she had spent so much time in here! She had to get back to her desk. She put the file in the drawer, closed it, and backed out of the closet. As she was reaching for the light switch, she heard Lisa Odom's voice calling from the outer office. "Nga? Nga, where are you?"

Blind panic swept through her. Miss Odom! My God, what could she do? She was trapped in here. For a moment, she clung to the door, paralyzed with fear. Then her mind began to work again. At least she could close the closet! She had every right to be in the outer file section.

She pulled the door shut and locked it. Then she ran to a file cabinet and pulled out a local-hire file, not even noting the name on it.

"Nga?" Miss Odom called again. She had to answer. She couldn't pretend not to hear. But where could she hide the key and ring? Her *ao dai* had no pockets, and she had left her purse on her desk. Closer and closer to panic, she dropped the key on its ring inside the file jacket and put her hand over it to hold the file.

She ran to the outer door and pulled it open. "Here I am, Miss Odom," she called, trying to appear normal. She felt flushed and disheveled. She was sure Miss Odom would notice. She was very clever, for an American.

Miss Odom, who was halfway out the door into the hallway, turned around at the sound of Nga's voice. Her face, which had a stern expression on it, cleared at the sight of Nga. "There you are," she said brightly. "I couldn't imagine that you had left the office unattended."

"Oh no. I was just doing some filing."

"You shouldn't have closed the door to the file room while you were in there, Nga," said Miss Odom. Nga's heart sank. Was she suspicious?

"Someone could have come in and taken your purse. It's in plain sight on your desk."

Nga felt as if she might faint from the overwhelming relief she felt. Thank God. Miss Odom didn't suspect a thing. "I'm sorry, Miss Odom. I didn't even think about that. It was silly of me."

"Well, never mind. All's well that ends well. You may go get your lunch now."

Oh, God! The key! Miss Odom was sure to open her desk drawer at some point this afternoon and notice that the key was gone. She would certainly remember that Nga had been in the file room and accuse her of having taken it. Nga would deny it, of course, but the damage would be done.

Fear flooded her mind. What could she do? The key under her hand in the file jacket felt the size of a papaya. Her legs begin to tremble under her. She leaned against the file closet door for support.

"Oh, could you wait just a minute more to go to lunch, Nga?" Miss Odom asked her. "I need to go to the bathroom. I won't be but a minute."

Saved! Nga felt tears begin to form in her eyes. Her smile felt tremulous. "Of course, Miss Odom. Go right ahead." My God, how could the woman not notice her condition? She was afraid she was going to fall right down on the floor.

Miss Odom gave her a smile, turned, and walked off down the hall. Nga carried the file to her own desk and put it down. Miss Odom looked back as she turned into the women's restroom. Nga smiled at her. As soon as the American was out of sight, she snatched the key from the file jacket, raced into Miss Odom's office, threw the key in the desk drawer, and tore back to her desk.

She looked at the name on the file. Patom Keovilay. She didn't have a thing in the world to do with that file, and Miss Odom knew it. She couldn't leave it lying on her desk. She ran back into the file room, stuffed the file back in the drawer, and riffled through the cardboard file jackets, looking for one that she could legitimately be handling. Here! Boun Sayavong. That would work.

When Miss Odom came out of the ladies' room, Nga was back at her desk again, leafing through the file. Her hands were shaking so badly that she could scarcely hold it. She put down the file and put her hands in her lap before Miss Odom got close enough to see them trembling.

"All right, Nga," the American woman called. "Off you go!"

Nga waited until Miss Odom went into her own office before she got up. She was quivering all over. The American couldn't help but notice, if she saw her. She hurried to the ladies' room, collapsed on the floor in front of one of the stools, and vomited into it. Never, never again, she swore to herself. Not even for Uncle Huu.

✲ ✲ ✲

Out of the corner of her eye, Lisa caught a glimpse of Nga, as she almost ran out the door. She had looked very strange just now.

In spite of her best intentions, Lisa had never been able to like Nga. She did good work, but there was an aura of dislike, even contempt, for her American employers that radiated from the beautiful Vietnamese metisse. Lisa had felt it from the first day she met her, and the longer she had known her, the more she sensed it. She had even mentioned it to the Chief of Personnel, but he had looked at her askance. Of course, C/Personnel was a man, and a man of any age was unlikely to see beyond Nga's face and body.

That thought brought to mind her noon encounter with Peter Ivorson. She had put him in his place good and proper, the hypocrite! His fear and suspicion of Vietnamese hadn't lasted long after he got a look at Nga! That thought upset her. She forced him out of her mind and focused on the things she had to do this afternoon.

Walt Swan, in Public Works, was rotating back to the States. She needed to cut travel orders on him. She pulled open her desk drawer and reached into it for the file closet key.

Now, where was it? She had left it right there before lunch. She pulled the drawer out further and reached deeper into it. Ah, there it was, almost at the very back of the drawer. That was funny. How had it gotten back there? She was sure she had left it right in the front. And her file cards looked different, too.

Could Nga have been in her drawer? Surely not. She wouldn't do that. Lisa shrugged. The key must have slid back there when she closed the drawer. She took it out, got up, and walked to the inner file closet.

She passed between the rows of file cabinets in the local-hire area, inserted the key in the inner door, twisted it, and pulled the door open.

The light was on.

She stopped in her tracks and stared at it. Something was very wrong here. Lisa remembered distinctly having turned it off when she locked up before lunch.

She looked down at the key in her hand. She was quite certain, now that she thought of it, that she had dropped it in the front of her desk drawer.

There was only one possible explanation for the changed location of the key and the light: Nguyen thi Nga must have taken the key and stolen into the American employees' files.

A wave of anger swept over Lisa. This was a serious infringement of the rules. Nga knew better. There was no excuse for it.

But why had she done it? What on earth could she have been looking for? Lisa looked at the file cabinets in front of her. The middle drawer of the center cabinet was pulled out, ever-so-slightly. Lisa opened it fully and looked at the files. One was off-center, as if replaced in a hurry. She looked at the name.

Peter Ivorson.

Lisa was stunned. Their original confrontation flashed into her mind. Could Peter's violent, anti-Vietnamese obsession really have some basis in fact? He had been suspicious of Ly, but could it be Nga, instead, who was some kind of spy?

Lisa had to get to the bottom of this immediately. She might not like Peter, but what he had said to her that first day was right: like him or not, it was Lisa's job to protect him and his cover.

She recalled his furious insistence that no local hire employee, especially Vietnamese, be allowed to handle his personnel file. Oh my! He would blame Lisa for what had happened, even if she weren't to blame at all. And what about the fact that he spoke Vietnamese? That was in the file. Had Nga seen it?

Sick with apprehension, Lisa put Ivorson's file back in the drawer, just has she had found it, closed the file cabinet, relocked the door, leaving the light on, and returned to her desk.

She heard the door to the ladies' room shut and the clicking of Nga's high heels in the hall. "Nga," she called, her voice tremulous, "please come in here for a moment."

The Eurasian girl entered the outer office, reluctance visible in every movement. Lisa stood up and started for the file room door. "Come with me to the files, Nga."

Nga stopped in her tracks, and for a moment, Lisa thought she was going to turn and flee. Very slowly, she followed Lisa into the outer file room. Her face was very pale, almost white.

"Nga," Lisa said to her. "When you were in the bathroom just now, I looked for my file room key in my drawer. It wasn't where I left it when I went to lunch. It was in the very back of the drawer. Did you take it out of the drawer while I was gone?"

Nga shook her head vehemently, but guilt was written large on her face. Lisa was certain she was lying.

"When I left for lunch," she told the Vietnamese girl, "I locked the inner file door. I distinctly remember turning off the light." Nga's face twisted at the words, as if Lisa had slapped her. She might as well have written out a confession.

Lisa fitted the key in the lock, turned it, and pushed open the door. The light of the fluorescent bulb inside flooded over the two of them. "When I re-opened the door a minute ago," Lisa said to Nga, "the light was on, just as it is now."

She went to the file cabinet. "I checked the drawers, Nga," she said, "and found one of them slightly opened. When I looked inside, one file was out of position. Peter Ivorson's file." Nga began to shake as if she were having an attack of malaria.

Lisa confronted her, hands on hips. "You got into this room and looked at his file, didn't you, Nga? You know that that is a very serious offense, don't you?"

Tears began pouring down the Eurasian's cheeks. Lisa hardened her heart and voice. "I'm going to have to tell the Security Office about this, Nga."

Nga broke out into loud sobs. "Please, please Miss Odom, don't tell Security. I'm sorry. I won't ever do it again." Her face contorted with fear. Lisa steeled herself against feeling pity. She had to get the truth out of Nga.

"You knew it would cost you your job if you were caught," she said severely. "Why on earth did you do such a thing?"

Nga's eyes rolled wildly for a moment, and Lisa thought she was going to bolt. Then she sobbed, "I love him. I wanted to see if he was married."

Lisa felt her mouth sag open. She closed it again and stared at the Eurasian girl speechlessly for a moment. Peter Ivorson really had got over his fear of

Vietnamese! He hadn't been in Vientiane for six weeks, and already Nga was sufficiently involved with him to risk her job for a peek at his file!

Lisa's distress over Nga's dereliction was suddenly overridden by anger at Peter Ivorson and embarrassment at her own melodramatic imaginings. Nga was no spy! She was a pretty, small-town Eurasian girl looking for a western husband. Nga had developed a crush on the handsome American and wanted to make sure he didn't have a wife back in the States!

Nga's interest in Peter Ivorson was understandable. She hadn't seen the violent side of his nature, as Lisa had. Lisa recalled that she too had looked in Ivorson's file, before his arrival and hoped that he would be as attractive as he sounded. No, if there was a villain in this scenario, it was not Nguyen thi Nga, but that lecherous Peter Ivorson!

Still, what was she going to do about the present situation? Nga's claim that she loved Peter was no excuse. She had committed a serious violation of USAID rules. Under the regulations, there was really no suitable course of action but dismissal.

She had almost decided on it when her conscience caught up with her. Did that punishment really fit the crime? Or was Lisa being subconsciously motivated to get rid of Nga because of her own dislike for the Eurasian?

The idea that she might be influenced by an ulterior motive made Lisa feel ashamed of herself. Besides, there would have to be a hearing, and the facts would come to Peter Ivorson's ears. Suppose his paranoia about Vietnamese was re-awakened. What would he do to Nga?

For that matter, what would he say, or do, to Lisa? He would be certain to resurrect the whole stupid business of that first interview and accuse her of carelessness with his cover file. He might well carry out his threat to take up the matter with the Ambassador!

Nga was crumpled against the side of a file cabinet, sobbing, her face contorted. There was no arrogance or contempt about her now. Only remorse and apprehension. Lisa felt a surge of pity for her. She might not like the girl, but she couldn't rob her of her livelihood for a romantic indiscretion like this.

The fair thing to do was just to give Nga a good talking-to about what she had done, and that would be that. It wasn't necessary to involve Peter Ivorson.

As soon as she had made that decision, Lisa felt much better. But, she promised herself, Nguyen thi Nga wouldn't soon forget the lecture Lisa was about to give her. USAID/Laos/Personnel was not running a dating service for its local employees!

Chapter Seven

It was 9:40 at night on the 18th of April, and ferociously hot. Miraculously, both air conditioning and water were still on. Ivorson had just taken a shower and was getting into his pajamas to do some reading (the cost of electricity was sky-high in Laos, and USAID would pay only for air conditioning the bedroom) when there was a frantic banging at the front door.

Who could that be? He wasn't expecting anyone. He drew the PPK from the drawer in the bedside table and went to the door, turning out the living room lights on the way.

Standing to one side of the door frame, he called out, "Who is it?"

Wilbur's agitated voice answered. "Quick, Mistair Petair, Cam call my sister. He want to meet her."

Ivorson's nervousness became euphoria. At last! He unlocked the door and threw it open. Wilbur entered, dancing with excitement. His eyes widened at the sight of Ivorson's pajamas. "Habillez-vous, Mistair Petair," he urged Ivorson. Get dressed. "Vite! He meet her at ten o'clock. We got to hurry. No shit!"

Wilbur drove them to the meeting place in the taxi. It was one of the most frightening automobile rides Ivorson had ever lived through. He tried to ignore the multiple near-misses and concentrate on Wilbur's briefing, which he insisted be in French. This was no time to risk misunderstandings.

"I've already gone over everything we talked about again with my sister," Wilbur told him, steering vigorously around a buffalo cart. "She is to learn from Cam how he got out, and when and where he can do it again. Also, she is to play on his emotions as much as she can and plant the idea of defecting."

"Good work, Wilbur," Ivorson praised him. He hoped Sengdara could carry off her role. They had rehearsed her time after time. She was not as enthusiastic about her part in the operation as he would like for her to have been, but Wilbur assured him that they could rely on her.

For his own part, he castigated himself for not having had the tape recorder at home. He had left it in his office, and there just hadn't been enough time to stop by the USAID compound to get it.

They arrived at the little café, located on a narrow back lane in Silom quarter, only five minutes before ten o'clock. Wilbur led Ivorson down a stinking alley toward the rear of the building. The odor of hot peppers frying in fish oil poured overpoweringly through a tiny window high in a concrete wall. Ivorson's eyes began to water.

Wilbur knocked softly on the flimsy wooden door that was the wall's only other feature. Almost immediately, a bolt on the inside withdrew. Sengdara let them in. Her pretty face was tense. She snapped a phrase in Black Thai at Wilbur.

He responded a soothing tone of voice, then pulled on Ivorson's sleeve and motioned with a jerk of his head at the rickety flight of stairs which lead upward from just inside the door. "She says we must hurry," he whispered in French, as they tiptoed up the squeaking steps. "Cam is due any minute."

Ivorson, who couldn't see a thing in the dark stairwell, was too busy trying to combine silence with safety to answer. He reached the top of the steps and, still unable to see, waited for Wilbur to catch up with him.

Wilbur led him over to the far side of the room, where Ivorson could see a pencil-point red glow. He smelled citronella-laden smoke and realized that he must be looking at the lighted tip of a mosquito coil, the universal, 90% useless, anti-mosquito technology of Southeast Asia.

Wilbur led him over to one side of the mosquito coil and gently pushed him down on the floor. He himself squatted down on his haunches—he preferred that position to sitting—on the other side.

As Ivorson's eyes began to adjust to the darkness, he could make out a faint line of yellow light coming up through a crack in the floor in front of him. He untied his shoes, took them off, and placed them carefully on the other side of the crack. Then he silently lowered himself to a prone position and applied an eye to the opening. He could see the concrete floor of the room below, but that was all.

There was a slight commotion, then the sound of a door opening, and then Sengdara's voice, followed by the voice of a man. Hoang Bac Cam had arrived! Ivorson still couldn't see anything through the crack. He quit trying and put his ear to it, instead.

✡ ✡ ✡

Sengdara smiled brightly at Cam and held out both her hands to his. "I didn't believe I would ever see you like this," she said. He tried to kiss her, but she avoided him with a light laugh. "Don't be so bold," she said teasingly. "You may frighten me away! Come, sit down here, beside me."

Cam was so excited to be alone with her and at the same time so fearful of what would happen to him if they were caught, that he could hardly sit still. He had always seen her before in her market clothes. Tonight she was even lovelier to look at, in a crisp white blouse and fine Lao skirt with gold thread shot through the stiff silk of the border. She had made herself beautiful for him. The thought made him swell with pride.

After a token struggle, she left her hands in his. Their softness thrilled him. After almost two weeks of not talking to her, he was famished for the sight of her and the sound of her voice. "I was afraid you wouldn't come," he told her.

"Silly," she answered, "of course I would come. But I had to make excuses to my brother. He is the head of our family, and I'm not sure he believed me. He might not let me go out again on short notice like this, after dark. You must call me earlier in the day, the next time."

The words tormented him. "I can't," he told her. "I can't call until I am outside, and only rarely can I be gone longer than an hour."

She pouted. "If you cared about me as much as you say you do, you would find a way."

He gripped her hands tightly. "You don't know how much I care for you, how miserable I am alone in there with all those Vietnamese,"–He used the vulgar, pejorative slang word— "thinking about you all the time, but never able to see you."

"You have the car," she said. "If I could go with you while you do your errands, we could be together longer."

The idea of her beside him in the car was as delightful as it was frightening. "I don't have the car when I go out at night," he told her. "I have to go on foot. By the time I have called you and done my errand, there is very little time left."

She looked incredulous. "No car? I don't believe it! Why should a chauffeur be sent to town without a car? What kind of errand are you doing anyway? I don't believe that story. I think you are seeing another girl at the same time!" She tried to pull her hands away.

He held them fast. "Sengdara, please! You know I have no other girl. Don't waste the little time we have together with foolish games."

She wouldn't be placated. "I am not being foolish! Tell me what you are doing, if it is not seeing another woman."

"I cannot tell you. It is business for the Embassy."

She snatched her hands out of his. "Ha! Business for the Embassy that you have to do on foot? You expect me to believe that?"

He caught her hands again. "Sengdara, my sweet, please believe me! I have to carry messages to and from people we know. The Lao authorities are very hostile to us. They follow me every time I go out in the car. I don't want to get our friends in trouble. That is why I go on foot."

It was the wrong thing to say. Her face contorted with anger. "The Lao authorities are hostile, are they? I can't imagine why! Could it be because there are twenty-five thousand North Vietnamese soldiers in Laos? And how can you say 'hostile to us,' when they are all Viets and you are Black Thai? I must have been crazy to come out at night to meet a running dog of the Vietnamese!" She pulled her hands violently from his and stood up.

He was devastated. He had taken such frightful risks to see her, and yet everything he said made her angry. It wasn't at all as he had dreamed it would be. He could feel tears of frustration welling up in his eyes. "Sengdara, my precious, please sit down again, and listen to me. I said 'us' from habit. I hate them. They all insult me. But I don't have any choice. They are in total control now, even in the highlands. There is nothing to do but cooperate. Would you rather I was sent home to labor on some project as a coolie?"

She sat down again, but when she spoke, her tone was bitter. "Why do you want to meet me, then, if you have no choice? Do you think I will return to North Vietnam with you, even if your precious uncles would let me? Never! Vietnamese soldiers killed my father. You are wasting both my time and yours. I am leaving."

Anguish overcame him. "What do you want from me, then, woman?" he wailed, heedless of the patrons in the front room of the café.

"You could leave them," she said intensely, looking him straight in the eyes. "That is what my family did. We would not stay in a place ruled by Vietnamese, where we had no freedom. If you truly cared for me, that is what you would do, too."

He was horrified. "Be quiet," he shushed her. "If anyone hears you tell me that, I will be sent home to a prison camp, or worse."

She looked at him for a moment without answering and then said quietly, "You are in a prison camp now, Cam." She pulled away from him on the bench. "I was foolish to ever talk to you in the first place," she continued, sadly, "more foolish to see you tonight, and triply foolish to care for a man who is an enemy of his own people."

In spite of his anxiety, her last phrase brought him a ray of hope. He caught at her hands again. "Do you care for me?"

She shook her head. "It is idle to talk of my feelings, when there is no future for us. I will not see you again."

The words struck him like a blow. He had risked his freedom only to be rejected. "Don't say that!" he hissed. "There must be a way. Give me time! Let me think! Please, meet me again."

She shook her head sadly, looking at the tabletop. "Why? It only hurts us both."

His heart leaped for joy at the words. It hurt her, too! She did care for him! "Please Sengdara! Angel! Meet me again, just once. I will try to get more time."

She looked dubious, but she didn't reject him out of hand. He redoubled his pleas. "Only once more, Sengdara. Give me time to think about what you've suggested."

She looked at him sharply. "Will you really think about it? You aren't lying just to make me say yes?"

He took her hands again. "I'm not lying. I—I know you couldn't go home with me, even if you were willing. Yes, I really will consider it. See me again!"

She frowned, her lower lip thrust out in thought. She glanced sideways at him. "When?" she finally asked him.

"I don't know," he said helplessly. "I must wait for orders from Nguyen van Huu, but it shouldn't be too long. I am going out much more often now. There are many messages back and forth these days. I received one tonight. If I deliver a reply the next time, that would give me more time."

She shook her head dubiously. "I don't know..."

"Please, Sengdara. Oh, please. Just once more." He had never begged a woman like this before. It was unmanly, but seeing her again had suddenly become the most important thing in his life. He pressed her hands to his lips and kissed them feverishly. "Please!"

She looked at him solemnly over her outstretched arms. "Very well," she whispered. "Once more."

Joy poured through him. "Thank you, my precious, thank you." His voice broke. He was too full of emotion to speak clearly.

She gently pulled her hands away from his. "When must you go? I don't want you to get in trouble because of me." He glanced at his watch. Oh! It was very late. He had to go and catch a taxi immediately, or he would arrive so late that it would arouse suspicion. He stood up. "I must go now."

She rose beside him. "Be careful," she told him with a sad little smile. "I will wait for your call." She seemed so small and sad and vulnerable. He tried again to kiss her, and this time, she let him. Her lips were like hot velvet. "Goodnight, Cam," she murmured. "Go in peace."

✲ ✲ ✲

With tears in his eyes, Cam turned and left the back room. He put a five hundred kip note on the counter, nodded silently to the café owner, and walked out into the dark lane. The other customers, four old Chinese men, deep in rice wine and conversation, didn't even look up when he passed their table.

He hurried toward the lights of Khoualouang, two blocks away. It was terribly late. He prayed to Buddha—something he hadn't done in years—that he could find a taxi nearby.

He did, parked in front of an open-fronted noodle shop. The driver was at a table in the front of the shop, eating soupe chinoise. At Cam's urging, he reluctantly left the bowl of soup half-finished on the table and got into his cab with Cam.

Sitting beside the driver in the sputtering, squeaking taxi, Cam's mind reeled with what had happened to him tonight. She cared for him! She had told him as much. But her demand that he run away from the Embassy was terrifying. Where could they go together? They couldn't possibly stay in Vientiane, or anywhere in Laos. Sooner or later, Vietnam and its Pathet Lao allies would win the war, and then they would track him down and kill him.

Thailand, then? The language was not so different. But would the Thai let him in? And how would he earn his living? Was it possible in Thailand to make a living driving a vehicle? He had no other urban skill. That he had left his native village for a job with the government in Hanoi was in itself a miracle, due to the influence of his uncle, one of the very few Black Thai to espouse Ho Chi Minh's revolutionary cause.

And, above all, if he defected, what would happen to his family at home, his brothers and sisters? Would they be sent to die in a forced labor camp somewhere in the lowlands? It was possible. The Vietnamese were ruthless in exacting revenge for betrayal.

He shrank from the ideas that were whirling about in his brain. He needed time to think. He became aware of the location of the taxi. Only three hundred meters from the Embassy! Too close. Much too close! "Stop here," he told the driver urgently.

The cab lurched to a halt. He paid the fare and got out. "I'll give you another hundred kip if you will return the same way we just came," he said, holding the banknote in through the open window.

The driver took the offered bill and turned the cab around in the middle of the street. Cam began trotting down the dusty road toward the Embassy. It was still very hot, even at this hour of the night, and perspiration broke out on his brow almost at once.

He reached the Embassy gate, let himself in, and locked the gate again behind him. He paused for a moment at the water tap by the garage to splash some water on his face and neck, then rang the bell on the door of the chancery. The duty officer let him in. He ran up the staircase and knocked on Huu's office.

"Come," came the usual barked command from inside. Still slightly out of breath from his run down the road, Cam dug the short piece of bamboo he had retrieved from Mango's dead drop out of his pants pocket and handed it over.

"Where have you been?" Huu demanded. "You are late. And why are you wet?"

"I'm sorry," Cam answered, panting in spite of himself. "There were police roadblocks on several streets tonight. I had to backtrack three times before I could get back here. I ran to make up the lost time and washed off the sweat before I came in."

Huu looked at him penetratingly. Cam felt a deep unease. Did Huu have some means of checking whether there were indeed roadblocks in town tonight? Sometimes there were but, in fact, he had seen none tonight. Suppose Huu could find out that he was lying! He tried to conceal the sudden pang of fear that froze his bowels.

"Very well," Huu dismissed him. "You may go."

Almost stumbling with relief, Cam left the room.

✲ ✲ ✲

Huu looked thoughtfully after him. Cam seemed very agitated, in addition to being late. Was that cause for suspicion? Of course, if it was true that there were police checks, he had grounds for agitation. He carried no identification when he went out on these missions. Had he been stopped, he would surely have been questioned and perhaps arrested. He would ask Mango to determine the truth of Cam's story.

Huu wished he didn't have to rely on the chauffeur. The Black Thai were a race of traitors, in his view. Unfortunately, no one else in the Embassy looked enough like a Lao to pass unnoticed, even at night, in the neighborhoods where Mango left his messages. Cam was indispensable, whether Huu trusted him or not.

He pried open the sealed end of the bamboo with a letter opener and pulled out the rice paper folded inside. It contained the usual description of the next dead drop's location and a short message. "In reply to your standing requirement of me, I have been informed that the Americans believe large numbers of troops of the Peoples Army of North Vietnamese are infiltrating South Vietnam. The Americans are attempting by all available means to determine the facts."

Damn! Huu crumpled the message in his fist and hurled it across the room. Then, ashamed of his emotional outburst, retrieved the sheet of rice paper and smoothed it again, as best he could.

He had been in a foul mood all day, ever since receiving the long written message from Papaya this morning. The silly girl had been caught red-handed looking the new American's personnel file at USAID.

That in itself had not been as disastrous as it might have been. She had apparently been as clever after the event as she had been clumsy during it and had convinced her American supervisor—also a woman, happily–that her curiosity was the result of love. She had got off with an oral reprimand, and the American woman had even agreed not to tell this man Ivorson–however it was pronounced–about the incident.

The worst part of the matter was that Papaya was terrified by the close call and now refused to have anything further to do with Peter Ivorson. And he was almost certainly the replacement of the CIA man Huu had killed in February! He had a separate file in the USAID Director's office and was concealing the fact that he spoke Vietnamese.

Huu had been trying all day to decide what to do next. He had not yet told the Ambassador about Papaya's misfortune, and he would give a great deal not to have to, since it was going to reflect adversely on Huu himself. In view of Mango's message, however, that painful interview could not be postponed any longer.

He reread the message. Huu himself had heard nothing of such PAVN movements. He hoped it was not true. It would be an extremely risky move and, in view of the success of the recent Tet offensive, it was completely uncalled for.

True or not, however, if the Americans believed it, then it caught Huu on the horns of a dilemma.

This new CIA man, Peter Ivorson, would certainly be involved in trying to ferret out the details of the supposed PAVN troop movements. Could he have a source with access to Huu's Embassy?

Huu had been haunted for the past two months by the possibility that the treasonous electrician suborned by the last Yankee spy might not be the only traitor among the local Vietnamese community. Huu had not believed that such a thing could happen, but he had been proved wrong.

And the discovery had not been the result of Huu's efforts or cleverness, but a happenstance; the happy outcome of sheer luck. A loyal cadre, passing by a spot where he would not have been on any other day of the year, had observed the traitor leaving a house on the outskirts of town, followed shortly by an American, and had reported the matter to Huu. The Ambassador was not aware of how great a role luck had played in the Embassy's deliverance, but Huu was. Acutely aware.

Suppose there WAS another traitor? The Americans' belief that the PAVN was entering South Vietnam would certainly cause this new American spy, this Ivorson, to contact that traitor and task him to learn the facts. Now that Ivorson had been identified, this was the moment for a maximum effort to watch him and observe his contacts. But how, since Papaya was paralyzed by fear?

Huu pounded his desk with frustration. She had always been a fearful agent, softened by her life here in Laos. She had no true revolutionary fervor. Had her access to the Americans in USAID not been so good, Huu would long ago have discharged her.

Even as he thought it, however, the image of her lovely face appeared in his mind's eye, and he knew he was lying to himself. The mere idea of her made his sex stir. He grimaced at his body's reaction. His lust for Papaya was his greatest weakness, the secret chink in his revolutionary armor. It was disgraceful, the way she made him feel! If she knew of it, she would never speak to him again.

He ordered his mind to return to the immediate problem. This Ivorson must be closely watched. Somehow, Huu must persuade Papaya not only to continue seeing Ivorson, but to get close to him. The image evoked by the words made him wince. The idea of the American making love to her was agony. Nonetheless, not only must Huu endure it, but he must convince Papaya to do it. Force her to do it, if necessary.

Their homeland was at war, fighting for its survival against the Americans. No sacrifice was too great in such a struggle, neither for Papaya, nor for Huu.

He pulled out a sheet of rice paper and began composing a letter to her. Phuong could deliver it to her mother tomorrow morning.

☆ ☆ ☆

Sengdara was already back at the safe house when Ivorson and Wilbur burst through the door. Wilbur picked up his little sister in his arms and whirled her around the room.

Ivorson, infected by Wilbur's jubilation and delighted by what Wilbur had told him of the proceedings on their way back from the café, smiled at Sengdara until his lips ached. "Bien fait, bien fait," he told her repeatedly. Well done.

Curiously, her response was subdued. She was probably emotionally exhausted by the demands of her performance, which had succeeded beyond Ivorson's wildest expectations.

When the mutual felicitations were over, the three of them settled down to a debriefing and translation of her conversation with Cam.

It was a painful and time-consuming process. Sengdara spoke very little French, so she and Wilbur reviewed her conversation with Cam in Black Thai, until they got it as close to verbatim as possible. When they were satisfied with a sentence or paragraph, Wilbur rendered it into French for Ivorson's benefit, and he, in turn, wrote it down in English.

Acutely aware of the possibility of errors inherent in a double translation, Ivorson made them go over the ground twice. By the time it was over, after midnight, everyone involved was exhausted. Sengdara, in particular, was gray-faced and grim.

In spite of his best efforts to remain cool and professional, Ivorson's excitement got the best of him as read back over his notes. "This is incredible, Wilbur," he chortled. "We've got a really, really good chance of recruiting this guy. On the plus-side, we can offer him safe haven and re-settlement in Thailand, and on the minus side, we can threaten to send Nguyen van Huu a tape recording of his next conversation with Sengdara. Hell, he can't say no!"

It was a fantastic operational prospect. As the Embassy chauffeur, of course, Cam wouldn't attend meetings where sensitive documents or correspondence from Hanoi were read, but Ivorson didn't care about that. He was after the main chance.

It was a good bet that Cam slept in the dormitory—the building where the code room was. If he could be persuaded to plant a device to monitor the electrical emanations of the code machine on the second floor, the code could be broken, and all of North Vietnam's diplomatic cable traffic, world-wide, would be an open book in Washington!

He looked up from his thoughts to smile his appreciation one more time at Sengdara and was startled to see her looking from him to Wilbur with an angry frown on her face. She stood up abruptly, delivered a burst of rapid-fire Black Thai, turned on her heels, and stormed out the air-conditioned safe house bedroom.

Ivorson was completely baffled. What was going on?

Wilbur looked after his sister with an expression of utter incomprehension and dismay on his handsome face.

"What's the matter, Wilbur?" Ivorson asked him. "What did she say?"

Wilbur swallowed and shook his head, like a boxer trying to shake off a hard blow. "Sengdara says she feels sorry for Hoang Bac Cam. She says he is a good man in a very bad situation, but you and I don't care a bit about him. She says that we are only trying to use him, and that we are no better than Nguyen van Huu. She says she isn't going to help us do this anymore."

Chapter Eight

"What the hell do you mean, she won't go on with it?"

It was two in the morning. Ivorson was in the Chief of Station's living room and not at all happy about it.

Even though COS obviously had to learn what had happened, it was only with the greatest reluctance that Ivorson had obeyed Riley's directive to come brief him at his home. Even at two A.M., there might be hostile surveillance on COS's house. If there was, and Ivorson's nocturnal visit was noticed, whatever cover he presently had at USAID would be absolutely destroyed.

He was not pleased, either, that he had to conclude his glowing report on the progress of the Cam operation with the news of Sengdara's revolt. As he had anticipated, Riley was furious.

"I mean, she absolutely refused," he answered Riley. "Wilbur and I tried every ploy we knew, from blandishment to threats, for over an hour. It just bounced off her. That's the most stubborn young lady in Southeast Asia."

"But, God damn it, why? What happened? She did so well earlier in the evening. Has she fallen in love with this frigging chauffeur?"

"She says she's not, but who knows? She has certainly become emotionally attached to him. She says she feels sorry for him, all by himself in the middle of all those Viets, and she's just decided that she's not going to add to his woes by deceiving him with false promises of love."

Riley's eyes were red, probably from lack of sleep, but that didn't detract from the malignancy of the look he gave Ivorson. "In sum, then, you have awakened me in the middle of the night to tell me that the most important operation this Station was running has turned into a piece of shit."

The assessment startled Ivorson. "That's not what I'm telling you at all," he protested hotly. "Cam doesn't know that Sengdara's backed out. He's going to meet her again, only when he does, Wilbur will meet him, instead. Sengdara mentioned her brother to Cam tonight. Maybe we can talk her into writing a note to Cam, and Wilbur will have a photo of Sengdara to prove who he is.

"As the head of her family, he'll offer Cam Sengdara's hand in marriage and safe-haven for the two of them in Thailand. I really don't see that we're in a lot worse shape than we would be in if Sengdara were present. Cam is crazy about her. I think we've still got a hell of a good chance."

Riley grunted and then surprised Ivorson by pointing to the bar in the corner of the room. "Fix whatever you want, Peter," he said, "and mix a stiff scotch on the rocks for me while you're at it."

They sat in a pair of white rattan peacock chairs in the center of the terrazzo-tiled living room with a low, glass-topped rattan table between them. Riley threw down half his scotch at the first swallow. "All right," he said. "Go on and write up what happened tonight, along with your proposal to pitch Cam. Send it down to me tomorrow morning via the courier. I'll transmit it to Headquarters and ask for approval to proceed."

Coming right on the heels of Riley's earlier anger, his present moderation inspired suspicion in Ivorson, "Yes, sir," he said neutrally.

"What do you think will happen when that message reaches Langley?" Riley asked him.

Ivorson's suspicions deepened. This sounded like a set-up. "I expect there'll be a certain amount of excitement," he ventured.

Riley smiled mirthlessly. "That's the understatement of the year. All hell will break loose, is what will happen. First of all, the Chief of the Vietnam Task Force will be called up to the communications center to read it."

Riley finished the scotch at a gulp and began tallying the route of the message on his fingers. "C/VTF will run it down to the Director of Operations. He'll take it up to the Director of Central Intelligence, who will call the White House. In less than an hour, it will be on the President's desk, and in less than two hours, I will have to receive an Eyes Only message from the White House. Not from Headquarters, CIA, Peter, but the White House."

Riley went to the bar to pour himself another scotch. He looked over his shoulder at Ivorson. "What do you think the message will say?"

Ivorson was definitely being set up. He kept his mouth shut.

"It will say something like this," Riley said: "'Operation cited your message of utmost interest to highest levels US. Government. Cannot overstress importance C/USG–'" Riley broke off his monologue and speared Ivorson with a look. "You do know who C/USG is, don't you, Peter?

"Yes, sir. Chief/US Government. Lyndon B. Johnson." Ivorson became convinced that he was not going to like the punch line, when he finally heard it.

"Excellent, Peter. Right on the mark. Where was I? Oh, yes–'Cannot overstress importance C/USG attaches to breaking the Vietnamese code. Request you keep this addressee advised progress this operation in greatest detail on daily basis. End.'"

Riley took a large swallow of the still almost undiluted scotch and put his glass down on the bar with a bang. "Have you ever been in daily contact with C/USG, Peter?"

Ivorson shook his head.

"Would you like to be?"

He shook his head again. Emphatically.

"Well, I don't like it either, Peter," Riley assured him. "I don't like it worth a shit, because C/USG is the biggest shark in the ocean, and he is severely frustrated. If he gets upset at me, he might bite me in two."

COS's eyes locked with Ivorson's. "I don't like it," he repeated, "but I'm stuck with it. So now I'll tell you what I expect from you. Whenever this meeting between Cam and Wilbur comes off, I expect you to handle it so that I can advise the President that there are no problems, and that Cam has agreed to plant our gadget in the code room. If I am able to do that, C/USG will be very happy with me, and I will be very happy with you. Clear?

"If, on the other hand," Riley went on, "Cam should refuse the proposition, regardless of his reason for refusing, C/USG will be very unhappy with me, and I will be VERY unhappy with you."

The red-streaked gray eyes had neither wavered nor blinked throughout Riley's presentation. Now they turned to polar ice. "What I am saying to you, Ivorson, is this: if you fuck me up with the White House, you'll wish you hadn't been born."

Sometime in the early morning hours, Ivorson had a nightmare: Wilbur had put the proposition to Hoang Bac Cam in accordance with Ivorson's scenario. Cam punched Wilbur in the nose and rushed from the room out into the street, screaming, "Save me from the American imperialists," at the top of his lungs.

In his dream, Ivorson ran after him, calling for him to wait, shouting that he had something terribly important to tell him. He caught up with Cam at the end of a blind alley, and, as he reached for the chauffeur, Cam pulled a snub-nosed revolver out of his pocket and shot Ivorson in the middle of the forehead.

He woke up trembling as violently as if he were having a malarial attack. Drenched in sweat, he lay on the kapok mattress, taking deep breaths and listening to the air conditioner groan under its load of BTU's. He shook his head to rid his mind of the dream. It was the worst he'd had since his first week in Laos.

He couldn't let COS psyche him this way about the Cam operation. Despite Sengdara, they had a really good chance to recruit Cam. What Ivorson had to do was to make damn certain that it happened.

If it did, he'd be rich and famous. If it didn't, well, he'd be on Riley's shit list, but he still had another chance to get the code key. In a month or so, the blimp prototype would be delivered.

Cam wasn't the only string to Ivorson's bow, and an angry COS wasn't the worst threat he'd ever faced, either. Compared to his situation when he arrived here, he was in good shape. No one was trying to kill him, and the Fear was dormant.

After a while, he fell asleep again. This time, he dreamed of making love to Nguyen thi Nga.

✡ ✡ ✡

The Ambassador of the Democratic Peoples Republic of Vietnam looked over his glasses at Huu, who was seated in a straight-backed chair in front of the desk. In spite of the avuncular appearance his round face and gold-rimmed spectacles gave him, the Ambassador was not a man to be trifled with. He was a personal friend of Ho Chi Minh's, and a seasoned guerrilla fighter against the French.

Huu had just finished telling him about Mango's message and about Papaya's having identified the new CIA operative. He had unfortunately had to include the fact that she had been caught in the USAID files. He thought he had put a good face on the matter, emphasizing her cleverness in extricating herself from the situation, but the Ambassador was obviously disturbed. Anger glinted in his eyes, and a line appeared between his sparsely-haired brows.

He continued to stare at Huu in silence for a moment, then got up and crossed the floor to his office safe, which was already unlocked. He pulled from it two sheets of type-written rice paper and returned with them to his desk. "I received this information from Hanoi on Monday night," he told Huu as he sat down again. "In view of the information you have just given me, I believe I must share it with you." He cleared his throat and began to read.

"By Order of the Central Committee of the Communist Party of Indochina, this message is for the eyes of Ambassadors only. Only the most trusted subordinates may be made aware of its contents." Huu leaned forward, on the edge of his chair. It was a great honor to be allowed to hear such a communication, whatever its contents.

"The offensive launched ten weeks ago by the Viet Cong forces in the south has now completely concluded," the Ambassador read. "It achieved great gains and inflicted heavy losses on both the American and puppet Armed Forces. However, the local population did not support the fighters to the degree anticipated."

Huu stirred uncomfortably. Mao Tze-tung's treatise on guerrilla warfare stated that in the third and final phase of a people's war, the guerillas left the countryside to attack and overwhelmed the counter-revolutionary forces in the cities with aid of the urban population, which would rise up in support of the attackers.

The Tet Offensive had clearly been phase-three and had achieved complete surprise. If the populations of Saigon and Hue had not risen up in support of it, then either Mao was wrong—unthinkable heresy—or the Central Committee had made a mistake of colossal proportions in the timing of the offensive. Huu could only imagine the ferocity of the accusations and recriminations which must have preceded the Committee's decision to make that fact known.

The Ambassador continued reading. "Although the southern fighters inflicted heavy losses on the Americans and their puppets, casualties among the attackers were very heavy as well, particularly during the final phase. Losses are estimated at between twenty and thirty thousand dead and wounded."

Huu's heart contracted with dismay. Those casualties far surpassed anything he had imagined in his worst nightmares or even in the exaggerations of the western press. It was a disaster.

The Ambassador continued to read, in an expressionless voice. Huu admired his self control. "The neo-colonialist and puppet forces may be expected to take the offensive before the beginning of the rainy season. Should they succeed in seizing the initiative during this critical period, while the fighters in the south are reequipping and reorganizing, a situation might result which would indefinitely prolong the division of our country. To prevent this, the decision has been make to reinforce the Viet Cong in the south with elements of the Peoples' Army of Vietnam."

Huu sat bolt upright. Mango's report had been correct. The PAVN was entering the war in the South! The fact disturbed him profoundly.

After decades of struggle and privation, Ho Chi Minh could not accept a divided Vietnam. If the Viet Cong could not win alone in the south, and North Vietnamese troops were needed, so be it. But suppose the Americans turned the full weight of their awesome military power on the north? It could mean the loss of everything the Party had fought and suffered for since 1945—it could be the end of the Revolution. "It is of the utmost importance that the presence of the PAVN in both South Vietnam and Laos be continually and forcefully denied," the Ambassador read on. "Nonetheless, it must be expected that the American forces in Vietnam will, in time, become aware of the presence of these units. The American government can be expected to mount a massive intelligence effort to determine their strength, composition, and mission.

"Should this anticipated American effort succeed in determining the full extent of PAVN participation in the armed struggle," the Ambassador read, "it will provide the reactionary elements in the American government with justification for invading the territory of the Peoples' Republic of Vietnam. This effort must, therefore, NOT succeed."

The Ambassador looked significantly at Huu before going on. "Embassies located in countries where American diplomatic missions are also present can expect to receive the full force of the American effort and are directed to be especially vigilant. All, repeat, all measures are authorized to thwart these attempts. Guidance on new propaganda measures will be provided in a separate message. Message ends."

The Ambassador put down the papers and looked fixedly at Huu. "Do you understand, Comrade Huu, the importance of assuring that the Americans do not succeed in placing a spy within this Embassy?"

Huu nodded emphatically.

"How do you intend to prevent them from doing so?"

DAMN Papaya, thought Huu. Of all the possible times for her to refuse further cooperation, this was absolutely the worst. Of course, he hadn't mentioned that facet of the situation to the Ambassador. To admit that he was not able to control his agent would produce a total loss of face. He might even be relieved of his post.

The Ambassador was waiting for his answer. He had only one option remaining. It was risky, but under the present circumstances, the risk was justifiable, and it would allow him to get at least some idea of what the American was doing while he tried to get Papaya back in line.

"I believe that the greatest danger to our Embassy still lies in the possibility that the American has suborned someone whom we trust," he said. "So, first, I will conduct another complete physical search of the compound.

"Second, Mango has told us that the Americans have already detected the PAVN movement and are seeking to determine its scope and meaning. It follows that, if there are other traitors in our midst, they must presently be in close contact with the new CIA man, this Peter Ivorson. I propose, therefore, to mount a surveillance of him. Payaya has learned where he lives. I will have that house watched, twenty-four hours a day, to see who visits him. If he goes out after dark, our watchers will follow, to learn whom he meets."

"Do you have people skilled in such work?" the Ambassador asked. "If he detects our surveillance, he will be alerted, and our task will become much more difficult."

That was, indeed, the weak point of Huu's plan. "They are not yet fully trained," he admitted. "They are only local cadre. Still, they know the city well, and the American's neighborhood is mixed enough so that they can loiter there. In any case, the Americans are famous for not being able to distinguish between one Asian face and another. I will work with them as closely as I possibly can. They should certainly be able to do the job better than the clumsy Lao who follow me around town."

The Ambassador thought for a moment then nodded agreement. "All right. Go ahead. And speaking of the watchers who follow our car, has there been an increase in their activity lately?"

"No. On the contrary, they seem to be paying less attention than before. Where there were two or three behind us, now there is only one. I believe their lack of results has discouraged them."

"Good," said the Ambassador. "Nonetheless, we must continue to be vigilant. We must not let ourselves be lulled into complacency. Not after the lesson we received in February."

Huu nodded silently, his lips compressed. He had no need to be reminded of that lesson. Its memory was as bitter as gall. He would not be taken unawares again. He would have this Ivorson watched, as a cat watches a mouse hole. If he led Huu to another traitor, Huu would destroy them both, just as he had the last time.

Chapter Nine

A week passed. For Ivorson, it was a very unsatisfactory week. Cam didn't call for another meeting with Sengdara. There was no word from Tech/Hqs On progress with the blimp prototype, and he got absolutely nowhere with Nguyen thi Nga. In fact, he seemed to have lost ground. She hadn't flirted with him at all during class, and her handshake, which had previously contained a very definite element of promise, was now as perfunctory as a Soviet diplomat's.

Her coldness dismayed him. He couldn't understand it. It wounded his vanity, too. Why the hell couldn't Nga react to him like the Thai whore at the Morocco Bar? She claimed she loved him and wanted him to move her into a house somewhere.

It had been a long time since a woman had occupied as much of his thoughts as Nga did. He realized that she was becoming an obsession with him, and that disturbed him. If he were smart, he'd give up the English lessons and get her out of his head and life at the same time. He had too many important things to do in Vientiane to waste his time mooning over an uncooperative female, no matter how beautiful and sexy she might be.

The fact that he was striking out with Nga didn't make Lisa Odom's obvious dislike for him any easier to take, either. Every time he ran into her, she stuck a needle in him. He found himself avoiding her. His own cowardice irritated him almost as much as she did.

After dark on Monday evening, April 22, he left home for an eight o'clock meeting with Wilbur. They had been working together on reorganizing the team's surveillance of the North Vietnamese Embassy. Ivorson wanted to be certain that the Viets weren't getting away with clandestine activity under the team's nose.

Nguyen van Huu's daily outings, for example. Ivorson had about decided that they constituted a red herring. He had directed Wilbur to reduce surveillance on Huu and watch the Embassy personnel who did the shopping in the market, instead. That had been going on for a week, now. Wilbur should have some reports for him tonight.

He always gave himself half an hour to get to the safe house where he and Wilbur met and went there by a very circuitous route, making three or four stops on the way, and being extremely alert for anyone behind him who stopped and started off again when he did.

It was something he did routinely on the way to an operational meeting. So far, since his arrival in Vientiane, he'd seen nothing alerting, but it was a habit that he firmly intended to continue. It had saved his life once, in Vietnam.

His first stop tonight was the P.T.T. building, where he inquired if he could book a call immediately to the United States. The answer, of course, was no. He didn't want to call anyone, in any case. His mother's smothering love was irritating enough in her weekly letters. He had no desire to feel it at closer range.

He left the P.T.T., started his motorcycle, and turned northwest up Lan Xang Avenue. Even at thirty miles an hour, the air was still as hot as the inside of an oven. Wilbur said it was the worst hot season he could remember. Ivorson had no idea how any of the locals could sleep, in their non-air-conditioned houses.

He turned left at the USIS American Library and cruised gently for two blocks to the antenna farm of the Lao National Radio, checking his two rear-view mirrors as he drove.

Just before he reached the driveway that led to the transmitter, he saw a single headlight turn off Lan Xang. Another motorcycle, coming in his direction. Probably normal traffic. A left turn back to the south here would help determine that.

He made the turn. As he reached the stop sign at Khoun Boulom, a block away, he saw the motorcyclist in his rear vision mirror continuing straight ahead through the intersection behind him. Good.

The traffic on Khoun Boulom was unusually heavy. He had to wait almost a minute for a break. He finally got it and put the Honda in gear.

Just before he pulled out and turned left, he flicked another glance at the mirrors. There were no headlights, but he got a sense of motion on the street behind him. He didn't have time for a doubletake. He had to concentrate on the traffic in front of him.

After he was established on Khoun Boulom, he tried to get a look in the mirror at the intersection he had just left, but the lights of the cars behind defeated him.

Could that have been a motorcycle, coasting down the hill behind him with no lights? Could the bike he'd seen coming off Lan Xang have turned after passing the corner where Ivorson had seen it and come back?

Maybe. He checked his watch. He had to meet Wilbur in fifteen minutes, and it took only five minutes to get there. He had enough time to dry-clean himself. The first step was to get out of this heavy traffic and into a residential area.

He turned left on Lan Xang again and took his time back up the hill to let the tail, if he had one, catch up. He passed the intersection by USIS again, but this time he continued straight up the hill toward the traffic circle around the Monument to the Dead. He couldn't distinguish anything in the jumble of headlight in his mirrors.

He swept left around the monument, passed the National Assembly building, and after a short block, turned right on the road that encircled the USAID compound. As he made the turn, he was momentarily caught in the beam of a single headlight coming off the traffic circle behind him.

He slowed down and putt-putted down the dark street in front of the quarters of the senior USAID officials, watching intently in the mirrors. He reached the left turn toward the guesthouse, but the headlight never re-appeared. Whoever had followed him off the traffic circle had stopped short of the street he was on now. Or he had turned off his headlights.

As he turned left toward the USAID compound gate, Ivorson threw a look back over his shoulder down the long block behind him. There was a heavy shade cast by the trees and no streetlight, so he couldn't be certain, but again he got a feeling of movement. A chill settled in his stomach. He took a quick look at his watch—it was 7:55. Too late for Wilbur now. He'd have to wait till tomorrow.

The entry gate to the USAID compound was just ahead. He thumbed on his left turn indicator and turned into the compound, slowing down to let the Mission Guard in the gateshack see his face.

As soon as he was inside the gate, he flicked off his headlight, swung around to the left in a big circle, and came to a stop next to the wall in back of the guardshack. He shut off the ignition and waited.

He heard the sound of a motorcycle approaching, its engine accelerating. It sounded like a big Honda, with perhaps twice the engine his bike had. As the motorcycle roared past the gate, Ivorson got a quick impression of a single rider in a dark shirt, wearing a plastic helmet.

There was only one way the cyclist could have passed the gate so soon after Ivorson turned in. He had been behind him on that long dark stretch, with his lights out.

Ivorson was under surveillance. He was someone's target. In an instant, the chill in his gut transformed itself into panic. The Fear, asleep for the past month or more, leaped to life and seized him by the throat. How long had he been under surveillance? Had his meetings with Wilbur been observed?

How had he been blown? Probably by that night visit to COS's house a week ago. The thought infuriated him. He'd KNOWN that was a stupid thing to do. His pristine USAID cover had been destroyed by COS's unwillingness to wait until morning to learn what had happened in the Cam case.

Ivorson's fear and anger turned on the surveillant. No sonofabitch was going to get away with surveilling Peter Ivorson!

The PPK was in the bedside table. Ivorson hadn't even thought about bringing it with him tonight, but gun or no gun, he was going to apprehend the watcher and find out, by whatever means necessary, who had ordered him watched. Until he knew that, he was completely helpless—a sitting duck.

He looked around him for something he might use as a weapon. Stacked against the compound wall a few feet behind him was a pile of scrap lumber. In the pile was a two-by-four, about three feet long. He pulled the motorcycle back on its kickstand, jumped off it, and ran to the lumber pile. He picked up the piece of lumber, vaulted back into the seat, and with the two by four under his left arm, rolled the motorcycle off the kickstand and into gear.

He turned on the light as he roared back out the entry gate in the wrong direction. The Lao gate guard raised his arm in protest, then dropped it again and shrugged as Ivorson turned left onto the street. Bless the Lao, Ivorson thought. They were such graceful losers.

The surveillant probably thought Ivorson was trying to lose him by cutting through the USAID compound and going back out the other side. That would explain his acceleration as he went past the entrance. He was trying to get to the exit gate before Ivorson did.

Now, having gotten there and not seeing Ivorson ahead of him, he was probably parked on the dark road outside the compound, waiting for Ivorson to come out. Well, Ivorson was out, all right, and that fucker on the Honda was going to get more of him than he wanted!

He reached the intersection that marked the apex of the triangle-shaped compound and turned left. The street light at the corner didn't reach even half-way to the lights of the exit gate. In between was a pool of inky darkness.

That was where the surveillant would be, probably parked against the wall on the right side of the road. From there, he would have the best view of the exit gate.

That location created a problem for Ivorson, however. He wanted to swing the two-by-four with his right hand, but that was the throttle side of the handlebar. When he let go of the throttle to grip the two-by-four, his motorcycle would immediately slow down, and the sudden drop in engine noise might alert the watcher.

A motorcycle appeared at the outer edge of Ivorson's headlight beam. It was a 350cc Honda, parked up on its kickstand with its helmeted rider in the seat. Ivorson rolled down toward him, staying near the center of the street so as not to give the watcher early warning of his intention.

At the last minute before reaching the man, he released the throttle, grasped the front of the two-by-four with his right hand, and pulled it from under his left arm.

Damnation! The air pressure of his forward motion, combined with the awkward grip he had on the wood, kept him from getting the club into position to strike.

Ivorson was right on top of the watcher. He had indeed been alerted by the drop in speed of Ivorson's engine and was turning his head toward Ivorson. In two seconds, Ivorson would be past him.

He wound up doing the only thing left to do: he steered his motorcycle with his left hand into a collision with the watcher, hoping that the roll bars in front and back of his lower legs would keep them from getting crushed in the impact.

He tried to use the two-by-four as a lance, to deliver a disabling blow to the watcher's back or kidneys, but the Asian recognized the threat and twisted on the motorcycle a split second before the impact, so that the wood only grazed his ribs.

They collided in a din of screeching rubber and metal. Ivorson dropped the two-by-four and swung his shoulder into the smaller man's side, trying to slam him against the concrete wall he was parked next to.

The watcher's motorcycle helmet banged hard against the wall. Ivorson heard the plastic crack, and then both machines fell against the wall together in a flailing pile of motorcycles and bodies.

Aiming any kind of effective blow was impossible in the close quarters and, in any case, might well result in breaking his fist on his adversary's plastic helmet. Ivorson's best bet was a choke hold. He threw his right arm around the Asian's neck and pulled it as tight as he could.

The effort brought the calf of his right leg up off the road and into contact with the red-hot muffler of his motorcycle. The pain made him cry out and momentarily slacken his grip on the watcher, who had recovered from his initial impact with wall and was trying to fight back.

The Asian was thirty pounds lighter than Ivorson, and even though he was heavily muscled, in a stand-up fight, it would have been no contest. The trouble was, it was a lying-down fight, and Ivorson was sorely distracted by the burning flesh of his calf.

Frightened by the suddenness of the attack, the Asian was fighting desperately. He wriggled violently, trying to loosen Ivorson's grasp on his windpipe. Fortunately for Ivorson, the watcher's motorcycle had pinned his right leg against the wall, and severely restricted his movement.

Ivorson managed to tighten his grip again, and the Asian's struggles weakened. Just a few seconds more, and he should lose consciousness. Thank God. The pain of his burnt leg was sapping Ivorson's strength.

The Asian had been striking at him with elbows and fists, but due to their closeness and Ivorson's being partially behind him, the blows had not done much damage. Now, just as he felt a distinct weakening in the Asian, Ivorson saw the man's left hand drop and begin groping for his pants pocket.

Oh, my God! The sonofabitch had a knife or gun! He saw the brown hand find the pocket, drop into it, and come out again with a red-handled pocket knife. It wasn't very big—only about four inches long—but a four-inch blade would reach Ivorson's eyes. Or, for the matter, his heart.

He tried to ignore the pain in his leg and grabbed the hand holding the knife with his own left hand, while he pulled the Asian's neck as tightly as he could in the crook of his right arm.

The Asian brought his right hand down into the battle for control of the knife. He grasped Ivorson's left thumb in his right hand and pulled it upward, trying to break Ivorson's grip.

Why didn't the little fucker pass out, for God's sake? He was getting weaker, but as weak as he was, he was still able to pry Ivorson's thumb off his wrist. He succeeded, and then slammed his left hand, with Ivorson's over it, down on the gas cap of the Honda.

The unexpected pain cost Ivorson his grip on the knife hand and loosened his hold on the man's neck as well. The Asian's right hand darted to the knife, trying to open the blade. If he succeeded, Ivorson was going to lose not only the fight, but his life.

The choke hold wasn't working and, in any case, the knife had first priority. Ivorson released his stranglehold to grasp the right side of the man's motorcycle helmet, turning his face toward the wall, against which both machines were still leaning, and used the weight of his body to bang the Asian's face into the concrete. He heard the nose bone crack and the cry of pain from the Asian, but it didn't distract him from his efforts to open the knife.

Ivorson tried it again, but the Asian yanked his head left at the last minute, and it was Ivorson's right hand, caught between the helmet and the wall, that absorbed the blow.

Tears sprang into his eyes, and he released his hold on the helmet. He looked down, and, through his tears, saw that the Asian had almost succeeded in opening the pocket knife. He slammed his left fist down on the Asian's two hands, smashing them against the gas tank, and—thank God!—the half-open knife fell to the road surface under the Honda.

Ivorson got his right arm around the man's throat again and was reaching across the back of his neck with his left arm to apply a locking choke hold, when the Asian suddenly slammed his left elbow back and downward into Ivorson's testicles.

The pain was instantaneous, overpowering. Ivorson could feel the strength leave his arms. He was in real trouble, now. He tried to hang on to the smaller man, but the Asian, feeling the effectiveness of the blow, made a desperate lunge and succeeded in getting his right leg out from between the Honda and the wall.

He turned and rained blows on Ivorson's face. Ivorson tried ineffectively to cover up, but the blow to his gonads had paralyzed him. He was practically helpless. Goddamit, this little shit was going to beat him!

There was a shout from the USAID exit gate, and the sound of people running. Ivorson was vaguely aware of flashlight beams approaching. The Asian apparently became aware of them, too, because he stopped hitting Ivorson, scrambled frantically over him onto the road surface, struggled to his feet, and began running shakily away.

Ivorson wanted to follow him, to stop him, but all he could do was curl up in a ball and groan in agony. The Mission Guards tried to help him to his feet, but the pain was too great for him to stand. He lay in the road until the American Medical Unit ambulance came to get him.

The State Department doctor, not at all pleased to be called in at night, examined Ivorson and pronounced him to be suffering from facial abrasions, a bad burn on his leg, and a pair of bruised balls. He prescribed a powerful sedative and put Ivorson in the only available private room in the medical unit.

Ivorson knew he needed to, at least, tell the Station where he was before the sedative took effect, but how to do it securely? He didn't want to call any of the

Station numbers, least of all Riley's residence. If there had been a surveillance there, the lines could be tapped as well. He didn't have a lot of time, either. He could feel his mind begin to fade.

Not for the first time, he bitterly regretted being isolated from the rest of the Station. Whom could he call? It would have to be a cover contact. The USAID duty officer, for example. Yes, but that was a rotating schedule. This week's incumbent might not be, probably wasn't, cleared.

Lisa Odom, then? Hell, no. He didn't want to ask that smart-ass for favors. She probably wouldn't do it, anyway. Maybe not, but he couldn't think of anyone else, and he had to do something fast. He was getting woozy. He swallowed his distaste and asked the USAID operator for her number.

Her initial coldness changed to what sounded like real concern, when he told her where he was. "The Medical Unit? Why? Are you hurt?"

His rapidly dulling brain made it hard for him to think of a reasonable cover story. He obviously couldn't tell her he'd been under surveillance. She probably wouldn't believe it, anyway, the Pollyanna. "I ran into a guy on another motorcycle outside the USAID compound," he told her. "He got mad and clobbered me. Could you please go see my boss tonight and tell him what happened?"

There was a long pause. "Can't you call him yourself?" she asked, the coolness back in her voice.

"I don't want to bother him on the telephone." He stressed the last words, thinking, "Come on lady, you're cleared to deal with people like me. Use your head."

She finally seemed to get it. "Ah. Okay, you want him to know in person, is that it?"

"Right, that's it. I'm sorry to saddle you with this chore, but there really isn't anyone else who can do it."

"Well," she said, with obvious reluctance, "all right."

Ivorson's grip on consciousness was fading fast. "Thanks a lot. I 'preciate it." He hung up, lay back on the pillow, and was instantly asleep.

When he woke up, it was 7:30 on Tuesday morning, and he felt as if he'd been hit by a truck instead of a hundred and thirty pound man. Every movment made him grunt with pain.

Worse yet, the Fear was perched on the foot of his bed like a gargoyle, leering at him. "No one puts surveillance on a USAID supply officer," it told him gleefully. "Ergo, whoever did it knows, or at least suspects, that you are CIA.

Your USAID/Supply cover is blown, Ivorson. Which means that you're dead meat. They can kill you anytime they want to. You'd better get the hell out of Vientiane while you're still alive!"

Before Ivorson had a chance to summon Reason to his defense, he heard the sound of crisp footsteps in the hall, and COS entered his room. He closed the door behind him and demanded, "What the hell is this about your getting into a fight over a fender bender? And why didn't you call me yourself instead of sending Lisa Odom to see me?"

The approach didn't calm Ivorson's nerves. "I had to let you know where I was, and I don't trust your telephone," he snapped. "Furthermore, there wasn't any accident. The guy I fought had been surveilling me on my way to meet Wilbur."

Riley's eyes, which were noticeably red, widened. "Surveillance? Are you sure?

"Hell yes, I'm sure. I must have picked it up when I came out to your house a week ago."

Riley looked at Ivorson sharply, and frowned. "You don't know that for a fact," he said sharply.

"No," agreed Ivorson, "I don't, but I damn sure know that I never had any surveillance before then."

They stared at each other disapprovingly for moment. "How did the fight start?" Riley finally asked.

"I jumped him," said Ivorson. "When someone tails me, I aim to find out who he's working for."

Even has he said it, he realized that he shouldn't have. His attack on the surveillant had been triggered more by his reaction to the Fear than by sound tactics. Viewed in the cold light of this morning, it was obvious that what he should have done was call Wilbur from the USAID compound and set up a counter-surveillance trap with Wilbur's team.

Riley lost no time in pointing out his error. "That was dumb," he said bluntly. "By trying to take the guy single-handedly, you not only failed to do so, you also revealed that you knew you were being watched. Our chances of identifying him now are zero."

Ivorson didn't like being called dumb, even if it was true. "He left his motorcycle when he ran off," he pointed out. "The cops can trace the serial number."

Riley snorted. "Could they trace the serial numbers on Wilbur's team's bikes? The motorcycle is a dead-end street. The guy's gone. You fucked up."

He was probably right about the motorcycle angle, Ivorson recognized glumly. He was being badly out-pointed. "Anyway, we don't have to guess who did it," he said defensively. "It was the Viets."

"Not necessarily," Riley said. "Not if you picked it up at my house. We've got the Soviets and the ChiComs in town, too. Both of them would be interested in my night visitors, and the chances are that they've both got surveillance capability. For that matter, the Lao Special Branch might be watching me, although I doubt that. Tran van Cao would certainly have alerted me."

Reason finally made its appearance in Ivorson's mind. "He's right," it whispered to him. "You just assumed it was a North Vietnamese surveillance because that's what you're involved with. And no matter who it was, it's still not the end of the world. Okay, you alerted them, but they alerted you, too. In fact, what happened was really a blessing. It shook you out of a false sense of security. From now on, you'll be a lot more careful."

"That's bullshit," countered the Fear. "The fact is, you're blown. And if it WAS the North Vietnamese, and they can't follow you around anymore to see who you're meeting, what's to keep them from just killing you, like they did Jim Reagan?"

Ivorson looked up from his internal debate to find Riley studying him intently. "You're acting like you've got the wind up, Ivorson," he said. "Have you lost your nerve? If you have, say so. I've got too much at stake here to risk your crapping out on me."

"Admit it," shrieked the Fear. "This is your chance to get out of here in one piece. Tell him, 'Yes, I've lost my nerve. I want to go home.'"

It was one of the greatest temptations that Ivorson had ever faced, and, in the end, what kept him from giving in to it wasn't Reason, but Pride.

He simply couldn't admit to fear, no matter how frightened he was. He was Peter Ivorson, a professional case officer. If he asked to be sent home, he would lose everything he'd spent the past six years obtaining: rank, reputation and, above all, self-respect. If he went slinking back to Langley with his tail between his legs, he would simply cease to matter in his own eyes.

Worse than that, no matter how much longer he stayed in the Agency, or what other tours of duty or assignments he might draw, he would always be watching for the significant glances between his peers when they thought he wasn't looking; always be listening for innuendos in what they said to him.

He couldn't live with that. He had to stick it out here. If he couldn't overcome the Fear, then he'd just have to learn to live with it and work around it any way he could.

He looked Riley straight in the eye. "Let someone slug you in the balls," he said, "and you won't look so hot either. I'm fine."

The Chief of Station looked back at him with cold calculation. "All right, Ivorson," he finally said. "If you say your nerve's okay, I'll take your word for it. I'll even accept the possibility that you might have picked up that surveillance at my house the other night. But you're through running wild with this operation."

Ivorson jerked up his head at the words, then winced at the pain the movement cost him.

"I asked for you for this operation on the basis of your reputation," Riley said coldly, "but the more I see of you, the more I think I was over-sold. Since you've began working for me, everything you've touched has turned to shit. You've managed to alienate the girl who is the key to the Cam operation, and now you've alerted a hostile surveillance, whose-ever it might have been."

"That's bullshit," said Ivorson angrily.

"Don't talk, Ivorson," snapped Riley. "Listen! From now on, you're going to do only what I tell you to do, when and where I tell you to do it. This Vietnamese code operation is my ticket to the Big Leagues, and I'm not going to let you screw it up for me." Before Ivorson had a chance to respond, Riley wheeled around and left the room.

✲ ✲ ✲

It was fifteen minutes before eight in the morning when Lisa pulled her car into one of the visitor's parking spaces at the State Department Medical Unit.

She really couldn't explain to herself why she was here. She was still resentful of the high-handed way Peter Ivorson had called her last night and practically forced her into helping him with his nefarious business. She probably should have refused to help him.

She had certainly regretted her agreement when she reached Mr. Riley's house last night. The Chief of Station had been absolutely rude to her. Some of his behavior might have been due to the water glass of Scotch whiskey he was determinedly emptying, but, whatever the reason, he had been very unpleasant. He hadn't even thanked her for coming out in the night to deliver the message. Maybe lack of manners was something the CIA taught its employees.

She hadn't had to come in person this morning. It wouldn't have given away any secrets if she had just called him and told him she'd done what he had asked of her. "Still," she told herself, "as long as I'm here, I might as well go ahead and tell him."

She crossed the parking lot in the already oppressive heat, entered the coolness of the Medical Unit lobby, and came face to face with a frowning Terence Riley. The scotch he had been drinking last night was visible in his eyes this morning.

She stepped out of his path and said, "Good morning."

He flicked a brief glance in her direction, grunted "Morning," and stiff-armed his way out the front door.

Well, she thought indignantly, I get even less thanks from him this morning than I did last night!

She hesitated again. Since Mr. Riley must have just come from Peter's room, there was hardly any sense in her telling Peter she had carried out his request. She was just wasting her time here.

She vacillated for several seconds and finally decided she would just poke her head in the door and say hello. He really HAD sounded in a bad way when he called her last night, and Mr. Riley—to judge from his demeanor just now—hadn't been here on an errand of mercy. Peter might want Lisa to send a telegram home, or something.

She got his room number from the Filipina nurse, found the room, and peeked around the door frame. Peter was sitting up in bed. She found herself looking directly into his eyes.

His appearance shocked her. One eye was swollen shut and colored in rich hues of purple and black. Other bruises were visible on his face, and the corner of his mouth was torn. She felt a surprising surge of pity for him. The poor man!

"Hi," he grunted. His voice was anything but friendly, and his features were contorted by a scowl of anger.

She recoiled, her initial feeling lost in a fluster of confusion and irritation. "Your boss just ran over me in the lobby," she said tartly, "and now you're looking at me as if I were a cobra. Have I committed some crime against you people?"

His scowl deepened at the words, and she cringed. That had been dumb of her! She'd said, "You people." It was the same phrase that made him so furious with her the first time they met. Would he explode at her again?

His frown became a grimace of pain, and he eased himself back down in the bed. "The look was left over from my last visitor," he told her. "I wish I hadn't had you call him. What brings you here, anyway?"

She couldn't tell if her rising temper was directed at him or at herself for getting into this situation. "I came by to tell you I'd done what you asked," she snapped. "Which, as you've apparently forgotten, was NOT to call Mr. Riley, but to go see him in person. I might add that he wasn't any happier to have me mixed up in his business than I was to be in it."

"He just now conveyed that same feeling to me," he grunted. "He doesn't seem to realize that you were the only option I had."

Lisa didn't like being described as an option. "Thanks for the compliment," she said acidly. "The next time, you can darn well go take your own messages."

"I would have done it last night," he retorted, "if I could have, but they'd just shot me full of pain-killer. I passed out within a minute of talking to you."

Her irritation faded. No wonder he'd sounded so weak over the telephone! "I had no idea you were so badly hurt," she said. "Your face looks awful. Do you have internal injuries?"

The question seemed to embarrass him. "It's nothing permanent," he answered evasively. "I should be out of here in a few days."

Well, she thought, if he won't even talk about what happened, that pretty much exhausts the conversational possibilities. And still not a single word of thanks from him, either! "That's good," she heard herself say. "I'll be on my way, then."

"Uh, I wonder if you'd do something else for me?" he asked her, in a somewhat defensive tone. "Would you tell Nga where I am?"

The request made Lisa furious. What a colossal nerve this man had! Carrying messages to his Asian mistress wasn't one of Lisa's official duties! She was on the point of saying so, when she decided that it would make her look childish. She nodded silently.

He said, "Thanks." Then he added, "I'm surprised you didn't make a snide comment about how I've got over my fear of Vietnamese."

As a matter of fact, that was exactly what she was thinking. "What you do with Nga is none of my business," she said shortly.

"Well, for your information," he said grimly, "I'm still scared of Viets. More than ever, in fact. I was wrong about Ly and Nga, though, and I'll admit it."

That's big of you, she thought caustically. Still, it was the closest thing to an apology that she was ever likely to hear from him. She decided she'd better leave while she was ahead.

It had been a bad mistake to come see him, she decided, as she walked down the hall. Even though the visit had ended on a somewhat conciliatory note, he still had never thanked her for her nocturnal mission on his behalf.

The fact was Peter Ivorson was an egotistical cretin who regarded Lisa as an errand girl, and his errands, whether they related to Nga or his other sneaky affairs, were not something she wanted to be involved in.

She wondered what had happened to him last night. He certainly had been hurt. He winced every time he moved. Could his saying that he was more afraid of the Vietnamese than ever have been a result of his injuries, or had that just been a face-saving statement to keep from apologizing for the awful way he'd behaved in her office that first day?

Well, it didn't matter. What Peter did with the Vietnamese—including Nga—was his business, not Lisa's. But if he ever asked her for another favor, she was going to turn him down flat. The next time, he'd just have to exercise some other option.

Chapter Ten

Wilbur's surveillant covering the area of the evening market sat back in the wicker chair and yawned hugely. It was 9:00 at night, over three hours past sundown. The glass of tamarind tea on the table in front of him was half-empty. He had been nursing it for the past hour. Tonight, as every night for the past week, had been absolutely dead, and to make it even worse, the café owner's daughter, with whom he used to flirt to pass the time, had recently accepted a proposal of marriage from a fat Chinese lumber merchant and now ignored him.

He glanced northward for perhaps the five hundredth time since arriving in the area of his coverage at 6 P.M., and then looked again, sharply. The old Mercedes with the CD plates was coming down Khoualouang Road toward him. The Vietnamese were out!

He dug two twenty-kip notes from his shirt pocket and dropped them on the tiny table. "Thanks," he called over his shoulder as he strolled casually toward the street corner a few meters away. The Mercedes rolled past him while he was walking. It contained only Cam, the driver, and one passenger, sitting beside the chauffeur in the front seat. It had looked like Phuong, one of the minor functionaries.

The surveillant rounded the corner without changing pace, then raced to the motorcycle parked at the curb a short distance back from the main road. He put the key in the ignition, turned it, and hit the electric start button on the handle bar. The well-tuned engine caught on the first turn of the crankshaft. The surveillant switched on the light, toed the gear selector down to first, and let out on the clutch handle. The motorcycle shot forward.

When he got out onto Khoualouang Road, the Mercedes was still in sight. The surveillant pulled a compact beeper off its case on his belt and pushed the button on it three times. There was no answer. He pushed the triple beep again.

Where was his teammate? Older cousin would raise hell with him if he didn't respond.

Even as he thought it, he saw the small red light flicker and heard the three answering beeps. Excellent! His teammate was alerted and waiting.

They had practiced this new technique for several weeks now and, by trial and error, had discovered the routes by which they could arrive at various intersections in town before the Vietnamese did. So far, nothing of interest had resulted, but this was the first time since the new system went into effect that the Viets had come out after dark.

Rolling at a moderate pace in third gear, the surveillant remained about a half-block behind the Mercedes. He saw his surveillance partner pull out from an alley ahead of him and take up position close behind the Viets. Good. Everything was ready. Now, then, which way would the bastards go?

✲ ✲ ✲

Huu squirmed uncomfortably, lying prone on the back seat of the elderly black embassy Mercedes. Hoang Bac Cam was at the wheel. Phuong, Huu's deputy, sat beside him. As they approached the intersection of Khoun Boulom, Cam looked carefully in the rearview mirror. "We are being followed," he said.

"Is he close behind?" Huu demanded.

"Not very. Perhaps forty or fifty meters."

Good, thought Huu. It was more than enough room. "You know what to do, Cam," he told the chauffeur. "Keep watching him."

"Yes, Comrade." The chauffeur's hill-country Black Thai accent grated on Huu's ears and irritated him.

He had been in a vile mood all day, ever since receiving the message passed to Phuong this morning in the market.

Huu's watcher had been spotted by the American the very first time he had been followed. And not only had the American seen him, he had attacked! Only a lucky blow had enabled Huu's man to escape.

It was a very narrow escape! Had the American captured him, he would certainly have turned the watcher over to the Lao police. Under interrogation, he would undoubtedly have revealed both his sponsorship and his instructions, with repercussions for the Embassy and for Huu, personally, that did not bear thinking about.

Huu's interview with the Ambassador on the subject had been quite unpleasant enough as it was. Huu grimaced at the memory of it. The Ambassador had been coldly furious and had calmed down only a little at Huu's assurance that there was no risk of official embarrassment. The motorcycle had been stolen in Thailand and its license plates were false.

There had been ample personal embarrassment for Huu, however. The loss of face stuck in his craw like a chicken bone. Furthermore, this damned Ivorson's discovery that he was being followed would make him much more careful in the future. Huu's chances of discovering his contacts with any traitors in and around Huu's Embassy were now greatly diminished.

Indeed, he had only one remaining chance to learn that information. He had to persuade Papaya to become Ivorson's lover; to move in with him and stick to him like glue.

The idea was abhorrent. The mental image of the American's white, hairy body, on top of and inside of Papaya's slender golden one had angered and disgusted him to such a degree this morning that he had not been able to sit still at his desk. He had flung himself out of the chancery building and tramped around the Embassy compound in the wilting heat, trying to overcome his emotions with sheer physical exertion.

Furthermore, it was by no means certain that he could convince Papaya to cooperate. She had resisted all his earlier urgings that she pretend to fall in love with the American, and, of late, she had even been ignoring the notes he'd sent her through her mother. The same hatred for white men that had enable Huu to recruit her was working against him now.

He almost hoped that she would refuse. It would spare him the pangs of jealousy that had tormented him this morning. He resolutely quashed that bourgeois sentiment. He must be firm and not allow his personal feelings to influence him. It was Papaya's revolutionary duty to become Ivorson's lover, just as it was Huu's to persuade her to do so.

To distract his mind from that unpleasant reality, he tried to determine the position of the car as they drove through the city. He recognized the left turn onto Khoun Boulom Road and the climb up onto the levee which protected the city center from flooding. Ahead, he saw the floodlights at the municipal stadium. Some children of the feudal Lao ruling families were no doubt amusing themselves at tennis. It was a game that Huu had never even watched.

✲ ✲ ✲

The Viets had turned left on Khoun Boulom and his teammate was right behind them! The surveillant dropped into second gear and twisted the throttle. The motorcycle leaped forward. He ran rapidly up through the gears, weaving through sparse traffic.

When he reached the Khoun Boulom intersection, he flicked a quick glance in both directions to check on-coming traffic, then knifed across it, straight south, leaving a flurry of squealing brakes and profanity behind him.

The road took him down off the levee. He raced passed Lulu's or, as the faded sign over the door proclaimed it, *Le Rendezvous des Amis*—it was an infamous brothel run by an ugly old Corsican widow woman.

At the first corner, he turned east, parallel to Khoun Boulom and accelerated to a dangerous speed through the darkness, speeding toward the lights of the national stadium ahead of him.

He held the beeper to his ear. At intervals he heard a series of staccato beeps. Each one indicated the passage of a street intersection and permitted him to visualize where the targets were. He was gaining on them!

He reached the park in front of the stadium. There was no time to detour legally around it. He heaved the front wheels into the air over the curb and continued straight ahead over the lawn of the park, past the lighted tennis courts. Ignoring the shouts of the strollers who scattered out of his way, he reached the far side of the park, lifted the wheels over the curb again, swerved north thirty yards, then turned back east on Rue Phai Nam.

Throughout, the beeper continued to sound in his ear. The Viets were still ahead of him. This was going to be a closely run race.

Two beeps. They were signaling a turn into Rue Phai Nam, straight at him! He braked to the curb with a squeal of rubber, turned off the engine, pulled the machine up on its stand, and leaped off it to squat down in the shadows of the service driveway of the wall that surrounded the Presidence du Conseil.

✲ ✲ ✲

Huu felt the car turning right and slowing down. They must be approaching the intersection with Phai Nam Road. Huu felt for the door handle. Why didn't Cam tell him what was happening? "Where is the surveillant?" he snapped.

The driver looked deliberately in the mirror. "Out of sight around the curve," he finally answered, and even as he said it, Huu felt the car turn sharply to the right. They had entered Rue Phai Nam. As soon as the wheels were straight again, the car came to a stop.

Huu opened the right-side door, jumped out of it and hurried across the sidewalk toward the arched entrance in the wall surrounding the Forestry and Water Service.

The car began moving again the minute his feet touched the sidewalk. The door closed by itself under the impetus of the acceleration. By the time Huu passed through the archway and was inside the courtyard, out of sight of the street, the Mercedes was already twenty meters away, on its way to make a cover purchase at the French bakery.

Huu stood dead still inside the archway, his back to the high wall, his eyes darting around the courtyard, probing the dark corners. He was alone, but he still didn't relax. A true revolutionary never relaxed. He heard the purr of the surveillant's motorcycle as it passed his location and faded off away in pursuit of the Mercedes.

He wondered whether it was the Lao or the Americans who directed the surveillance and what they thought they were gaining from it. Whoever they were, they were not a match for him. He had them running aimlessly around circles. The idea pleased him.

He waited a full minute after he could no longer hear the motorcycle then left the courtyard, turned left on Phai Nam Road and began walking eastward, toward the intersection of Lan Xang Boulevard.

It was the widest street in the city, designed after the Champs Elysees, and, like the more famous avenue, it also climbed a hill toward a military monument. In the darkness, Huu couldn't make out the concrete skeleton of the memorial rising from the traffic circle a kilometer away, but the thought of it made him smile again. There was no race on earth who needed a war monument less than the Lao. They hadn't won one in a thousand years.

✲ ✲ ✲

The surveillant had seen the headlights as the Mercedes turned into Rue Phai Nam and had heard the sound of the car door slamming. His head still buried in his arms, he had heard the sound of its engine as it passed him, followed, a moment later, by his teammate's motorcycle.

He risked a peek as the car went away from him. It definitely was the Viets. Furthermore, the two people he had seen in the front seat in Khoualouang were still in the car! So what had the slamming car door been about? He peeked around the corner of the gate post and strained his eyes to see up the dark street.

Ha! Someone had just come out of the doorway of the Forestry and Water compound, and was walking eastward, back toward the intersection of Lan Xang. The surveillant got up and started walking after him, very slowly, remaining in the shadows of the buildings.

As the man who had come out the Forestry and Water courtyard reached the corner and passed under the streetlight, the surveillant got a clear look at him. It was Nguyen van Huu! He must have been hiding in the back seat of the Mercedes. He was up to dirty business, for sure, and they had caught him at it. The new system had paid off!

He needed to call his elder cousin and get the rest of the team downtown to cover Huu, but now? There weren't any available telephones in this neighborhood. He'd just have to stay in sight of Huu and hope he found a shop with a telephone that was still open, somewhere along the way.

Keeping well back, he shadowed Huu eastward to Lan Xang Avenue. He had to stay even further back as they approached the main street, because of the higher light level there.

Huu crossed the avenue ahead of the surveillant and continued to the east in front of the Post Office. The surveillant waited for the next green light, then followed, his eyes glued on Huu. He almost got run down by a bicycle rickshaw. Its driver's curses followed him to the east side of the avenue.

Huu was still walking steadily eastward. Suddenly, he veered north across Khoun Boulom and entered the darkened grounds of the morning market. He must be going to Khouadine Quarter!

The surveillant had to make a decision. Either he stuck with Huu or he stopped in the Post Office to use the phone and call for reinforcements.

The object of the surveillance, of course, was to identify whoever Huu was going to meet, but in Khouadine, the surveillant's chances of doing that were almost zero. The place was a rabbit warren of lanes and alleys. Huu could disappear in a second.

Besides, the surveillant was so obviously a Black Thai that he risked being accosted by some hostile Vietnamese before he got a hundred meters. The better plan was to call out the rest of the team and cover the area so as to pick Huu up again when he left. He might make another meeting somewhere else before he returned to the Embassy.

Making up his mind, the surveillant entered the Post Office to use the phone.

✲ ✲ ✲

From behind the protection of a vendor's booth in the darkness of market grounds, Huu watched the man who had crossed Lan Xang Avenue after him enter the Post Office. He had heard the faint slap of rubber sandals behind him on rue Phai Nam just before crossing Lan Xang and had veered into the morning market. Now he continued to wait and watch. In a few minutes, the man came out again and walked back to the west toward Lan Xang.

Huu drew a deep breath. The man was an innocent citizen whose business had taken him along the same path as Huu. Had he followed Huu into the darkness of the marketplace, he would have died there. Huu folded and re-pocketed his knife and continued on his way. Time was short.

Picking his way through the filth left behind that morning by the merchants, he passed the rows of shuttered stores. A few Indian tailors were still open for business. He detoured wide around their shops to avoid the light shining out of their doors.

He left the marketplace, crossed Mahosot Road, and entered the dimly lit, narrow lane that let into Khouadine, the second-largest Vietnamese neighborhood in the city. Most of his trusted collaborators in the local community lived here.

As he passed between the tightly-packed wooden houses, built Lao-style on stilts, the stench of the swamp over which the slum was built assailed his nose. Trust the Lao to force the Vietnamese into the most miserable, stinking, mosquito-infested part of the town. Well, the day of reckoning would come.

The deeper he moved into Khouadine, the higher the sound level rose. All around him now he could hear Vietnamese being spoken: northern dialect, loudly, proudly, a bedlam of sound as husbands, wives, children, and neighbors all shouted to be heard above each other, and the transistor powered amplification of radio receivers. Huu chuckled at the racket. No one could accuse his countrymen of being mousy.

A few meters beyond the rickety footbridge over the sewage-laden canal beside Khoun Boulom Road, he turned abruptly left onto a narrow wooden walkway between rows of shanties. As soon as he was round the corner, he stopped, flattened himself against the wall of the structure in front of him and slid an eye back around the corner. The presence of the man on Rue Phai Nam had made him extra cautious.

The few people in the lane all looked normal. None of them were looking at the place where he had disappeared from view. He waited there and watched for over a minute. People came and went in the lane, but no one else entered the walkway, nor was anyone visibly stalling to keep from doing so.

Satisfied that he was not being followed, Huu continued on his way between the rows of houses. The walkway groaned and sagged under his feet. In some places, it became so narrow that he could have touched the wall of the houses on both sides.

When he had almost reached the end of the walkway, he stopped in front of a flimsy wooden house from which came the sound of Radio Hanoi. A glance behind him revealed no one in sight. He rapped softly on the door.

"Who is it?" demanded a shrill female voice.

"Uncle Huu," he answered, speaking no more loudly than was necessary to be heard.

The door immediately swung open. An elderly woman, dressed in black silk pants and a white blouse, greeted him warmly. "Welcome, uncle! Come join us for tea."

Huu smiled at her. "Thank you, sister. I will be pleased to, in just a moment. First, however, may I sit for a little while in your bedroom?"

The old woman beamed a gap-toothed smile at him. "Of course, uncle. Come!" She led him across the tiny wooden room and threw open the burlap curtain which served as the door to the bedroom. Three cots were crammed side by side in a space even smaller than the one he had just left. Children in stairstep sizes lay on each cot under mosquito netting. "Up, up, lazy ones," shrilled the woman. "Say hello to the uncle who has come to visit us."

The children awoke with a start, blinking in the light from the living room. At the sight of Huu, their faces lit up. "Uncle, uncle!" they shouted in chorus and climbed from their cots to surround him. He knelt and hugged them, calling each by a pet name before the old woman shooed them out of the bedroom and pulled the burlap down over the doorway, leaving Huu in semi-darkness.

He sat down on the center cot and pulled aside the flimsy cotton curtain that covered the window. Directly across from his window was the darkened rear window of a shanty like the one he was in, but which fronted on another walkway. Between the two windows was a meter of open air. The mixed smells of feces and swamp mud came to his nostrils from the mire ten feet below.

Papaya was waiting on the other side of that air space, in the bedroom of another trusted local cadre. They could communicate, but never be seen in the same place at the same time. Huu had set up the system, and he was proud of it.

"Good evening, sister," Huu said quietly.

"Good evening, uncle," she answered. The mere sound of her voice in the darkness excited him, just as it always did. It was shameful, unrevolutionary. He tried to think of Ho Chi Minh.

"What can I do for my uncle tonight?" Her voice, normally soft and sweet, held a petulant quality tonight, as if she suspected the aim of his visit. It irked him, and the irritation brought his mind back to safe ground. What did she have to complain about, when her brothers and sisters in the south were dying in battle with the imperialists?

"A great change is taking place in the struggle in Vietnam," he began. "One which will change the course of the war there and determine the fate of our homeland. Now is the time when all of us must make a maximum effort and sacrifice."

"What do you want me to do?" He could hear the doubt and unwillingness in her voice. Papaya was soft, bourgeois, Huu thought. She had not been hardened by the deprivation of the northern struggle against the French. He made a special effort to keep the irritation out of his voice.

"You have done extremely well in learning the true function of the American, Ivorson," he praised her. "I am proud of you. Now that we know who and what he is, the time has come to take the next step. I must know who his contacts are, his agent. You must learn that for me, Nga. You must become his lover, move into his house, and watch his every move.

He had anticipated objections on her part, but he was surprised by her vehemence. "You want to turn me into a white man's whore!" she cried. "How can I do such a thing? My mother will die of shame! She and I will both be ostracized. No one will speak to us."

He was moved by her appeal, but he steeled himself. He was in Laos to fight the Americans, not to pamper Papaya. "I know how distasteful the idea is to you," he said softly, trying to calm her, "but it is your duty. You can be a decisive figure in one of the most critical moments in our history."

"I don't care about such things," she cried, in a tear-and-fear choked voice. "You do, but you are a patriot and a soldier. I am not. I've never even been in Vietnam. I don't want to be a decisive figure!

"I wish I had never agreed to work for you," she continued, a tinge of hysteria in her voice. "I hate Peter Ivorson, with his hairy arms and his breath stinking of red meat. You've ruined my life! I have no friends left, and I'm frightened all the time. I won't do it. Leave me alone, uncle! Leave me alone!"

The sympathy Huu had felt for her vanished. How dare she accuse him of ruining her life? When their race and nation was fighting for its very soul, what did her peace of mind matter, to him or anyone else? She was a silly, shallow, girl. He had let her beauty blind him to her faults and been too lenient with her.

"Listen to me, Nga," he said severely. "Stop saying stupid things. You are not a whore, you are a patriot, and when we have won, and your true role is revealed, you will be admired by the whole community. Besides, what has happened in your life is not my fault at all. It is the fault of the American neo-imperialists who have invaded our homeland. You should be angry with Peter Ivorson, not with me."

Repeated refusal was her only response. "I can't do it," she sobbed. "I hate him. You can't make me do it."

Damn her, Huu thought furiously. The security of his Embassy was at stake, perhaps even the outcome of the war, and all she could say was, "I can't." He had to find some way to make her change her mind. He struggled to retain his self-control, to think of something that would satisfy her and win her cooperation.

Suddenly, it was there in his mind, full-blown. He leaned back away from the darkened window and tried to shut out the sound of her sobbing while he examined his idea for flaws.

He could find none. In fact, the more he considered it, the more it appealed to him. Indeed, he was ashamed of himself for not having thought of it before. It would not only remove Ivorson as a threat to Huu, but at the same time it would enable him to learn the identity of the American agents. And it could be done. All the necessary ingredients were available. All, that is, but Papaya's consent. Could he make her agree?

"Listen to me, little sister," he said softly across the fetid darkness separating them, "I understand how much this mission disgusts you. Poor child, you have been betrayed and mistreated by westerners all your life. I know how hard it will be for you to pretend to love one of them. But soon, very soon, you will have your revenge, and that revenge will make all your fear and shame worthwhile. Furthermore, you will run no risks at all. Listen to me, and I will explain my plan to you."

✲ ✲ ✲

From his vantage point inside a vendor's booth in the market, the surveillant who had followed Huu from Rue Phai Nam watched him come out of Khouadine again. There was no mistaking him. Huu stood for a moment under the dim streetlight at the corner of Khouadine Lane and Mahosot Road, then he turned south and began walking along the sidewalk in front of the shops on the east side of Mahosot, in the direction of Khoun Boulom.

The surveillant pushed the button on his beeper four times in rapid succession to alert the motorcycle surveillant on the east side of the market. His own machine was still back on Rue Phai Nam. There hadn't been time for him to go back and get it.

His beeper sounded with an answering series of beeps. The other members of the team, in place near the other exits from Khouadine, were starting their motorcycles and moving into position to track Huu, wherever he went next.

The surveillant wished he had been able to follow Huu into Khouadine and see who he met in there. His elder cousin would have been very proud had he been able to do it, but one man could only do so much, and his elder cousin had agreed that he had made the right choice in breaking off and summoning the full team.

The surveillant left his vantage point and began walking toward Mahosot Road. As he approached the street, he was passed by a taxi, cruising southbound in search of a late-night fare. The cab's headlights fell on Huu, who glanced over his shoulder, and then raised his arm to hail the taxi.

Damn! The team wasn't fully in position yet. The surveillant frantically pushed his beeper button to summon his teammate who was covering the north end of the market.

Huu got in the cab, which continued south on Mahosot. It passed in front of the Pathet Lao residence. Where was his teammate? The surveillant pushed imperiously on the beeper button. If the lazy bastard didn't get moving, they'd lose Huu!

The cab reached Samsenthai, turned right, and disappeared from the surveillant's view. At the same time, his teammate came into view, gunning his motorcycle. The surveillant ran out into the street and flagged him down. The motorcyclist recognized him and skidded his machine to a stop. The surveillant jumped on behind him, and they roared off again in pursuit of the cab. At the intersection of Khoun Boulom, they were joined by another motorcycle coming from the east, and at the corner of Setthathirath, by yet another.

All three of them were comfortably established behind the taxicab, cruising north on Khoualouang Road, three miles away, when Nguyen thi Nga left Khouadine and walked the two blocks north on Mahosot to her home in the Chinese cemetery. No one at all saw her go.

Chapter Eleven

It was Friday morning before the doctor let Ivorson go home, and, even then, he still moved very carefully. That little shit on the motorcycle had really pounded him.

Despite Oum's joyous welcome—his housekeeper had acted as his cut-out to Wilbur throughout the week—he was in a bleak mood as he lay down on his bed. He might not have asked Lisa Odom to tell Nga where he was, for all the good it had done. He hadn't heard a word from her during the whole time he had been laid up.

It made him furiously angry. He wasn't used to being ignored by women, least of all Asian women. He was through with the English lessons. He'd be damned if he'd waste his time on her.

After Oum had finally left him alone with his telephone, he called Nga at the office. "Personnel. Nga speaking." Her English was careful, overly precise, but the sound of her voice endangered his resolution. Damn, he thought, I really let her sink her hooks into me.

"Hi," he said, in what he hoped was a neutral tone.

"Peter? Hello! I'm so glad you called. Where are you?" Amazingly, she sounded delighted to hear from him. He could scarcely believe his ears.

"I'm back at home. I—."

She didn't let him finish the sentence. "Oh, I'm so glad you're out of the Medical Unit! Miss Odom told me you were there. I was so worried about you, and I wanted to come see you, but I didn't dare. Every tongue in the city would have started wagging. How do you feel? When will you come to work again?"

"Oh, on Monday I guess. I'm basically all right. I just need to take it easy for a while."

"Peter, I really want to see you." His intention to stop seeing her died, still-born. "Tomorrow is Boon Bahng Fie, the rocket festival. Would you be able to take us–Ly and me?"

The euphoria vanished like a popped soap bubble. Ly, too? Shit! He was back to square one. He didn't answer for a moment, and she whispered, "Peter? Don't be angry because Ly is coming. We'll find some time to be alone. I promise."

Suddenly, the prospect of taking the two girls to the rocket festival seemed like the best idea he had heard in years. "All right, then," he told her. "What time shall we go?"

It was only mid-morning on Saturday when they arrived at the site of the festival, out in the bone-dry rice paddies behind the That Luang stupa, but it was already very hot. The dust of the road puffed under their feet with each step. The girls both wore Lao skirts and blouses instead of their usual *ao dai*s. He supposed it was to avoid drawing hostile attention in what would be an overwhelmingly Lao crowd.

Thousands of people were there ahead of them. A great many of the young men were already well in their cups and making loud, bawdy comments to all the women they saw. Ly and Nga clung to Ivorson's arms. He could feel Nga's breast under her thin cotton blouse and bra. It was almost as if she were deliberately holding his arm against it. He began to be aroused and, embarrassed, changed his position between the girls.

The rockets were great, long stalks of bamboo, packed with black powder and launched from V-shaped wooden troughs mounted on the back of trucks. About half of them fizzled on their ramps or corkscrewed erratically after launching and tumbled to the ground, but the ones that worked were quite impressive, soaring hundreds of yards into the sky, with trails of thick black smoke behind them.

"What's the idea of all this?" he asked the girls. Ly covered her mouth and giggled.

"Don't be silly, Ly," Nga said to her sharply. "The Lao believe the rockets will make the rain fall," she explained to Ivorson. "It is a stupid superstition, but it is amusing to watch."

As the morning went on, however, and the Lao men got drunker, Ivorson began to see some of them sporting bamboo dildos, and it finally dawned on him that the rockets were phallic symbols, and the whole festival was a fertility rite, designed to bring on the monsoon rain. He decided that it was time to take the girls home.

They walked back to That Luang through the now-blistering heat and caught a taxi to his house, where he offered them a light lunch prepared by Oum during their absence. He had given her the day off after preparing the food, calculating that her Black Thai distaste for the Vietnamese girls would have definitely chilled the atmosphere he was trying to create.

Oum's food was delicious, and they had a good time, with much joking and laughing. Nga had never looked more alluring, but when the hell was this opportunity to be alone with her going to come along?

After lunch was over, the girls declined his offer to go find a cab for them. They were going to Nga's home, which, as Ivorson had long since made a point of finding out, was only two blocks away from his, in the Chinese cemetery. Ivorson began to feel cheated.

Ly went to use the bathroom before she left, and suddenly, for the first time since he had met her, he and Nga were alone together in the living room.

"Thank you so much for today," she said to him. "I haven't been to Boun Bahng Fie for many years. Without a father or older brother to protect me, it is frightening when men look at me that way." She looked straight into his eyes, dropped her voice to a whisper and added, "I see you look at me like that sometimes, too."

Ivorson was so startled he didn't know what to say. God knew it was the truth. Then, amazingly, she added, "I don't mind, since it's you." And standing on tiptoe, she kissed him on the lips.

It was a quick kiss, but its intensity, together with the words that preceded it, shook Ivorson. He pulled her tightly against him and kissed her back, hard. Her lips opened under his, and she pressed her body against him for a moment, before pulling away.

"We can't, now," she whispered. "Ly will come back."

He wouldn't let her go. "When can I see you alone?" he murmured. "Can you come back tonight?"

She shook her head. "We have to be very careful."

He heard the bolt on the bathroom door snap open. "Please," he begged.

She stared at him silently for a moment, hesitating, and then put her mouth next to his ear, and whispered, "All right. I'll come tonight at nine. Leave the gate unlocked."

When Ly re-entered the room, she was six feet away from him. He was so aroused he didn't see how Ly could fail to notice. He chatted with her from behind the furniture while Nga took her turn in the bathroom.

Ten interminable minutes had passed since the clock's hands stood at nine. He was in the living room, where he had been waiting since eight-thirty, trying vainly to read TIME magazine. He turned the pages and scanned the articles but didn't retain a thing he read. He became more and more excited and anxious with the passage of each endless minute. She'd better not stand him up, damn her!

The hinges of the garden gate squealed, and he literally jumped out of the chair. He threw down the magazine, ran to the door, and opened it wide. She was coming up the porch steps. She practically fell off the porch in her haste to get out of the light streaming through the open door. "Turn it off!" she snapped. "I mustn't be seen here!"

Startled by the vehemence of her voice, he snapped off the switch for the overhead light. The only other light was the table lamp by the sofa. She slipped into the room, closed the door behind herself, and stood with her back to it, looking at him. Her eyes were wide, and a pulse beat rapidly in her throat.

"What was that about?" he asked.

"I must not be seen going into your house at night," she whispered fiercely. "What would people think?"

He felt a twinge of guilt. He had been so wrapped up in his lust that he hadn't even given that a thought.

His remorse apparently showed on his face. She softened her tone. "I don't think anyone saw me." She took a deep breath, then, more composed, gave him a timid smile. "May I sit down?"

"Yes, yes, of course. Come over and sit on the sofa." He picked up the TIME magazine from the floor where he had thrown it. "Can I get you something to drink?"

"Yes, thank you. It's so hot outside. Perhaps a Perrier?" She sounded quite formal now.

He had already put some ice in an ice bucket in the bar, and some Perrier was there, as well, so he didn't have to go to the outside kitchen. He poured a drink for both of them, handed one to her, and sat down by her side.

He raised his glass to her in a toast. "Here's to having you with me. I can't think of anything nicer than that."

She hesitantly clinked her glass against his, her face unsmiling. "Yes," she said, "I think that is nice, too." She didn't sound as if she meant it, though. Was she having second thoughts?

She sipped her Perrier, her light brown eyes avoiding his. She had on no makeup at all, and her face was solemn. He had no clue of what she was thinking. Still, she had come here, at night, alone, and that spoke for itself.

They sipped their Perriers in silence until he couldn't make himself wait any longer. He put down his glass on the coffee table, took hers from her passive hand, and put it beside his own. Taking her face between his two hands, he began gently kissing it: brow, cheeks, ears, neck, and finally, lips.

She didn't respond at first, but when his lips met hers, she opened her mouth to him. He pulled her close, kissing her deeply, and ran his hands down her back and over her hips. He felt her stiffen for a moment, and then she slumped against him. Her arms crept around his neck.

He felt a bead of sweat roll down his brow. He released her, stood up, and took both her hands in his. "Come on," he said. "Let's go where it's cooler." She let herself be led into the bedroom, her eyes on the floor.

The only light was the faint glow of a street light coming through the upper glass panes. He pulled her down beside him on the bed, kissing her and unbuttoning her blouse. She rolled on her side, so he could undo her bra. His fingers were trembling so much he had a hard time unfastening it.

He raised himself up on his knees beside her and began kissing her large, soft breasts, one after the other, sucking the hard nipples deep into his mouth.

He felt her fingers slide up his thigh, searching for and then finding his sex. Even though he was fully dressed, her touch excited him so much that he almost came. He hadn't been so aroused since he was a teenager.

He pulled off her clothes in a frenzy of desire. His eyes had adjusted to the darkness, and he could see her full nakedness. Her knees were parted, her lower legs hanging off the bed. He had never seen a lovelier woman's body: full breasts, a tiny waist and swelling hips surrounding the black splash of pubic hair.

Her flesh felt like heated silk. It smelled and tasted like sandalwood. She was moans and wetness against and under him. He was steel flesh and unthinking lust when he slid into her. She flinched and groaned, and sighed. She was so much smaller than he that all he could kiss was the top of her head.

He wanted to be gentle, to make it last for her, but he couldn't. Her body devoured his senses. He came in a ferocious burst of desire, bucking against her with a force that made her grunt, and then, spent, he collapsed on top of her. She wrapped her arms and legs around him and held him tightly.

When he could breath normally again, he looked down at her face. Her eyes were clenched tightly shut, and a trail of tears ran down both sides of her face. He kissed them away.

"You were so strong," she whispered, her voice ragged. "You hurt me."

He was conscience-stricken. "I'm sorry, sweetheart. I was so excited I couldn't control myself."

She opened her huge eyes to look up at him. "Did you like it?"

His mind reeled at the question. Had he liked it? He couldn't remember ever having liked anything more in his life.

Before he could answer her question, someone began knocking on the front door of the house.

Beneath him, Nga turned as rigid as stone, then jerked into panic-driven motion, trying to wriggle out from under him, beating him with her tiny fists when he continued to hold her.

The knocking continued. God DAMN whoever was out there, he thought savagely. He rolled off of her. She scrambled out the bed and began frantically searching for her clothes. In spite of his surprise and anger at the interruption, the sight of her naked breasts bobbing in rhythm with her movements stirred him again.

"Don't be frightened, Nga," he whispered. "It can't be anything to do with you. Just relax. Stay in the bedroom. I'll go find out who it is."

She had already pulled on her underpants. He took her by the shoulders and pushed her down on the bed. "Don't be afraid, sweetheart," he repeated. "I'll be right back."

He pulled on his pants and slipped out of the bedroom. Who the hell could be out there at this time of the night? Of course, he reminded himself, it was only 9:30. It could be anyone at all.

Well, whoever it was, he was in for a cold welcome. Ivorson was going to send him packing and get back to the bedroom! He unlocked the heavy deadbolt and opened the door. The porch light was still off. All he could make out was the silhouette of a man standing on the porch.

The Fear suddenly gripped him in talons of steel as he realized his utter defenselessness, outlined in the doorway. "Who is it?" he croaked, scarcely recognizing his own voice.

"Mistair Peetair." It was Wilbur. "I must see you. Very important."

Ivorson's relief was overwhelming but, Jesus Christ, what a time for Wilbur to show up! Trembling with reaction, he opened the door and joined Wilbur on the porch, closing the door behind him.

His mind began to recover from his fright and grappled with the situation. This was tricky from every point of view. He didn't want Nga to see or hear Wilbur. Or vice-versa, for that matter.

He put his finger to his lips and pulled Wilbur by the arm, off the porch and around to the garage, on the side of the house away from the bedroom. "What is it, Wilbur?" he whispered, when they were there. "What's the matter?"

"Mistair Peetair," Wilbur began in English. Then, apparently too pressed for time to use English, he lapsed into French. "You must come quickly. Hoang Bac Cam has called. He wants Sengdara to meet him."

Oh, shit! Of all the goddamn times for Cam to get free! Ivorson shook his head violently, trying to clear his mind of the fragrance and feel of Nga's body and focus it on this new situation.

The first thing he had to do was get Wilbur out of here—arrange to meet him elsewhere, so Nga could leave without seeing him. God, he didn't want her to leave! Maybe she could stay in the house until he came back. No, that was a bad idea, and she wouldn't do it, anyway. He had to send her home and go meet Wilbur and the team. Damn. Damn! DAMN!

"Where does he want to meet her?" he asked Wilbur, who was wearing his police uniform.

"A little café in Oupmoung. Hurry! He wants to meet her at ten o'clock. We have to go! My brother is waiting out there in the taxi."

Ten o'clock! Ivorson looked at his watch. Nine thirty-five. Jesus! He had to move fast. Oupmoung was on the way to the airport, on the other side of town. He made up his mind. "Go on out there and get into place," he told Wilbur. "Tell Orville to wait for me on Wattay Road, opposite Oupmoung. I'll get there as soon as I can."

"Why wait, Mistair Peetair? Come with me now."

"I have to go to my office and get some things, Wilbur," he lied. "Have you got the beeper?"

Wilbur nodded. "All right, then," said Ivorson. "Get going. You know what to do. Good luck." He turned and ran back to the porch, forestalling any further conversation. Behind him, he heard the sound of Wilbur's departing footsteps.

He let himself back in the house, hastily crossed the living room, and tried the bedroom door. It was locked. He tapped on it softly. "It's me, Nga. Open up. It's all right."

After a few seconds, he heard the bolt snap, and the door opened. Nga was fully dressed. He took her in his arms. She was shivering. "Who was that?" she demanded. "Were they looking for me?"

He kissed her hair, her face, and her throat, while he tried to think of some believable story he could tell her. "No, silly, don't be so frightened. No one knows you're here. It was the USAID duty officer, for me. They've received a telegram from my family. My father is very sick. I have to call home."

She looked dubious, but when he began pulling on his clothes, she relaxed and even put a sympathetic hand on his arm. "I am sorry to hear about your father, Peter. Is his life in danger?"

"I don't know." He pulled on his socks and shoes. "I have to go down to the Post Office right now, and place a call. I'll drop you near your house on the way."

"No!" She shook her head violently. "I'll walk. I don't want anyone to see us together."

Her insistence on not being seen with him was nettling. Was she ashamed of him? God, he wished he could stay with her and talk about it. They had gone from acquaintances to being lovers so fast that he knew her carnally better than he did as a person.

He finished dressing and pulled her back into his arms. Her body felt wonderful! Still half drunk with the memory of their love-making, he murmured into her hair, "Nga, I have to see you again. Can you come back tomorrow?"

She stiffened against him, her eyes closed.

"What's the problem?" he asked her.

She drew a deep, shuddering breath and said, "I am afraid."

"Please, darling, there's nothing to be frightened of. No one knows you're here. Come back tomorrow." It wasn't like him to plead with a woman, but he couldn't help it. He wanted her again, right now. God DAMN Hoang Bac Cam and his infatuation with Sengdara! The irony of the thought didn't even occur to him.

Finally, her eyes still lowered, she nodded. "All right," she whispered, "I will come back tomorrow night. Leave the gate open, and turn off the lights before you open the house door."

He pulled her into his arms for another kiss. "I'm so glad you came tonight," he told her. "It was wonderful."

She didn't answer, just kissed him briefly, then vanished into the darkness of the garden. As soon as she was out of the gate, he locked the door and ran to the carport for his motorcycle.

✡ ✡ ✡

Nga paused at the gate and looked nervously in both directions, but couldn't see anyone loitering about. She crossed to the other side of the road, where there was a sidewalk, and began to walk toward home through the hot, charcoal-scented night.

She heard Peter's motorcycle behind her, driving off in the direction of Lan Xang Avenue. She lengthened her stride, winced and slowed again. What a brute he was! He was so strong, and he had come in her so hard that she felt bruised all over. Thank God he had worn a prevantatif. She had felt it. If he hadn't, she would certainly have his half-breed baby starting in her womb now. The idea made her shudder.

She tried to analyze her emotions as she walked along. She had expected to be upset, but aside from a vague feeling of disgust, all she felt inside was emptiness. White man or Asian, in bed all men were the same.

But, my God, when the knocking on the door began! She couldn't remember ever having been more frightened. It was even worse than when Miss Odom caught her getting into Peter's file. She couldn't stand much more of this tension. Huu would have to hurry up with his plan, or she would refuse to continue with it, that was all.

He would be delighted with what had happened tonight, although he would doubtless scold her for not having identified the visitor. Well, to hell with him. If he thought that Nga was going to risk her life sneaking around in the dark for him, he was wrong. He would just have to wait until his plan had come to fruition to find out who had been at the door.

One thing was certain, though, it hadn't been the USAID duty officer. Peter's story was a bald-faced lie. His father had been dead for several years. She had seen that in his file. Miss Odom must have kept her promise not to tell Peter about Nga's looking at the files, or he wouldn't have told her that story just now. What a simple, foolish woman! They were a nation of fools.

She winced again at the pain between her legs, and hatred for the American bubbled up inside her. She would pay him back for that, and it would not be long now, either. He had used her tonight, but her sacrifice had achieved what it was supposed to do. Peter Ivorson was mad about her. He had practically begged her to come again tomorrow night. Before long, she would be able to make him do anything she wanted him to do. And then her turn would come.

Chapter Twelve

Cam paid off the taxi and entered the dirt road that divided Khounta and Oupmoung quarters. The track was ill-lit by comparison with Wattay Road, but it was still too bright for comfort, and it was too early, too. Many people were still about.

That might make it hard for him to securely leave the message for Mango, even though, dressed as he was in the *paa salong* and cotton shirt of the country Lao, there was nothing about him that would cause anyone to pay him special attention.

His appearance, of course, was why the Uncles chose him for these dangerous missions. A Black Thai looked enough like a Lao to pass even close scrutiny. Cam's Lao was good, too, although he hadn't completely been able to overcome the buzzing quality that his native language gave to the Lao "jaw" and "yaw" consonants.

Nguyen van Huu never ceased telling him how important Cam's nighttime missions were to the country and to the war effort, but Cam could sense his dislike and distrust. Cam's coloration and his features were what Huu used him for, and as the lowest-ranking member of the staff, and a non-Vietnamese into the bargain, Cam was expendable.

As usual, he carried no diplomatic credentials. If he were questioned or arrested, he was under orders not to admit any connection with the Embassy, but to stick to a story that he was a refugee from up-country, recently arrived in Vientiane.

Tonight, that cover story would be much harder to maintain. What refugee had enough kip for taxi fares? Still, he himself had chosen to take that extra risk. Instead of walking to the site of the message drop, as Huu had directed him, he had caught a taxi. He would take another back to the vicinity of the Embassy. The time thus saved would be spent with Sengdara.

He was taking a fearful risk by lying to Huu, but he couldn't help himself. She had been on his mind constantly. He simply had to see her again, even if he still didn't know how he was going to answer the angry challenges she had made to him at their last meeting.

He didn't blame her for being against the Hanoi government, or for hating the Vietnamese. He hated them himself. Only the influence of his uncle, who had been recruited by the Viet Minh while a student at the Provincial Lycee, had kept Cam's own village from feeling the heavy hand of the victorious Viets following Dien Bien Phu.

Still, dared he break with the Embassy for Sengdara's sake? The question tormented him. He wanted her desperately, but the thought of the price his siblings would have to pay for his defection appalled him. His uncle, too, who had taken the place of his father in their family, would also suffer greatly. He would certainly lose his position in the government and might even be sent to prison.

Cam arrived at the east-west path that joined Khounta and Oupmoung and turned to the west. The night was very warm, and the combination of his fear and rapid pace had brought perspiration to his brow. He wiped it off with him arm. He was very pleased to see that there were fewer people here.

He walked for another two hundred meters in the stifling night. On either side of him were Lao houses. They were modest homes, some barely more than shanties, all built up on stilts. Soon he should reach the first check-point along the route he must follow to leave the message from Huu to his agent, Mango.

✡ ✡ ✡

Ivorson parked his motorcycle a block behind the team taxi. As he trotted down the uneven sidewalk toward the car, he scanned the neighborhood for an open business establishment with a telephone. COS had ordered him to call for approval before making any operational moves.

The problem was, it was almost ten o'clock at night; the stores were almost all closed, and the few that were still open didn't boast the luxury of a telephone.

He should have called before he left the house, but he had been so totally involved with Nga that he had forgotten all about Riley's orders until after he was on the way to meet Orville.

He reached the taxi without finding a telephone. Well, to hell with it. He'd tell Riley there hadn't been time to call. Anyway, he didn't need Riley to tell him how to run his operations. He'd coerced Ivorson into taking this job, and he could damn well trust him.

He put both Nga and Riley out of his mind and concentrated on the *Service Geographique* city map that he'd brought with him. Orville had parked on Wattay Road, at a point from which they could see both of the narrow lanes which led into Oupmoung Quarter from the north. It was a good location. These lanes were the routes most likely to be taken into the area by someone arriving by taxi.

The south border of the neighborhood was the Mekong River, so the rest of the surveillance team would be scattered along the lanes which led into the area from the east and west, watching for Cam's arrival. When he reached the café, they would move in close, to provide muscle for Wilbur in case Cam reacted violently to the pitch.

They heard a double beep on Ivorson's beeper, which meant that Wilbur was in place. Wilbur had the cassette recorder and a photo of Sengdara with him. Ivorson hoped to God the recorder worked. He hadn't had a chance to check it.

He looked at his watch. Ten o'clock exactly. Nothing to do now but wait. That was the worst part about this damned business, waiting around while some agent did your work for you. Ivorson would have given every penny he had in the world to be in there delivering the pitch to Cam himself. Of course, a surer guarantee of its failure would be hard to imagine.

The minutes ticked interminably by. He and Orville sat in silence, the Black Thai behind the wheel, smoking Disque Bleu cigarettes, Ivorson in back. An occasional car passed. A mosquito whined in Ivorson's ear.

A noodle vendor was pushing his hand cart down the street in their direction, rhythmically clapping a length of bamboo against a hollow piece of hardwood to announce his presence to potential customers. The repeated "whack—whack—whack" added to Ivorson's tension.

Suddenly, Ivorson's beeper emitted four muted yelps. Four beeps! That meant Cam had been spotted, entering Oup Moung from the east! Ivorson pushed an answering beep on his beeper transmitter, hastily unfolded the *Service Geographique* map again and studied it in the dim light of the streetlamps.

According to his map, the only access of any kind into the neighborhood from that direction was a dirt track which ran parallel to the Mekong and about halfway between the river and Wattay Road.

Cam must have got out of his cab further east and made his way through Khounta Quarter. Ivorson's map showed a rabbit warren of tiny paths and tracks without names. How had Cam been able to find his way?

Well, who cared? He had. What mattered was his impending conversation with Wilbur. Ivorson checked his watch for perhaps the twentieth time since they parked. Five minutes after ten. It wouldn't be long now.

✲ ✲ ✲

Ahead of him, Cam saw the landmark he was looking for. The track he was on dead-ended into the wider north-south road that formed the eastern border of Oupmoung Quarter. At that point he had to turn south. After only twenty meters, another east-west track began. He was to turn west again there, and then place the glued-together leaves in a vertical crack in the westerly-most pillar of the first house on his right.

He made the turn to the south. No one was near him on the road. He walked the twenty meters toward the next corner, the dust of the road as dry as powder under his rubber sandals.

Here was the track going west. He made the turn, hugging the pillar of the corner house. He looked ahead after the turn and saw no one. He pulled the leaf bag out of his pants pocket.

He was approaching the next pillar. Where was the crack? The instructions said it was one hundred thirty centimeters off the ground. Ah, there it was! With scarcely a pause in his forward motion, he slipped the leaf bag into the crack. It fit well, and enough of it still protruded to make it easy for Mango to find it and take it out.

Perspiration was pouring off his face, but he felt a great weight lift from his mind. Despite the earliness of the hour, he had successfully put the message in place. Now, to see his sweet Sengdara! He wiped the sweat from his brow again and strode happily forward.

The sight of the café, however, dismayed him. He had never been there before and knew of its existence only because it was described as a landmark in the instructions given to him for leaving the site of the message drop. It was not nearly as suitable as the café in Khoualouang had been. This was just a wooden shack, built at ground level, and open in the front.

Disappointed and anxious, he approached the door and looked in. Sengdara wasn't there. The café owner was standing behind the counter, staring at Cam with a strained expression. He barely returned Cam's greeting. "Has a lady come in here recently?" Cam asked him. Surely she wouldn't fail him! Not after all the risks he had run to see her!

The man mutely shook his head. Cam looked at his watch. He was a couple of minutes early. Perhaps she hadn't arrived yet. He turned to step outside again and look up the road for her, when he sensed someone's presence close behind him. A hand touched his arm, and a male voice, speaking Black Thai, said, "Excuse me, brother."

Cam jumped with fright and whirled around. He found himself looking at a uniformed—and armed—Lao policeman.

He felt his testicles shrivel up against his body. Before he could react further, however, the policeman smiled and held out something for Cam to look at. "Don't be frightened, brother," he said soothingly. "I am Sengdara's brother. I am here to speak on her behalf. Come. Let's sit back in the corner, where we can talk." He held out something toward Cam.

Cam stared at the offering. It was a glossy studio photograph of Sengdara. Clipped to it with a paperclip was a message. "This man is the head of my family. He speaks for me."

Cam was torn between the lure of the photo, note, and familiar language, and his fear of the uniformed stranger. The policeman took him gently by the arm. "Don't be afraid," he repeated. "I mean you no harm." He shot a significant glance at the café owner, who immediately left the café. They were alone.

The policeman tugged Cam toward a tiny table against the back wall. He took a chair and waved Cam into another. "Please sit down. Let's talk."

Still staring at the photograph of Sengdara, Cam slowly sat down. Was this real, or was it some sort of trap? The policeman was certainly Black Thai, and Cam could see a family resemblance. His racing pulse began to slow.

"My sister," said the policeman, gesturing at the photograph, "tells me that you love her, and that she loves you. Is that true?"

Cam's heart gave a mighty leap in his chest. She loved him! She loved him enough to have sent the head of her family to talk for her. That was normal Black Thai protocol for the marriage bargaining of a decent girl. He felt himself relax a bit. "Why are you wearing that?" he asked, gesturing at the uniform.

"Because I am a policeman, and on duty," answered the man with an easy laugh. More of Cam's tension seeped away.

"Do you love my sister?" the policeman repeated.

Cam hesitated for an instant, then, looking at the lovely face on the photograph, said, "Yes. I do."

The policeman smiled broadly. "Thank goodness for that," he said. "She would be heartbroken if you had said no."

Came felt a wave of utter delight well up inside him. He couldn't remember ever having been happier.

"I am pleased for both of you," said the policeman. "Were you a member of the local community, you would have my blessing on the spot. However, we both know that in this case, there are some serious problems. That is why I came here tonight." He looked directly into Cam's eyes. "Do you want to marry my sister?"

Faced with the point-blank question, Cam answered without hesitation. "Yes." It was true. He did.

"But you cannot take her back to North Vietnam, can you?" the policeman asked him.

That was the dilemma that had been tormenting Cam for the past weeks. Miserably, he shook his head.

"Then the matter is simple," said the policeman. "You must leave the Embassy."

"It isn't simple at all," snapped Cam. He had brooded over it during many sleepless nights. "The Uncles have sympathizers everywhere. They would hunt me down and kill me. And your sister, too!"

The policeman nodded. "I believe you. They killed my father and uncles. Killing Black Thai is something they delight in. But they cannot hunt you down if you settle in Thailand."

Cam stared at the policeman in disbelief. Thailand? The idea had occurred to him, but he had dismissed it as a fantasy. The Thai had troops fighting alongside the Americans in South Vietnam. If Cam appeared in Thailand, they would put him in jail. Who knew what would happen to him? "I have no way to settle there," he stammered.

The policeman nodded. "Not by yourself," he agreed. "But with my help, you do. That is another reason I am here in uniform tonight—so that you can see my official status. As a matter of fact, I have a very close friend in the Thai Immigration Police at Nong Khai, just across the Mekong. I have already indirectly raised the subject with him."

The words alarmed Cam. "What did you say?" he demanded. "You didn't tell him my name, did you?"

The policeman raised a reassuring hand. "Of course, not, brother. Of course not. I asked him to find out what the Thai reaction would be if a Lao-speaking functionary of a hostile Embassy in Vientiane fell in love with a local girl and, with the blessing of the Lao government, asked for asylum in Thailand."

For the first time since he realized that he loved Sengdara, a faint ray of hope gleamed on the horizon of Cam's mind. "What did he say?" he asked.

"He said that he would make inquiries and let me know," said the Sengdara's brother, "and when I saw him the next time, he told me that he had asked the head of the Provincial Special Branch in Udorn, and that the response was favorable." The policeman beamed at Cam. "So, there you are. The way is clear!"

Cam's mind reeled. "Is it really that easy?" he asked dubiously.

The policeman nodded. "They need some advance warning, a day or two. The rest is simple. When all is ready, you can meet me secretly, just like tonight. Sengdara and I will accompany you across the river at Nong Khai and introduce you to the Thai officials who will arrange your immigration papers. You and Sengdara will be married and depart immediately for Bangkok, safe from the Uncles forever!"

Looking at the bland face of the policeman in front of him, a seed of doubt germinated in Cam's mind. *This was too easy. There had to be something else, some further price to pay.*

"Are you sure that is all there is to it?" he asked sharply.

The policeman shrugged deprecatingly. "A very small matter. Before you leave the Embassy, the Thai want you to place a small object in the dormitory building. A tiny thing, actually. By the time it is found, you will have long since disappeared."

The seed of doubt in Cam's mind grew instantly into a large, ugly weed. He was being asked to take part in an intelligence operation! And, furthermore, one that would not work. Only last week, Nguyen van Huu had given the staff a lecture about such devices and then had led them on a two-hour search of every nook and cranny in the Embassy compound, looking for one. Thoroughly alarmed, Cam stammered, "I can't do that. I will be caught."

The policeman shook his head. "No, no, you will not be caught, and you can do it, very easily. In fact, if you are to marry my sister, you must do it, for that is the price the Thai demand for your settlement."

Cam looked at the picture in his hands. She was so lovely, and he yearned for her so desperately. But fear paralyzed him.

Of all the Uncles, the one he feared the most was Nguyen van Huu. Huu, with his sharp tongue and those bulging, darting, eyes that watched Cam with disdain and distrust. It was that same Huu who was the watchdog against such things as the Thai wanted him to plant.

And of course, it was not the Thai at all who were behind this plot, but—far worse—their American masters. That was obvious. The Thai had no such listening devices. The thought of what would happen to him if he were caught planting such a device for the Americans made Cam's manhood shrivel.

"No," he said softly, almost to himself, and then more loudly. "No, I cannot do that. I will be caught." He leaned across the tiny table between them and grasped the policeman's hand. "I will do anything else they want," he promised. "I will tell them all I know about the Uncles, but I cannot do what they ask."

The policeman looked at him sadly. "Does my sister mean so little to you, then?" he asked.

Cam felt as if he were being pulled apart by water buffalos. "Please," he begged. "Some other way."

The policeman shook his head. "I am sorry, brother. It is not my requirement, but the Thai's. They say that it is a very small object and that you can leave it in perfect safety." His voice became urgent. "Come, brother! This is for your future life with my sister. A good life, in a free country. Come on, man. Courage!"

Cam stared at him for what seemed like hours, while his brain reeled and raced between hope and determination, fear and hesitation. In the end, it was the fear that won. He shook his head. "No. I can't," he said. He found himself on his feet. "No. It's too dangerous." He backed toward the door of the café, the photo of Sengdara still in his hands.

The policeman remained seated, his arms stretched out toward Cam. "Don't throw away this chance for happiness, brother," he pleaded.

Cam reached the door of the café. He looked again at Sengdara's face in the photo, but in his mind's eye, the only features he could see were those of Nguyen van Huu. He gave a cry of despair, threw the photo on the dirt floor, and ran, weeping, into the night.

Chapter Thirteen

Orville suddenly became rigid. "Ah, merde," he muttered. Ivorson's eyes followed the direction he was looking. Across Wattay Road, a man had just come out of the entrance to one of the lanes leading into Oupmoung. He turned east on Wattay Road and ran along its shoulder as fast as he could, his arms pumping. From time to time, he darted glances over his shoulder at the traffic coming up behind him.

Ivorson's heart sank. He knew who the runner was long before he could recognize his face. It was Haong Bac Cam, and he was running away from Wilbur. Damn. Damn! DAMN!

A taxi came from the direction of the airport. Cam ran out into the street to flag it down. The cab skidded to a halt. Before it had even come to a stop, Cam yanked open the rear door and dived into the rear seat. The taxi started off again, east-bound.

Ivorson's first instinct was to order Orville to pursue it. He opened his mouth to say the words, and his eyes caught Orville's in the rear-vision mirror. "Monsieur?" Orville asked expectantly.

The impulse died. It was stupid. There was nothing Ivorson could do with Cam, even if he caught him. He shook his head dejectedly. "Rien," he said to Orville. Nothing.

The operation to recruit Cam had failed. And so much had been riding on it! So many lives might have been saved; so many billions of dollars spared.

What had gone wrong? Ivorson had coached Wilbur well, and he had a lot of faith in the Asian's native charm and intelligence. Cam had not bolted immediately. Enough time had passed for him to have heard out the proposition and given it some serious thought. Something had certainly frightened him, though. He had been running as if the devil were after him.

Orville grunted. Ivorson looked up to see Wilbur come out of the mouth of the same lane Cam had just exited and stand on the edge of Wattay Road. The dejected slump of his shoulders proclaimed defeat.

He crossed the road, climbed into the back seat beside Ivorson, and turned an anguished face to him. "I don't know what happened, Monsieur Peetair," he said glumly. "It started well. He was surprised, of course, but did not seem very frightened. After I showed him her photo and the note, he seemed to relax more and listened to what I said."

Wilbur frowned with concentration of his recollection. "He showed a lot of interest in the offer of settling in Thailand, and at that point, I was sure I had him. But when he learned about leaving the listening device, he became very frightened. He said he couldn't do it, that they would catch him, and once he had that thought in his mind, I couldn't reach him any more, no matter how much I talked about Sengdara. Finally, he just ran away."

Wilbur's handsome features were distorted with the pain of his failure. "I am desolate, Monsieur Peetair," he said. "I have failed you." Ivorson was shocked at how old he suddenly looked.

He patted the Asian's shoulder. "It's not your fault, Wilbur. It sounds as if you handled it perfectly. We just didn't know enough about Cam's situation back home. He may have a wife and five kids being held hostage back there."

Wilbur wasn't cheered by the rationale. He looked as if he might break into tears at any moment. The taste of the debacle was like ashes in Ivorson's mouth, too. Now he had to go tell the Chief of Station about the evening's disaster. That was likely to be a very unpleasant interview. His only consolation was that he didn't think it could make him feel any worse.

An idea occurred to him. Perhaps something could be salvaged from the wreckage of the operation. "I want you to go back in there with the team, Wilbur," he said, "and go over the route that Cam took on his way into the café, looking for a dead drop. Start at the point where your men first saw him and work in both directions from there."

Wilbur looked like a tired hunting dog who'd just caught a new scent of game. "Do you think he left a message?"

"Maybe. Remember? He told Sengdara that he was sent out at night to deliver messages to Embassy sympathizers, but how many Viets live in Khounta or Oupmoung?"

Wilbur's eyes widened. "None at all. And he was dressed like a Lao! He could pass through the neighborhood unnoticed. I believe you are right!" He put a hand on the door latch and looked at Ivorson resolutely. "If a message is there, Mistair Peetair, I will find it for you. I guarantee that. No shit."

☆ ☆ ☆

COS's eyes were as hard as armor plate. "So that's it?" he demanded, at the conclusion of Ivorson's dreary recital. "I have to tell the White House that the operation they've been banking on is kaput?"

He took a long swallow of the drink he'd had in his hand when he let Ivorson in. "Is there any chance of getting it back on track?" He took another swallow that finished the drink. It was obviously not his first of the evening, either. That could make a difficult interview much tougher.

Ivorson answered warily. "If Sengdara would cooperate, maybe we could have her meet Cam again at the market parking place and try to put things back together. I'll have Wilbur talk to her about it, of course, but realistically, I don't think there's much of a chance that she'll go along."

"Do you understand just how bad this fiasco is, Ivorson?" Riley asked sharply.

"Of course I do," Ivorson told him soothingly, "and I feel as bad about it as you do, but they don't always say yes. You know that. We gave it the best shot we had, and it just didn't work, that's all. Besides, it may not be a total loss. We think that Cam put down a dead drop out there. Wilbur and the boys are looking for it now."

Riley dismissed the prospect of finding the dead drop with an angry wave of his hand. "Fuck that! We need an agent in place, not a dead drop."

He reached for the bottle on the coffee table. "We're in a war with North Vietnam, Ivorson," he snapped. "That's the biggest political fact in our country, and in war, best shots don't count. Only winning counts. That's what I'm going to hear from the White House. They're going to shove this up my ass."

He poured himself a new drink. "This could cost me my chance to go to Europe," he said querulously. "For twenty-one years I've served in every armpit post the Agency's got, Ivorson. Medan, Katmandu, you name it, I've been there, and I'm sick of it. I want a European post. I want Paris. I deserve Paris, God damn it! And I had the operation that would have gotten me there. Until you fucked it up."

Ivorson knew that a lot of what he was hearing had come out of the Scotch bottle, but it stuck in his craw, anyway. Tonight wasn't going to do HIS career any good, either, but the prospects that had been lost along with the operation were of incomparably greater magnitude than either his, or Riley's job.

"I'm sorry about that," he told Riley evenly, "but I'm a lot sorrier for the G.I.'s in Vietnam who're going to die because we didn't get that code."

Riley's face turned red. "Don't preach to me, Ivorson," he snapped. "None of this would have happened if you hadn't disregarded my orders to call me before you did any operational acts."

Ivorson had been expecting COS to raise that issue, but the utter unreasonableness of the statement stunned and stung him. "That's bullshit," he retorted hotly. "You'd already agreed on the recruitment scenario. Besides, there wasn't time to call. Wilbur and I had only twenty minutes to cross town and get into place."

Riley wasn't listening. "When I give orders, Ivorson, I expect them to be carried out!" He glared at Ivorson for a long moment. "You're a fuck-up, Ivorson. You blew your chance to catch that surveillant, and now you've blown the biggest recruitment attempt you'll ever have. And that last bit's a promise, Ivorson, because you're fired. You're through. I'm sending you back to Washington."

Ivorson stared at him in disbelief and in growing fury. Riley had sandbagged him into taking this damned job in the first place, without proper Station support and with a woefully inadequate cover—last week's surveillance proved that—and now, because Riley's ambition was threatened, he was tossing Ivorson onto the garbage heap of the Directorate.

"What excuse are you going to use?" he demanded. "The disobedience angle won't wash, and you know it."

"I'll think of something," Riley growled at him. "Now get out of here."

Ivorson flirted with the idea of hitting him. In his present mood, he would have welcomed the emotional release of a fight, and, after all, what did he have to lose? He swung around on his heels and stormed out of COS's house, before the temptation became irresistible.

The drive home through the hot darkness didn't improve Ivorson's disposition. He had risked his neck for Riley, and he was getting shit on, in return. Riley wasn't likely to back down tomorrow, either, despite the fact that a lot of what he'd said had been fueled by alcohol. He couldn't admit that he'd been drunk, any more than he'd admit to being wrong.

As Ivorson brooded over the situation, however, it occurred to him that perhaps going home was the lesser of the available evils. His cover was blown. He'd been surveilled. Every additional day he stayed in Vientiane put him in greater danger.

Besides, he'd had it with Riley. COS's view that his own career was the primary casualty of the blown-op infuriated Ivorson. He didn't want to work for a man he couldn't respect, and he damn sure didn't want to get killed working for one.

He pulled up in front of his house.

The gate was open.

But he had left it closed.

The Fear leaped out at him from the darkness like a tiger. He jumped off the motorcycle, letting it fall to the macadam road. Thank God he had brought the PPK! He clawed it out of the holster in the small of his back, and dived across the ditch for the cover of the wall.

Just as he reached it, he heard Wilbur's voice hissing urgently from the other side. "Gently, Monsieur Peetair! Don't shoot! C'est moi."

His heart pounding, Ivorson got slowly back to his feet and re-holstered the weapon. Jesus! His terror had made him react instinctively, on a surge of fear-driven adrenaline, without a rational thought in his head. Let Riley fire him. It was time to get out of this town.

He righted and re-started his motorcycle, drove through the open gate and into the garage. Wilbur was waiting for him there, literally jumping up and down.

"I am sorry to make you nervous, Mistair Peetair," he said, "but you must come quickly. We have found the dead letter box left by Cam. My brother and the others have it under observation."

Ivorson's fright dissipated in a flood of excitement. "Are you sure it's the drop?" he asked the Black Thai.

"Certainement! It is a tightly folded piece of paper, glued inside two leaves and stuck in the pillar of a house that Cam passed on his way to the Café."

"Great, Wilbur," Ivorson said jubilantly. Good job. Let's go!" he kicked the motorcycle back into life.

A thought made him hesitate. Should he call Riley? COS had rejected the idea that Cam had put down a drop. It would be sweet revenge to tell him he was wrong, but if he did, there was an even bigger chance that COS would pull him off the case and send some other Station Officer out to cover it.

Ivorson couldn't afford that. He needed a victory, and a successful counter-intelligence coup on Ivorson's part would go a long way toward erasing the stigma of having been sent home short of tour.

Anyway, there was no time. He and Wilbur had to get back out to Oupmoung before the recipient of the drop came over to recover it. Then Wilbur, using his police credentials, could arrest the Viet agent, interrogate, and, using the threat of imprisonment, try to turn him around and make him a double agent.

He turned to Wilbur. "Go on back out there and stand by," he said. "I have to stop by my office for a minute. Wait for me in the taxi, in the same place it was parked earlier."

Wilbur nodded his assent and dashed out the gate. Ivorson followed him on the motorcycle, as fast as he dared, but at the Monument to the Dead, he turned off toward the USAID compound. He let himself into Jack Lawrence's shop and got a black wig and some dark brown pancake makeup. He wasn't going to run this operation by beeper. He'd had enough fiascos for one night. He intended to be on the scene in person, this time, and make sure things went right.

When he reached Oupmoung, the taxi and Wilbur were waiting for him. "I just talked to my brother," Wilbur announced. "The drop is still in place."

Ivorson got into front seat beside him. He pulled the black wig out of its plastic sack, tugged it onto his head, and looking in the mirror to straighten it. Wilbur grinned for the first time that evening. "Are we going back to the swamp?" he asked.

"I'm going into Oupmoung with you," Ivorson told him.

"Good," Wilbur sounded relieved. The failure to recruit Cam had clearly taken its toll on his self-confidence, too.

Ivorson opened the flat jar of theatrical pancake makeup and began sponging it on his face, neck and hands. Up close, it wouldn't fool anyone, but it should keep him from being spotted immediately as a white man in a place where a white face could only arouse curiosity.

You weren't supposed to do this sort of thing in public, of course, but Ivorson had learned, shortly after getting out of training and into the catch-as-catch-can of real operations, that you often wound up doing whatever you had to do any goddamn way you could and hoped for the best.

He finished his makeup job. They locked the cab, crossed Wattay Road, and walked together down the narrow dirt lane into Oupmoung Quarter. As they moved away from the lights of the main road, the light level fell dramatically.

After a time, they turned left, onto a path so narrow that they had to walk single file. It was even darker here, but Ivorson's eyes had begun to adjust to it. On either side of them were Lao homes, built up on posts. The lights were out in most of them, but a few families were still up, talking or listening to battery-powered transistor radios by the light of kerosene or white-gas lanterns.

They met no other pedestrians as they made their way to the drop site, but at one point, Ivorson heard someone's fingers snap in the darkness. It must have been a team member, for Wilbur responded with snap of his own. Ivorson couldn't see a soul.

When he saw the dead drop site, he had to give the Viets grudging credit. The site was a good one. After dark it would have been impossible for anyone following Cam to have seen him putting the device into the split in the house pillar.

Wilbur and his boys deserved a lot of credit, too, for finding the thing. Ivorson made a mental note to pass out a healthy cash bonus.

Wilbur pulled Ivorson after him into the shadows under a nearby Lao home. The hunkered down, Asian-style, on their haunches, behind an enormous pottery klong jar, used to store water for washing.

The family who lived above them had gone to sleep, but the sound of Asian music and laughing voices, and the smells of garlic, and hot peppers in fish sauce wafted to their ears and noses from the houses around them.

They waited, and Ivorson wondered who the agent could be. In this neighborhood, the chances were that he was a Lao. Had the Viets recruited a penetration of the Lao government?

After fifteen minutes of squatting, Ivorson's thigh muscles began protesting. He put a hand down behind him to assure that he could sit safely and felt a mass of fur.

He felt the hair on his neck rise. "There's an animal behind us," he whispered to Wilbur. At the same time, his hand encountered a sticky substance.

"It's the dog of the house," Wilbur whispered back. "He barked."

Fighting down nausea, Ivorson wiped off the dog's blood on the side of the klong jar, and tried to ignore the ache in his thighs.

A full hour passed. He had lost all the feeling in his legs, when a soft hiss sounded in the middle distance, and Wilbur nudged him in the side. "Someone is coming," he whispered.

Ivorson leaned forward on his knees, and the pain almost brought an exclamation to his lips. Damn! He should have shifted positions more often. If he had to move fast, he was going to be in trouble. He massaged his thighs and wiggled his legs.

Wilbur nudged him again. "Quiet," he cautioned. "Someone is approaching. It may be our man."

Ivorson could hear the sound of steps coming around the corner of the house on the other side of the path. A faint shadow, cast by a light somewhere behind the new arrival, fell on the path at the house's corner, and then the man turned the corner toward them. They saw his hand come quickly up, feel the pillar of the house, find the protruding leaf bag, and then drop into his pants pocket. Had they not been perfectly positioned, they would have missed it.

The man continued toward them, approaching their position. The pinpoint of a cigarette glowed in front of his face, and the smell of Turkish tobacco reached their noses, but it was still too dark to make out his features.

The man continued toward the west, passing their hiding place. Ivorson heard a soft gasp from Wilbur. What was wrong? Then, despite the darkness, he, too, recognized the diminutive, limping figure of Tran van Cao.

Chapter Fourteen

The two of them sat frozen in the darkness as Cao passed their position and disappeared down the lane. Wilbur recovered first. "Monsieur Peetair," he hissed, "I know that man. He is Monsieur Cao, the head of the Vietnamese Section of the Police Special Branch."

Ivorson mumbled, "I know him, too, Wilbur." He was in a state of shock. Cao, COS's prize agent, was working for the Viets. The enormity of the discovery finally prodded him out of his trance. "Come on," he whispered. "We've got to arrest him."

He tried to get to his feet, but his cramped thigh muscles refused to operate. He fell back down on his knees. The pain of the effort almost brought a cry from his lips. He massaged his crippled thighs furiously.

"Arrest?" repeated Wilbur incredulously. "Monsieur Peetair," he protested, "I cannot arrest Tran van Cao. He is the protégé of Colonel Saly, the Chief of Police. He will deny his guilt. He will claim I planted the dead drop on him after the arrest. It will be my word against his. I will probably be removed from the police, and worse yet, Cao will cause the North Vietnamese Embassy to move against me and my family. Our lives will be in great danger."

Ivorson had never heard Wilbur sound so agitated. He continued whispering, urgently. "I must kill Cao, Monsieur Peetair. I will hit him over the head and leave the body where it will not be found until the morning. The dead drop in his pocket will let Colonel Saly learn that Cao was a traitor, but he will not be embarrassed. The death will not be investigated. The Viets will lose their chief agent. I and my family will be safe, and so will you. It is the only way."

Wilbur's logic was flawless. Saly was Cao's patron. Rather than face an enormous loss of face from the public revelation of Cao's treason, he would use the classic Lao method of dealing with unpleasantness: publicly praise the dead Cao as a loyal public servant and quietly try to cover up the damage he had done.

Ivorson's frustration was even more painful than his leg muscles. God damn Cao! He was a sleeper, sent south with the thousands of other Communists after the defeat of the French, to set the stage for the next phase of Ho chi Minh's plans for Indochina.

And Cao had certainly given Uncle Ho his money's worth. He had subverted all the Lao Police operations against the Vietnamese for a decade. No wonder they didn't amount to shit!

He had been in liaison with the Station for eight years, too, systematically blowing every case officer and joint operation to which he had been exposed. How many agents had died because of him? He was undoubtedly responsible for Jim Reagan's death.

And for identifying Ivorson to the Viets, as well. Ivorson's alias had been no defense. All Cao had had to do to learn his true name was request the Foreign Ministry to send over the visa applications of all the recently arrived American officials.

He was as deadly as a viper. Ivorson opened his mouth to give Wilbur the go-ahead and then, slowly and reluctantly, closed it again. As much as he wanted to, he couldn't do that. Cao richly deserved it, but Ivorson just couldn't sentence him to death in cold blood. He was prohibited from it by the laws of a government that didn't sanction assassination and by his own personal moral code, as well.

He had killed the Viet Cong intruders in self-defense. If confronted with an armed enemy, he wouldn't hesitate to pull the trigger, but he was not an assassin. He actually hoped that Cao would resist the attempt to arrest him and thereby justify his death, but the arrest attempt had to be made.

He shook his head. "No, Wilbur," he whispered. "We can't do that."

In the gloom, he saw Wilbur's eyes widen in amazement. "What are you saying, Monsieur Peetair?" he hissed. "Of course we can do that. And we must. This is the one who killed Monsieur Jim, and if we don't get him first, he will kill you and me, too." He leaped to his feet.

Ivorson put a restraining hand on his arm. "I know exactly how you feel, Wilbur, but I have to follow rules..."

Wilbur's eyes hardened. He shook off Ivorson's hand. "Non, Monsieur Peetair," he said. "You do not understand. My family's survival is at stake here. This is a war, Monsieur Peetair, and in a war, there is only one rule: kill the enemy or be killed by him. That is the rule I will follow." He wheeled around and silently stalked toward the lane.

Ivorson lunged for him, but he was already out of reach. Ivorson struggled to his feet to follow. The pain of the effort brought a groan from his lips. He hobbled out from under the Lao house and limped down the narrow lane in the direction Cao and Wilbur had taken. Both of them were already out of sight in the darkness.

He started after Wilbur. His cramped muscles screamed, but he was able to move. He gritted his teeth and tried to make himself go faster.

His eyes, accustomed to the almost total darkness under the Lao house, made out the form of someone trotting down the lane ahead of him.

He tried to close the distance, but his legs were not yet up to running. The form ahead of him—it must be Wilbur—suddenly disappeared from sight. Where the hell had he gone?

It took him, perhaps, twenty seconds to reach the spot where Wilbur had vanished. It proved to be the turn into the dirt track leading north toward Wattay Road. There was more light here. Ahead of him now, he could definitely make out Wilbur, silhouetted against the lights on Wattay Road. And there, beyond him, was the unmistakable form of Tran van Cao.

Ivorson broke into an agonizing, hobbling trot, knowing even as he did so that he could never catch up with Wilbur in time to prevent whatever was about to happen.

Wilbur was only ten or fifteen yards behind Cao, now. Ivorson saw him pull his service revolver from its holster and reverse it, holding it by the barrel. He was going to club Cao with the handle of the pistol!

Suddenly, the little Vietnamese whirled around. He must have heard Wilbur's footsteps. He momentarily froze, perhaps confused by the sight of the police uniform. Ivorson heard him snap out a question in Lao. Wilbur, still running full tilt toward him, said something in response.

Whether it was the spoken exchange or something else, Cao's semi-trance was broken. He turned around again and began running, skittering like a crab on his lame legs. As he ran, he reached into his right hip pocket and pulled out an automatic pistol. It was a toy-like thing, probably no bigger than .25 caliber.

Wilbur was now almost on top of him. He raised the hand holding the revolver over his head, but before he could deliver the blow, Cao stopped, whirled around, and pointed the little gun at him.

Fire spouted from its barrel. Two high-pitched cracks came to Ivorson's ears. Wilbur stumbled and fell, almost at Cao's feet. Cao turned and began running again, a panic-stricken hobble eastward on Wattay Road. He disappeared from Ivorson's view.

Ivorson came panting up to Wilbur, who was lying face-down in the dirt track, absolutely still. Ivorson had seen that stillness before. An awful chill settled in his gut. He knelt beside Wilbur.

There was no blood visible. He grasped Wilbur by one of his out-flung arms and turned him over. "Are you all right?" he asked.

It was a wasted question. There were two small holes in Wilbur's forehead, directly above his staring eyes. Wilbur would never be all right again.

For an instant, Ivorson's sense of loss paralyzed him, and then a tide of violent anger and lust for revenge brought him back up on his feet. He yanked the PPK from its holster, snapped back the action to arm it, and rushed out of the alley after Cao.

The little man was still running, as fast as his crippled legs would let him, along the dirt shoulder of Wattay Road, but with his disability, he hadn't put more than forty yards between himself and the site of the shooting.

Ivorson broke into the best run his still-aching thighs permitted. A deadly red rage enveloped him. All he could see or think about was killing Tran van Cao.

He was only ten yards behind Cao now. The Vietnamese still had his tiny automatic in his hand. The sight of the gun deprived Ivorson of the last shreds of reason. "Now, you fucker," he silently raged at Cao's back. "Now you get yours!"

He stopped, raised the PPK and held it in both hands to steady it against the movement of this heaving chest. He centered the sight picture on the middle of the little Asian's back, took a deep breath, and began to take up the slack on the trigger.

There was a loud screech of rubber and, simultaneously, Ivorson received a violent blow on the left shoulder. It staggered him. The bullet he intended for Cao roared off harmlessly into the night. He fell onto his right knee and jerked up his head to see who his assailant was.

A jeep, full of Lao military police, was right beside him. An MP officer, sitting in the front passenger seat, had a pistol pointed at Ivorson, and an enlisted man in the back was in the process of aiming the M-I carbine he had just butt-stroked Ivorson with. They were both shouting at him in Lao. He couldn't understand them, of course, but the meaning was crystal clear. If he didn't drop the gun and put up his hands, they were going to shoot him.

He let the automatic fall in the dirt and raised his hands. Out of the corner of his eye, he saw Cao stop, turn around and start back toward him. Once he started talking, Ivorson would be in even more trouble than he was in now. Ivorson had to get the first explanation in, somehow. "Parlez-vous francais?" he asked the MP officer.

Ivorson wasn't too clear on Lao military insignia, but he though his captor was either a first or second lieutenant. He was a young man. He shook his head to Ivorson's question. No French.

Cao was coming toward them fast, now. "Do you speak English?" Ivorson asked the MP in desperation. The Lao officer shook his head negatively again, and then Cao arrived, his tiny pistol was out of sight now, but his National Police credentials very much in evidence. He broke into a flood of high-velocity Lao.

Ivorson's situation was rapidly becoming desperate. Cao would soon recognize him, if he hadn't already, and if he got these MPs to turn Ivorson over to him...

Cao was still talking fast to the MP and waving his credentials under the young officer's nose. Ivorson would have given everything he had for minimal fluency in Lao. His Vietnamese wouldn't help him here, and the MP officer didn't speak any European languages. Jesus Christ, what was he going to do?

He toyed with the idea of making a break for it but gave it up almost immediately. They would shoot him down inside of five yards.

Cao fell silent, and the MP officer shrugged. Ivorson realized that he was just about to relinquish custody to Cao. Whatever the hell Ivorson was going to do, he had to do it right now.

He raised his right arm to his head. The muzzle of the M-I carbine centered on him, and for a horrible split-second, he thought he was going to be shot. He snatched the black wig off his head, and threw it on the ground, then wiped his hand across his brow, revealing his white skin. He looked at the little Vietnamese spy. "Bon soir, Monsier Cao," he said loudly. "C'est moi, Peter Ivorson."

Cao's mouth dropped open. He stared, struck dumb. Ivorson pointed at him, for the benefit of the MP officer. "Look!" he said in French. "He knows me!" He tapped his own chest. "American Embassy!" Pointing back at Cao, he said, "Vietnamese spy!" He gestured behind him. "He just murdered a Lao policeman."

The expression on the young Lao officer's face was a study in absolute bafflement. In any other circumstances, Ivorson might have found it comical, but not now. If he couldn't make this MP understand him, he might never laugh again. "American Embassy," he repeated, pointing to his own face again.

Tran van Cao recovered from the shock, and began speaking again. Ivorson could tell that his revelation of identity had shaken the Vietnamese. His voice was pitched much higher, and there was a note of desperation in it. His hands were shaking. Could the MP see them?

The Lao officer was listening to Cao, but his eyes kept straying to Ivorson's face and hair. Ivorson tried to make the most of his interest by pointing at Cao and saying, over and over, "Espion vietnamien! Vietnamese spy!"

A loud shout suddenly drowned out his and Cao's voices. It was a multi-voiced cry of grief and rage that turned all their heads, including the MPs. From the mouth of the alley that he and Cao had run out of came Orville and four or five other members of Wilbur's team. They were carrying Wilbur's body on their shoulders. His unseeing eyes were toward the sky, and his arms hung grotesquely down. His hands jerked in reaction to the movement of the men carrying him. It looked as if he were gesturing.

Orville looked in Ivorson's direction, and then, seeing Cao and the MPs, came running toward them, screaming at the top of his lungs in Lao and pointing from Wilbur's body to Cao. Ivorson didn't understand a word, but it was apparent that he was accusing Cao of the murder of his brother.

At a point about half-way between the alley and where Ivorson was, Orville abruptly stopped, stooped down and came up with something in his hand. He held it up over his head and began shouting again.

It was the leaf bag Cao had picked up from the dead drop. He must have thrown it down as he fled after shooting Wilbur. Ivorson turned to look at the little Vietnamese. At the sight of the leaf bag, his eyes narrowed, and his features twisted into a grimace of hatred, directed first at Orville, and then at Ivorson.

The little man's left hand still held his police credentials, but his right hand now darted toward his hip pocket, and came out with the tiny automatic pistol.

He swung the muzzle toward Ivorson, who was standing not a yard away. Expecting to feel the bullet's impact at any second, Ivorson flinched, but before Cao could line up the gun, the MP officer, who had caught the movement out of the corner of his eye, let out a shout and raised his own pistol. Cao shifted his aim from Ivorson to the MP officer and opened fire. There was a series of sharp cracks and darts of flame from the muzzle, right in Ivorson's face. The MP officer was hit. Ivorson saw him jerk and then slump. The soldier with the carbine grunted and began to topple backward in the seat.

Cao fired again and again at the two remaining MPs in the jeep. Realizing that he was going to be next, Ivorson lunged at Cao, and caught the wrist of the hand holding the gun with both his own hands. He pushed Cao's arm skyward, pivoted his body under it, and holding Cao's arm straight over his shoulder, he heaved forward and down with all his strength.

Cao was jerked off his feet and through the air over Ivorson's shoulder. Ivorson heard the bark of the automatic again. A puff of dust between Ivorson's feet showed him where the round had hit.

Fear gave him additional strength. He slammed Cao down on the ground, as hard as he could. He heard the wind whistle out of the Asian's lungs. Still holding Cao's wrist firmly between his own two hands, Ivorson stamped his left foot down with all his force on the back of Cao's arm.

The bone cracked with the sound of a breaking branch. Cao screamed like a woman, and dropped the pistol.

"You didn't like that, did you, fucker?" grunted Ivorson viciously. "Try this!" Still holding Cao's wrist, he kicked him in the ribs with his right foot. He had never hated anyone so all-consumingly in his life.

The little man grunted in agony and rolled into a protective ball. Ivorson drew back his foot for another kick, this one aimed at Cao's head, when he became aware of Orville, standing beside him and pulling on his arm.

"Monsieur! Monsieur!" Orville shouted. "We will deal with this serpent. You must go now, quickly, before the police come. Our family's connection with you must not be known."

Ivorson's mind climbed slowly out of the murderous rage that possessed him. He was ashamed that Orville, even in the sight of Wilbur's body, had the presence of mind to evaluate the operational situation, while Ivorson, a trained case officer, wanted only to avenge his dead agent.

"You're right," he panted. "Thank you."

He took the leaf bag from Orville, put it in his own shirt pocket, and started around the back of the jeep toward his motorcycle, parked across the street, when his eyes fell on Wilbur's body, lying on the side of Wattay Road at the feet of his relatives and team members.

The full weight of his loss crashed down on Ivorson. Wilbur was dead. Handsome, smiling, courageous Wilbur, who was afraid of nothing and would do anything, was gone. It was the hardest thing Ivorson had ever had to accept in his life. Tears welled in his eyes. Blinded by them, he groped for Orville's shoulder. "Toi dau long lam," he said in Vietnamese, knowing that he understood that language much better than French. "I am sick at heart. I loved your brother, too."

Orville looked startled at the fluent Vietnamese, then gravely nodded. "Thank you," he replied. Then his eyes jerked away from Ivorson's face and, wide with shock, fixed on something behind him. Ivorson wheeled around.

Tran van Cao was slithering in the dust like a wounded python. His teeth gleamed in a grimace of agony as he dragged his broken arm and ribs over the rough ground, but his eyes gleamed with triumph as he reached out with his good arm and seized Ivorson's Walther PPK, which was still lying by the side of the road where he had dropped it when the MP hit him with the carbine butt.

Before either he or Orville could move, Cao had picked up the still-cocked pistol and rolled over on his side to point it at Ivorson. "You son of a whore," he whispered, in a voice as malignant as terminal cancer. "Drag them out of the jeep." He motioned with the muzzle of the gun to make it clear that he was talking about the dead Lao MPs.

The PPk tracked Ivorson like a radar as he tried to lift the young officer's body out of the passenger seat. He was sprawled against the corpse of the driver.

"I said, drag him out of there!" snapped Cao. "He's a corpse, not a virgin girl."

Furious with himself for having left his weapon unattended so close to Cao, Ivorson roughly pulled the MP officer out off the seat. The body collapsed on the ground beside the vehicle.

"Now the driver." Cao's hiss sounded like a cobra's. "If you do something wrong, I will kill this one." He pointed the gun at Orville.

Ivorson went around to the other side of the vehicle, where the body of the driver was slumped forward against the wheel. Now that he was partially screened from Cao's view by the vehicle, Ivorson saw a chance to turn the tables. He could pull the driver's sidearm, drop to the ground along with the body of the driver, and shoot Cao from under the jeep.

He felt for the pistol on the driver's belt. There wasn't one. He was the only person in the car who didn't have a weapon. Sick with disappointment, Ivorson dragged the body out from under the wheel and let it fall to the macadam.

"Come back around to this side," Cao ordered him.

Ivorson experienced an almost irresistible urge to run for his life, make a dash for it across Wattay Road, keeping the jeep between himself and Cao. If he did, however, Cao would kill Orville. Ivorson was already responsible for one death in their family tonight. He forced himself back into Cao's line of fire.

"Come here," ordered the little Vietnamese, "and help me to get up."

Ivorson approached him. Cao had the gun in his left hand. The other arm was broken. He had broken ribs, too. Perhaps there was an opportunity here.

Cao was too clever for him. He trained the PPK on Ivorson as soon as he was in sight and ordered him, "Stand in front of me and pull me upright by my belt. If you do anything at all that displeases me, I will kill you."

Ivorson could do nothing but obey. He knelt beside the little man, who thrust the muzzle of the automatic painfully into Ivorson's ribs.

"Lift me up," Cao ordered.

Ivorson put both hands on Cao's belt and pulled him slowly upright. His left arm was still numb and weak from the blow on the shoulder.

Suppose he suddenly let go of the belt and slammed Cao's broken ribs as he fell. Impossible. Cao had the automatic right in his side. He would be dead before Cao even began to fall.

Ivorson felt the little man's weight leave his arms as Cao got his feet under him. "Help me into the driver's seat," Cao ordered him. "Don't let go of my belt."

Ivorson half-carried Cao around the back of the jeep. Thirty yards away, the rest of the surveillance team was still clustered around Wilbur's body, frozen in tableau vivant by the menace of the weapon in Cao's hand. Its muzzle was still jammed into Ivorson's side.

They reached the driver's side of the jeep. Cao stepped up on the body of the dead Lao MP. "Help me get in," he hissed.

Ivorson obeyed. They grunted together as Cao's right leg swung up into the jeep: Ivorson from the effort, Cao from pain.

Cao settled into the seat. It came to Ivorson, with a horrible sick feeling in his gut, that his life was about to end. Cao's right hand was useless. To turn the key and start the jeep, then put it in gear, he would have to use his left hand. But that was the one holding the pistol against Ivorson's side. It presented Cao with an insurmountable problem.

Unless he did the obvious thing.

Shoot Ivorson.

Cao's eyes met his, and in them, Ivorson could see nothing but death. The only chance he had left now was to drop suddenly to the ground and roll under the jeep. He prepared himself to do it, knowing full well that it wasn't going to work.

At that instant, the center of the jeep's windshield disappeared in a spray of flying glass, and the sound of a shot roared out. One of the surveillance team members must have taken advantage of Cao's concentration on Ivorson and opened fire with Wilbur's service revolver!

Cao flinched at the assault of the glass splinters, and Ivorson dropped to the ground like a stone. He landed on the corpse of the driver.

The PPK roared, almost in his ear, and searing pain sliced across his right shoulder. Cao was shooting at him, at pointblank range, and Ivorson couldn't get out of the way. The driver's body blocked his access to the underside of the jeep. The next round would kill him.

Overpowering, soul-consuming fear possessed him. It was worse than the assassination attempt in Saigon. Now he had no means to defend himself. It took every ounce of willpower he had not to plead for his life. Instead, he jerked, gasped, and lay still, feigning death.

The next three seconds lasted an hour. His shoulder hurt like fire, but he dared not even breathe. Please God, he pleaded with the Creator of his Lutheran childhood, let him think I'm dead. Please, dear God, please. He had never known such terror.

Another shot from Wilbur's pistol rang out. Ivorson heard the bullet slam into the back of the jeep. Jesus! Suppose it hit the gas tank? He would be burned alive.

The engine of the jeep cranked one, twice and then caught. The gears grated, and the little vehicle lurched away from Ivorson's side, over the arm of the dead driver, and away down Wattay Road. The service revolver behind Ivorson roared three more times.

Ivorson opened his eyes and looked after the vanishing jeep. He saw no apparent effects from the shots. It continued straight ahead to the east and finally disappeared from view in the traffic. Tran van Cao had escaped.

Chapter Fifteen

The Filipina nurse shut the door and Ivorson was left alone in the room of the Medical Unit. He spat out the sleeping tablet he'd been hiding under his tongue, and dropped it in the waste basket beside the bed.

The bullet wound on his shoulder felt as if it were on fire, and his testicles had swollen again, but he didn't dare go to sleep. It was almost two o'clock in the morning now. The daytime nurses came on duty at six A.M., so he had to make his move at five, or even before.

He started to sit up in bed, and pain stabbed him from both ends of his body. The painkiller the doc had given him was not doing much good. It was going to be a long three hours.

Thank God Orville had driven him here in the taxi. He would never have made it on the motorcycle. He'd just barely hung onto consciousness as it was.

Moving very slowly and carefully, he made it to a sitting position, slid his feet to the floor, and stood up. His head went light, and for a moment he thought he would faint, but he hung onto the bed, and the weakness left him. He inched his way over to the closet. He found his trouser on the hangar, where the nurse had put them, and felt for his billfold. He got it out of the pocket, opened it, and from it pulled the leaf bag that Tran van Cao had recovered from the dead drop.

He made his painful way back to the bed, switched on the bedside light, and carefully pulled apart the glued leaves that formed the concealment for the message. Wilbur had died for this thing, and Ivorson almost had, himself. Before he had it out with the Chief of Station, he needed to know what it said. He separated the leaves enough to slip out the folded sheet of rice paper inside. He opened it up, held it under the light and read the message. It was printed in precise Vietnamese: "Mango. The American Ivorson detected and attacked my surveillant. Stay away from him. I have made arrangements to remove him."

The Fear suddenly leered at him from the sheet of paper. Ivorson's hands began to shake. He almost tore the rice paper while re-folding it, but he finally managed to slip it back inside the leaf bag and return that to his billfold. By the time he crawled back into the bed again, he was shaking all over. God, he was weak! Before he could pull the sheet over himself, he fainted.

When the throbbing of his shoulder woke him again, it was after three. The Fear was inside him now, lodged deep in his soul, and the words of the message were burned in his mind: "I have made arrangements to remove him."

The writer had to be Nguyen van Huu, the Vietnamese intelligence chief. Not only COULD he kill Ivorson at will, but he apparently intended to do just that. It could happen anytime he left the refuge of the USAID compound; on any street corner, perhaps even in his own house. It was like being back in Saigon but without the protecting armies.

The realization corroded the resolve he had formed in the taxi, on his way to the Medical Unit. Wasn't it better to let Riley send him home and defend his reputation as best he could in the safety of Headquarters? What good was reputation or pride to a dead man?

Then into his mind's eye came the image of Wilbur's lifeless body, sprawled in the dust alongside Wattay Road. Never mind that Wilbur's disobedience of Ivorson's orders had exposed him to Cao's bullets. He had been there in the first place on Ivorson's business, at Ivorson's orders, and he had died fighting their common enemy in this strange, shadowy war that they were both engaged in.

And the incarnation of that common enemy was Nguyen van Huu. Cao may have pulled the trigger, but the willpower, the evil genius behind Wilbur's death, was Huu. Huu had killed Wilbur.

A devastating sense of loss filled Ivorson's heart. He was the only child of a martinet father, fifty when Ivorson was born and a younger and insecure mother. He had not had many friends as a youngster. All through his childhood, he had longed for a brother; someone who could share his joys and woes with, as well as his father's disapproving attention.

And only now—too late—had he finally found him. Wilbur was not just an agent. Ivorson had lost agents in Vietnam, during Tet, and it hadn't affected him this way. Wilbur had become the brother Ivorson had always wanted. Brown-skinned Wilbur, whose true name Ivorson's mother couldn't even pronounce.

The thought of his mother's reaction to that concept produced chuckle, which instantly became a spasm of pain, but when the chuckle and the pain were past, the truth of the emotion remained.

Of all the men Ivorson had ever known, the only one he could truly say he'd loved was Wilbur. He had loved him for his infectious gaiety, his charm, his success with women, and above all, for his indomitable courage. God, how he had envied Wilbur that bravery!

And now Wilbur was no more. He had been taken from Ivorson and from the ranks of free men everywhere, by Nguyen van Huu, who even now was "making arrangements" to remove Ivorson, as well.

Ice-cold rage flooded into Ivorson's heart, a rage so cold that even the Fear fled its presence. From the core of that rage came a new resolve: Ivorson wasn't going home, no matter what Riley said, or what "arrangements" Huu was making. Ivorson was going to stay in Vientiane and build a memorial to Wilbur: a memorial of video tape, filmed through the window of the North Vietnamese Embassy code room.

He checked his watch. He still had over an hour to wait. He lay back on the bed. He needed to get some rest. It was a five block walk to the safe site.

☆ ☆ ☆

Cam slept very badly. He was tormented by a dream in which he saw Sengdara, seated at a table, weeping. She repeatedly refused her brother's offers of food. As Cam watched, she became thinner and thinner, until she finally just faded from sight. It was the small hours of the morning when he finally fell asleep.

He was awakened, both suddenly and violently, to find Nguyen van Huu screaming curses and shaking him. Cam, at first, thought he might be having another nightmare, but a hard slap across the face quickly disabused him of that idea.

Sudden, mortal, dread overcame him. Huu had found out about him and Sengdara! The policeman claiming to be her brother had really been an agent provocateur of Huu's. Scarcely able to speak for fear, Cam stammered, "What is it, Comrade Huu? What is the matter? Why are you treating me like this?"

"You viper," screamed Huu. "You villain! You traitor! When did you tell Ivorson about the message?"

Ivorson? The message? Cam was utterly confused. He was guilty of betraying his trust but not of talking about the message, much less to anyone with such a strange name. "I told no one, Comrade," he stammered. "No one! What are you talking about?"

Huu hurled him back on the cot and stood over him, panting with rage. Cam had never seen Huu display emotion like this before. His face was white, and his large eyes bulged so that they seemed about to pop out of his face.

"You know perfectly well what I am talking about! Mango was attacked last night after he picked up the message," he hissed viciously. "First by a Black Thai member of the Lao Police and then by the American intelligence officer, Ivorson. You are their agent. Admit it!"

Cam's stomach tied in a knot. He was doomed! The Black Thai policemen had to be Sengdara's brother.

He was on the verge of confession when a last vestige of reason saved him. He had put the message properly in place before he even saw Sengdara's brother, and he really had not mentioned it to anyone. Re-convinced of his innocence, he defended himself. "No, it is not true. I spoke to no one. I know no such people. I placed the message exactly according to instructions, and no one saw me do it."

Huu's face was implacable. "Then how did they know when and where to attack Mango? You lie! You Thai are all the same. Traitors! Lovers of foreigners!"

For a horrible moment, Cam thought Huu was referring to his love for Sengdara. Then he realized that the reference was to the Black Thai's support for the French during the first Indochinese war and with that realization came a glimmer of hope.

"You are not only accusing me of treason," he said, in what he hoped was a properly indignant tone of voice, "but all those of my race. Are you also accusing my uncle of loving foreigners more than his country?"

Cam's uncle, to whom Cam owed his position in Vientiane, was a senior functionary in the Foreign Ministry. Although he was not in a position to directly threaten Huu, who was employed by the Ministry of Interior, he might well have friends from the Viet Minh days who could. It was a desperate ploy on Cam's part, but the only one available to him.

Having delivered the veiled threat, he held his breath. Would Huu knuckle under to it, or would he return to the attack? If he chose the latter course, Cam was as good as lost. The attack on Mango might not be his fault, but his conscience was as black as night, and Huu, with his nose for deceit, would smell his guilt.

Huu stood beside his cot, breathing heavily. "Don't you dare threaten me with your uncle's political influence," he barked, but the tone of his voice had subtly altered, and Cam knew that he had won at least a momentary reprieve. He carefully concealed his relief.

"I would not dream of threatening you, Comrade Huu," he disclaimed. "I merely want to be judged for what I myself did or did not do, and not on the basis of your prejudice against my race. Our revolution," he continued, carefully keeping from his voice the malice he felt, "was, after all, made for all the citizens of our country."

Huu struggled visibly to regain his lost self-control. Cam mentally braced himself for the inevitable interrogation. It was not long in coming. "Tell me exactly what you did and where you went last night," Huu demanded.

Cam did, omitting only the fact that he went to and returned from Oupmoung by cab rather than on foot, and (obviously) the fact of his meeting with Sengdara's brother.

He concluded the factual recital by saying, "I was, as always, very alert for surveillance. I saw no one, either following me or loitering along the route Mango provided."

The thought that his route had been provided by Mango led him to add, "As you know, you gave me the direction for getting to the message site for the first time just before I left here last night." The statement was calculated to remind Huu that the directions had been received sealed inside the previous week's leaf bag and had been in Huu's possession ever since.

"Could some enemy have seen it before Mango sent it to us?" Cam continued, thinking furiously. The success of the false trail he was laying would depend on Huu's ability to communicate with Mango under the new circumstances. "You should ask Mango about that."

"Are you deaf? Huu snapped at him. "I told you, Mango was attacked by a Lao policeman and the American CIA man, Ivorson. He killed them both in self-defense and fled the city. I have only now received a message from him through a cut-out."

It required an act of supreme will on Cam's part not to reveal his relief. Mango, whoever or wherever he might be, was not in a position of refute Cam's hypotheses about the cause of their misfortunes.

"I am sorry to hear that, Comrade Huu," he said in as sincere a tone as he could muster. He paused. "I do not mean to imply any carelessness on the part of Mango, whom I, of course, do not know, but the only cause I can see for this misfortune is that he was followed when he went to pick up the message. I am certain that I myself was not."

He hoped that his voice conveyed the confidence he felt in the truth of the last statement. He had been as nervous and as wary as a jungle deer last night. If someone had been following him, he would have noticed them.

Huu did not react further to Cam's suggestions, but stood silently at the foot of his cot. Cam felt that he had to keep the initiative at all cost. He could not allow Huu to be the arbiter of his fate. "Whatever the cause of Mango's misfortune," he said, "it is clear that I no longer have your confidence. I therefore ask to be sent home. I prefer to suffer the American bombings in Hanoi rather than remain under suspicion as a traitor."

Huu acknowledged the offer with a nod. After another moment of silence, he said stiffly, "I will ask the Ambassador to forward your request. He may wish to speak to you later, himself." He turned and marched toward the door of Cam's dormitory room, his back as straight as a ramrod.

At the door, Huu turned and said, "You are to say nothing of this matter to anyone." That was a good sign. Huu had lost face with his unproven verbal and physical attack on Cam. He knew he would lose even more if others learned of his uncontrolled outburst.

Not trusting his voice, Cam nodded silently. Huu hesitated, as if about to say something else, then turned and left the room.

Shaking with reaction, Cam got off his cot and went to the window. It was still very early. There was only a hint of gray in the sliver of sky he could see above the compound wall. He stood in front of the screen, taking in deep breaths of the hot air in an effort to compose himself.

He had just had a very, very narrow escape. He wasn't sure whether he had survived due to Huu's lack of evidence or his fear of Cam's uncle's connections. Probably the latter, he decided. Lack of evidence had never prevented the Vietnamese from working their will on the Black Thai in the past.

It wasn't over yet, either. Not by any means. His present reprieve could be nullified by some new word from Mango or by any number of other factors over which Cam had no control. He had done well to ask for reassignment to Hanoi. He needed to get away from Nguyen van Huu, as fast as possible.

If only he could relive last night! He had begun having second thoughts about cooperating with Sengdara's brother even as he ran away from him last night, but it was too late to re-consider, now. Huu would certainly never allow Cam to leave the Embassy alone again.

No, Sengdara was irretrievably lost to him, and he was therefore safer in Hanoi under his uncle's protection, even with the bombs falling, than he was here under Huu's suspicious scrutiny and tormented by thoughts of her nearness. Her face appeared in his mind's eye, and he blinked away the tears.

✲ ✲ ✲

"What the hell do you mean by getting me here at six o'clock in the morning?" demanded Riley. "What's this all about?" The Chief of Station's red-veined eyes glared accusingly at Ivorson.

"I couldn't get hold of you last night," Ivorson answered, at the door of the safe site. "The doc locked me into the Medical Unit and gave me a sleeping pill. This was the soonest I could reach you."

"Medical Unit?" Riley echoed from behind him. "What the hell were you doing there?" Then, after a short pause, during which Riley took a seat, "You do look banged up. What happened to you?"

"I got a bullet crease across my right shoulder," Ivorson told him, "and my balls have swelled up again." They had, too. The walk through the dark streets to the safe site had been agony.

"You got shot?" The pitch of Riley's voice rose noticeably. "Ivorson, God damn it, I'm the Chief of Station! If one of my people gets shot, I want to know about it right then! Who shot you? What the hell happened?"

Ivorson sat down, very gently. "Actually," he said, "my getting shot is the best news I've got for you."

Riley's face tightened. "Oh, God," he said warily. "What have you fucked up besides the Cam recruitment?"

Ivorson took out his temper on the arms of his chair before he answered. "Cam did leave a dead drop out there last night, and the party who picked it up was Tran van Cao."

Riley's eyes opened wide. His jaw dropped. Then he exploded. "That's insane!"

Ivorson shook his head. "That's a fact."

Riley peered at him closely. "Are you high on something? Cao can't be a Viet agent. He's a Catholic, he's as anti-Communist as he can be, and, furthermore, he passed his polygraph."

"What I'm on," retorted Ivorson, "is reality. Cam beat the polygraph. He's a North Vietnamese intelligence officer and a murderer."

Riley's eyes got even wider. "A murderer? Bullshit! Who'd he kill?"

"Wilbur." It was hard for Ivorson to say. "Also four Lao MPs and me, if his aim had been better. That's how I got the bullet wound."

Riley's face was a study in disbelief. "If you're shitting me, Ivorson," he said hoarsely, "so help me I'll destroy you."

The threat burst through the flimsy veneer of Ivorson's self-control. "You'll destroy nothing?" he shouted. "You're the one who's been destroyed. Can't you understand plain English? Tran van Cao is a double-agent. You think I might cost you your career? Your career is history. Cao took it from you, along with all this Station's Vietnamese operations!"

COS's face paled. "You can't talk to me like that," he growled.

Ivorson gave him scowl for scowl. "I just did." For the space of ten seconds, they stared at each other like hostile dogs.

Riley finally broke the silence. "Did you say that Cao killed Wilbur?" His voice betrayed the massive self-control he was exerting. "What happened?"

"Wilbur went for him. Cao shot him."

"Wilbur went for him?" Riley's self-control disappeared. "God damn it, how could you have let that happen? That was incredibly stupid!"

"I agree," Ivorson answered, trying desperately to keep his own temper under control. "I ordered him not to. He disobeyed me."

Riley blinked. "For Christ's sake, what got into him? No wonder Cao shot him. I mean, Wilbur was a great agent, and I'm sorry he's dead, but you can't blame Cao for defending himself."

Ivorson's temper flared. "And the four MPs?" he demanded. "And me? Was that self-defense? Cao was trapped, caught red-handed with a dead drop put down by the North Vietnamese Embassy. His only chance was to kill all the witnesses, and that's just what he tried to do."

Riley shook his head. "I just can't accept that. There has to be some mistake."

"Mistake, my ass!" Ivorson snapped. He pulled the leaf bag out of his pocket. "This is the drop Cam left for Cao. He threw it away as he fled. See what it says!" He pulled the square of rice paper from the leaf bag and handed it to Riley, who reluctantly unfolded it and looked at it.

"I can't read Vietnamese," he said, and handed it back to Ivorson. "Read it for me."

Ivorson did, trying to keep his voice normal as he translated the note word for word. The last line frightened him as much this morning as it had last night, but now he had an agenda of his own.

"Mango is obviously Cao," he said. "The writer has to be Nguyen van Huu."

Riley glared at the thin sheet of paper. Ivorson could almost see his mind at work, seeking an exit from the dilemma. Apparently finding none, he transferred the glare to Ivorson. "So what happened to Cao?" he asked.

The memory was bitter. "The last time I saw him, he was headed east on Wattay Road in the MPs' jeep. He probably headed straight out of town to join the Pathet Lao."

Riley grimaced his displeasure at the theory and lapsed into a prolonged silence, his eyes fixed calculatingly on Ivorson's face. Ivorson braced himself. The confrontation he had spent the night preparing himself for was about to begin.

"Coming on top of the Cam recruitment debacle," said Riley finally, "this puts me in a completely untenable position with Washington. In one night, you have managed to completely fuck up over twenty years of hard work.

"If Tran van Cao WAS a Vietnamese asset," Riley went on, "which I still think is bullshit, your proper move was to let him go his way and report back to me. Telling me that Wilbur attacked him against your orders is unbelievable. Wilbur is—was—too good an agent to disobey orders. You told him to arrest Cao, he obeyed you, and he died because of your stupidity. You caused this disaster, Ivorson, and I'm going to make damned sure that you pay for it."

Ivorson shook his head. "Nice try, Riley, but it didn't work. Even if I had directed Wilbur to attack Cao, which I didn't, the real disaster was Cao himself. He blew every Station operation known to him, he was almost certainly responsible for Jim Reagan's murder—God knows he tried to be responsible for mine—and you're the one who recruited him. If anyone's at fault here, it's you."

"You're a naïve child, Ivorson." Riley's voice was cobra-cold. "I haven't spent a lifetime in the assholes of Asia to lose my position now. Not over Tran van Cao, or Wilbur, or for any other reason. Washington will demand someone's head for last night's fiasco, and the head they get will be yours."

The statement was made with total conviction. In spite of his hole card, Ivorson felt a twinge of apprehension. "You can't make it play," he said.

"Sure I can," responded Riley. "I control the communications from this Station. All Headquarters knows is what I tell them, and that will be that I had long suspected Cao of being a double-agent. Your bungling last night kept me from mounting a major deception operation against Hanoi by passing them false information through Cao."

Pleased with his inventiveness, Riley actually smiled. "When you arrive in Langley a week later with your side of the story," he went on, "the decisions will have already been made. They won't be overturned on the basis of your unsupported word against mine. I've got a spotless reputation."

Ivorson stared at him with unfeigned disgust. "You're a sorry sonofabitch," he said.

Riley nodded calmly. "You're absolutely right, but who are you to complain about it? You've been scared shitless someone was going to shoot you, ever since you got here. Well, it's happened, and judging by this," (he waved the sheet of rice paper) "that's only the beginning. Hell, Ivorson, I'm your friend. I'm sending you home, safe and sound. Losing your job is a small price to pay for saving your life."

Chapter Sixteen

Ivorson fought off the temptation to let Riley have his way. He took a series of deep breaths to make sure his voice was under control, and said, "Hang on just a minute. I've got something here that may change your mind." He rose and walked painfully to the long rattan couch against the living room wall. He picked up a cushion at the end closest to their chairs, pulled out the small tape recorder he had hidden there, and held it up for Riley's inspection.

COS's eyes blinked, and then narrowed. A line of white showed along his jaw. Ivorson rewound the tape as he limped back toward his chair. He sat down carefully, stopped the rewind and pushed the "play" button. Riley's voice cam clearly out of the speaker. "—control the communications from this Station, Ivorson. All Headquarters knows is what I tell them—"

Ivorson pushed the stop button again and looked across at the Chief of Station. "Let's make a deal," he suggested.

Riley's eyes reminded him of those of a tiger he had seen in a cage at the local animal buyer's compound. The white line along his jaw had expanded to cover his whole face. "You bastard," he hissed. "You're trying to blackmail me."

"Turnabout is fair play," Ivorson responded mildly.

That wasn't true, of course. The offense he had just committed was unforgivable. If Riley didn't buy it, Ivorson was finished. Even if he established Riley's evil intentions to the Inspector-General's satisfaction and forced him out of the service, no other COS would touch Ivorson thereafter. The question was, would Riley risk his own career by pushing the matter to a showdown?

"What kind of deal?" COS ground out between clenched teeth.

The question cheered Ivorson enormously. He struggled not to let if show. "Easy deal, he answered. "You put the best face you honestly can on what happened last night, and I stay here and finish the job you saddled me with."

It was enormously satisfying to see Riley's jaw drop. "You must be crazy, Ivorson," he said, when he had recovered from his surprise. "If your story about Cao is right, and if you translated this note correctly for me, you're a walking target. If you stay here, you'll be dead inside of a week."

The grim reality of the prognostication chilled Ivorson. He tried to swallow the coppery taste of the Fear at the back of his throat, but it wouldn't go away. He hoped Riley couldn't hear it in his voice.

"What the hell do you care?" he asked. "If you're prepared to destroy my career to cover your ass, you ought to be willing to see me risk my life to make you COS, Paris."

He saw calculation replace rage in Riley's eyes, and he knew he'd won. "All right," he said, "I'll make a deal with you. You give me that tape, and I'll report last night's events to Headquarters straight. I won't impute any blame for what happened to you."

Ivorson struggled to keep the triumph out of his face, but he didn't have to struggle long. Riley's next words put him back to square one.

"However, you can forget about staying here." I'll be goddamned if I'll have a case officer who's blackmailed me strutting around the Station. I'll advise Headquarters that in view of Cao's attempt on your life and the language of this note, I'm sending you back home for your own protection."

Accept, you idiot, the Fear screamed in his ear. The temptation was almost overwhelming. He could leave here in one piece, with his reputation intact and a good career still ahead of him. What did he really have to gain by staying? After all, Cao was history now, and no matter what Ivorson might achieve against the North Vietnamese, it wouldn't bring Wilbur back to life.

With a supreme effort of will, he shook his head.

Riley scowled. "Don't you get it, Ivorson? You've won. You've got what you want. I mean it. Hell, you can write the cable yourself and watch it being transmitted."

Ivorson shook his head again. "No deal. Either I stay here, or this tape goes to the Inspector-General."

Riley looked utterly baffled. "Why, for Christ's sake?"

The awful sense of loss that had overcome Ivorson last night in the Medical Unit had not departed with the light of morning, but he knew that Riley wouldn't accept the idea of a personal vendetta. Ivorson's ostensible motivation had to be one that Riley could empathize with.

"That code is the most important intelligence target on earth," he said. "I want it."

Riley's brows rose. "What is this, Ivorson? Are you bucking for the Intelligence Medal?"

"You're damn right I am," Ivorson told him. "This is the mission you brought me here for, remember? That blimp the techs are building is my idea. When it's ready, I intend to be the one who takes it out in that swamp and uses it. I'm entitled to do it, not that asshole Jack Lawrence!"

"Why not Lawrence? He'll have a better grip on the equipment than you will. That's his business."

Ivorson snorted. "We're not talking about operating a piece of machinery. We're talking about wading around neck-deep in a swamp full of leeches and pythons. I've done it once, and I can do it again. If you think Lawrence can handle that, I wish you luck. You'll damn sure need it."

"What have you got against Lawrence? He's a good tech."

"He's a phony, who takes credit for work that was really done by dead case officers," snapped Ivorson. "The first time somebody sneezes inside that Embassy compound, Lawrence will cut and run."

The mention of dead case officers made Riley frown. Then he pursed his lips in thought. "As a matter of fact," he mused, "I got a cable about the blimp the other day. They flew the prototype last week. It apparently worked quite well."

Ivorson pressed his advantage. "You see? We're not talking about a long time. A month at the most."

Calculation returned to COS's eyes. "All right, Ivorson," he said. "You want a month. I'll give you till June 1st to fly the blimp at the code room and bring home the bacon."

Ivorson felt a surge of delight. Riley immediately burst his bubble. "But if you think you're going to stay here while you wait for it to be delivered, you're crazy. If the Viets kill you, you're useless to me, and, besides that, I can't stand the sight of your smirking face. I'm sending you to the Fifth Field Hospital in Bangkok for the care of your wounds, and that's where you'll stay until the blimp gets here."

The idea of being in exile, three hundred miles away from Nga, appalled Ivorson. "Hell, that could be weeks," he protested.

"Tough," Riley said tersely. "That's the deal, Ivorson. Take it or leave it."

Ivorson twisted in his chair, and a twinge from his aching testicles reminded him that his relationship with Nga was going to be platonic for quite a while anyway. Besides that, considering the "arrangements" that Nguyen van Huu was making for Ivorson, a couple of weeks in Bangkok might not be a bad idea. "Okay," he agreed. "It's a deal."

Riley held out his hand for the tape recorder. Ivorson handed it over. "Can you give me a ride back up to the Medical Unit?" he asked. "I hurt like hell."

He still hurt when he left Vientiane at three o'clock the same day, on the same dilapidated Royal Air Lao DC-3 that had brought him to town months before. Every muscle and tendon ached. His testicles throbbed excruciatingly with every heartbeat, and the bullet crease across his shoulder burned as if he had just been branded with a red-hot iron.

As much as his body pained him, the pain inside was worse. They took off to the east, over the city, and Ivorson peered out of the small porthole, looking for the That Luang parade ground. Oum, when she brought his suitcase to the Medical Unit, had tearfully told him that Wilbur's cremation would take place there this afternoon.

He spotted the race track and stadium through shimmering waves of heat. A hundred yards to their north, a thin column of black smoke rose like a pencil stroke in the air. At the bottom of that column of smoke, Wilbur's body, in a rickety wooden coffin atop a bier of dry hardwood, was being consumed by fire.

Ivorson could visualize the scene. He had attended several cremations during his tour in Vietnam. In his mind, he could see the faces of Orville, Oum, Sengdara and the rest of the mourners, sweat pouring from them in the hundred-plus degree heat, vastly increased by the flames of the pyre. He could hear the monks chanting over the roar of the flames and the crackling and spitting of the body fat.

He felt like a traitor, not being there with them to show his love and respect for Wilbur, but Riley wouldn't hear of delaying his departure to attend the cremation, and, anyway, his unexplained presence would have constituted a real hazard to the security of Wilbur's family.

Besides that, Wilbur's mother had seen both her husband and first-born son die in white men's wars, first at Dien Bien Phu and now in the streets of Vientiane. Ivorson's presence at the cremation might well have offended her.

He watched the smoke column for as long as he could, craning his neck to keep it in sight, until the plane turned south, toward Bangkok, and the last trace he would ever see of Wilbur vanished behind him. Ivorson blinked back tears. "I'll get even," he silently promised the hot Asian sky. "I swear, I'll get even."

✲ ✲ ✲

Huu crushed the note from Papaya, hurled it into the waste basket, and swore viciously. Two weeks had passed since Mango's disastrous flight from Vientiane. Papaya had just reported that Ivorson was still in Bangkok for medical treatment. She had no idea what the problem was. Her supervisor, Miss Odom, would not discuss it. She had no idea when he would return. Her supervisor was going to Bangkok this weekend. Perhaps she would bring news of Ivorson when she returned on Monday.

Huu swore again and retrieved the paper. He crumpled it in the large ash tray on his desk amid the cigarette butts and lit a match to it. He wanted with all his heart for Ivorson to return to Vientiane, so that his plan could go forward.

Everything was ready: Papaya was briefed and even enthusiastic. The Pathet Lao unit, with a partially-recovered Mango at its head, was standing by. All that was lacking was the victim.

Huu left the paper crackling in the ashtray and walked to the open window. It was well into May now, and even at this early hour, the heat was almost unbearable. He looked down at Hoang Bac Cam, washing the old Mercedes in the driveway, after the morning trip to the market.

The sight aggravated Huu's evil temper. He had been unable to acquire any further evidence against the chauffeur. The one note he had received from Mango since his departure contained nothing new, only self-serving excuses for his own behavior on the night of his unmasking.

Furthermore, the Ambassador had proved to be an acquaintance of Cam's uncle during the war against the French. He had counseled patience and watchfulness in dealing with the Black Thai while they waited for his replacement to arrive from Hanoi. The decision infuriated Huu, who could almost smell the aura of guilt radiating from the chauffeur.

Would that the Ambassador's tolerance had extended to him! Following Mango's bloody escape, the Lao Foreign Minister had called in the Ambassador and handed him a note accusing North Vietnam of, "sponsoring activities inimical to the sovereignty of the Kingdom of Laos," a clear reference to Mango's successful career. The Ambassador had taken out his embarrassment over the note on Huu.

He closed the wooden shutters to spare his eyes any further sight of the treasonous chauffeur, turned on the air conditioner, and went back to his desk. He leaned back in his chair and eased his frustrations by imagining the terrible things he would cause to be done to the American, Ivorson.

✡ ✡ ✡

The elevator doors opened on Peter's floor. Lisa hesitated. She still wasn't at all sure that she ought to be here, but when Mr. Montgomery, the USAID Director, had told her in confidence a week ago that Peter had been sent to Bangkok for the treatment of a bullet wound, she had been surprised by how much the news concerned her. She had found herself thinking about him often since then, and today, when she got to Bangkok, she had been drawn to the hospital as if by a magnet.

Now that she was here, though, she felt embarrassed. She supposed that they weren't sworn enemies any more, following their conversation in the Medical Unit, but he certainly still thought of her as no more than an errand-girl. He might even think she had a crush on him, coming to see him like this.

That idea almost made her push the "down" button, but then she decided it would be silly to leave again after having come all the way out Sukhumvit Road to the American Army Field hospital. She squared her shoulders and set off down the hall in search of his room.

She knocked at the open door. "May I come in?"

Peter looked up at her from the magazine he was reading. "My gosh, what a surprise," he said. "Sure, come on in. Sit down." He gestured at the only chair.

Lisa took a seat. "You look pretty chipper," she said. "Are you feeling better?"

"Oh, yes, practically a hundred percent. I'm bored to death, though. How's Nga? Did you give her my address?"

Darn the man, she thought. Here, she'd come to visit him in the hospital, and all he wanted to talk about was Nga. "She's fine," she told him, "and, yes, I gave her your address here, as you asked me on the phone before you left. I really haven't talked with her much lately. She did ask me if I was going to see you while I was down her, but she didn't give me a message for you."

"Oh." His disappointment at Lisa's lack of information about the Vietnamese girl was obvious. And irritating. It was puzzling, as well. Surely Nga had written him?

"What are you doing in Bangkok?" he asked her.

"I came down to meet my father. He's arriving here tomorrow from the States. I'll accompany him back to Vientiane. Since I was free today, I thought I'd drop in. Hospital calls on you seem to have become part of my duties." She felt her cheeks getting warm at the transparent excuse.

"I'm glad you did." His tone was no more than polite. "I haven't had any news from Vientiane since I got here."

So Nga hadn't written him! Lisa had got the street address of the hospital for her too, so that she could use the local mail. She couldn't understand why Nga hadn't written. If she loved him, as she claimed to, you'd think she would have written him every day. That was really very strange.

"So your Dad is coming for a visit?" Peter said. "I know you're happy about that. How long will he stay?"

"Indefinitely. That is, until he gets so bad that he's got to go home."

Peter gave her an inquiring look. "My father has cancer," she explained, talking past the now-familiar lump in her throat. "It's terminal. This will be our last visit. Since no one knows how long he'll continue to feel good, we decided it would be better for him to come to me rather than have me go home on leave."

Ivorson's face reflected pain and sympathy. "I'm really sorry," he said, "but it's wonderful that he's able to make the trip. That will give you a lot of time together."

She felt tears begin to fill her eyes. She had cried every day for weeks, it seemed to her. She no longer bothered to apologize for it.

"You and your Dad must be very close." His voice invited her to share her pain.

"We are," she told him. "I was the only child, and Mama died when I was young, so I was his whole family. He coached all the Little League teams I was on—I was a tremendous tomboy—and we went to model meets and fly-offs the whole time I was growing up."

"Fly-offs? Was your Dad a pilot?"

"Sort of. He was—still is—a fanatic model airplane builder and flyer. The big remote controlled models, you know? He's won the NATS twice."

"NATS?"

"It's the national championship competition for remote-controlled models. We went every year all the time I was growing up."

He was looking at her curiously. "Did you like that?"

It was the first sign of real interest that he'd ever shown in her. She laughed nervously. "Well, what I really liked was being with my Dad. But I enjoyed it enough. I built and flew my own models. I came in third in the children's competition once."

He seemed intrigued. "You did? Third place nationally?" She nodded. He chuckled ruefully. "I wish I'd known that a month ago. I would have picked your brains."

"Picked my brains? About modeling? Whatever for?"

"Oh, I was working on a project that involved something like that a while back," he said evasively. "It's in the hands of the experts now. How much time do you have? Want to go to lunch?"

The invitation startled her—as did the depth of her pleasure upon receiving it. "Can you leave the hospital?"

He laughed. "No, but there's a little snack bar downstairs. Come on. My treat."

They dawdled for an hour over their hamburgers, and Lisa saw a side of him that she had never known existed. He was intelligent, witty, and a terrible tease. In fact, he was one of the most attractive men she had ever known. What a pity that they had got off to such a bad start!

They talked about Indochina. His grasp of both the current situation and its historical background was very impressive. In the elevator on the way back upstairs, she complimented him on it. "You ought to be in the Foreign Service."

He shot a speculative look at her. "I already am, sort of, but I gather you were thinking about something a bit more reputable than my present employment—the State Department, for example?"

She felt a surge of embarrassment, and a little apprehension, too. Surely he wasn't going to start that business again? She looked at him nervously. He didn't seem to be angry. In fact, he was smiling. He was teasing her! She felt unaccountably happy about it.

Buoyed by a feeling of camaraderie, and since they were alone on the elevator, she dared to ask the question that had been haunting her for the past week. "Peter, Mr. Montgomery told me that you were in the hospital in Bangkok because you had been shot. Is that true?"

His smile vanished, and he snapped, "I don't know where Mr. Montgomery heard that, but he had no business repeating it, not to you or anyone else."

She mentally flinched from the anger in his voice, but she didn't let it deter her. Was his life in danger? She felt a compulsion to know. "Is it true?" she insisted.

He looked at her for an instant in silence, then shrugged. "I don't guess I have to worry about defending my non-existent cover from you," he said, "but I can't answer that question, Lisa. You don't have a need to know."

Hearing him take refuge behind the legalistic phrase made her suddenly angry. Maybe she didn't have a "need to know", but she cared more about what happened to him than that beautiful Nguyen thi Nga he was so obsessed with, who wouldn't even write him when he was in the hospital!

"All right," she snapped. "Forget I asked you."

"Hey," he said in an injured tone, "don't get mad. You know the rules. I really can't talk about it."

The evasion was a good as an admission. He HAD been shot! When he returned to Vientiane, his life would be in danger, and here he was, talking to her about rules! It made her furious.

"I called you paranoid the first time we met," she told him hotly. "I was wrong. You're not paranoid, you're a psychopath! How can you possibly live like this, with people beating you up and shooting you? What kind of strange person are you, anyway?"

Her voice broke, and her eyes stung with tears. Her anger turned inward. She was making an utter fool of herself with this man!

He looked startled at her outburst. "Well," he said, trying to make a joke of it, "at least you don't think I'm paranoid anymore." That made her angrier.

The elevator had stopped at his floor. "Come on in and visit some more," he invited her, obviously trying to calm her down.

She shook her head angrily. "No, I have to go."

He shrugged. "Well, okay, if you have to." He stepped out of the elevator and turned around to face her. "Do me a favor, will you?"

She blew up. "No, I will NOT carry any more messages to Nga for you," she snapped and stabbed the DOWN button. The door started to close in his face.

He reached out an arm and stopped it. "I was going to ask you to say hi to your Dad for me," he said quietly. "He sounds like quite a guy."

He let the door close, and the elevator started down. Lisa had never felt so foolish and embarrassed in her entire life. The first really normal, friendly, contact she'd ever had with him had turned into a complete disaster. How had he managed to make her do that?

She tried to sort out her churning emotions and failed. She was certain of just one thing: this was absolutely, positively the last time she was ever, ever going to see Peter Ivorson!

Chapter Seventeen

Ivorson watched Lisa's pretty, angry, face disappear between the closing elevator doors and thought, now what in the hell was that all about?

It really was strange, the way he seemed to rub Lisa wrong. It was a shame, too. She was a good-looking woman and a high-class, all-American girl, even if she did make snide comments about the Agency. He'd bet that she wouldn't let HER lover spend two weeks in the hospital without writing him!

He really couldn't understand Nga. She knew his address, and yet he hadn't heard a single solitary word from her. If he had any brains, he'd put her out of his mind. The trouble with that, of course, was that his feelings about Nga were being driven by his balls, not his brains, and his memories of their lovemaking guaranteed that he wouldn't forget her, no matter how angry she made him.

But DAMN her for not writing!

He still hadn't heard from Nga eight days later, when the USAF C-130 deposited him on the transient ramp at Udorn Air Base, after a thermal-tossed afternoon flight from Bangkok.

It was incredibly, mind-numbingly, hot. The wet monsoon should have begun weeks ago, breaking the heat and bringing rain to the baked lateritic plateau of northern Thailand and south Laos, but the rains were very late this year, and every day the thermometer rose above 120 degrees.

Captain Ken Stein was waiting for his plane, along with Jack Lawrence and two technicians from Headquarters, whose names Ivorson made no effort to remember. They weren't interested in being polite to him, either.

They all piled into an Air Force van, with Captain Stein at the wheel and drove to a warehouse inside a restricted area, segregated from the remainder of the Air Base by a high cyclone fence and gates manned by Thai sentries. It was

Saturday, and routine activity on the base was at a low ebb, which suited their purposes well.

Captain Stein dropped them off in front of the warehouse door. Lawrence unlocked it to admit them, and locked it again after they entered. The warehouse was made of metal, and the two air conditioners laboring in its windows didn't begin to cool the oven-like interior. Within a minute, they were all drenched in sweat.

The mini-blimp sat in the center of the warehouse floor, its gas bag uninflated. It was held upright by two .50 caliber ammo boxes, placed against either side of the sheet metal framework which held the mounts for the electric motors and their battery.

Lawrence proudly displayed the blimp's features to him, and Ivorson had to admit (only to himself, of course—the tech would be insufferable enough without any further ego inflation–) that it was a very ingenious piece of work.

One visiting tech unzipped the forward section of the bag and inserted the television camera, its battery pack and transmitter, securing them with clamps against a vertical sheet metal section inside. The tech explained to Ivorson, rather pompously, that this feature made the machine a hybrid blimp/dirigible. Ivorson couldn't have cared less, just so the sonofabitch worked.

They reclosed the black neoprene around the camera. The lens protruded from the nose and responded gratifyingly to electronic commands from the command module, zooming obediently in and out.

Jack Lawrence, acting like a proud father, enumerated its virtues. "The video transmitter has a range of two miles," he said. "That enables us to monitor and record what we're looking at, and if, for some reason, we should lose the blimp, we've still got the pictures it took. Here, come see."

He led Ivorson to the monitor. Sure enough, the picture on the screen—a section of the warehouse wall—grew and diminished as the camera lens moved in and out. The image was extremely clear, and at full zoom, even in the dim interior of the warehouse, very fine details of the wall were visible. Ivorson could feel enthusiasm beginning to bubble up inside him. He tried to keep Lawrence from seeing it.

The techs hooked up hoses from two bottles of helium, one to each of the two interior gas compartments located behind the camera, and began the filling process. In less than three minutes, the blimp was straining at its tethering ropes.

Filled with helium, the blimp looked positively sleek. It was painted a dull matte black over its full ten-foot length, including the battery for the motors, which the techs now secured in the metal frame beneath the bag. Next to it was the on-board control module, which received and relayed instructions for the motors and controls from the command module.

Lawrence had appropriated that item, and Ivorson didn't like it. This wasn't the time or place to have it out, but he watched every move of the tech's fingers on the controls. This was his idea, by God, and he'd fly it, or know the reason why.

The tech tested the controls. The rudder and elevators moved through their full ranges of direction from the command module. Lawrence directed the electric motors to start, and they did, instantly and silently. The blimp tried to move forward against its restraining ropes. The motors were reversed, and it wallowed backward.

"The motor mounts are on gimbals," Lawrence explained. "They can be moved independently through ninety degrees in both the vertical and horizontal planes, not only to climb and descend, but also to counteract the wind and hold the balloon stationary, while filming is going on." He demonstrated. The balloon moved sideways, first in one direction, then in the other. In spite of himself, Ivorson was impressed.

"The really slick thing about this baby is the altitude control mechanism. We load ballast on board to achieve neutral lift. The amount of ballast will depend on the air temperature, of course."

Not understanding, Ivorson nodded. "Then," Lawrence continued, "we drive the thing into the air by tilting the motors downward. When we get it as high as we want it, we center the motors, and it stays at that height. We can fine tune it either with the motors or by dropping small amounts of the birdshot which makes up part of the ballast."

The techs suited action to words and loaded the ballast until the blimp hovered, untethered, six inches above the floor. Lawrence tilted the motors down; the propellers whirred silently, and the machine moved forward and up. At two feet off the floor, Lawrence centered the motors vertically, reversed them in fore-and-aft plane, and gave the propellers little shots of power until the forward motion stopped. The blimp hovered motionless above the floor.

Lawrence gestured to Ivorson. "Come over and take a look." Ivorson joined him and watched the television monitor. Lawrence applied power on the left propeller, and the nose of the blimp drifted slowly right. The interior of the warehouse drifted at the same rate across the screen of the TV monitor. A burst of power on the right propeller stopped the drift. Another burst on the same propeller, and the camera began tracking back to the left.

"How do you like that?" Lawrence crowed triumphantly. Ivorson nodded his head. Had it been anyone but Lawrence, he would have kissed him, but his determination to regain control of the operation enabled him to restrain his enthusiasm.

"Great, Jack," he said. "Now, if we can just figure how to keep the leeches out of our assholes while we use it, we'll be in business."

Lawrence's reaction to that caused the blimp to hit the warehouse floor with a bang. The techs yelped a chorus of protest. Lawrence gave Ivorson a dirty look. "Very funny, Ivorson," he said coldly.

"I'm not kidding, Jack. The controls are complex as hell. Are you going to be able to operate them in total darkness, up to your neck in that swamp?"

"I won't be in the swamp, Ivorson," Lawrence answered coldly. "Using the camera to navigate, I can control the blimp from the launching truck on the road, a quarter of a mile away."

"We won't even be able to see the blimp from the truck, Jack, and the camera has to have some light to work with, too. Are you sure we can get the thing on target without a lot of hunting around that will run down the batteries?"

"We thought of that, of course." Lawrence's voice had resumed its habitual tone of an impatient teacher dealing with a retarded child. "There are small hooded infrared lights mounted at the rear of the blimp."

He pointed them out to Ivorson. "They're invisible to the naked eye," he continued, "but by tracking them through IR goggles, we can guide it to the Viet Embassy from the launch site as straight as an arrow. Any other questions?" he asked with a smirk.

Ivorson restrained the urge to wipe it off his face. "No," he said. "It looks good to me. Shut it off and let's get out of here before we all die of heat prostration. We'll put it through its real paces tonight."

He spent the afternoon in an air-conditioned room of the Spartan BOQ, trying not to let optimism completely overpower him. Everything he had seen in the warehouse looked like the answer to his prayers. After a struggle with his ego, he finally decided that in Wilbur's absence—a thought which still depressed him tremendously—he could live with Lawrence in charge of the command module. Tonight's session could thus become a dress rehearsal and save him precious time.

They did the actual testing that night, after dark, in the bomb storage area behind triple fences and sentry dogs. Through some miracle of persuasion, Captain Stein got the base commander to shut off the perimeter lights while they ran the tests, and the bomb dump was Carlsbad-Cavern black. The illuminated flight area was behind them to the east. To the west, the only light was a flicker of heat lightning on the horizon. There was no breeze, and night had brought no relief from the heat.

In an attempt to simulate actual operational conditions, Ivorson and Jack Lawrence drove to the test site alone in a ton-and-a-half truck with the already-inflated blimp hovering, tethered, under the tarpaulin. They checked all systems with the blimp still tethered. Then, with Lawrence manning the control module, Ivorson released all the tethers except the nose rope, which he held firmly in his hand.

He led the blimp out of the tailgate. It followed him like Mary's little lamb. Both he and Lawrence were wearing goggles which permitted them to see the infrared position lights of the blimp.

When he got ten feet away from the truck he heard the faint hum of the motors. "Power is on," Lawrence hissed. "Let it go."

Ivorson released the nose halter, and the blimp began to move forward and upward, very slowly, almost majestically. It passed within three feet of Ivorson's head, yet he could scarcely make out its form against the black sky. The sound of the propellers made no more noise than humming of night insects. By God, he thought, this thing is really going to work!

Lawrence leveled it off at twenty feet above the ground, then brought it to a stop. Through the IR goggles, Ivorson could see the tiny position lights on the stern, glowing in the dark like the ash of lighted cigarettes. He took off the goggles, and he could see nothing at all. He couldn't hear anything, either. Wonderful!

For thirty minutes they played with it, making it climb, descend, turn, and hover; sending it away from them and then bringing it back again by keeping the image of the truck centered on the TV monitor. When Lawrence brought it down and hovered it, nose to nose with Ivorson, he couldn't conceal his pleasure any more.

"This is a terrific gadget, Jack," he enthused. "Your guys have done a marvelous piece of work."

Lawrence accepted the praise with his customary graciousness. "Damn right they did. There's nothing wrong with the Directorate of Operations that the techs can't fix. Tell you what: let's give it the acid test. We'll fly it back to that first hangar–" He pointed to an illuminated hangar on the air field, over half a mile east of them. "–and see how well the camera will see for us from thirty feet up and, say, fifty feet out. Then we'll navigate it back here."

"Okay," Ivorson agreed. "Should we change the battery first? We've pulled a lot of amps from this one."

"Leave the technical decisions to me, Ivorson," Lawrence said coldly. "There's still plenty of juice in this battery."

Ivorson bit down on the reply that leaped to his lips. The blimp moved off eastward, toward the hangar, and vanished silently into the night sky. They followed its flight as long as they could with the IR goggles and then shifted their attention to the TV monitor.

The hangar came into view and loomed slowly closer. Lawrence pulled the control labeled "climb" on the control module, and the camera turned skyward. After a few seconds, he pushed the control forward, and the camera came back down again. When it was level with the horizon, he neutralized the vertical controls, moved the motor control to "hover" and the forward motion stopped.

They were looking directly at the red warning light on the top of the hangar. The video image seemed to float in mid-air. The tech zoomed the lens, and the eye of the camera appeared to move to within inches of the light. The resolution was still crystal clear.

"See the control tower?" Lawrence asked him. Ivorson did. It was perhaps five hundred yards from the roof of the hangar they were looking at, in the center of the airfield. "Let's drive it on down there and give it a real workout. We've got plenty of juice."

"Suits me," said Ivorson. He wanted to see how well the camera would work against a target comparable to the real target. He just hoped Lawrence was right about there being enough juice left to get back again.

Lawrence manipulated his levers, and the blimp turned and moved forward again. The image of the control tower appeared on the TV monitor. Lawrence maneuvered the blimp until the glassed-in control room at the top of the tower was centered in the monitor. They could clearly see the men inside.

With the camera lens in normal position, they moved to within what looked to be about thirty feet away, then directed the blimp to hover and zoomed the lens. The interior of the control tower rushed at them on the TV screen. Lawrence gave tiny bursts of power to the motors until he had centered the lens on the face of one controller, then zoomed the lens as far as he could.

The controller's face filled the monitor screen. "Incredible, Jack," breathed Ivorson. "We're going to be able to see that code clerk's fingers on the keys of the machine. We're going to be able to break that code in a walk. This is the greatest intelligence operation since the Berlin tunnel!"

"Don't jiggle me!" Lawrence said sharply. "I'm concentrating like hell here."

The warning put both Ivorson's enthusiasm and Lawrence back in their proper perspectives. "Sorry," Ivorson mumbled. "Better bring it back now, I guess. A breeze seems to be coming up."

Lawrence grunted agreement. The picture on the monitor swung away from the tower and into the darkness. It remained dark, with the occasional twinkling of light patterns which Ivorson supposed must be runway or taxiway lights. "Which way are you headed?" he asked the tech.

There was a rather lengthy silence. "I'm not sure," Lawrence finally said. "I can't identify anything on the screen."

Ivorson's euphoria vanished like a pricked soap bubble. "Uh oh. Better put everything into neutral and just let it sit for a minute while we try to get located. We sure don't want to lose this baby."

"I already have," Lawrence snapped. "It's in neutral now." Ivorson could hear the edge of tension in his voice.

"You turned left from the tower, didn't you?" Back in our direction?" Ivorson asked.

"Yes."

"How far did you turn?"

"How the hell would I know? We have to rely on the camera to tell us that if we can't see the infrared beacon!" Lawrence's voice rose in pitch with every word.

"Relax, Jack. I'm trying to help you, not bug you. Let's do a slow turn back to the right until we pick up the tower again. Once we've got that, we can start over."

Lawrence pulled on the appropriate toggle lever, and the view on the monitor began changing, but the tower didn't come back in sight. Instead, the first thing they saw was a lighted dispersal area sprinkled with F-4 fighter-bombers.

"Where in the hell is that?" Lawrence's voice was half an octave higher than normal.

"Further east along the airfield," said Ivorson. He felt the rising west wind on his face and was suddenly alarmed. "The wind has come up, and the blimp is drifting east. Keep turning it. We've got to spot a landmark we recognize." Damnation!

If they couldn't get the blimp down soon, it was going to get beyond the range of the control module!

The picture on the monitor began moving again. First a taxiway appeared, then the World War 2 Japanese hangar at the east end of the field. God almighty, the blimp was almost two miles east of them! They were never going to get it back to their location.

Ivorson made a decision. "Jack, keep it turning until you get the tower back in the picture. Then fly it at full power in that direction. I'm going to drive us down there to recover it."

He jumped up into the cab of the truck, twisted the key in the ignition, and slammed the ton-and-a-half into gear.

The idea of losing the blimp made Ivorson sick. He had to get it back. If some sentry saw it in the process, that was just too damn bad. It was by far the lesser of the possible evils.

He roared down the narrow macadam road between the half-buried ordinance bunkers. Captain Stein was waiting for them at the gate of the area, and there was a telephone there, too. They needed to pass the word to the Air Police not to fire on the blimp.

The gate and gate house appeared in his headlight beam. Captain Stein and two sentries, one Thai, one American, ran out as he screeched to a stop behind the closed gate. Captain Stein opened the passenger side door. "Is something wrong?"

"Yeah. It's got away from us. We're going after it. You stay here and call the Officer of the Guard. Tell him to pass the word to the sentries: Don't shoot at anything in the sky, or at this truck."

Stein grasped the problem immediately. "Okay. Will do."

Ivorson opened his own door and shouted into the rear of the truck. "What's happening, Jack?"

Lawrence's voice was almost a scream. "I've got the tower in the camera, but I can't make any headway toward it. The wind's too strong!"

The batteries were probably getting weak, too, thought Ivorson. "Drive it onto the ground, Jack," he shouted. "We've got to get it out of the air." He turned back to Captain Stein. "Get on that phone man, and open the fucking gate!"

"Roger that!" Stein backed out of the cab, slammed the truck door, and made an imperious gesture at the gate to the two sentries, who ran to open it. Ivorson had to back up a bit to let it swing clear of the nose of the truck, then he stomped the accelerator pedal to the floor and ground the transmission up through the low gears toward the lights of the airfield ahead of him.

When he reached the field perimeter, he had to make a decision. He could either stay on the perimeter road, the way they had come, or he could turn left and reach the taxiway, which would take him directly east, past the control tower. The latter would be by far the faster route, but it might take him into the path of a bomb-laden F-4 or, worse yet, into the gun sights of a startled and trigger-happy Thai sentry.

He tried to ignore the last thought and turned left toward the taxiway. Sure enough, his headlights picked out the figure of an armed guard ahead of him at the taxiway intersection. The Thai sentry, startled by the sudden appearance of the lights and the sound of the revving truck engine was un-slinging his M16.

There was a sudden banging on the roof of the truck cab. He stuck his head as far out of the window as he could. "What is it?" he shouted, taking his foot off the accelerator.

"It doesn't want to land." Lawrence's voice, now completely panicked, came to him faintly over the rush of wind past the truck. "The batteries are fading."

Shit! The only hope to save the blimp was to get the truck under it and hope they could get it close enough to the ground to be able to catch the ten-foot long tether line that dangled from its nose. He didn't have time for a palaver with the Thai sentry, now just ahead, his rifle in his hands.

He twisted the headlight switch, and the dome light inside the cab flashed on. Hoping to hell that the Thai wouldn't open fire on an obviously American face in a USAF truck, he flashed the headlight dimmer switch, roared past the blessedly indecisive guard, and turned right down the taxiway.

The blue taxiway lights seemed to stretch out to infinity on either side of him. He pushed the accelerator to the floor. The control tower was almost half a mile ahead of them. The blimp was well beyond that, maybe as much as a mile away. If the wind blew it beyond the perimeter of the airfield, they were out of luck.

That idea made him shove the accelerator down even harder. The blimp was indispensable. There was no way to get a replacement here before June 1st. The speedometer rose to sixty miles an hour and then stuck. The truck wouldn't go any faster. It must have had a governor on it.

He passed the control tower. Out of the corner of his eye, he could see people running from it toward a vehicle. Hell! Were they coming after him? Hadn't Stein notified the Officer of the Guard?

Never mind. He'd square his mad ride through the air base later, if he could. The only thing that mattered now was to save the blimp. He kept on going, toward the east end of the field.

The end of the taxiway loomed in his headlights. He put on the brakes. His hope was now that he was downwind of the blimp, he could spot it through the infrared goggles he had shoved up on his brow and could drive the truck beneath it.

He reached the end of the taxi way, braked to a stop, and shouted out of the window. "What can you see in the monitor, Jack? Where is the thing?"

Lawrence answered in a near-scream. "It's hovering, about thirty feet up. I've still got it pointed at the control tower, but we're losing ground. It's drifting downwind. Goddamit, Ivorson, do something!"

Before Ivorson could answer, there was a burst of automatic weapons fire behind them and to their left. Reacting instinctively, he hurled himself sideways on the seat of the truck. Jesus Christ, were they under fire?

There was another burst of firing, even more sustained, but no rounds hit the truck, and he couldn't hear any bullets whining by. An awful premonition drove the initial fear out of his mind. Was it the blimp they were shooting at?

He scrambled back upright in the cab, yanked open the door, and looked behind him. In the dark area between the runway and the taxiway, about half way between him and the tower, he saw the muzzle flash of an automatic weapon and, a second later, the sound of more firing reached him on the wind. God DAMN!

"Hang on, Jack," he shouted and pulled himself back under the steering wheel again. He banged the shift lever into low and hurled the protesting truck onto the grass, heading straight for the site of the firing.

A feeling of hopeless, helpless fury washed over him as the truck lurched over the infield at what seemed like water buffalo velocity. Some rice-planting Thai draftee was out there shooting the shit out of the greatest intelligence operation in the history of the Vietnam war, and Ivorson was utterly helpless to stop him.

The figure of a man appeared at the extreme outer range of the truck's headlights. Ivorson pointed the nose of the vehicle at him and began honking the horn. Maybe he could distract the trigger-happy bastard and save something from this disaster!

The figure proved to be a uniformed Thai soldier with an M16 at his shoulder. He was pointing the weapon at something on the ground ahead of him. While Ivorson watched in helpless fury, the Thai fired another full clip at his unseen target.

Overcoming the temptation to run over the sentry, Ivorson roared past him, toward his target. The headlights picked up something. As he approached, its form coalesced. What remained of the blimp was lying on its side on the grass.

Ivorson braked the truck and jumped out to kneel beside the blimp. It had been riddled by at least fifty rounds of rifle fire. The camera was shattered, the battery was leaking acid from a dozen holes, and the precious, irreplaceable, on-board control module was a smoldering, multi-punctured wreck.

Behind him, Ivorson could hear Jack Lawrence, sobbing audibly. He tried to despise the tech's display of emotion, but it was hard to do, when he felt so much like crying himself.

Chapter Eighteen

Ivorson sat in the back of the crowded, bouncing bus and tried unsuccessfully to keep his legs from going to sleep. He was wedged into the narrow bench between two Thai peasant women on their way home from the Sunday morning market in Udorn, and his knees were jammed against the back of the seats in front of him. Both the women held large wicker baskets on their laps, in which they'd taken their ducks to market. The ducks were sold, but their aroma and loose feathers remained.

Ivorson had caught the bus in Udorn half an hour before. There weren't any Air America flights available to Vientiane on this Sunday morning, and, in any case, he didn't want to risk being seen at Wattay Airport by one of the Viet mechanics out there. He figured he had a better chance of keeping his return to Laos from Nguyen van Huu by coming across the Mekong.

And for that matter, until he got his plan well under way, he didn't want Terence Riley to know he was back, either.

He hadn't seen Jack Lawrence or the visiting techs since the screaming match that followed the demise of the prototype blimp last night. The techs were probably still in a state of shock this morning, but they could afford that luxury. He couldn't.

It was the eighteenth day of May. The Chief of Station had given him until June 1st to launch the blimp operation against the North Vietnamese code room. That was less than two weeks away, and the blimp was no more. A replacement couldn't possibly be had in less than six weeks. Ergo, Ivorson's tour in Vientiane was finished.

That idea ought to make him happy, he reflected. After all, last night's disaster wasn't his fault. He had done his best. He could leave Laos alive, with his reputation intact, and go on with his career in other, safer, places.

But he couldn't forget what he'd seen last night. If not for Lawrence's bull-headed refusal to change the battery, Ivorson would now be on the verge of a tremendous intelligence operation. The blimp had not only worked, it had worked to perfection. There wasn't any doubt in Ivorson's mind that it could successfully film the operation of the code machine in the North Vietnamese Embassy.

But that was history for the time being, and Ivorson knew COS well enough to bet that he hadn't forgotten how Ivorson had a June 1st deadline. COS would make him wait for a replacement blimp.

Unless.

Unless Ivorson could devise a substitute, before the deadline. It was probably a futile hope, but he intended to try. His desire for a look through that code room window was so strong now, after seeing what the blimp could do, that the idea of someone else carrying out his idea was bitter gall. Besides, Wilbur's ghost still haunted him every night, crying out for revenge.

What he had in mind was by no means a sure bet, but if Ivorson was able to present the Chief of Station with another accomplished fact, there was at least a chance that Riley might let him go ahead. After all, he needed a victory, too.

When the bus reached Nongkhai, an hour north of Udorn on the banks of the Mekong, he stiffly pried himself out of it and hobbled through Thai Immigration and down the concrete steps to the edge of the Mekong, where he hired a long-tailed boat—a slender, wooden craft powered by a V-8 automobile engine—to take him across the drought-diminished river to the Lao customs and immigration point at Tha Deua.

After waiting half an hour for a Lao immigration official to appear and stamp his passport, he was declared legally in Laos. He caught a taxi for the twenty-kilometer ride to Vientiane and directed the driver to take him on through town to Rainbow Village, a small USAID housing complex located in the rice fields alongside of Route 13, about four kilometers north of the city.

All along the route the land was brown: brown bare rice paddies, brown wooden houses built on stilts, brown wilted leaves hanging from sun-seared trees. The only color was an occasional splash of vivid red from a blooming flame tree. They came into bloom at the hottest time of the year, after six months of drought. He'd never been able to fathom how they did it.

His ID card got him past the Mission Guard at the compound gate, and after peering at the names on the bungalows for a few minutes, he found the one he was after.

He climbed the steps and rapped on the door. A man's voice inside called out, "There's someone knocking, honey. Shall I answer it?"

"Sure, Dad," he heard Lisa Odom's voice answer from further back in the house. Ivorson heard the sound of footsteps approaching the door, the latch snapped, and the door opened to reveal a slender, gray-haired man in his sixties, with the same china blue eyes Lisa had.

"Good morning, Mr. Odom," Ivorson said. "I'm Peter Ivorson. I've come to see if I can interest you in building a remote control model flying machine for me."

"Call me Herbert," said Mr. Odom, shaking Ivorson's hand. "A model flying machine, huh? Well, you've come to the right man. I know a lot about that. Put your bag down and have a seat. It tires me to stand for very long."

Ivorson could see traces of the disease that was taking Herbert Odom's life: he was very thin, and there was an unhealthy gray tinge under his tan.

"Who is it, Dad?" Lisa called from the bedroom wing. "Who are you talking to?"

"A Mr. Ivorson, honey."

There was the bang of something being dropped, then the sound of rapid footsteps, and Lisa appeared in the living room. At the sight of Ivorson, she flushed pink, and gave him a brilliant smile. She wore a cotton sundress and had locally made rubber flip-flops on her feet.

"Hi!" she said. "What a surprise! What are you doing here?"

"He wants to build a model," replied her father.

The welcoming smile slid slowly off her face, to be replaced first by a look of puzzlement, and then by a frown. "Excuse us a minute, Dad," she said. "Come out on the porch with me for a minute, will you, Peter?"

Once outside, she closed the door behind them and turned on him. "If you're trying to involve my father in one of your sneaky operations," she said sternly, "forget it. I don't want any part of that."

"I know you don't," he answered, trying to find soft words for hard facts, "but it's your Dad I'm asking for help, Lisa, not you. He's got expertise that our country needs, and that I can't find anywhere else on short notice."

The frown deepened on her flushed forehead. "Peter, I don't have 'need to know'"—he could hear the quotation marks in her voice—"about what you do, but I know it requires you to tell lies to people, and that it seems to put you in the hospital on a regular basis. I don't like either one of those things. My father is a very sick man, and I am absolutely not going to have you involve him in your dirty business."

"Hadn't I better be the one to decide that, honey?" Herbert Odom's voice came through the screen wire behind Lisa.

She gave a start. "You were eavesdropping, Dad," she said reproachfully.

"Of course I was," he agreed cheerfully, pushing open the porch door to join them. "This young fellow's offered to let me have some fun." He turned to Ivorson. "What is it that's so dirty about your business, Peter?"

Ivorson had hoped to finesse that question. To answer it, he had to violate a number of Agency regulations. Not only did he not have authorization to recruit Herbert Odom (and he being an American, that was particularly a requirement), but he didn't even have any basic background checks.

That bothered him, but not enough to make him give up. Herbert Odom was his last hope. And, anyway, his sins were becoming progressively less heinous. Compared to blackmailing a Chief of Station, this was small potatoes.

"I'm a CIA operations officer, Mr. Odom," he told the older man, "and I need your help in a very important operation. It could shorten the war in Vietnam by years, and save thousands of American soldiers' lives. I can't tell you any details about it, but I need a way to control the movement of a tethered balloon with an instrument package under it."

Lisa's eyes flew open. "Well, for God's sake," she sputtered. "What happened to your famous 'need to know'?"

"Your Dad needs to know because I need him to," he told her. "What do you say, Mr. Odom? Interested?"

Lisa broke in. "Dad, I really don't want you to get involved in this. You're here on a tourist visa, and—"

Her father spoke over her objections. "Honey, being a tourist doesn't have a thing to do with it. I served in the US Army for four years during World War Two, and I saw a lot of fine young men die. If I can help Mr. Ivorson here save the lives of American soldiers, I want to do it. Besides, this sounds like a lot more fun than I ever figured to have again before I cashed in my chips." He turned his blue eyes to Ivorson. "Count me in."

Ivorson felt as if a huge weight had been lifted from his shoulders. Now he had a fighting chance. There was still one more hurdle he had to get over, however. Looking at Lisa's worried, angry face, he knew that what he had to say next wasn't going to please her at all. Still, it was a bullet that he had to bite. He liked Herbert Odom. A lot. He didn't want to get his cooperation with lies.

"I need to warn you, he said, "that there's a real element of danger involved in this. You will have to remain absolutely silent about what you do for me, especially while you're here in Laos."

Lisa broke in, her voice tight with fear. "That does it! I am not going to have you put my father's life in danger, Peter Ivorson. It's bad enough you spend half your time in hospitals, but I will not have you make a target out of my father. Absolutely not. No!"

"Honey," her father told her gently, "I'm going to be dead in six months anyway."

Tears welled up in Lisa's eyes. Ivorson felt a surprising urge to put his arms around her. Her father beat him to it. "It's all right, sugar," he told her soothingly. "Are you talking about physical danger?" he asked Ivorson. "Guns and so forth?"

Ivorson hated to answer that question. If he scared the older man off, he was out of luck, but Lisa's wet eyes forced him to tell the truth. "Yes, sir," he admitted. "Danger including guns. That's why this is going to be our only visit until the gadget is ready to go. Lisa can carry messages back and forth for us.

"What Mr. Montgomery told me was true, wasn't it?" Lisa demanded suddenly. "Someone did shoot you, didn't they?"

He didn't dare tell her again that she'd had no need to know. She'd probably hit him. Besides, he needed to have her believe in him, to be on his side. "Yes," he said simply. "I didn't think I ought to tell you. I'm sorry. From now on, I won't lie any more. I promise."

She snorted her disbelief. A long, awkward silence followed, which her father mercifully broke. "Since we shouldn't be seen together," he suggested, "let's go inside, and you can tell me exactly what it is that you need."

He led the way back into the living room. Ivorson held the door open for Lisa, but she shook her head. "I'm sure I don't have a need to know any of this," she said in a voice rich with anger. "I'll just stay out here on the porch."

It was over an hour later when he asked her to give him a ride back to town. She greeted the request with an angry stare, but at her father's quiet, "Honey, our guest needs a ride," she got her car keys and marched ahead of him out the door and down the steps.

Behind her, Ivorson shook hands with her father. "She'll come around," the latter said to Ivorson. "She's always been a worry wart, but,"—his voice dropped confidentially —"she's a really sweet girl. You take care of her, Mr. Ivorson. Yourself, too."

Not knowing what to make of that non-sequitur, Ivorson shook hands again with him and went down the steps to join Lisa in the car.

The silence on the way to town was broken only by the air- conditioner's hum. She wouldn't answer his conversational gambits, wouldn't even look at him. He wanted to be able to reassure her, to ease her worries about her father, but he couldn't think of any honest way to do that, and he didn't think she was in any mood for a lecture on security.

When they passed the Operation Brotherhood Hospital, he said, "There ought to be some cabs up at That Luang. If there are, you can just drop me, and I'll walk over and catch one."

She shot him an irritated glance "I've brought you this far," she said shortly. "I might as well take you all the way home."

"I don't want the wrong people to see us together," he explained, unhappily aware that he was lying to her again. He was actually going to the safe house to call the Chief of Station.

There were a couple of cabs parked at That Luang. She pulled off the road to let him out. As he reached into the back seat for his carry-on bag, she turned toward him abruptly and asked, "Did Nga ever write to you in Bangkok?"

Startled, he said, "Uh, no. Why?"

She reached over the top of the front seat, caught his wrist in her hand, and squeezed, hard. He winced at the pain of her fingernails digging into his flesh. "If anything happens to my father because of you, Peter Ivorson," she whispered intensely, "I'll never forgive you. Never!"

Before he could even begin to think of a response to that she released his arm. He barely got his bag out of the car and closed the door before she drove off, leaving him in a cloud of hot, red dust, and wondering what the hell Nga's failure to write him had to do with Herbert Odom's safety.

Riley arrived at the safe house thirty minutes later. He listened with uncharacteristic patience to Ivorson's detailed account of blimp testing. When Ivorson finished, he said calmly, "I already know all that. Jack Lawrence called my office on the encrypted radio system from Udorn two hours ago."

Ivorson was startled. "Oh?" he said lamely. "He did?" He hadn't ever been told that there was a secure radio link between the Air Base and the Embassy. COS must have briefed Lawrence on it before he came down to test the blimp.

"Yes, he did," said Riley, "and, surprisingly enough, there's only one difference between his version of what happened and yours." COS smiled coldly. "Can you guess what it is?"

Apprehension filled Ivorson. He didn't like either the question or COS's tone of voice. He shook his head.

"Why, naturally, whose decision it was not to change the battery before making the long test flight."

Ivorson exploded. "Did that lying sonofabitch tell you that I told him not to change batteries?"

"Of course he did, Ivorson. You didn't expect him to admit that it was his fuck-up, did you?"

Relieved by what seemed to be COS's skepticism about the tech's story, Ivorson shrugged. "I guess it would be out of character."

Riley's cold smile broadened. "Of course it would be. Unfortunately for you, however, I choose to believe Lawrence's version of the facts. The blimp was lost as a result of your incompetence. You're finished here, Ivorson. Pack your bags."

An icy chill struck the pit of Ivorson's stomach. "Wait a minute," he stammered. "It wasn't my fault. And you gave me until June 1st!"

"I gave you until June 1st to mount the blimp operation," Riley said icily, "but the blimp operation is dead for another month and a half, and by the time it's replaced, you can be replaced, too.

"You blackmailed me into keeping you after the Cam and Cao fiascos, with that fucking tape of yours," COS continued, his fury mounting, "and I had nothing but shit from Washington the whole time you were in Bangkok. Well, the tape is burned now, buddy, and so are you. I've got a brand-new reason for getting rid of you, now, and I intend to make the most of it."

Ivorson tried to interrupt, but Riley went on, almost shouting. "You thought you could put me in a box, didn't you? Well, I didn't get where I am today by letting smart-ass junior case officers best me." His eyes blazed venom.

Ivorson's heart sank. He debated with himself. Should he tell Riley what Herbert Odom was doing? Probably not. This was not the moment. In Riley's present mood, it would just feed the fire of his anger.

"I'd have you out of here this afternoon," Riley told him icily, "except they need your Vietnamese language ability down in Pakse. A Lao snatch team captured what they think is a Viet officer over on the Ho Chi Minh trail, and they've agreed to let us work the case jointly. A Porter is laid on to take you down there this afternoon at thirteen hundred hours."

Pakse! This afternoon! Shit. That wouldn't even give him a chance to talk to Nga, let alone see her. He started to protest, then thought better of it. After all, it was a reprieve. It gave him time. Time for Riley to calm down, and time for Herbert Odom to produce something that might induce COS to let Ivorson have one more try before he left Laos.

"All right," he said. "I'll see you when I get back from Pakse."

"No you won't," snapped Riley. "I don't have anything further to say to you. You'll leave Laos as soon as you get back from the south. Now get out of here."

Ivorson trudged home through the blistering hot streets, as dejected as he had ever felt in his life. The gate and doors of his house were locked, but the interior was clean and tidy, and there was a small supply of fresh food on hand. Oum had been faithfully holding the fort in his absence.

Being back in the bedroom where he had made love to Nga brought her vividly into his mind. He could almost smell her champa flower scent on the air. His anger over the fact that she hadn't written him in Bangkok dissolved into lust.

He desperately wanted to see her, but there was no way he could contact her on the weekend. He toyed briefly with the idea of calling Lisa and asking her to pass a message but reluctantly dismissed it. That would be like throwing gasoline on a fire. She was mad enough at him as it was.

He did need to call her, though, and let her know that he was going to be out of touch. Hell, he reflected despondently, maybe he just ought to tell her Dad to forget it. The odds were very great that Riley wouldn't go for the homemade blimp idea anyway, and, under those circumstances, did Ivorson have the right to put her and her father at risk?

He ate a morose early lunch, brooding about the situation, then packed his bag. Just before it was time to leave for Wattay, he made up his mind. Odom might as well go ahead and build his flying machine while Ivorson was out of town. It probably wouldn't convince Riley—in fact, it would probably infuriate him—but it gave Ivorson one tiny last straw of hope to grasp at, and he was already in so much trouble that one more sin wouldn't matter.

It was late on Friday afternoon, five days later, that he returned from Pakse, after a tremendously bumpy ride through swollen clouds. The rains had begun the same day he left for the south, and it had poured virtually nonstop the whole time he was there.

Nature had made up for the late arrival of the wet monsoon. Ivorson had never seen such heavy, protracted storms. Flash after flash of lightning had cast stark shadows on his bedroom wall every night, and the thunder sounded like a twenty-four hour artillery barrage over Pakse.

As the Porter that brought him back to Vientiane made its approach to Wattay, he could see signs of heavy rain here, too. There was standing water everywhere.

The captured Vietnamese had broken on the third day of interrogation. He proved to be a lieutenant in the People's Army of Vietnam, a northerner, and he admitted that he was part of a massive PAVN movement south for a new offensive in South Vietnam. Ivorson's Lao hosts were ecstatic, and so were the Agency people in Pakse.

Ivorson felt good about his part in the interrogation. It wasn't like breaking the enemy's code, but at least he had contributed to an early warning for the allied armies in Vietnam.

Oum received him royally when he came in the door of his house, clapping her hands like an overjoyed child. He was moved by her pleasure at seeing him. She wept when he presented her with the golden chain and locket he'd brought for her in Bangkok.

When she recovered her composure and had gone to the kitchen to prepare his dinner, Ivorson made for the telephone in the bedroom. His first call was to Lisa, at the office. Her voice was not as cool as he had expected it to be, but the news she had for him could hardly have been worse.

"I've got orders here for you to return to Washington," she told him. "The word came down on Monday. Did you know about that?"

The glow created by Oum's reception vanished in a flash. Riley had obviously been as good as his word. "I heard about the possibility just before I left town," he told her, "but I was hoping it wouldn't materialize. I guess I was wrong. When am I supposed to leave?"

"No reservations have been made yet. We didn't know when you'd get back from Pakse." She didn't seem as pleased as she might have been, he thought, considering she was getting rid of him. Good manners, he supposed.

"My Dad wants to see you," she told him. "The last of the material he needed to finish the thing he was doing for you arrived today in the APO. Shall I tell him to expect you tonight?"

No, he thought. Not tonight. Tonight might be Ivorson's last night in Laos, and he didn't intend to spend it with Herbert Odom. In light of Lisa's news about his orders, his chances of persuading Riley to try Odom's contraption were probably about zero, anyway.

"I'll come by tomorrow, if that's okay."

"Morning?"

He hoped he'd be sleeping very late. "Maybe afternoon would be better."

"All right. Goodbye." She hung up. She'd sounded downright sulky. He couldn't understand why. She ought to be delighted to be getting rid of him.

He looked at his watch. It was almost quitting time at USAID. He had to make another call, fast.

"Personnel, Nga speaking," she answered the phone on her desk.

"Hi," he said. "It's me."

"Oh? Oh!" He could hear her surprise. "Are you in Vientiane?"

"Uh, yes, I just got back. When can you come to my house tonight?"

"Yes, of course."

"Seven?"

"Yes. I can hardly wait," the last words were a whisper.

He hung up, quivering with desire.

He thought about calling COS, but decided against it. He didn't have anything to show him now. His best bet was to wait until he had Odom's gadget in hand.

They were in bed within five minutes after her arrival. The intensity of their reunion rivaled the thunderstorm outside. It almost made his absence worthwhile. She clung to him with arms legs and mouth. Enormously aroused by her passion, he spent himself in her totally, utterly. He no longer even cared why she hadn't written him. The idea that he would have to leave her again so soon, and forever, was devastating.

When it was over for the second time, and they were resting, their bodies still touching, she said to him, "The countryside is so beautiful, now that the rains have come. Let's go for a picnic."

"A picnic?" he echoed. "Where in the world could we go for a picnic? The town is surrounded by the Pathet Lao."

She laughed. "Oh, no. We'll only go out to the Teachers' College at Don Dok. That is just at kilometer twelve. It's perfectly safe. A little way to the west of the college is a place I know on the banks of the Nam Khen. It will be very pretty there, now that everything has turned green again."

It was an attractive idea. He had never been further into the countryside than the USAID housing area at kilometer six, and the countryside would be pretty, now. His own garden had amazed him this afternoon. The grass and bushes glistened with moist new greenery, and the stark, gnarled branches of the champa tree had sprouted leaves.

She propped herself up on an elbow. The movement made her breasts bob temptingly. "Come on," she urged him. "We can go very early, when it's still cool. We'll take a picnic breakfast, and be back by mid-day, before it starts to rain."

He had never seen her so enthusiastic about anything before. Well, why not? Nguyen van Huu couldn't possibly know that he was back in Vientiane, and it was probably the only opportunity he would ever have to enjoy a normal boy/ girl outing with her. It could even be the last time he would ever see her.

"All right, then," he agreed, "but are you sure you want to do this? You've always been so frightened of someone seeing us together."

She threw her arms around his neck. "When you were gone," she whispered in his ear, "I missed you so very much." Her tongue flicked his ear lobe. "I don't care anymore what people say about me, I just want to be with you."

Her mouth dropped to his throat, then began sliding down his body, kissing his chest. "Besides, no one will see us at Don Dok. There are no Vietnamese people there, just Lao farmers." Her lips closed over one of his nipples. "You will love it, Peter."

If it was anything like what he was feeling right not, he was sure he would.

Chapter Nineteen

She came to the house by cab in the gray light of early morning on Saturday, carrying a basket of food and wearing the same white blouse and Lao skirt she'd worn to Boon Bang Fie. The sight stirred his erotic memories of that day, but he still had qualms about what they were doing, too. If any of Nguyen van Huu's people saw them leaving town and followed them into the countryside, they would be in very big trouble.

Still, he figured that the odds were strongly in his favor. There was no way Huu could know that he was back in the city. They didn't have to pass through any Vietnamese neighborhoods between his home and Route 13, and once they were outside town, there would be no problem.

Finally, he had his gun, although the .380 Walther PPK, holstered inside his jeans in the small of his back, wouldn't help much if they ran into a PL patrol, and it would be awkward if Nga saw or felt it. He'd even toyed with idea of leaving it at home, but decided not to. He'd feel naked out in the Asian countryside without some sort of weapon.

Actually, what bothered him the most about the situation was simply that no one would know where he was. That was something you just didn't do, and it bothered him, but who could he tell?

Riley was out of the question. That would only result in an order not to go. How would he square that with Nga? He couldn't very well tell Oum, either. She fully shared Wilbur's hatred of all things Vietnamese. If she discovered he had a Viet mistress, the least that would happen would be that he'd immediately lose a servant–and a surveillance team, too, probably, when she shared the information with Orville.

He and Nga packed the contents of her basket, plus some cold soft drinks, in the saddlebags of his Suzuki and prepared to set out. He wanted to get away before Oum's arrival at six. Nga acted as a happy as a bird, dancing around the motorcycle and humming. "Come on, Peter," she pleaded. "We want to get there while it's still cool."

"All right. Let's go." He straddled the Honda and started it with a touch of his thumb on the electric starter. Nga walked beside him as he rolled slowly through the gate, pulled the motorcycle up on its kickstand, and dismounted to lock the gate.

As he pulled the hasp of the padlock through the heavy chain, however, another wave of misgiving swept over him. God damn it, he was taking an unprofessional chance! They might have an accident or a flat tire. Anything could happen. He hesitated a second, then opened the gate again. "Forgot something," he called to Nga over his shoulder. "I'll be right back."

He unlocked the front door, trotted over to the coffee table, and picked up his American Express bill. Turning the envelope over, he printed on the back of it in pidgin French, for Oum, "Pique-nique at Don Dok/Nam Khen. If no return by noon, go tell Orville come look for me there." He replaced the envelope with the new message face up and went back out to rejoin Nga. He felt better. He wouldn't need Orville, of course. They'd be back from their outing long before noon, but at least he wasn't being completely irresponsible.

They reached the edge of town beyond the Lao Army camp at Pone Kheng without drawing so much as a curious glance and set out on the road to Don Dok.

Ivorson breathed a sigh of relief when they got past the entrance to Rainbow Village. If Lisa saw him and Nga going off together after he'd postponed the meeting with her Dad, her respect for him would sink to rock bottom. Not that it made a damn.

The countryside had changed radically during the single week of rain. Where there had been bare, red paddy fields, there were now an infinity of shimmering squares of water, being ploughed by bare-legged farmers behind their plodding, docile water buffalo.

The ditches on either side of the road were full of water, too, and their banks were lined with people, fishing with cumbersome square nets suspended from bamboo poles. Ivorson saw one fisherman pull up his net and dump out a catch of squirming fingerlings. The miracle of the rains amazed him, as it had ever since he first saw it in Vietnam. A week ago, these ditches had been salt-dry and rock-hard.

There was fresh greenery everywhere. The air was still cool on his face as they rolled along. It would be warm again this afternoon, although a good twenty degrees cooler than it had been a week ago in Udorn. Could that really be only a week ago? The pressure of Nga's breasts against his back made it hard for him to keep his mind on anything else.

They reached the dirt road that led to the left, toward the Lao National Teachers' College. Ivorson took one last look in his rearview mirror. No one there.

They passed the Teachers' College, made a short jog north, and then continued to the west again on a newly-graded dirt road, away from rice fields and into what the French called "clear forest"—mostly scrub vegetation with occasional towering solitary trees and patches of dense vegetation.

There was only a very occasional thatched hut to indicate human presence, the dark-skinned inhabitants gaping at their passage. Ivorson was amazed at how few people there were in the Lao countryside, compared to Vietnam. There was abundant unsettled land here, less than twenty miles from the capital.

"How much further?" he called over his shoulder to Nga. "We're already more than a mile west of Don Dok."

She squeezed his waist. "Not far now. Just a kilometer or so more."

Sure enough, at the end of another three-quarters of a mile, they came to a wooden bridge over a creek. "Take the track to the right before the bridge," Nga spoke in his ear "There is a pretty beach by a bamboo grove."

Ivorson followed her directions. They burbled along slowly for fifty yards on the muddy track Nga had indicated, with dense foliage on either side and came out in a clearing by the edge of the stream. Ahead of them, a massive grove of bamboo, eight-inch thick stalks towering seventy feet high, blocked further progress.

"Here we are," Nga told him. Ivorson killed the engine, and Nga slid off. He pulled the motorcycle up on its stand, and looked around. On the opposite bank of the stream was more of the dense jungle they had just driven through. Wild orchids hung down from the branches. It was a secluded, idyllic Eden. "This really is a lovely place, Nga," he told her, taking her hands in his. "I'm glad you talked me into coming here."

She looked up at him with a complacent smile. "Yes," she said. "It is the perfect place." She glanced at her watch. "We made good time. It's not even six thirty yet. Let's go and look at the water."

Hand in hand, she led him down to the banks of the stream. On the map, the Nam Khen was no more than a creek, but the recent rains had vastly increased its volume and produced a slight current, on which clumps of vegetation, some of them quite large, floated leisurely south toward the Mekong.

Nga kept looking at her watch.

"What's the matter?" he teased her. "Time for your breakfast?"

She shook her head, pulled her hand from his, and walked away from him a few yards down the bank. "It is time," she said, "but not for breakfast." The remark made no sense to him.

Puzzled, he turned to follow her, and as he did so, out of the corner of his eye he caught a hint of motion and the gleam of metal in the foliage across the creek. His stomach froze into a steel knot. Someone was hidden over there! Someone with a rifle.

He tried to think through his fear and confusion. They could scarcely be in a worse position, standing in the middle of an open field with tree lines on all sides. The only hope was to go for cover in the jungle and hope it wasn't already occupied by another concealed watcher.

"Nga," he said quietly, walking after her and trying to appear casual, "keep on moving toward the trees downstream."

"What, Peter?" she asked over her shoulder.

"Don't look around, or act frightened honey," he said, "but we're not alone out here."

She turned to face him, and smiled. It was a smile he had never seen on her face before: a hard, mirthless smile that held not the faintest hint of humor or affection. "Oh, I know that, Peter," she told him. "I brought you out here for them."

He stared, uncomprehending.

"You don't understand, do you?" she asked him, her voice ice-cold. "You thought I like having you in my body. You think I am honored to be chosen by a white man to spill his seed into."

He shook his head, trying to clear his shocked mind. This couldn't be happening. Beautiful, passionate Nga, couldn't be talking to him like that.

"You are all alike," she hissed. "French and Americans, my father and you." Her voice became more agitated. "You come to Asia, sire your half-breeds, and then expect us to love you. Well, I don't love you, Peter. I hate you! I hate you, do you hear me?" Her voice shrilled upward in a crescendo of fury, and the sickening reality of what he was hearing could be denied no longer.

She had set him up. She had played the oldest trick in the history of espionage on him, and he had fallen willingly into the honey trap, just like all the previous suckers.

She'd said she brought him out here for "them". That meant the one across the creek wasn't alone. Christ, there could be a platoon or more of them! He could be completely surrounded.

The Fear washed over him, inundated him, drowned him. He couldn't fight against odds like these. He didn't have a chance. God, it wasn't fair! He wanted to just lie down on the grass and cry, to surrender, to throw himself on the mercy of his unseen captors.

His suddenly treasonous mind tried to rationalize surrender. Why not? After all, what did he know that would really damage the US? He wasn't running any agent operations. Tran van Cao had proved a traitor, and Wilbur was dead.

Wilbur was dead. The thought brought him a measure of self-control. Wilbur would never surrender, no matter what the odds, and neither would Orville, but if Ivorson surrendered, their whole family was doomed. Those people depended on him for their survival. For that matter, so did all of his fellow case officers in Vietnam and Laos, whose identities would be tortured out of him if he surrendered.

Nga was looking at him with a face of such terrible malignancy that he could scarcely recognize her. She started to raise a hand to her mouth, as if to call someone, and he realized that if she did that, all of his options were ended. If he was going to fight, he had to start now.

"Don't be so angry, sweetheart," he said to her. Only part of the words came out coherently over his fear-dried vocal cords, but the conciliatory tone reached her. Her hand stopped in mid-motion, and she looked at him with angry disbelief. Holding his arms out, he moved slowly toward her.

"Are you deaf, you fool?" she asked him, speaking Vietnamese for the first time. "Don't you understand plain English?"

Come on, Ivorson, he thought. If you've ever played a convincing role in your life, do it now. Still approaching her, he threw back his head and tried to laugh. It was a pitiful excuse for the real thing, but it caused her to stop in her tracks and stare. She was still four feet away. He kept edging forward, his arms extended to her.

"Come on, Nga," he said, hoping he sounded like the buffoon she had played him for. "You know I can't understand Vietnamese. Tell me why you're so angry with me. You know I love you." He almost choked on the words, but he'd tell her anything to keep her attention focused on him. Two feet to go.

"Love?" She spat the word at him as if it were an obscenity. "You pig! You fascist! Don't you understand? I have led you to your death!"

Smiling foolishly, he touched her fingertips.

She saw her danger in his eyes then, but she was just a heartbeat too slow. He got her by the wrist and pulled her tightly against him. She opened her mouth to cry out, but his other hand clamped down on her throat and squeezed her voice to an anguished croak. He bent his face over her, feigning a kiss.

He sensed some sort of motion behind him, near the bamboo grove. His spine crawled at the thought of the rifle bullet which might already be flying toward him. He had move NOW!

Maintaining the charade of a kiss, he lifted her bodily and began moving toward the edge of the jungle in front of him. She tried to struggle, but another vicious squeeze on her throat froze her against him again.

He had to keep his ambushers from guessing his intentions; keep them immobilized until he got to the tree line. Only how the hell could he do it?

The idea seemed outlandish at first, but it might conceivably work. His ambushers had probably been living without women for months. Anyway, it was all he could think of. He shifted the hand he had around Nga's waist until he felt the thin woven copper belt that held her Lao skirt. He closed his fist on it and twisted. He felt it break in his hand. He tossed it aside. The Lao skirt loosened. He yanked at its waistband and felt it start to slide down her thighs. Pray God his audience was as horny as he hoped they were!

He rolled his eyes along the edge of the tree line ahead of him. At first he could see nothing. Then, ten yards to his left, bushes moved, and a brown face appeared through the leaves, its eyes glued to Nga's bared thighs. Below the face, the barrel of an AK-47 poked out into the clearing. Jesus, an assault rifle!

Not letting himself think about the gun, he carried Nga forward for another ten feet, looking feverishly for signs of another ambusher. If there were another one, closer to the stream, he really wouldn't have a prayer.

He couldn't see anyone but the brown face with the AK. Now he was less than five feet from the trees. Right ahead was a very large hardwood of some sort, which formed part of the jungle's edge and, behind it for a short space, the brush was less dense. If he could get in there, behind the tree, it would protect him from fire. It was a very faint hope and a very temporary refuge, but it was absolutely all he had.

Nga was semi-conscious now from lack of oxygen, but feeling her skirt fall around her knees, she began to kick again.

He was almost there. He abruptly threw her to the ground, his body on top of hers. They landed hard on the rain-softened turf. He heard the wind whistle out of her lungs. He rolled over on his left side, pulling her with him, so that her body was between him and the clearing, released her throat and grabbed the waist of her underpants with both hands. He yanked them down her thighs with a motion that brought him to his knees and half-turned toward the trees.

The big hardwood was no more than a yard away. He launched himself for it with all his strength, every nerve screaming in anticipation of the awful impact of bullets. He brushed by the tree and dived headlong into the hollow in the vegetation behind it. He heard the first rounds thump into the tree a microsecond before his ears filled with the roar of AKs firing on full automatic fire. The sight of Nga's beautiful ass had diverted them just long enough for him to get to cover!

He wasn't covered from all sides, however. Slugs were whipping through the leaves close over his head. Maybe from Brown Face. An instant later, the roar of automatic rifle fire not thirty feet away showed him his error. THAT was brown face. The rounds lashing the vegetation above him must be coming from the guy he'd seen across the creek.

As close to the earth as he could get himself, he wormed his way deeper into the vegetation. Vines caught at him and thorns gouged him, but, thank God, there was some kind of small animal trail that led away from the tree into the bush, which let him wriggle his way deeper into the jungle. Above him, bullets were still tearing at the leaves, but the level of fire had dropped a lot.

That encouraged him until he realized that it must mean the ambushers were on the move, running from their original positions toward his present location. The thought was devastating. He'd been lucky as hell to make it this far, but as outnumbered as he was, his liberty was likely to be very short-lived. All they had to do was surround the area he was in and beat the bushes until they found him.

Viciously banishing that thought from his mind, he kept wriggling, deeper and deeper into the jungle. It was incredibly dense. Had he been standing, or even crawling on his knees, he couldn't have moved at all.

Suddenly he heard a shout behind him, and the sound of firing ceased. From an incredible din, the jungle fell into a deathly silence. Ivorson froze. Brown Face was close enough to hear him, if he continued thrashing through the undergrowth.

He tried to control his panting and strained his ears for any rustling of leaves that might indicate the approach of Brown Face. He could hear nothing but insects.

He rolled his eyes around as far as he could without moving his head, but he could see nothing but leaves on either side. He looked ahead of him. Beyond his torn and bleeding hands, the tunnel, made by whatever animal it was, continued. It was a couple of feet wide at the widest. He couldn't move further without making noise. Until they started firing again, all he could do was lie here.

"Monsieur Ivorson!" The voice was so close behind him that he almost cried out in fright. "Come out, monsieur," the voice continued. "This is quite useless. You are completely surrounded. You cannot possibly escape." The words were spoken in familiar, chirping, sing-song French. The voice belonged to Tran van Cao.

Chapter Twenty

Ivorson was paralyzed. Not so much by the presence of Tran van Cao as by the magnitude of his own incredible blindness and folly. He had made himself Nguyen van Huu's prisoner here in this few acres of jungle, as surely as if he had walked into the North Vietnamese Embassy and sat down in a chair. What was worse, between Cao and Nga, he had been in Huu's clutches from his first day in Laos.

Nga. His mind still couldn't fully adjust to that reality. She had played him like a violin; made an absolutely, unmitigated ass of him. He could hear her voice now, faintly, speaking in Vietnamese. What wouldn't he give for one clear shot at that bitch!

He mentally shook himself. If he didn't quit bemoaning his past blunders and start thinking, she was the one who would have the clear shot.

He tried to recall the burst of firing that followed his dive into cover. It seemed to him that there hadn't been more than five or six weapons involved. Plus Brown Face, who'd fired later. Say seven, plus Nga, but she didn't have a weapon. Cao might be armed, but only with a hand gun. His right arm couldn't have healed to the point of firing an AK.

Eight altogether, then. Six of them armed with automatic assault rifle, against Ivorson and his pathetic little PPK. The PPK! Jesus, did he still have it? He could feel the holster against his skin. He arched his back slightly and felt the butt touch his lower spine. Very quietly and carefully, he brought one of his hands back along his body to the hem of his sports shirt. He tugged it upward until his fingers closed on the butt of the gun. He pulled it from the holster and returned both hand and gun to a position ahead of him, pointing down the tiny game trail he was in.

Now he could hear a number of voices, including Cao's and Nga's, and they were speaking in Lao. His ambushers must be a Pathet Lao unit. That might make a lot of difference before the day was out. Ivorson's experience with the VC had left him greatly impressed with both their courage and their cruelty. The Lao were not noted for either quality.

The voices fell silent, and for a time he lay there, straining his senses for some clue as to what was happening; not daring to move for fear that they were listening as hard as he.

Then, behind him, he heard a faint rustling of leaves. He cocked his head, first to one side and then to the other, trying to isolate and locate the sound. Finally, he understood. Someone was very stealthily slithering toward him along the game trail!

His mouth went dry with the adrenalin surge that accompanied the realization. Whoever was coming would catch up with him in a lot less time than it had taken Ivorson to get where he was, because he had enlarged the trail by his passage. For that same reason, he couldn't possibly outrun his pursuer, and, anyway, the noise of the attempt would bring a concentration of automatic weapons fire upon his position. He had only one option: to kill his pursuer before he could get off a shot of his own. Of course, that, too, would bring counter-fire, but the brush was thick. Maybe it would miss him.

The furtive sounds in the underbrush were getting closer. He needed to get himself in position to fire back down the trail behind him, but the narrow tunnel which formed the game trail was tightly encased in brambles and vines. Any movement at all was difficult, and silence much more so.

Very quietly, he pulled his arms back underneath his chest and shoulders and then tried to roll over on his back. It didn't work. The additional bulk of his arms pinned him against the green roof of the tiny tunnel he was in.

The sounds behind him were becoming very clear now. In just a few more seconds, his pursuer would be in position to put a 7.62mm round clear through Ivorson, from bottom to top.

The thought moved him to Herculean effort. He put both hands out ahead of himself again, then attempted to roll over on his back. A dozen thorns drew blood, but he was able to effect the maneuver.

Now, on his back, he pulled his gun hand back down, wriggling and undulating his shoulders to slip the weapon past his face. He had almost succeeded when his wrist got caught by a slender vine. The muzzle of the automatic was pressed firmly against his own ear. He carefully took his finger off the trigger and moved the weapon back above his head an inch or so. The vine released him, and he tried again. This time the gun slid by his face unimpeded.

The rustling in the undergrowth behind his feet sounded very close indeed. Still working his gun hand down to his side, he pulled the toes of his sneakers apart and raised his head as high as he could, trying to see down the length of his body and through the narrow tunnel in the foliage behind him.

It was very hard to do. The view was obscured by leaves and vines, and a small branch was pushing down on his head. He gritted his teeth and shoved the branch up with his skull. It gave a couple of inches. Now he could see better.

But not very far. A few feet beyond his shoes, the tunnel bent in the undergrowth. The sounds of approach were completely obvious now. As Ivorson strained to hold his head up against the downward pressure of the branch, he saw the muzzle and foresight of an AK-47 slide into view around the bend in the game trail. His pursuer was pushing his weapon ahead of him, ready for a shot.

Ivorson's automatic was still only waist high. Its muzzle was caught on the trunk of a slender tree which formed one side of the tunnel, and his elbow was wedged into the matted wall of vine which composed the other side. He strained to push the elbow deeper into the vines and free the gun barrel.

The barrel of the AK appeared, and then a shock of straight black hair came into view at the edge of the bend. Its owner raised his head to look in front of him, and his eyes locked with Ivorson's.

Ivorson read the surprise and fear in them. The Pathet Lao gave a violent heave, and the muzzle of the AK began to swing toward Ivorson.

With a furious effort, Ivorson jerked his elbow, pointed the pistol between his spread feet, and pulled the trigger three times, as fast as he could.

The sharp cracks of the PPK's fire filled his ears. A hot, ejected cartridge bounced off something on the tunnel wall and hit his cheek, burning him. He involuntarily jerked his head aside for an instant. When he centered the barrel of the PPK again, he could see only darkness beyond the gun smoke.

Then he realized that the darkness was the black hair of the Lao, who lay face down, very still, on the barrel of the AK.

He didn't have time for a sigh of relief. A hailstorm of lead exploded in the leaves around and above him. His instinctive desire to curl up in a ball was thwarted by the narrow confines of the game trail, and, in any case, it was silly. What he needed to do was get away from this location while the sound of firing covered his movements.

He wriggled toward the Pathet Lao on his back until his feet touched the barrel of the AK. His previous passage had widened this portion of the tunnel, and he could easily roll back over onto his belly. He holstered the PPK and began slithering forward again, as fast as he could.

The firing ceased as suddenly as it had begun. Ivorson stopped moving. What would his ambushers try next? Actually, his position was not so bad, now that he had time to think about it. The body of the dead PL would keep anyone else from following him through the game trail, and they had lost one of their number.

They didn't have enough troops to be sure of driving him either toward the road or the stream, where he could be seen and captured or killed. The undergrowth was so dense that he might easily slip through their line. That is, unless they had reinforcements in the neighborhood.

He could hear faint talking again. He strained his ears to make some sense of the talk. All he could get was unintelligible sound, but there was a sense of disagreement. The voices became louder and began overriding each other. Fine! The longer they palavered, the more time he had to make his getaway. He began moving forward again.

A movement in the foliage above him froze him for an instant before he realized that it was the wind, moving the leaves of the trees. The terrain was beginning to warm in the morning sunshine, creating a little breeze. He pulled his left hand back to his mouth, licked the forefinger and held it up beside his face.

The back of the finger cooled. The air was moving from the clearing toward the road, roughly from north to south. That might explain why he could hear the voices. If so, it would also carry the sound of his movement away from them. He resumed his forward motion.

"Monsieur Ivorson!"

It was Cao again. The voice was definitely further away than it had been the first time. That was heartening.

"This is your last chance, monsieur. If you come out now, with your hands above your head, you will be treated humanely, as a prisoner of war. If you do not give up, you will die horribly."

Ivorson just kept wriggling along the ground. Whatever death Cao had in mind for him here was sure to be preferable to what would happen to him as a known CIA officer in the hands of the PL or the Vietnamese.

He raised his head and wrist to look at his watch. My God, it wasn't even seven o'clock in the morning! Five hours to go until Oum even notified Orville that he was missing.

Despite that fact, however, time might now actually be on his side. It was unlikely that his ambushers had a lot of reinforcements this close to Vientiane, and they had done a hell of a lot of shooting. The distinctive sound of the AKs must have been heard by some farmer along the road to Don Dok, perhaps even in Don Dok itself. A Royal Lao Army patrol might be on its way to investigate right now, and Cao and his cohorts must surely be as aware of that possibility as Ivorson was. They might just give up and fade away. God, he hoped so!

He could still feel the faint breeze on the back of his neck. Despite the twisting and turning of the game trail among the trunks of the trees, the clearing must still be behind him. He could hear nothing. He inched forward again.

And then he smelled smoke. He raised his head as high as he could and sniffed frantically. There was no question about it. Wood smoke was coming down the wind from the tree line behind him. The bastards were going to burn him out!

The idea of burning to death, trapped helplessly in the constricting walls of the game tunnel, appalled him. He scrambled forward with all his strength, heedless of the noise he was making. The jungle was so thick that bullets probably couldn't reach him anymore, and even if they could, death by gunshot was infinitely preferable to being burned alive.

Now the smell of smoke was unmistakable. Would the forest burn? This time last week he wouldn't have stood a chance—the woods had been tinder-dry—but it had rained hard every day for four or five days now. Surely that moisture would impede the fire, perhaps even bog it down completely.

Hopeful, he seized a handful of dust from the dirt floor of his game trail. It was bone dry. The jungle was so thick that the rains had not been able to penetrate to its floor. It would still burn—and fast.

The discovery very nearly robbed him of all rationality. He clawed frantically at the shrubbery. He wriggled. He slid. He tried every possible combination of movements he could think of which might produce more rapid progress. None of it worked. A yard a minute was all he could do.

The smoke was getting thicker, making his eyes sting and his nose tickle. He paused for a moment to dig the handkerchief out of his pocket. He moistened it with sweat from his brow, made a mask of it, which he tied over mouth and nose. He started bellying forward again.

He didn't have any idea where the game trail was leading him, but it didn't matter, just as long as it was away from the fire. If the little tunnel ended at the road or stream, there would be someone waiting for him, but that was a chance he had to take. With his pistol, at least he had a chance against the Pathet Lao. Against the fire, he had none.

The smoke got thicker. The foliage was so dense near the jungle floor that the breeze couldn't disperse it. He began to cough. He couldn't feel any heat yet, but behind him, he could hear the fire beginning to crackle.

He kept on pulling himself along the floor of the jungle, following his burrow like a mole. His fingers began bleeding, rubbed raw by pulling his weight over the ground. The smoke was still getting worse, and he could hear the crackling of fire, both behind him and now, more and more, to his right.

That frightened him terribly. He couldn't understand it. The stream should be on his right. How could they have torched the forest along the stream bank? Where had his game trail taken him?

The fire was roaring now, loudly, and he was beginning to feel heat. The smoke was thicker than ever; yellow-white smoke, the kind you get from burning wet grass. It made him gag, but he kept on crawling.

A spark fell beside his outstretched hand. It went out when it hit the dirt, but soon there was another one, and then another, and then one fell on his back. He let out a yelp of pain, but the roaring of the fire was so loud that he could hardly hear his own voice.

He bulled his way along on his belly with all his might, sobbing with the effort, but even as he struggled, into the back of his fear-fogged mind seeped the ice-cold knowledge that he wasn't going to make it; that the fire would catch him and kill him. It was the most horrible feeling that he had ever known.

Panic-stricken, he reached out another hand-hold with which to pull himself forward and found nothing but air. Startled, he looked ahead. Under his outreaching hand, the earth fell sharply away. He wriggled forward and peered downward.

A yard below him, under the overhang of a thick bush, was water. Brown, moving water. It was the stream! The game trail had led him to the Nam Khen!

The fire was very close. Its roaring was mind-numbing. Heat shriveled his back and legs. He slid down the stream bank and crawled head-first into the muddy stream. It was shallow. It didn't even cover his body. Flames were all around him. The heat was so intense that he could feel the skin of his back sizzling.

He snatched a lung-scorching breath and pushed off from the bank, out into the center of the stream. He dived, trying to find the bottom of the stream bed, feeling frantically for something he could hang onto and hold himself under the surface, away from the flames.

He groped in the mud, but the remaining air in his lungs kept pulling him back to the surface. Then something hit him on the side. Terror-stricken, he tried to fend it off. Were there crocodiles in Laos?

After an instant of total panic, he recognized the feel of vegetation and mud, and realized that it must be a large clump of debris floating down the stream. Thank God!

His lungs were about to burst. He clawed his way up the vegetation toward the surface. He opened his eyes and saw sunlight above him. It took every ounce of willpower he possessed to move slowly, but if he burst to the surface and got spotted by the PL, it would be all over.

Every fiber in his body was screaming for oxygen when his head broke the surface. He sucked in a greedy, gut-deep breath and opened his eyes. He was about ten feet from the far shore of the Nam Khen, and on the bank, straight in front of him, was a Pathet Lao with an AK-47.

Ivorson's brain gave his body the order to submerge again, but his fuel-deprived muscles were incapable of obeying. That probably saved him. The PL trooper was staring beyond and above Ivorson, fascinated by the roaring furnace that had just been Ivorson's sanctuary. The splash of a panicky submersion would have attracted his attention.

Ivorson took in another huge breath and pulled himself silently under the water at the front of the floating island. He stayed down as long as he could, then, very slowly and carefully, surfaced again, tipping his head backwards so that only his mouth and nose would break the surface.

When he had satisfied his air-starved body, he risked a careful look around. On his left, the fire was still raging. Flames leaped almost two hundred feet into the air. Even with water on his face, the heat singed him. The right bank looked empty, but ahead of him, no more than fifty yards away, was the bridge, and on it, looking in his direction, stood an armed PL trooper and Nguyen thi Nga.

He hastily re-submerged and groped along his belt for the butt of the PPK. It would be easy to shoot both her and the PL as he floated under the bridge. The idea was immensely attractive. She had betrayed him; led him to slaughter like a water buffalo and was still trying to kill him now. It would be so satisfying to see the look of terror on her face just before the bullets struck her.

The trouble was, the sound of shooting would reveal his location and result in his own death or capture. He reluctantly postponed vengeance in favor of survival and began pulling himself around the undersurface of the floating island to its rear, where he could surface to breathe without being spotted by Nga and her gunman.

When he came carefully up again for another breath, he seemed to be about half-way to the rear of the clump of vegetation. The main mass of the fire had burned past him, and the heat above the stream's surface was greatly diminished.

He hoped the gravel road proved an effective fire break. He hoped even more that the towering column of flame and smoke attracted the attention of a Royal Lao Army patrol.

His attackers must have recognized that danger, too. It was one thing for a dozen people to infiltrate this close to town at night, but to remain here in broad daylight under a beacon of smoke and flame, after all the shooting they had done, was almost suicidal. Surely they would withdraw soon!

He continued to make his way underwater toward the upstream side of the clump of vegetation. When he surfaced the next time, he was almost there, and was overjoyed to discover a very broad-leafed bush of some sort, right at the water's edge. One of its leaves spread out horizontally over the stream and provided a perfect hiding place for Ivorson. He wouldn't have to keep submerging and surfacing.

He slid in under it and looked downstream again. The bridge was a lot closer now. He could make out Nga's face very clearly. She looked worried. Almost panicky. Well she might. If she couldn't be certain of Ivorson's death, would she dare to return to Vientiane? She might have to stay with the PL. He hoped she came back to town. He wanted to settle his score with her in person.

The sound of the fire was greatly diminished. The road must have proven an effective firebreak. A few patches of green still remained here and there near the stream, but the great majority of what had been dense jungle half an hour ago was now a smoking charred wasteland.

A shout from behind him made him submerge hastily. Had he been seen? He heard no shots. No bullets pierced the water. He cautiously re-surfaced. A shouted conversation was in progress between the PL on the bridge and someone on the west bank of the stream—presumably the PL soldier he had seen earlier.

A careful peek at the bridge now showed him four PL soldiers, but no Nga. He caught a glimpse of her walking off the bridge to the east, past another PL. They were all gathering on the road, hopefully preparing to pull out.

One of the PL said something to the others. They all raised their AKs and pointed them at his clump of vegetation, which was now only about thirty feet north of the bridge. One of the assault rifles was aimed directly at Ivorson's covering leaf. He gulped a quick breath of air and submerged, just as the first bullet threw up a gout of water in his face. The last thing he heard before his ears filled with water was the staccato thunder of the automatic weapons fire.

Chapter Twenty-one

"What am I going to do, uncle?" Nga asked Cao. She couldn't control the rising edge of panic in her voice. Everything had gone so horribly wrong.

He looked sourly at her. She could see fear in his eyes, too. "Go on back to town, of course."

"But how can I?" she wailed. "We don't know that Peter is dead. Suppose he appears at work on Monday? Suppose he sends the police to arrest me?"

"Don't be a damned fool!" Cao's voice was sharp. "How could he possibly have survived? We had people watching both the stream and the road. They didn't see anyone. He burned up in the fire."

"That's easy for you to say," she snapped back at him. "You can't go back to town in any case. Uncle Huu promised me that I would be in no danger at all, but if Peter is not dead, I am ruined." She softened her tone, tried to appeal to whatever male was left in the wizened little man. "Don't you see, I have to make sure. The fire is out now. Make them look for his body."

"That's out of the question," he said coldly. "It will take a day for that ground to cool off enough to walk on with our rubber sandals. We have to go immediately. We have already taken an enormous risk by staying here this long. With the fire and smoke, someone will come at any moment."

A burst of firing broke out behind them, and they both jumped. Hope leaped inside her. "What are you shooting at?" she called to the men on the bridge. "Did you see him?"

"No. We're just making certain that he was not hiding under this floating vegetation," the PL corporal called back. "If he was, he's dead now."

Crushed by disappointment, she turned back to Cao. "I can't take such a great chance, uncle," she wailed. "You must help me."

"Listen, girl," Cao told her severely. "If I believed that he might have survived, I would stop at nothing to kill him. He broke my cover and my body. He forced me to flee to the jungle and live like an animal. But he is not alive. He cannot be." He gestured furiously at the blackened wasteland behind them. "You may return home in safety."

He studied her fearful face for a moment, and then added, with a sly smile, "Of course, if you don't want to believe me, you may go with us and join the liberators in the forest. The Lao comrades would be very happy to have you."

She repressed a shudder. Never, no matter what, would she follow these Lao peasants into the forest. They had been leering at her ever since Peter made his escape. Damn him eternally for showing these animals her bare bottom! Oh, how she wanted him to have burned to death. If only she had heard just one scream!

"Make up your mind," Cao ordered her. "We are leaving now." He turned to the three men lying in the roadside ditch behind them and ordered them to join the others on the bridge.

She was horrified. "You can't leave yet! Someone has to give me a ride back to Don Dok."

"Ivorson shot our man in civilian clothes," Cao told her sullenly, "and thanks to your ineptness, we have no time for that in any case. Get yourself back to Don Dok. The keys are in his motorcycle."

"The motorcycle is supposed to be dropped in the Nam Khen, after I am delivered to Don Dok," she wailed. "Where am I supposed to hide it? You are making me take all the risks!"

He shrugged callously. "If you like, push the machine into the stream and walk back to Don Dok. Either that, or come with us. Make up your mind. We are leaving now."

Her mind reeled back and forth between fear and fury. Had she been armed, she would have shot him where he stood. "Uncle Huu will hear how you bungled this," she hissed at him. "It was not my fault. I delivered him to you like a trussed up chicken, and you botched it."

He grimaced angrily. "One cannot avoid the unexpected in war. Tell Huu what you like." He turned and began limping after the PL soldiers. They fell into single file, with Cao bringing up the rear. As they began to move, he turned toward her one last time. "If I am wrong, and you DO see Ivorson again," he called out, "tell him that he hasn't heard the last of Tran van Cao."

The mere idea of seeing Peter Ivorson again made her want to retch. She watched the PL column cross the bridge and disappear into the scrub at the right side of the road. In a moment, the thick vegetation beyond the stream had swallowed them, and she was alone.

She glanced at her watch. My God! It was already after seven-thirty. She had arranged to meet Ly at nine, so she would have an alibi. She could never make it if she walked back to Don Dok. A sudden surge of panic engulfed her. She raced back to the muddy track that paralleled the stream and ran along it, past the charred and smoking remnants of what had been the jungle, until she reached the clearing.

Her sandaled feet splashed in the puddles of rainwater and muddied her clothes, but she didn't care about that. All she could think of was getting away from here! The motorcycle was on its kickstand, just where Peter had parked it. She shoved it off the stand and straddled the big machine, her Lao skirt hiked to her thighs. God damn Tran van Cao, she thought viciously. I would have worn pants, had I guessed this would happen.

By the time she was within half a kilometer of Don Dok, she was in a state of near-panic. She had passed five farm families, and every one of them turned and stared after her. At least some of them must have noticed the AID license plates. When the motorcycle was discovered, there would be an investigation, and at least one of those farmers would remember the girl with the light-skinned legs.

Her mind whirled around in circles, seeking some way out of her dilemma, but everything she thought of promised new disaster. Even if Peter had burned up, his body would be found. There would be an investigation. Lisa Odom would tell the authorities that Nga was Peter's girlfriend. She was sure to be questioned. She began crying from fright.

When she could make out the college buildings in the distance, she braked and checked the road ahead and behind. Only one man was in sight, and he was behind her, walking the other way. She found a shallow spot in the ditch and drove the motorcycle off the road. She paralleled it for almost a hundred meters, steering carefully between stumps and termite mounds, looking for a place to hide it.

She finally came to a small clump of thicker vegetation. She stopped the machine behind it, pushed it as far into the foliage as she could, and let it fall on its side. She couldn't conceal it completely. It was just a matter of time until the thing was found, but what else could she do?

She regained the road and walked as fast as she could to Don Dok. There were a number of students up and moving around the college grounds. They looked at her strangely. Every sideways glance increased her fear. When she finally saw herself in the mirror of a women's toilet, she understood the looks. Her clothes were torn and mud-splattered, her hair was bedraggled and dusty, and her face was marked with sweat and the traces of tears.

She tidied herself up as much as she could and made her way to the bus stop. There were a number of students waiting. They didn't pay her much mind, and she had begun to feel a little better when a Royal Lao Army convoy passed, going in the direction of the fire.

There were four big trucks, full of troops, all of them armed to the teeth. The sight made her fragile self-confidence melt in an instant. They would find the bodies—Peter's and the PL he had shot—and an investigation would begin. She couldn't possibly go home now!

Terror consumed her. She had to see Uncle Huu! He had promised her that if she did as he told her, she could stop this business forever. She had done her part. Now he must keep his word.

Cao had broken all of the promises Huu had made to her, but that was his fault, not Huu's. Uncle Huu was honorable, the only good man she had ever known. He would protect her.

When the bus arrived five minutes later, she took a seat as far to the rear as she could. She spent the journey back to Vientiane with her face buried in her arms, feigning sleep. Every time she heard the exhaust of a passing vehicle, her heart almost stopped beating from fright.

She left the bus at its first stop in town and spent her last few kip on a taxi to Khoualouang. It seemed to her that every pedestrian on the street turned and stared at her as they passed by.

She paid off the taxi and began walking down the dirt road that led to the Embassy. She passed a man beside the road polishing his motorcycle under the shade of a flame tree. He glanced incuriously at her and then looked at her again, this time with a startled expression on his face.

His attention turned her fear to stark terror. He must be a policeman, taking note of visitors to the Embassy. He must have recognized her! Unable to control herself any longer, she broke into a run. Sweat broke out on her face and arms. By the time she reached the Embassy gate, it was pouring from her. She grasped the bell rope inside the iron gates and pulled on it as if it was a lifeline, and she were adrift in an angry sea.

✲ ✲ ✲

Aghast at the news that Nga was on the Embassy grounds, it was all Huu could do to keep from running as he went to meet her in the little room behind the garage where the chauffeur had taken her.

"Are you mad?" he snapped, as soon as he had locked the door behind him. "What do you mean by coming here?"

She seized his hand in hers. "Please don't be angry, Uncle," she sobbed, her face shining with sweat and tears. "I could do nothing else."

Huu disentangled his hand from hers. "Calm yourself, Nga," he told her, trying to overcome his own agitation. "Why did you come here? What happened?"

Her story enraged and horrified him. How could his clever plan possibly have gone so terribly awry? Even the Pathet Lao should have been capable of handling that operation! And what had come over Mango? If Papaya's story were true, he had destroyed her cover by refusing to take her to Don Dok and to dispose of the motorcycle.

Still, no matter how badly things had gone for Papaya, for her to have come to the Embassy was incomprehensible, criminal.

"Why did you do it?" he demanded sternly. "You were almost certainly seen by the Lao surveillance."

Her tear-reddened eyes were wide with fright. "Where else could I go?" she gibbered. "I would have been arrested. I have to remain here. You have to give me asylum, uncle."

"Asylum?" The idea was absurd. "That is completely out of the question," he snapped. "The Ambassador wouldn't permit it. Suppose there IS a criminal investigation, and the Lao government learns you are here. They could demand that we hand you over for trial. The diplomatic and political embarrassment would be endless. No, it is impossible. You must return home immediately. The sooner, the better."

But even as he said it, it became apparent to him that it was not a valid solution. Papaya was right. Given the inevitability of finding both Ivorson's body and his motorcycle, there certainly would be an investigation, and she would sooner or later be interrogated.

"No, Uncle Huu," she wailed piteously. "It is too late. I will be arrested. You must keep me here!"

He heard the crackle of panic in her voice. She would never be able to resist interrogation. To save her own skin, she would reveal his plan to kidnap Ivorson. It would be a disaster. Both for the Embassy and for him, personally.

Should he dispose of her permanently? The threat she posed under the present circumstances justified such action. He tried to look at her dispassionately; to weigh the matter correctly in its revolutionary context. She was still the most beautiful and desirable woman he had ever seen, but she was weak, self-centered and cowardly.

Her eyes were fixed on him with a mixture of hope and dread. Her breasts rose and fell rapidly in time with her anxious breathing. He found his eyes drawn to their movement, and, frowning at his own weakness, shook his head violently to clear his mind of improper feelings.

She must have taken the frown and headshake as his final decision on her fate. She threw herself out of the chair she had been sitting at and fell at his feet, her arms around his legs. "Uncle, please, please, don't make me go! I will do anything you ask of me—anything—but don't let them arrest me."

She rose to her knees, her arms tight around his legs. He could feel the pressure of her breasts trembling against his thighs. Her face, turned up to his, was at the level of his waist. He tried to step away from her, but she held onto him as if for life itself.

"Uncle," she whispered, "You have always treated me properly, not like other men. I have always admired and liked you so much. Please, uncle, be kind to me. Take care of me." She buried her face in the front of his trousers.

Huu felt as if a gigantic electrical shock was running through his body. He looked wildly around. If anyone saw this, he was ruined! The door was locked, however, and the curtains were drawn over the windows.

Through the thin cotton trousers, he could feel her face against his sex. Betraying him, it rose to meet her. She felt it. She gave a little gasp, and pulled her head away. She looked up at him, tears flowing down her face, with an expression of hopeless desolation.

For a long moment they remained frozen like that. Huu wanted to tear himself away from her, but his body, paralyzed by desire, refused to obey his mind.

Before he could recover, she whispered, "As you wish, Uncle." With a sigh, she pressed her mouth against the bulge in the front of his trousers.

The sensation drove the air from his lungs in a long whistle. Slowly, reluctantly, as if in a dream, he reached down and took her face in his hands. "Perhaps we can send you to Hanoi," he heard himself say hoarsely.

Between his hands, her flushed, tear-streaked face produced a sad smile. "Thank you, Uncle Huu," she whispered. "I knew that you would help me."

Her grip on the back of his legs relaxed, and one of her tiny, shapely hands came into sight. It fluttered up his pants leg, caressed his aching penis for an instant, and then felt for the zipper on his pants. "I love you, Uncle Huu," she murmured, and pulled the zipper down.

Deeply ashamed of himself, Huu turned her face downward again and guided her lips over himself.

✡ ✡ ✡

Ivorson kicked very softly with his legs, trying not to make a splash, or even a ripple. The massive clump of foliage and debris scarcely responded to the impetus. Nonetheless, after a minute or so, he could see that he was slowly driving it toward the bank of the stream.

The little bridge had been out of sight behind him for a long time, and he had seen no more PL troops during his careful peeks at the jungle-clad banks, but he was taking no chances.

Jesus, that had been close! He had been certain that he was going to be killed by the fusillade of AK rounds. Their impact against the floating island and in the water around him had felt like a rain of massive fists against his head as he desperately clung to the roots of the mass of vegetation.

He had almost been out of air when the firing finally stopped. Thank God for the bridge! Its cover had let him get some oxygen back in his famished lungs before he floated back into the gunners' sights again. He had burst into silent tears of relief when he realized that they weren't going to fire any more.

He felt the mass of mud and plants lodge against the bank, and stopped kicking. He took a long, careful look at the vegetation on both banks from under his bullet-pierced cover of broad leaves. He saw nothing. Far upstream, only a faint haze revealed the site of the earlier forest fire.

Very slowly and quietly, he pulled himself around to the downstream side of his floating haven and then, feeling utterly exposed, slid out of the water, up the shallow bank of the stream and slithered like a snake into the shelter of the jungle.

It was much less dense in this location than it had been above the bridge. He burrowed into the foliage for a few yards and lay still. Nothing moved. He could hear nothing. He pulled the PPK from its water-logged holster, poured brown water from its barrel, and blew several long breaths down it. He hoped to God it would fire. He didn't dare disassemble and clean it.

Gun in hand, every nerve alert, he began to move through the vegetation, away from the Nam Khen. If he never saw it again, he thought, it would be too soon. Nonetheless, it had saved him. But for the muddy, rain-swollen stream, he would now be dead or a prisoner.

The memory of his betrayal by Nga gnawed at him. God, he had been so incredibly vain and stupid, thinking with his balls instead of his brain. He was a disgrace to his profession. And he could never have the catharsis of confession. Who could he tell? COS? Not a chance. That would absolutely destroy whatever slim hope he might still have of using Herbert Odom's balloon against the Vietnamese Embassy.

He tried to put the humiliation out of his mind and concentrate on what he was doing. He must be at least a mile south of the road he and Nga had taken to the Nam Khen, maybe more. His plan was to walk due east across-country until he came to either Route 13 or Don Dok. There would be friendlies at either place. In the meantime, however, he had to assume that anyone he met was hostile.

He walked slowly, watching where he put his feet. His progress was slow. He had no idea what the hour was. His watch had stopped, its crystal awash in water. It didn't matter. The sun was not yet at it zenith. He could afford to take his time. What he could not afford was another ambush.

For what he estimated to be an hour, he made his way eastward. The jungle cleared, becoming clear forest. He saw no one, but once, the sight of a thin column of smoke to his left forced him into a long detour.

When he felt certain he must be approaching the area of Don Dok, he turned north. The sun was high now. The morning freshness had long since disappeared, and the sky had not yet clouded over. Perhaps the tempo of the rainy season was slackening.

Cover became scarce. He flitted between the termite mounds and the rare trees. His mouth became dry with thirst. He heard the sound of a truck passing not far ahead. That must be the road. Warily, he approached. It was screened from sight by a band of thick scrub that bordered it. He followed a little path into the scrub and followed it toward the road.

Chapter Twenty-two

Ivorson cautiously pushed his head through the brush and looked up and down the road. To his right, in the distance, he could see the rooftops of the Teachers' College at Don Dok. To his left, no one was in sight. He holstered the PPK, stepped out of the shelter of the foliage, and began walking.

Twenty minutes later, he approached the bus stop at Don Dok. A number of cars and motorcycles had passed him during his walk, most of them going to the west—the site of the fire had clearly become a local tourist attraction—and while his appearance had drawn a great many curious stares, no one had challenged him.

He had been surprised to see no military vehicles. He didn't know whether they had not responded to the fire and the sound of shooting or they had, and were still at the scene. He wondered if they had found the man he had shot, and if enough remained of him for the cause of his death to be apparent. If his ambushers hadn't retrieved the AK, that would identify him as a Pathet Lao.

He reached the bus stop. The students politely avoided staring at him. As he lined up with them to get on the next bus, he was startled to see Orville drive past in the team taxi, coming from the direction of the fire.

Ivorson broke away from the line of passengers and sprinted after him down the road, waving his arms and shouting.

Thank God, Orville glanced in the rear-view mirror and jammed on the brakes. The taxi slid to a stop in the dust. Ivorson reached it, puffing, opened the passenger door and climbed in. "I am so glad you're here," he panted in Vietnamese. "But it can't be noon already. Why did you come so early?"

Orville's eyes avoided Ivorson's, "About an hour ago," he said, "our surveillant saw Nguyen thi Nga running into the North Vietnamese Embassy. She was dressed in Lao clothing and was dirty and sweaty. The surveillant notified me, and I went to your house to tell you. When I saw your note to Oum, I feared that you had been out here with her, and I came to look for you."

"Nga ran into the Viet Embassy?" She must have panicked when there was no sign of Ivorson or his body and sought refuge there. That couldn't have made Nguyen van Huu very happy.

"Yes. The surveillant said that she looked very frightened." Orville's eyes finally met Ivorson's. "You were very foolish, patron. Nguyen thi Nga is the daughter of a notorious Northern sympathizer."

Oh? If that was true, foolish was the most charitable adjective Orville could have used. "I checked her out carefully when I met her," he heard him saying defensively.

"You did not check her out with my brother," Orville answered dryly.

Touché, Ivorson thought ruefully. He had deliberately not done so, knowing that the idea of his consorting with any Vietnamese would send Wilbur through the roof. "But what made you think I had come out here with her?" he asked.

"Oum found long black hairs in your bed when she made it this morning. She had found them once before. I put two and two together." Orville's gaze was accusing. "You should have told me, patron. Our family's life depends on you."

The Asian's quiet words made Ivorson feel deeply ashamed. What Orville had just said was true. Their family did indeed depend for its survival on Ivorson's professionalism, and he had utterly failed them.

"I apologize to you, Orville," he said. "To you, and all your family. I risked your lives foolishly."

The Black Thai shook his head and gave Ivorson a wry smile, which for a moment made him look a great deal like Wilbur. "My brother also took foolish risks over women," he said, "and he had some narrow escapes from husbands that he did not tell you about, either. The main thing is, you survived it." He gave a jerk of his chin at Ivorson's clothes. "What happened?"

Ivorson told him the story, briefly but honestly. The loss of face involved was immense. It would not be surprising if the whole team quit on him.

Orville maintained a poker face throughout the recital. Only at the mention of Tran van Cao's role did he reveal his emotions. "That cobra," he muttered. "Buddha strike me dead if I do not kill him some day!"

At the end of the recital, Orville said, "If the Viets learn that you survived the fire, they will stop at nothing to kill you. They must be made to believe the burned body the Army found in the jungle was really yours. Can your service arrange that with the Lao authorities?"

It was an excellent suggestion. Ivorson had already considered it. The problem, of course, was that it could not be arranged. At least, not without letting the Chief of Station know the whole story, and that was out of the question.

Ivorson was trapped in a web of deceit that he had spun himself, and he would have to get out of it, or perish in it, alone.

"You go ahead and start the rumor in the marketplace that a white man's body was found," he answered. "We'll see if we can get the cooperation of the Lao government. In any case, you're right. I'll have to find somewhere to hide out."

There was no question about that last statement. Nga was a source of enormous value to Nguyen van Huu. After all, she'd just barely missed turning Ivorson into the Vietnamese intelligence coup of the war. If Huu could get her out of the Embassy and back to work at USAID, where she could be targeted against other Station officers in the future, he would certainly want to do so.

But for that to work, Ivorson would have to have died in the fire. Huu would therefore do everything he could to be certain of that fact. He had probably already put Ivorson's house and the USAID gate under surveillance, regardless of the risk to his surveillants. He would also be watching the Guesthouse and any locations where his people might have observed Ivorson in the past. The safe house could be under observation, for all Ivorson knew. After all, he had no idea how long Huu had had him watched before he spotted the surveillance.

He might only have a few days remaining in Vientiane, but if he wanted to survive them, he had to go to ground at some location where he had never been before, where Huu and his local sympathizers would not be looking for him, but which still would give him access to the Station (without the need to explain the situation to COS, however) and also let him stay in touch with Lisa Odom's father. He could think of only one place in Laos that filled all those requirements.

✲ ✲ ✲

Lisa's eyes widened and her mouth dropped as she took in the condition of his clothes. "What on earth happened to you?"

"I fell off my motorcycle," he said shortly. "Is your Dad here?" Mr. Odom was a whole lot more likely to be on Ivorson's side than Lisa was.

She ignored the question. "Your eyebrows are singed off," she said accusingly, "you reek of smoke, and you're mud from head to foot. You haven't been in any motorcycle accident. You're lying to me again. You just can't help it, can you? It's as natural to you as breathing."

He wasn't in any mood for one of her sermons. "All right," he snapped. "You want the truth? I had a really serious kidnapping attempt made on me this morning, followed closely by several murder attempts. I have to stay out of sight until your Dad has that balloon ready to fly. I don't dare go home, or to a hotel, or to any other place I've ever slept since I got to Laos. I need to stay here. An empty servant's quarters will do, or I'll sleep on the floor."

Her features reflected horror, then fear, and finally amazed anger. "People are trying to kidnap and kill you, and you want to stay here? What about me? What about my father?" Her voice rose with each question, and her face turned pink. "What about your promise that you had been here for the last time until you came to get the monstrosity you conned my Dad into building?"

He didn't have any good answers for her. "I didn't think this was going to happen," he told her defensively, "but it's not as bad as it sounds. The Viets think I'm dead. I wasn't followed here, and the Mission Guard on the gate is a Lao. It should be all right."

Her cheeks were bright red now. "Should! Should isn't good enough for me, Peter Ivorson!"

"It's good enough for me, honey." Her father's voice came from the hall to the bedroom wing. Mr. Odom crossed the living room toward them. "Good morning, Peter," he said. "Glad you came by. I just got the thing finished. Let me show it to you."

He and Ivorson shook hands. Lisa sputtered then got her voice back. "No, Dad, this time I am not going to give in. Peter wants us to risk our lives to shelter him. I might do it myself,"—her face turned red again—"but I am absolutely not going to risk you. I'm sorry, Peter, the answer is no. You have to go."

The time had come for Ivorson to play his trump card. He hadn't wanted to use it, since it made him out to be an even bigger sucker than Lisa, but he had to do something to make her feel guilty about his situation.

"Do you remember the fit I threw in your office?" he asked her, "the first day I was in Laos, because Vietnamese employees might have access to my personnel records? Well, I was right about that, and you were wrong."

She scowled. "My God, Peter, you really aren't going to start that story again, are you?"

"Nguyen thi Nga is hiding in the North Vietnamese Embassy right this minute," he assured her, "after having failed in her attempt to turn me over to a Pathet Lao hit squad this morning out at Don Dok."

Lisa's eyes widened in disbelief. Then they began moving again over his torn, scorched and filthy clothes. When they reached his battered hands, the color drained from her face. She sat down very carefully on the arm of the rattan sofa.

"Peter," she said softly, "swear to me that you're not lying. Did Nga really do something like that? Has she really gone to the North Vietnamese Embassy?"

He could hear the first hint of self-accusation in her voice and tried to make the most of it. "It's true, I swear. She was seen going in there about nine o'clock this morning, after she tried to burn me alive in a forest fire. That's why I have to hide. If the Viets can be sure I'm dead, then Nga can safely go back to work at USAID, to look for another sucker."

Lisa shuddered. "Burn you alive?" she repeated. "How horrible." Her eyes suddenly grew enormous, and she turned pale. "I'm sorry, Peter," she whispered. "This is my fault. You weren't paranoid after all. Not at all. Later on, I caught Nga in the file room, looking at your file, and I didn't tell you. She told me she loved you, and I believed her."

She began to cry, and he knew he had her. He was shocked by what he'd just heard, and he supposed he should be furious with her for not having told him about the file room incident. Instead, idiotically, he felt wetness welling in his own eyes. "I thought she loved me too," he said.

✲ ✲ ✲

Half an hour later, after a bath, Ivorson, bulging out of a shirt and slacks of Herbert Odom's, was in the guest bedroom with the older man. "I had a hell of a lot of fun putting this thing together, Peter," Herb told him. "It's going to fly a lot better than it looks."

Ivorson hoped so. It was the strangest looking, jury-rigged apparatus he had ever seen. It didn't have the weather balloon inflated above it, of course, but once it did, it would look like the whimsical creation of a Victorian cartoonist.

"I'll need for you to get me a cargo net from one of the USAID-leased airplanes," Mr. Odom said. "We'll use that to tie the weather balloon to this wooden rod, which forms the backbone of the thing."

The rod in question was a four-foot long dowel of some tropical hardwood, about two inches in diameter. Clamped under the front of it was a small electrical fan, the kind you find in taxi cabs in Southeast Asia. Immediately behind the fan was the small 12-volt DC battery that powered it. Suspended from the midpoint of the dowel, and hanging well below the fan motor, was the sheet metal carrier which would hold the video camera, transmitter and its battery. From its bottom dangled a thick metal ring.

Behind the carrier came a series of three small gray plastic boxes, connected to each other by electrical wire. From the bottom of the rear-most of these protruded a flat metal wheel with holes drilled in its perimeter. Stiff metal wires ran rearward from two of the holes to metal arms protruding from each side of the eight-inch square plastic rudder that hung down from the rear end of the rod.

Mr. Odom pointed to the three plastic boxes. "I called back to the States for those. They just got here yesterday."

He made Ivorson hold the dowel while he threaded a nylon cord through a metal ring clamped to the top of it at its mid-point. Then he climbed on a chair and hung the loop on the cord's other end over a large hook screwed into the bedroom ceiling.

"This simulates the lift we'll get from the balloon," he said. "I've got it balanced right for its present load. That will change, of course, when you add the camera. You can add additional balance weights then, so it stays level in flight."

He completed his knot and motioned for Ivorson to release the dowel. It hung bobbing at the end of the cord, perfectly balanced.

Mr. Odom led Ivorson over to the chest of drawers. From the top drawer, he took a metal and plastic rectangle with an antenna protruding from its top and two small joysticks on its face. Ivorson recognized it as a radio transmitter for a model airplane.

"Okay, now," Mr. Odom explained. "You've got the balloon attached to the rod by the cargo net. If the weight figures you gave me for the camera, battery, and tether rope are correct, the total load will be right at thirty pounds, which you say the balloon can lift."

Ivorson nodded agreement.

"So," Odom continued, "the balloon lifts it up in the air. To keep it from flying off and to control its altitude, we'll have tethering rope run through that ring you see there on the bottom of the camera carrier."

Ivorson suddenly visualized how it would work. "I get it," he said, "and if we fill the balloon carefully, so that it just barely flies, one man should be able to handle the tether. So, we get in place and inflate the balloon. It goes up. We hold it with the—"

Mr. Odom interrupted him. "Not so fast. Before you let it go, you turn on the fan motor." He crossed over to the fan and suited action to the words. The little plastic blade became a whirling disk. Ivorson could barely hear its hum. In response to the little propeller's thrust, the dowel tried to move forward.

"It can't go anywhere when you're holding onto the tether rope," Mr. Odom explained, "but the airstream it creates over the rudder lets you turn it right or left to aim your camera."

He pointed the antenna of the transmitter at the wooden rod and pushed the right-hand joystick to the right. The plastic disc moved, the rudder followed it, and a moment later, the nose of the dowel began to swing in their direction. Mr. Odom centered the joystick. The dowel stopped moving. A push to the left sent the nose of the dowel back to, and then beyond, its original position.

"That's it," he said proudly. "The left-hand stick is the throttle control, which you don't use with this rig. The one on the right gives you full control over direction and altitude. You aim the lens at your target by looking through the monitor on the ground, and you make whatever corrections you need. Want to practice?"

Ivorson certainly did. This thing might not be as sophisticated as the blimp, and he'd have to get himself awfully close to the wall of the North Vietnamese Embassy compound to use it, but it would work, by God, and he wanted to be just as skillful in maneuvering it as he possibly could be when he demonstrated it to the Chief of Station.

Chapter Twenty-three

After dark, he had Lisa drive him to within a block of the safe house. The dowel (he couldn't think of anything else to call it) was in the back seat.

They didn't exchange more than two words on the way. The feeling between them was strained, even though there wasn't any anger left in it. It was almost as if they were too embarrassed to talk.

He got out on the corner and walked to the safe house, carrying the dowel and its cargo over his shoulder. He risked attracting attention, of course, with his strange burden, and the safe house itself could be under surveillance, but those were both chances he had to take.

What he couldn't do was put Lisa and her father at risk by calling COS from her house. Besides, he had to be able to demonstrate the thing to COS and talk about the operation, and he couldn't do that in their presence, so the safe house it had to be. As a last resort, he had the PPK with him.

If there was surveillance on the safe house, he couldn't see it. He let himself in and turned on the lights and window air conditioners. In spite of the rains, the interior was very hot.

The Chief of Station answered his call on the third ring. "Hello," Ivorson said. "I've got some good news for you."

"Where the hell have you been all day?" demanded Riley.

"I've been trying to reach you since noon."

That put Ivorson off his game plan. "What did you want me for?"

"To tell you to pack your bags," Riley said. "You're on the Royal Air Lao flight to Bangkok on Tuesday afternoon, connecting with Pan Am 2 that same night. It's the first flight we could get you on."

Jesus! COS really wanted to get rid of him. It didn't look good for the balloon operation, but this was his last chance. "Okay," he said, "Tuesday it is, but listen, can you come over to the usual place? I've got something to show you that

I know you'll be really interested in. I've been working on it all day. That's why you couldn't get me."

"I can't imagine anything you might have to show me that I'd be interested in, Ivorson," COS answered. Ivorson could hear faint traces of Scotch in Riley's voice, but he ploughed ahead. It was all he could do.

"You know the thing we lost last week in Udorn? Well, I've got a substitute for it, a damn good one. One we can use right now." An inspiration struck him. "Before the water in the swamp gets too deep to work in. I've got it here with me. Come on in, and I'll show it to you." He was practically pleading. If Riley saw Herb Odom's gadget, there was at least a faint hope that he'd get intrigued by it.

Riley's next words killed that hope and all others, as well. "Listen, to me, Ivorson, and listen good," he said. "I wouldn't come in and see you if you had the twin sister of what you lost in Udorn. You're a fuck-up, Ivorson. You fucked up everything you touched while you were here, and in the process you fucked me with Washington. Now it's my turn to fuck you, and I'm not only going to do it, I'm going to enjoy every single minute of it."

Riley's voice sounded as if he were already enjoying himself. "This is an order, Ivorson," he said. "Go home, pack your bags, and stay home until the USAID van comes for you to take you to the airport on Tuesday. The driver will bring the tickets with him. Don't see anyone else, don't call anyone else, and destroy what the hell ever cockamamie gizmo you've got there with you. Is that understood?"

Ivorson was in despair. He'd been attacked by snakes, hit in the balls and shot, lost the best agent in the whole world, almost been kidnapped, and damn near been burned alive for this operation, and now he was being shut out of it and sent home as Riley's scapegoat.

"Do you hear me, Ivorson?" It was almost a scream.

"Yeah," Ivorson muttered. "I hear you." He hung up the phone, and only then added, "But I'll be goddamned if I'm going to obey you."

✲ ✲ ✲

Nga felt frozen, suspended in an emotional void. All around her were the sights and sounds of the terminal at Wattay Airport, the lilting cadence of the Lao language, the smells of garlic and fish sauce and hot peppers. These familiar things had surrounded her since childhood, but she already felt divorced from them by an immeasurable gulf, as if the old four-motor Boeing out on the tarmac had already flown away with her into the night sky.

In the few hours since her panicked flight to the Embassy, she had lost everything she had ever had: country, home, job, mother, and—the most devastating loss of all—hope.

She had cried a Mekong flood of tears on the narrow bed in the servants' quarters behind the garage. She had said and thought, "If only" a million times, until it ran through her mind like the litany of the rosary the nuns had taught her at the French cathedral school when she was a little girl.

She used to feel sorry for herself, after her father left Vientiane, because no one came to get her after school or watched her perform in school programs. She would trade the merit of a million rosaries now to be that lonely little girl again.

Nguyen van Huu, whom she had always idolized for his kindness and proper behavior, had proved to have not only feet of clay, but a sex of hard flesh, just like all the other men who had used her over the years.

He sat beside her now on the concrete bench in the diplomatic passengers' lounge; cool, proper, aloof, without the least indication that less than two hours ago he had been grunting on top of her. She shifted her position a bit to keep from touching him. Of all that she had suffered, his treatment of her was by far the bitterest torment.

She had been cruelly disillusioned by his first sexual demand on her this morning; but still, knowing that he had always been attracted to her, she had at first believed that his passion had overcome his revolutionary Puritanism, and that what he had made her do was basically the result of a lover's ardor.

Nga could have pardoned, perhaps even welcomed, the comfort of physical love. But after that first time, he became completely depraved, and did things to her that no man had ever done before.

Love had no place in it. The kindness and consideration he had shown her in the past vanished with the satisfaction of his first erection. Nor had there been any more talk of her being a heroine in the war against the imperialists. It was as if her passage to Hanoi had become a whore's fee, and she had become the prostitute he had made her behave like in the name of patriotism.

It was even worse than that. It was as if he were using his body to punish her, to exact satisfaction from her for some crime she had committed against him.

But what had she done wrong? She had asked the question of herself again and again. She had obeyed his instructions. She had kept her side of their bargain faithfully. She had given him her body. Why then, had he become so cruel? She had begged him to explain, but he would not answer.

There had been no one else to turn to. She was held prisoner in her room behind the garage, with bolted doors and windows. Aside from Huu, the only other person she had seen until they arrived at the airport was the Black Thai chauffeur, Cam, who brought her lunch and dinner. He met her efforts at conversation with silence. She had asked to see her mother, but even that request had been refused.

A repetitive, insistent tapping sound imposed itself on her grief-numbed mind. Her eyes and ears slowly located the source of the sound behind the thick, louvered glass windows in the wall which separated the diplomatic lounge from the other passengers.

There, on the other side of the glass, were her mother and Ly! Nga sprang to her feet and ran toward them. Huu, instantly on her heels, grasped her arm roughly and pulled her back. "You are to tell your mother only that you are happy to be going home," he growled. "You are not to talk to Ly at all."

She tore herself loose and pressed herself against the wall, frantically turning the handle that opened the glass panels. She pushed her hands between the panes and grasped their fingers. "Mother!" she cried, "I am so glad to see you. Ly, my sweet Ly! How did you know I was here?"

"A friend in the International Control Commission office came by our home and told me your name had been added to the manifest," sobbed Ly, her plain face distorted by grief. "Why, Nga? Why? Where have you been? What has happened?"

"Do not answer her," repeated Huu, behind her. "Go home," he snarled at Ly. "You should not have come here. You will only upset her."

Nga's mother's face was ravaged by grief. "My daughter!" she sobbed, "what will I do without you? How will I sleep, knowing that you are under the bombs of the American warplanes? Where will you live? Where can I write you?"

Every word was a burning sliver of bamboo thrust into Nga's mind, setting it ablaze with terror of the unknown. "I don't know, Mama," she wailed. "They won't tell me anything."

"She will be well taken care of," said Huu, now at her side. "Arrangements will be made for you to correspond. Go home now, both of you. You are upsetting her and creating a scene." His voice was hard, angry, threatening.

"Ly," Nga blurted, "have you heard from Peter?"

She felt Huu's hands, like steel claws, dig into her arms. On the other side of the glass Ly began crying again.

"He is dead, Nga. He was burned up in a fire out by the Nam Khen this morning. The story was all over the market today. The Army found his body, and his motorcycle is missing. They say he was killed by robbers."

Nga burst into tears, too, but hers were tears of relief. He was dead. There would still be an investigation, no doubt, but no one would ever know what had really happened. Her full role would never be revealed.

Suddenly, Nga knew that she mustn't let Huu send her to Hanoi. She might lose her job or even go to jail if she stayed here, but no matter what the Lao government did to her, it would be better than life in North Vietnam, without family or friends, under the bombs of the Americans, and despised for her mixed blood by fanatics like Huu.

She clung to Ly's hands with all her strength. "I don't want to go," she cried aloud. "I have changed my mind!"

She heard Huu's gasp of rage. His grip tightened on her, hurting her. He began to drag her bodily away from the window. "Shut up, you idiot," he hissed in her ear. "It is too late for such nonsense."

Nga was beside herself with fear. "Save me, Mama," she cried. "I want to stay with you."

Her mother's face contorted with pain and confusion. Ly turned away from the window and ran off down the hall. Huu dragged Nga, still screaming and crying, bodily into the toilet of the waiting room. He kicked the door closed behind them and slammed her violently against the wall. Her head hit hard. She saw flashing lights and her knees gave out from under her.

Huu knelt beside her. "Listen to me, you half-breed bitch," he snarled. "You came sniveling to me for help. You insisted that you could not go home, even when I told you that you could. It is too late now to change your mind, far too late. The Ambassador himself intervened with the Ministry in Hanoi to get you out of Laos, and you are going."

His face swam back into focus before Nga's eyes. She had never seen such distilled hatred and contempt in a man's face before. "If you make one more outcry," he promised her, "you will be sent to a labor reform camp." His mouth twisted in a grimace of disgust. "I was a fool to let you tempt me," he hissed. "I should have had you killed."

When the ICC plane took off, half an hour later, she was on it. She had not said another word, either to the Lao officials summoned by Ly, to Ly herself, or even to her mother. Strapped into her seat, she watched the few faint lights on the ground fade away, replaced by the darkness of the night and the jungle below.

The blackness that pervaded her heart and mind was far, far darker. It's not fair, she kept telling herself. It's just not fair.

✡ ✡ ✡

Ivorson called Orville and told him to come get him, then mixed a very stiff drink from the bottle in the safe house. While he waited for the taxi, he worked on the drink and brooded about Riley's orders. He had to admit that COS had put the case very succinctly. Ivorson had fucked Riley. Ergo, Riley would fuck Ivorson. Tit for tat.

There were only two possible courses of action available to Ivorson, now: One, he could obey the Chief of Station like a good soldier, go home, and either quit the Agency or, over a period of years, patiently rebuild the reputation and career that Riley had destroyed. And incidentally, see someone else carry out and be rewarded for the operation that Ivorson had been brought here to do, and had made possible.

Or two, he could go ahead on his own, not only without authorization, but against orders, and use Herbert Odom's home-made masterpiece to film the decryption of the Monday night radio traffic from Hanoi.

If he chose the latter option and succeeded, the glory for all involved would be of such magnitude that Riley, in order to claim credit for it himself, would have no choice but to cover up Ivorson's disobedience. On the other hand, if Ivorson failed... Well, there were still two possibilities: If he just failed and didn't get caught in the process, he wouldn't be any worse off than he was now, so why not go for it?

On the other hand, if the Viets caught him at it, and the future operation with the blimp was foreclosed as a result, he would not only be finished with the Agency, he would be a pariah forever in the eyes of his peers.

Orville announced his presence outside with a soft toot of the horn. Ivorson packed the dowel out to the cab and asked Orville to drive him back out to Rainbow Village. He still hadn't decided what he was going to do when they arrived. He told Orville to take the dowel home with him and expect a phone call from Ivorson tomorrow or the next day. That way, he could preserve his options.

After a rough night on the rattan couch in Lisa's living room, tormented not only by his singed flesh and aching muscles, but also by dreams of Nga, he wasn't any closer to making up his mind. Disgusted with his own indecision, he decided that Hamlet had it right: Conscience really does make cowards of us all.

Lisa took her father to church and to lunch at the ACA. Ivorson stayed in the house, looking out the window over the water-filled rice paddies at the distant blue mass of Phou Khou Khoay, jutting into the sky. It was an idyllic scene, but up there, in the mountains, the Meo tribesmen were fighting and dying against the Pathet Lao and their Vietnamese advisors.

Lisa and her Dad came home around one o'clock. She was pale and wouldn't meet his eyes. "What's happened?" he asked her, when her father had gone into his bedroom. "You look as if you've seen a ghost."

"I'm looking at one right now," she told him, "if you can believe the story going around the ACA."

"What do you mean?"

"Everyone thinks you got burned up out at the Nam Khen yesterday," she said tersely.

"You didn't tell them I'm here, did you?" he asked in alarm.

She shook her head, with a frown. "No. You've succeeded in making me an accomplice to your lying."

He let that go by. After a moment of silence, she said, "There's more."

He looked at her questioningly. "Oh? What?"

"Nguyen thi Nga took the ICC flight to Hanoi last night." She started to say something further, then abruptly turned and went to her bedroom, leaving Ivorson alone.

His initial reaction was raging fury. The bitch had got away from him! He stormed around the living room, wanting to throw something and knowing that he couldn't do it without bringing both Lisa and her father on the run to find out what the matter was. He wanted desperately to get out of the house and run himself into exhaustion, but he didn't dare.

His inability to do anything but sit and brood was maddening. He was tempted to get drunk, but couldn't do that, either. He needed to think straight.

Later in the afternoon, in a moment of insight, he recognized that his anger was, at least in part, a mental subterfuge, a cover to mask the hollow feeling in his guts at the realization that he would never see her again. That knowledge didn't quench his anger, but redirected it at himself.

And also at Nguyen van Huu.

Huu was Nga's case officer. He was the one who had directed her to become Ivorson's lover, to lure him out to the Nam Khen; the man to whom she had run when the operation backfired, and who had sent her off to the dubious safety of Hanoi.

Huu was Ivorson's true nemesis. He had hemmed Ivorson in on all sides ever since his arrival in Vientiane. Ivorson had been humiliated, battered, and shot. He'd come within a hair's breadth of torture and death, all at Huu's instigation. And Wilbur had died.

Ivorson finally made up his mind. There was only one way he could continue to live with himself, and that was to even the score with Nguyen van Huu.

When Lisa came back out of the bedroom half an hour later, he told her, "I need for you to give me a ride into USAID tonight."

It was almost eleven when they were waved into the compound by the Mission Guard. Ivorson was lying on the floor of the back seat, covered by Lisa's dark blue beach towel. "Drive around behind the warehouse and park," he told her. "You can wait in the car. I won't be more than five minutes."

He let himself into the tech's shop and went to work picking up the items on his shopping list. First of all, the spare TV camera with its transmitter; then the receiver, the video recorder and its film; next came the small steel bottle of helium, brought back from the debacle in Udorn by Jack Lawrence; then two of the weather balloons he'd got from the weather officer during his first trip down there—it seemed like a lifetime ago; and finally, a waterproof watch; the fishing seine from his survival kit; and the same black wig and brown pancake make-up he'd had on the night Wilbur was killed.

Even at this distance in time, the memory of that night was hard to live with. Orville was a good, reliable, troop, but Wilbur had been one in a million.

He loaded his booty in the trunk of Lisa's Impala, climbed back into the back seat and lay down again on the floor. After they'd gone back out through the compound's exit gate, he permitted himself the luxury of sitting up and letting Lisa chauffeur him back to Rainbow Village in style. He saw her looking repeatedly at him in the mirror, but she didn't break the silence between them that had started after she told him about Nga.

She was on leave during her father's visit, so on Monday morning, she took him on an outing to the Five Five Five Cigarette Company's garden, out on the Tha Deua Road, leaving Ivorson alone in the house. He passed the treacle-slow hours reading *The Brothers Karamazov*. He also made a call to Orville.

Lisa and her father came back after lunch. She was visibly agitated. When her father went to take a nap, she whispered to him, "I went into the office for a minute. Did you know that you're supposed to leave Laos tomorrow?"

He nodded. "Yeah. Riley told me about that."

She bit her lip. "Shouldn't you go pack or something?"

"You'll have to put up with me just a little longer," he told her, "but I'll be leaving here this evening." She reddened, wheeled around, and returned to the bedroom. "I appreciate your patience," he called after her.

She didn't answer.

At four o'clock, the phone rang. Mr. Odom, who had awakened from his nap and was chatting with Ivorson, answered it. "It's for you, Lisa," he called. "A Mr. Riley." Ivorson jumped to his feet.

He wasn't surprised that Riley was looking for him. Lawrence would have noticed that the TV camera and helium bottle were missing, and he would have told the Chief of Station about it. When Ivorson didn't answer the phone at home, Riley would have suspected the worst.

But why was he calling Lisa? He couldn't possibly suspect that Ivorson was here. Or could he?

Lisa came out of the bedroom to answer the phone. Ivorson met her in the middle of the living room. "I'm not here!" he whispered in her ear.

She stared at him in amazement. "What do you mean, you're not here?" she hissed back. "That's your boss calling."

"I know it is," he snapped at her. "That's why I'm not here."

Her eyes grew enormous. "I can't lie to Mr. Riley, Peter."

He held her arm tighter. "You owe me Lisa," he told her fiercely. "If you had told me about Nga and my file, I wouldn't be hiding out here to begin with." It was a lie and a lousy thing to do to Lisa, but if Riley suspected what he was up to, one false note in her voice would bring a car-load of Station heavies down on Ivorson's head.

She gave him an angry, agonized look, tore her arm away from his hand, and marched over to take the phone from her father. Ivorson followed her, got hold of her arm again, and put his head against hers on the other side of the phone receiver. She smelled like apple blossoms.

"Hello? This is Lisa."

"Miss Odom?" Riley's voice came faintly to Ivorson's ears. "This is Terence Riley. Do you have any idea where Peter Ivorson might be?"

She threw Ivorson a pained look. He shook his head violently, and silently mouthed at her, "You owe me."

She bit her lip in indecision for an instant, and then said, in a pained voice, "Why, no, Mr. Riley. I heard he was dead. There's a rumor that his body was found out by Don Dok on Saturday. Isn't that true?"

There was a long pause at the other end of the line, then Riley said, "No, that's not true."

"Oh, I'm so glad to hear it," Lisa said, much less artificially. "I'm on leave, you know," she added, "so I haven't heard the official version."

"Yes, I understand that you've been out of the office," Riley said, "and I'm sorry to bother you at home. I just thought you might have seen him somewhere. If you do, let me know immediately, will you?"

"Yes, of course," she said. The instant she hung up, she rounded on Ivorson. "We're even now, Peter Ivorson!" she snapped. "I don't owe you anything, and I never want you to speak to me again! You've turned me into a liar, and I hate you!" She tore herself from his grasp and stormed back into the bedroom wing.

Her father looked at Ivorson quizzically. "She certainly does get mad at you a lot, Peter," he said calmly. "Why do you suppose that is?"

They ate a very quiet, very uncomfortable dinner. Lisa didn't say a single word, either to Ivorson or to her father. The two men tried to carry on a semblance of normal conversation, but the only effect was to increase the feeling of abnormality.

At a little after seven, the muted beep of the taxi's horn sounded outside. Ivorson threw down *The Brothers Karamazov*, got up, and walked over to shake hands with Mr. Odom. "Thanks very much for all your help," he said. "If you don't hear anything else about this business, you'll know it went okay. I hope that's the way it works out. Tell Lisa I'm sorry I had to impose on her the way I have."

The older man squeezed his hand tightly. "If that's how it is," he answered, "then I don't want to hear any more about you. Good luck, Peter. God bless you."

Embarrassed by the final phrase, Ivorson nodded and turned toward the door. He was halfway there when Lisa's bedroom door opened with a bang, there was a flutter of footsteps down the hall, and she burst into the living room. She crossed it at a dead run, and hurled her arms around Ivorson.

"Be careful," she sobbed. "Please be careful."

Ivorson had always fancied himself a pretty good judge of women. He'd been around a lot; he'd known a lot of them; he'd had at least his share of them in bed. But this girl left him absolutely baffled. "Uh, yeah, sure," he muttered, "I will."

She raised a tear-stained face to his. "Call me when it's over. Promise. No matter how late it is." She squeezed him with surprising strength. "Promise!"

Hugely embarrassed, he murmured, "Uh, okay, okay. I promise." Across the room, he was startled to see tears in her father's eyes, too.

"Yes, Peter, call her. Call us both," the older man said.

The two old cars, their headlights extinguished, thumped and banged their way across the dike between the rice paddies. The taxi led, driven by a family member to whom Ivorson was not introduced. Its other occupants were Ivorson, Orville, and Chan, Orville's cousin who had spotted Nguyen van Huu going into Khouadine before Ivorson went to Bangkok.

Thirty yards behind them came Wilbur's old Datsun, laden with their equipment and driven, surprisingly, by Sengdara. When Ivorson asked Orville why the girl was involved, he had replied, "She already knows your face. Also, she feels badly about what happened. She wants to help."

Ivorson almost responded that if she screwed up this operation the way she had the Cam recruitment, they'd be better off without her, but he'd clamped his mouth shut on it. He needed all the friends he could get this evening.

The cars stopped. The brake and interior light bulbs had been removed from both of them. Ivorson, Chan, and Orville got out of the taxi into the darkness and quietly closed the doors. They had rehearsed their next moves verbally, earlier tonight at Orville's house.

Ivorson ran back to the waiting Datsun, opened the front passenger door and carefully withdrew the wooden rod with its attached hardware, which was balanced on the tops of the front and rear seats.

From the trunk of the taxi, Chan removed the bamboo basket which contained his load: the black-painted weather balloons, the tether rope, and the helium bottle. He slung the basket on his shoulders and came to join Ivorson.

The taxi's trunk also contained the video camera, its battery, and the transmitter. Orville got them out and joined Ivorson. They loaded the camera and battery in the carrier under the wooden rod and secured them in place by the minimal light of a taped-over penlight bulb. Then Orville went to the Datsun's trunk for the backpack containing the video monitor, recorder and the fifty foot long nylon tether rope.

Just as he shouldered the pack with the monitor, headlights appeared at the intersection of the dike and the road they had just turned off of, two hundred yards to their south. "Hurry, Chan," Orville grunted, coiling the tether rope over his shoulder. "Into the swamp!" He closed the trunk and called softly to the drivers, "Go now! No lights until you are off the dike. Return at eleven. Go!"

Ivorson heard Sengdara say, "Good luck," and then the engines revved and the cars clattered away into the darkness.

"Come quickly," Orville urged Ivorson. "No one must see us." Ivorson needed no encouragement. If they were spotted at this point, the operation would be lost forever. He hoisted the dowel—it was surprisingly heavy—on his shoulder and followed Orville into the water.

He immediately sank to above his waist. He grimaced. The water was much deeper than it had been two months ago when Wilbur and he were out here the last time. The torrential rains of the last week had made a big difference.

Thank God it hadn't rained since Friday night. He needed to get away from the road as quickly as possible, and any more water would have made rapid motion impossible. He had to move very slowly as it was. He also had to be very careful of his footing. If he slipped or fell into a hole and the camera got wet, that was the end of everything.

The headlights were getting closer. He tried to ignore them and concentrate on following Orville, who, also heavily laden with water-sensitive equipment, was just ahead of him. Chan was already out of sight in the darkness.

The headlights were quite close now, no more than thirty yards. "Stop!" Ivorson hissed in Vietnamese, the agreed language of the operation.

They were all dressed in black, and with blackened faces and hands, even this close to the road, the greatest risk of their becoming noticed would come from motion rather than their forms.

They froze. An eternity passed as the car, a Peugeot diesel by the sound of it, labored past their position and disappeared to the north. Ivorson's lungs sucked in the night air with a whoosh. He hadn't realized he had been holding his breath.

Orville took the lead now, and Chan fell in behind Ivorson. They moved slowly and carefully. Time was not a problem; it was still fifty minutes until time for the Viets' ten o'clock radio schedule with Hanoi. The main thing was not to get the equipment wet and, above all, not to be seen or heard. Tonight was the only chance. Tomorrow, win, lose or die, Ivorson would be gone.

The water was marginally shallower now, but still waist deep. He could hear the boiling sound the leeches made around his legs as his passage disturbed them, but his pants legs and shirt cuffs were tied tight with cord, his sex sheathed with Trojan's finest product, and his bunghole securely plugged. Anyway, he had bigger problems to worry about than leeches.

He was reasonably confident about the operation of the equipment, despite the fact that their only rehearsal had been at Orville's house this evening while they waited for the time to move out. He, Orville, and Chan practiced what had to be done to load the balloon gondola and fill the black-stained neoprene sphere over and over, until they were able to do it in silence, without a bobble.

He wished he felt as good about their chances of escaping detection. The tether rope was only fifty feet long, and to get really useable quality video, they might have to get the camera even closer to the code room window than that. Everything was painted matte black, but even so, it was going to be a hell of a big, funny looking thing floating up there in the sky, and if they WERE spotted, they would be sitting ducks.

He tried to put that thought out of his mind and concentrate on some positive aspect of the operation.

He could think of only two, off-hand: first of all, it was wonderfully dark. The moon wasn't scheduled to rise until after eleven o'clock, and a thin cloud cover partially veiled the stars. The only light he could see, other than the lights of the buildings ahead of them, was an occasional flash of lightning from a cumulus cloud that half-filled the western sky.

The other good news was the simple fact that he was here at all, with the equipment in working order, with reliable people, and with a fighting chance to pull off what could be the greatest intelligence operation since the British broke the German Enigma code during World War Two.

Every other aspect of the operation was a real or potential problem, the most daunting of which was that if something went wrong, he was absolutely on his own. He tried to put that idea out of his mind. He had to make it work, that was all.

Orville's hiss brought him to an abrupt halt. "What is it?" he whispered.

"The Embassy is ahead," was the reply. "Do we go closer now, or stay here?"

Ivorson pondered. They were still a hundred yards from the east end of the Embassy compound, and fifty or more yards deep in the swamp. He checked the watch he'd taken from the tech shop. Only nine twenty-five. They had plenty of time. "Stay here," he directed and simultaneously realized that he had made a bad mistake in timing.

When he and Wilbur had been here before, they had squatted up to their chins in the swamp to wait out the start of the radio schedule. The leeches had a feast, but they had been impossible to see from the Embassy. Now, with the electrical gear on their backs, and the deeper water in the swamp, they couldn't enjoy that measure of concealment. They had no choice but to stand up. He should have waited until later to enter the swamp.

While he was berating himself for that error, Orville added another problem. "All the windows are open tonight."

It was true. In fact, the only windows in the dormitory building which were not unshuttered and illuminated were the radio and code room windows upstairs. The sight chilled Ivorson. The light coming from the open windows would greatly increase the chances of the balloon being spotted.

For a moment, his will almost failed him. There was a point at which the odds against him would make any further approach completely hopeless. Had he reached that point now? He would reap only condemnation for pressing on tonight and causing the operation to fail when it might be successfully carried out on a later occasion. It still wasn't too late to quit.

Yes, but damn it, he wanted that code machine. He wanted it more than he had ever wanted anything in his life. He wanted it to avenge Wilbur, and he needed it to avenge himself; to salvage his professional pride and self-image from the shambles that Tran van Cao and Nga had made of them.

Finally, if the Viet POW he'd interrogated in Pakse had told the truth, and the North Vietnamese army was truly entering the war, the United States of America needed that code machine, and needed it soon. The NVA's offensive could well start before the replacement blimp arrived from Langley.

That time crunch was the deciding factor. Having the code in hand could save thousands of lives. That was worth disobeying Riley for; worth risking his own career, and even his life, for. He had no choice but to push his luck as hard as he could.

Curiously, since the trial of fire and water at the Nam Khen, the Fear had vanished. He had no idea why; perhaps he had achieved some sort of personal saturation point out there in the jungle. Whatever the reason, he was hugely grateful.

He decided to wait as long as possible where they were. Even standing up, at this distance they wouldn't be visible in the darkness, and, who knows, maybe some of the lights would be turned off before they had to make their approach.

Maybe it would start to rain. The big thundercloud was moving closer. He could hear a faint growl of thunder. If the wind didn't blow too hard, the rain might screen them from view. It wouldn't hurt to wait here, and it might help. He could use some help.

Chapter Twenty-four

Hoang bac Cam stared at the ceiling through the gauzy mist of the mosquito netting. With the start of the rains, the mosquitoes had come out of the swamp behind the wall in such great numbers that the wire mesh window screens and smoke from the mosquito coils couldn't cope with them. He could hear their frustrated whining now, outside the net.

The orders had arrived from Hanoi. His replacement would arrive on next Saturday's ICC flight, and he would leave on the return flight that same night.

Ever since the disastrous night when he had fled Sengdara's brother, Cam's life had been barely endurable. He had not been formally accused of anything and was leaving with an unblemished record, at least on paper, but Huu had made certain that the mind of every functionary in the Embassy was poisoned against him.

The toleration and rough camaraderie that he had enjoyed from the lower-level cadre had been cut short by Huu's innuendos of treason as if by the stroke of a knife. A leper would not have been avoided more assiduously than he had during the past weeks.

Even worse than that was his yearning for Sengdara. He hadn't seen or spoken to her in over a month, but her face was as fresh in his mind's eye as if he had seen her this morning. The thought that he would never do so again was pure torture.

He had dreamed many times of going over the wall at night in search of her and the start of a new life, but that was only a vain fantasy. He didn't know where she lived. He couldn't go to the market in broad daylight in search of her.

A more realistic dream was to get out and then call her. The telephone number she had given him was engraved in his memory.

But even that was a daunting leap into the unknown. Would she talk to him? And even if she still loved him, how could they meet? Huu had told him that

Mango shot a Black Thai policeman that same night. It almost had to have been her brother. Did her family have any other way to contact the Thai authorities?

He had struggled with these temptations and fears every day for weeks, but had gradually come to accept the bitter reality that he had missed the great chance of his life when he ran away from the little café in Oupmuong.

And then, two days ago, Huu's agent—code name Papaya—had arrived at the Embassy gate.

Cam knew her true name, Nguyen thi Nga, from the old days, before she stopped coming to the Sunday afternoon open house for the local Vietnamese. Not that she had ever paid attention to Cam. Well aware of her beauty, she saved her smiles for the senior functionaries, especially Huu, with whom she had behaved like a daughter.

Or so Cam thought.

He had rarely been as shocked in his life as on Saturday afternoon, when he went to take Nga the evening meal before her departure and had heard, through the door of the servants' quarters where she was "talking" with Huu, the rhythmic creaking of the cot.

His shock had soon been replaced by furious anger and resentment. Huu, the hard, pure revolutionary who tolerated no human weaknesses and permitted no fraternization with local women by his staff, nonetheless was permitting himself the luxury of the flesh of Nguyen thi Nga!

The sounds of Huu sating his lust with her had instantly brought Cam's own desire for Sengdara back into agonizing focus. The damned hypocrite! And it might be even worse than that. After the creaking had reached it staccato climax and subsided, Cam was sure he had heard the girl sobbing. Had Huu forced himself on her?

Cam had been in torment ever since. What should he do? Too restless in spirit to lie still any more, he tore open the mosquito netting, got off his bed and went to the window. It was a dark night, still and humid, but there would be a storm later. He could hear the thunder in the distance.

He caught the faint glimmer of a star through high clouds. Starlight. Sengdara. He began to weep.

✲ ✲ ✲

The seconds ticked slowly away into minutes. Mosquitoes swarmed around Ivorson's head like a cloud, but the repellent seemed to be working, so far.

The weight of the fully-laden dowel grew with every passing minute. Ivorson hadn't realized what a problem the weight of their burdens would be. When he and Wilbur were out here before, they had had to carry nothing, except Wilbur's knife.

He wished to God that Wilbur were here with him now. His presence would have made Ivorson feel much better. Orville was reliable and steady, but Wilbur would have actually enjoyed what they were doing.

More minutes passed. His arms began to ache terribly from holding the thirty-plus pounds of the wooden dowel with all its cargo out of the water. The thundercloud climbed up the sky, his watch ticked on, and finally it was twenty to ten and time to start setting up. A good thing, too. His arm muscles had just about reached the limit of their endurance.

He hissed for Chan to approach him, and they began the silent ballet they had rehearsed at Orville's house. The difference was, now they were waist-deep in leech-filled water, and if they made a mistake this time, there would be no chance to try it again.

Ivorson gratefully handed Chan the dowel and its precious cargo. Chan took it and then turned his back to Ivorson, who fumbled around the top of the basket on Chan's back for the cord that secured its thatched palm-leaf cover. He finally located it and tugged it open.

From beneath the thatch, he pulled out one of the plastic packages that contained the weather balloons. He had brought both of them, in case one leaked. He opened the package and extracted the balloon, carefully jamming the empty wrapper into his pants pocket.

He felt in the basket again for the slender metal bottle of helium. He found its tube, inserted it into the mouth of the balloon, and opened the valve on the helium bottle. He heard a faint hiss. In a few seconds, he felt the balloon come to life in his hands.

Orville now came to stand beside him. From the basket, Ivorson extracted a finely-meshed, but very strong, nylon seine net, the sort used in US Air Force survival kits. Ivorson had taken it from his own personal survival bag at the office. It was an improvement over the cargo net suggested by Herbert Odom and was the means to secure the balloon to the dowel.

The balloon began to expand. Now came critical moment number one: lack of sufficient helium had prevented them from actually practicing this part of the operation.

The moment the balloon assumed a spherical form, Ivorson closed the valve on the helium bottle. If he had over-filled it, the balloon might tear loose from his grip. Holding its neck tightly shut, he held it out toward Orville, who threw the seine over it. The cords at each corner of the seine dangled down over Ivorson's hands and arms.

Orville carefully pulled on the four corners of the seine until the balloon was precisely centered within it. Then he began tying the sides of the seine to each other around the bottom of the balloon with short pieces of nylon cord.

Ivorson's arm muscles, strained by holding the heavily laden dowel, felt like mush. He had trouble retaining his grip on the balloon which, despite its light charge of helium, definitely wanted to fly. "Hurry up," he whispered to Orville.

"Wait," was the preoccupied answer. "Not long now."

Thirty seconds later, the sides of the seine were sewn shut with nylon around the balloon. Orville took the four cords at each corner of the seine, whipped them together in a knot and pulled down on it. The lift of the balloon disappeared magically from Ivorson's aching fingers.

With Orville now keeping the netted balloon under control, Ivorson reinserted the gas tube in the balloon's mouth and added more helium. This was critical moment number two, also unrehearsed.

His aim was to fill the balloon with just enough helium to gently lift the payload to the twenty-five or thirty-foot height he needed to let the camera's lens peek through the code room window. Any additional gas would only impose more work on Chan, whose job it would be to hold the balloon at the proper altitude.

Since Ivorson had never had a chance to determine how many pounds of pressure was required, he had to do it by trial and error, and, as a quick glance at his watch told him, time was beginning to be a factor. It was ten minutes until the radio schedule with Hanoi began.

He opened the valve and added helium, pressing his other hand against the side of seine-imprisoned balloon to gauge its degree of inflation. After twenty seconds of filling, he closed the valve, dug a length of cord from his shirt pocket, and whipped it around the neck of the balloon. This was another tricky moment. The closure had to be tight enough to seal it, but not so tight that he couldn't get if off again.

"Let's try," he whispered to Orville. Chan turned and faced him, the wooden rod with its payload in his hands. Orville ran the four cords of the now-secured seine through the metal ring Herbert Odom had clamped on top of the rod, and tied them securely.

"Let go of the rod, but hold onto the tether ring," Ivorson told Chan.

He obeyed. The balloon tugged upward. The rod with its payload, shifted and moved on Chan's outstretched palms, but didn't lift. They needed more helium.

"Leave it tied to the payload," Ivorson hissed. "I can add gas through the mesh in the seine." He had to hurry. He groped for the neck of the balloon, fished it out through the mesh of the seine, and untied it. He found that he was able to pull the filler hose over Chan's shoulder and leave the metal bottle in the basket on his back. He added more gas.

Over the hissing of the helium, Orville said, "Lights are on in the radio room." Then, a moment later, "The window shutters are opening."

Damnation! The radio schedule was about to begin, and they were still a hundred yards away and struggling to fill the balloon. Ivorson fought down the temptation to open the valve on the helium bottle wider. He gave it another ten seconds. The balloon strained against his hand. He shut off the gas and tied the neck of the balloon shut again.

"It is trying to fly," Chan whispered excitedly. "I have to hold it down."

"Hang on," Ivorson warned him. "Let me get the tether rope on it." He pulled the rope off Orville's neck and shoulder. A fifty-foot length of slender black nylon, it had a loop for Chan's hand at one end and a metal clip at the other. Ivorson found the clip and snapped it on the ring that hung down from the bottom of the camera carrier. He got a firm grip on the rope and said, "Let it go."

The enmeshed balloon lifted its payload majestically into the air. Ivorson paid out the tether rope. In a few seconds, the apparatus had disappeared from his view against the black sky. It pulled strongly against his arms. He had overfilled it now, but that was just tough luck. Right now, they needed to make their final approach.

"Let's get closer," he whispered. "Take the rope, Chan. I want you to get used to the feel of it." Chan's hands closed over his. When Ivorson was sure the Asian had the tether under control, he let go of it. They started toward the rear wall of the compound.

His watch showed four minutes until ten. They had cut it very close. He moved as fast as he could without splashing, but their progress was painfully slow. The dormitory windows were now all lighted and open, with the sole exception of the code room. The sound of radios came clearly to his ears. So much the better. That would afford cover for any noise they might make.

He threw a quick look over his shoulder for any sign of fishermen or other activity behind them. Nothing moved in the inky blackness of the swamp. The thunderstorm now covered most of the western sky, stabbing lightning bolts earthward every few seconds. The booms of its thunder became louder with each minute. Fine. More covering noise.

He realized almost immediately, however, that light, not noise, was his big problem. As they moved to within thirty yards of the wall, the light level increased dramatically. He glanced upward and was horrified to see that he could make out the outline of the balloon and its package in the glow emanating from the open dormitory windows. It wasn't obvious, but it was visible, and they still weren't close enough for the camera's lens.

The payload was nose-heavy, too. The fan pointed downward at an angle of about ten degrees. He decided that it was time to correct that.

He hissed them to a halt and helped Chan pull the balloon slowly back down. It was far too buoyant. He definitely needed to release helium.

As soon as they had the thing in their hands, he found the balloon's neck, untied the cord, and squeezed its sides for about five seconds to drive out the excess helium. Then he retied it, permanently. If it needed further adjustment, too bad! The radio schedule had already started.

"All right, Orville," he whispered, "let's get you hooked up." He reached into the backpack the Asian was carrying and turned the toggle switches for the receiver, monitor and recorder to the "ON" position.

He turned back to the dowel and its burdens for a moment and made himself go slowly and methodically over the checklist he had memorized with Herbert Odom's help. All right, they were ready. He snapped on the power switches of the camera and its transmitter. A very faint red light glowed under the black electric tape which covered them.

Now he shifted his attention back to the monitor in Orville's backpack. He rechecked its power switch. The taped-over light glowed, and the small screen glowed green as the electron tube flooded it with energy. Nerves taut, he waited for an image to appear. It didn't. What the hell was wrong? He glanced at the camera hanging under the balloon. It was pointed at the wall. He ought to be seeing that on the screen.

"Is it all right?" Orville whispered.

Ivorson was just on the verge of saying, "No", when another glance at the camera brought a gust of relief from his lungs. The lens cap was still on! He removed it, and immediately the back of the dormitory appeared on the monitor screen. It worked! With the camera lens set on full zoom, the wall looked to be right in front of them.

He looked at his watch. Christ! It was two minutes after ten. The radio schedule was under way. If it was a short one, the decoding could start while he was still fiddling around with the camera.

Don't panic, Ivorson, he told himself. Just a couple of seconds more.

He switched on the little fan at the nose of the payload. It whirred into life, and the payload began tugging forward. "Let it up a few feet," he whispered to Chan, who paid out the tether rope.

The balloon slowly rose and began moving forward toward the wall of the Embassy compound. "Stop," Ivorson hissed, and the payload came to halt in mid-air. Herbert Odom's calculations had been correct. It was almost perfectly balanced.

Now for the most critical moment of all. From a black-dyed cotton bag slung around his neck, he pulled out the remote control transmitter. He switched it on and moved the joystick to the right. The nose of the payload began to move right. He centered the stick. The payload, slowed, then stopped. He moved it back to the left, then stopped it again. It obeyed every command. There was a substantial lag time, but it was under control.

All right. Now to do what they'd come here for. So tense he could feel himself quivering, he whispered to Chan, "Let me have the tether rope. Hold it until I tell you to let go." The Asian passed it to him, and Ivorson made certain he had it under control before nodding to Chan.

The three of them were standing all together now, with the two Asians in front and Ivorson behind Orville, watching the monitor in Orville's backpack. He kept his eyes on it as he slowly paid out the tether rope. The eye of the camera rose over the wall. Now he was looking at the rear wall of dormitory building. The corner of a window appeared in the screen, then disappeared. Was that the first floor?

He shot a quick glance upward. No, the balloon was already too high for that. It had to be the second floor. He had to bring it back down a bit. He wound it back in. The top of the lighted window appeared again at the bottom of the monitor. "Lower still," he murmured to himself. The window moved up on his screen, and he pulled in more rope.

Suddenly, he was looking through the open window into a room in the building in front of him. He could see a chair and table, but no one was seated there. Which window was he looking at anyway?

From another quick glance upward, he got the impression that he was pointed too far to the left. He moved the joystick to the right, and the picture on the monitor swung away from the window. It passed over a drain pipe. The edge of another window came into view. Ivorson centered the control. The movement slowed, then stopped. He was looking at the back of a man's head. The man was seated at a table, and on the table in front of him was a large radio set.

Ivorson's heart gave a great leap. God Almighty, he was actually looking into the North Vietnamese radio room! The video was crystal clear. He could see the part in the radio operator's hair and make out the lettering on a label on the radio. It was in Cyrillic print. The radio must be Russian-built.

He needed to have just a bit more elevation, so he could see the radio operator's hands. "Up just a little bit," he whispered to himself, but before he could suit action to the words, the radio operator pushed back his chair and stood up. In his right hand he had a sheet of paper. He walked to the door, pulled it open, and walked through it into the darkness beyond. He turned around to close the door behind him, and his eyes looked directly into Ivorson's through the lens of the camera.

Chapter Twenty-five

Nguyen van Huu heard the approaching rolls of thunder and grunted with satisfaction. His office was hot. A downpour would be welcomed. He got up from the desk and opened the wooden shutter on the sidewall window.

Above the thatched roofs of the Lao houses beyond the Embassy garage and wall, the thundercloud towered into the night, its boiling energy vividly illuminated by almost constant flashes of internal lightning. The accompaniment of thunder sounded like an artillery barrage.

Nature's violence matched his own internal turmoil. Since the departure of the ICC flight Saturday night, he had been ill-tempered, vacillating, incapable of concentration, and useless to either the Embassy or the Party.

His eyes were drawn to the window of the servants' quarters behind the garage, and he snatched them away again. He hated the sight of the place! It was there he had betrayed his revolutionary trust. How he wished this was last Friday night instead of Monday! If it were, when Papayaa rang the gate bell tomorrow morning, he would have Cam throw her back out onto the street. Having her arrested by the Lao police would have been better by far than what had happened.

Between Saturday morning and night, when he had watched Papaya fly away, Huu had been a man possessed, completely out of control.

He had known, even as she manipulated him toward that first climax. He had seen the tears pour down her face and realized with horror that he was making a mistake, that she had not really offered herself to him in exchange for his official protection, and was now only complying with what she believed to be his demand.

He had realized it. He should have stopped what was happening and begged her pardon.

But he had not.

His years of sexual privation, his carnal fantasies about her and the American, and his anger over the botched kidnapping had all combined, not only to make her continue that first shameful act, but thereafter to deny the truth of his realization, and to continue making her his whore.

He, Nguyen van Huu, who had always prided himself on his revolutionary morality, had succumbed to the worst form of bourgeois decadence!

What was worse, Hoang bac Cam knew it. He had knocked on the door of the servants' quarters with Nga's dinner only minutes after Huu finished with her for the last time. The chauffeur had tried to hide his feelings, but Huu had seen his look of contempt.

Cam was leaving soon for Hanoi, but what if the driver had shared his knowledge with others here, before he left? Would they believe the Black Thai traitor? If so, Huu's face would be completely destroyed. He had looked ever since Saturday for the surreptitious glances of disdain that would spell disaster for him. He had seen none so far, but the dread of what tomorrow might bring weighed on his heart.

And what of Nga herself? Suppose she reported what had happened to the authorities in Hanoi? Would they believe her?

DAMN the American! He was the ultimate cause of Huu's disgrace. Were it not for him, Huu would never have forced Nga into the relationship with the white man that had produced his own jealous nightmares. He would never have disgraced himself with her, except for Ivorson.

He felt the bile of vitriolic hatred souring his stomach. In all his life, he had never even come close to hating someone as much as he hated Peter Ivorson. He would give anything to have heard the American's screams as he burned alive in the forest.

But was he, in fact, dead? There was a rumor in the market that government soldiers had found a foreigner's charred corpse at the scene of the fire, but Nga told him that she heard Ivorson shoot the PL who followed him into the jungle. If that were true, the PL's body must have been found after the fire, too. Why didn't the rumor mention two bodies?

It would be the ultimate disaster, if, after destroying the usefulness of Huu's two irreplaceable agents and driving Huu himself to disgrace and shame, Ivorson had somehow escaped.

Huu had ordered Mango to return to Vientiane and meet with him late tonight. It was dangerous, but Huu simply had to learn what had really happened at the Nam Khen. If there was any question about Ivorson's death, Huu would learn the truth, and if he were alive, track him down. It was no longer a political matter. He was going to make sure that Ivorson died, no matter what the cost.

Besides, if Nga's story about the events at the Nam Khen was true, Mango had much to answer for. According to her, it was Mango's disregard for Huu's instructions that made her seek refuge in the Embassy and led to Huu's present self-loathing. His note to Mango, directing him to present himself for the meeting, had not been couched in diplomatic language.

A brilliant flash of lightning jolted him from his bitter reverie. He looked at his watch. The radio messages from Hanoi were coming in, at this very moment. There might be something about Nga's arrival in Hanoi. Had she accused him? He couldn't bring himself to stay in his office and listen for the Ambassador's knock on the door. He would go see the code clerk himself.

✲ ✲ ✲

Ivorson instinctively ducked as the radio operator looked at him and then caught himself and looked again at the monitor. Had the Viet seen the camera lens staring at him from the darkness outside?

The Asian pulled the door closed with no change of expression, and Ivorson, with vast relief, was left staring at the back door.

"The other light is on," murmured Orville. Ivorson saw it at the same time and was jolted into action.

"Come on," he hissed. "We have to move that way, toward the code room." Open the window, you sonofabitch, he thought. Come on, open the goddamn window. The two small panes above the wooden shutters didn't provide enough of a view to guarantee that he could see the code machine.

In answer to his profane prayer, the shutters opened. The radio operator was clearly silhouetted in the window. Ivorson and the two Black Thai froze simultaneously. The Vietnamese looked out the window, in the direction of the thunderstorms, which was both growing and rapidly approaching.

Thank God they hadn't already got themselves in the proper location, thought Ivorson. If they had, the television lens would have practically poked the Viet in the eye.

The man left the window. Ivorson heard Orville's pent-up breath whistle out of his lungs. Ivorson's own relief left his legs feeling like rubber bands. "Let's get closer," he heard himself whisper. Moving almost in lock step, they made their way toward the west end of the dormitory, dragging the balloon and its cargo behind them.

Ivorson's eyes were glued to the monitor. If his calculations were correct, the door was at the east end of the code room, directly opposite the window. The code machine should therefore be located west of the window.

If so, then his best angle should be from about where he was presently located. Provided of course, that the machine was located against the inside wall of the room, as the radio had been. If it were set up against the outside wall, then Ivorson would have to get very close to the wall to get a view of it at all. More probably, he wouldn't be able to see anything except the code clerk himself. He glanced up, located the balloon, and began directing it via the joy sticks.

The window of the code room came into sight on the monitor. Any second now, and he would know whether he had an operation or a dangerous failure.

There was the code clerk! He was sitting in front of a table, and his back was to Ivorson! On the table in front of him was the code machine. Ivorson couldn't get a full view of it from where he was. The code clerk's shoulder obscured his view. "Move closer to the wall," he whispered to Chan. At the same time, he pushed the joystick on the control module to the right just a tiny bit.

The maneuvering increased his field of vision. He had to let it rise, just a little. A moment later, the viewpoint of the picture moved upward, and he was looking directly at the North Vietnamese diplomatic code machine.

It was a strange looking affair, a rectangular wooden frame with a series of wires running in both directions across it. On the wires were mounted what looked like wooden beads. The effect was of an oversized, two dimensional abacus.

The clerk's hands were moving the beads back and forth as he read from the encoded message, which Ivorson could see lying on the table beside the code machine. No wonder NSA couldn't do anything with it, Ivorson thought. It's completely oriental.

And completely manual, too. Even if he had recruited Cam to put an electrical device on the internal wiring in the dormitory, it wouldn't have done him a bit of good! The damn thing didn't use electricity. He realized with a start that he was wasting precious time.

He reached into Orville's pack and felt for the controls of the video recorder to which the monitor was plugged. He found them, located the "play" button by feel, and pushed it. He heard the whirring of the recorder. From now on, the picture on the monitor would be preserved on film. This was what would enable the NSA code breakers to understand how the Vietnamese system worked.

The picture on the monitor was incredibly clear. All Ivorson had to do was keep the camera centered on the code machine. He concentrated his whole being on the task. He was vaguely aware that the sound of thunder was getting much nearer, but so far there was no wind. All he needed was just a couple of minutes; just two or three lousy minutes more, and he would have pulled off the greatest intelligence coup in a generation. God, how he wished Wilbur were here to share this moment of triumph!

The hands of the code clerk flicked and jerked the beads back and forth on the code machine. The recorder whirred in Orville's backpack, but for Ivorson, time stood still. He was suspended inside the greatest moment of his life, like a fly preserved in a lump of amber.

And then there was a tremendous white light, and a crack of thunder like a bomb going off.

Both he and Orville jumped. The picture on the monitor leaped away from the code machine. When Ivorson looked again, all he could see was the outside wall of the dormitory. There was another tremendous crack of thunder, and lightning lit up the scene so brightly that he could actually see their three shadows on the wall of Embassy compound. At the same time, he was pushed by a powerful gust of wind.

That did it. The operation was over. It was time to go. Even as he thought it, he heard wooden shutters slamming shut on the rear of the dormitory building. That's it, you bastards, Ivorson silently praised the inhabitants. Close up!

He hastily amended the thought to exclude the code clerk. For the operation to end in disaster, all he had to do was leave the code machine and come to the window. The TV camera would be staring him straight in the face.

They had to get away from the code room window! "Come on," he whispered urgently to Chan and Orville. "Come on!" He tugged urgently at the tether rope. Never mind how much noise they made. Between the thunderclaps and the rising roar of the wind, that was no longer a problem.

Waist deep in water and vegetation, they slogged away to the east. The compound wall was no more than thirty feet away, but with the exception of one window, all the ground floor shutters had been shut now, and the light level had declined enough to provide an additional measure of security.

Then there was another arc-light white flash of lightning, a simultaneous bomb burst of thunder, and the wind and rain burst upon them with a force that made them all reel. Ivorson felt the nylon rope jerk violently in his hands, and at the same time he heard Chan cry out, "The wind has taken the balloon!"

Oh, my God! He looked aloft. Nothing. The rain had made the night as opaque as concrete. The tether rope in his hands kicked and bucked violently, as it disappeared into the darkness, but it wasn't going upward. It was almost horizontal, at an angle above ground level of no more than ten degrees. The balloon was being blown toward the wall of the Vietnamese Embassy!

✲ ✲ ✲

Huu had just reached the door to the elevated walkway which connected the chancery building to the dormitory, when the violent thunderclap made him jump. What a storm! If the radio contact with Hanoi was not already completed, it would probably be impossible to finish copying the transmission.

He opened the wooden door and stepped out onto the walkway. Although roofed, it was open on both sides, and huge raindrops were beginning to splatter on its concrete floor. At any moment, there would be a downpour!

Just as he readied himself for a dash to the shelter of the second floor porch of the dormitory, another brilliant flash of lightning and almost simultaneous thunderclap made him instinctively pull back. He closed his eyes against the white-hot light. That was very close, he thought. It must have struck in the swamp behind the wall.

He glanced out over the wall into the darkness beyond. In the last vestige of the lightning bolts light, he caught a glimpse of something that froze him in place. What in the world was that? A strong gust of wind and rain struck him in the face, but he didn't flinch. Something very strange was out there in the night. "Come, come," he mentally ordered the storm. "Another lightning flash!"

Obediently, it came. Squinting his eyes against the glare, Huu searched the rain-filled sky. There! Disappearing behind the corner of the dormitory was an object like nothing he had seen before in his life. It was indescribable. But it was unquestionably man-made.

Every defensive instinct aroused, he rushed out onto the walkway. Before he had taken two steps he was completely drenched. The wind buffeted him so strongly that it drove him against the metal handrail. His feet almost went out from under him. Recovering, he dragged himself onward until he reached the lee of the dormitory, and then he ran as fast as he could down the second-story porch toward the far end of the building.

☆ ☆ ☆

Ivorson was transfixed with horror for a precious half-second. Then he pulled with all his might on the tether rope, and at the same time shouted, "Help me! Pull it away from the wall!"

Orville immediately understood the danger. He joined Chan on the tether rope, and the three of them hauled on the runaway balloon as hard as they could. They absolutely had to bring it down before it was blown over the wall!

Half-drowned in the incredible volume of water falling from the sky, they heaved on the tether. It was like trying to tame an elephant. Driven before the tremendous wind gusts, the balloon had taken on a malignant life of its own. It refused to yield more than a few feet, even to their combined strength.

"Away from the wall," Ivorson shouted, heedless of the noise he was making. "Just hold onto it and walk away from the wall into the swamp."

They turned, and fighting both the force of the wind in their faces and the enormous pull of the balloon behind, they reeled away from the wall like a trio of drunks. Another lightning flash blinded them. Another tremendous gust of wind brought them to a virtual standstill, and then, as if by an invisible hand, they were all three jerked backward.

Ivorson and Chan both sat down, up to their faces in the swamp. Orville kept his footing. "What happened?" he gasped. Ivorson spit out a mouthful of filthy water. He didn't know what had happened, but whatever it was, it had to be bad. He staggered back to his feet and followed the direction of the tether, which, by a miracle, he had been able to hold onto.

It no longer disappeared into the black, rain-lashed sky. Now it lay atop the vegetation on the surface of the swamp. The balloon had hit the ground.

The tether rope pointed in a straight line toward the wall of the North Vietnamese Embassy. A presentiment of impending doom settled in Ivorson's gut. He began following the rope toward the wall of the compound.

☆ ☆ ☆

Hoang Bac Cam started at the first thunderclap. He heard the sound of excited voices in the rooms on both sides of him in the dormitory and then the slamming of wooden window shutters against the impending rain, but he didn't move off his cot. What did a rainstorm matter to a man whose life had ended?

He heard the wind rising. Another bright flash of thunder illuminated his dark room, and the wind became a howl. One of the shutters on his window tore loose from the hook that held it open and banged loudly shut.

The shutter continued to bang as the violence of the wind increased. Cam ignored it at first, but finally, irritated by the insistent clatter, he heaved himself off his cot and went to the window.

Rain blew in on him as he approached the screen. He unlatched it, opened it, and leaned out to catch the flying shutter. As he grasped it and pulled it shut, a brilliant flash of lightning seemed to strike the ground outside the wall. He involuntarily jerked away from it and lost his grip on the shutter.

Swearing, he reached out again, and another lightning flash revealed to him the most peculiar object he had ever seen in his life. Jerking at the end of a rope, not three meters above his startled eyes, was what appeared to be a large balloon! Underneath it hung a long horizontal stick, below which hung a variety of objects which he could not identify in the quarter-second of light.

Open-mouthed, Cam stood transfixed. The next lightning flash showed him an empty sky, but he knew that he had not been dreaming. Something extremely strange had been right outside his room. Something that definitely did not belong there. Leaving the banging shutter to do what it would, Cam headed toward the door.

✲ ✲ ✲

Ivorson pulled himself through the water and vegetation of the swamp along the tether rope. It had no give at all. Wherever the balloon had landed, it had hung up solidly on something. He didn't let himself think of what that might be. He'd find out soon enough.

And he did. His legs began to emerge from the water, mud, and vegetation, and he found himself staring at the wall of the North Vietnamese Embassy compound, not more than a yard in front of him.

The tether rope also rose out of the swamp and disappeared over the compound wall. The balloon, with its utterly incriminating cargo, had fallen inside the Embassy grounds! Ivorson grasped the rope and heaved on it with all him might. It didn't move so much as an inch.

Heartsick, stunned by the enormity of the disaster, he stared dumbly at the wall. The Viets would find the camera, realize its purpose and change their code. All of his effort expended, all the risks taken since his arrival in Vientiane had been in vain. Wilbur's death, his own betrayal by Nga, and his trial by fire and water at the Nam Khen had all been for nothing. The video images of the code machine in the cassette on Orville's back weren't worth the cost of the film they were exposed on.

☆ ☆ ☆

Huu reached the end of the balcony and craned his head around the corner of the dormitory. The rain was a solid wall of gray-black. Even in the lee of the building, water filled his eyes and made him blink constantly. This wouldn't do. He would have to get closer.

Cursing, he raced back along the balcony to the walkway end of the building, where the stairs were located, and ran down them as fast as his rubber sandals would permit. As he reached the bottom, there was another tremendous lightning bolt, and the electricity in the compound failed.

"Goddamned incompetent Lao," he growled under his breath. Every time there was a thunderstorm, the power went off! It was pitch black at the bottom of the stairs. He turned east again and began feeling his way along the front wall of the dormitory toward the other end. He moved as fast as he could, but to his anxious mind, it seemed as if he were creeping.

As he reached what he thought must be the east end of the dormitory, he collided solidly with another person. Instinctively, he struck out His fist hit someone's upper body.

"Hey," said and indignant voice. "What the hell are you doing?" Huu recognized the accent immediately. It was Cam. Suspicion leaped into his mind.

"What are YOU doing, out here in the dark?" he demanded harshly.

"I saw something funny out of my window a minute ago," the Black Thai answered sullenly. "I came out to take another look. And anyway, when I came out, the lights were still on."

The answer allayed Huu's suspicion somewhat. If Cam were a party to this business, would he admit having seen the object? "Ah!" he said. "You saw it, too? What is it?"

"I don't know exactly," Cam replied. "It looked like a big balloon with some strange things hanging underneath."

Huu felt for Cam's arm. "It is an American plot against the Embassy," he told the chauffeur. "Come with me!"

Cam heard the suspicion in the intelligence chief's voice, but let Huu pull him along only with the greatest reluctance. What terrible luck for Huu to find him out here, alone in the dark, just as some American scheme against the Embassy was under way!

The intelligence chief was perfectly capable of accusing him of complicity in whatever the strange balloon was doing. In fact, he was almost certain to do so. It would justify his character assassination of Cam following the Tran van Cao debacle.

The more Cam reflected on his situation, the more frightened he became. He was trapped. Huu would surely succeed in labeling him a traitor now. There were only the two of them out here. Who would take his word against Huu's?

The thought suggested a remedy. He stopped abruptly, just as they reached the end of the building. "Let's get some more help," he suggested, almost shouting over the roar of the wind and rain. "There are others just inside."

Huu yanked at his arm. "There is not time for that! Come on! Hurry!"

✲ ✲ ✲

Ivorson felt, rather than saw, Orville and Chan as they joined him at the wall. The rain was a solid, living thing. It struck his bare head and shoulders with such force that simply standing upright was difficult.

He saw Orville grasp the tether rope, and follow them with his eyes to the top of the wall. "The balloon is inside," he yelled in Ivorson's ear. "I will go in and get it."

At the words, the Fear, which Ivorson supposed he had banished forever at the Nam Khen, erupted into full force again. It sickened his stomach, sapped the strength from his legs.

He looked at Orville's rain-drenched face, bare inches from his own, and opened his mouth to shout his rejection of the idea, when the man's resemblance to Wilbur brought him up short.

Suppose Wilbur were still alive and here now? What would he do?

There wasn't any question about it. He would already be on top of the wall. And if he were, Ivorson would go and join him, because Wilbur's good opinion of Ivorson was more important than the Fear.

Wilbur wasn't here, of course, but his look-alike brother was, and he was ready to go over the wall, too. So what else could Ivorson do? Besides, that was the only option left. If the operation was to succeed, the balloon and its payload had to be recovered.

And the operation had to succeed. It was really the only thing left in Ivorson's life that had any meaning. Wilbur was dead. Nga had betrayed him. Of the things that had mattered to him in Laos, only the operation was left, and no matter how great the risk, he simply couldn't tell COS, "I had it, but I lost it." For Wilbur and for himself, he had to go over the wall.

But alone. All by himself. Orville was now the head of Wilbur's family, the last of his mother's sons. Ivorson's business had cost that woman her first-born. He had no right to risk her surviving child as well.

Before his resolution could weaken, he put it into words. "No. I'll go in. You wait for me on top of the wall, and I'll pass the thing up to you. Chan can stay here. Come on! Boost me up."

For a moment, Orville's eyes stared into his. Then he wordlessly turned and knelt at the foot of the wall, his back to Ivorson. Ivorson stepped up on his shoulders, one foot at a time, steadying himself with his hands against the wall as Orville slowly stood up under him.

The Asian's strength was amazing. In bare seconds, the top of the wall was at Ivorson's waist. He felt carefully for broken glass on its top.

It was there, but the concrete in which it was set was old. He was able to pull some pieces loose. When that possibility was exhausted, he pulled the PPK out of its holster in the small of his back and broke the sharp glass shards off with its butt, trying to let none of them fall inside the wall. If there were no clues on the ground, perhaps they wouldn't notice the absence of the glass atop the wall. He knew he must be making noise, but the roar of the wind was so loud that he couldn't hear anything but that. He hoped no one else could, either.

When he had a sufficient space cleared for two people, he reholstered the gun and crawled carefully upon the top of the wall. It was only about a foot thick. The force of the wind and rain made him teeter sickeningly. Trying to blot the idea of a fall from his mind, he gingerly turned around on his knees and held his hand down to Orville. "Come on up," he called softly.

Orville grasped his hand and, boosted from below by Chan, joined him on the top of the wall. Ivorson knew he had to move fast now or he'd lose his nerve. He let his feet slide down the wall behind him, then his legs, then his belly.

The Fear leered at him out of the darkness below, and for an eternal instant, the urge to scrabble back upon the wall and down the other side to the safety of the swamp was almost overwhelming.

He overcame it by simply letting go and dropping to the ground inside the North Vietnamese compound.

Chapter Twenty-six

Ivorson landed with a thump and wheeled around. Nothing moved in reaction to his presence. He was in an open space, which he remembered from the aerial photographs as the vegetable garden. Ten feet away or so, through the twin curtains of rain and darkness, he could barely make out the loom of the east wall of the dormitory.

Assured that his presence hadn't been noted, he looked for the balloon and its payload. It was directly in front of him, not three feet away. All that remained of the balloon was a tatter of rubber. It must have burst on some sharp object as it came down, perhaps a shard of glass on the wall.

The payload appeared to be intact and still attached to the wooden dowel that had supported it. Thank God for that. Now to pick the damn thing up and get out of here! He sprang forward, gripped the dowel at its midpoint and heaved upward. The rear section came off the ground easily, but the front end refused to budge.

The Fear, battened down in his gut, threatened to break loose again. He crushed it by sheer force of will, put the dowel down again, and knelt beside it on one knee to see what the problem was.

It was too dark to make out any details. He didn't have a light and wouldn't have dared use it, in any case. He felt along the rod to the back of the little fan motor. It seemed to be all right. He groped for the battery. Aha! There was the villain. A thin metal rod driven in the ground, probably a stake for some sort of vegetable, had gotten caught in the pierced metal strap that supported the battery.

Working by feel, he carefully lifted the front end of the dowel off the stake. As soon at its plastic propellers came clear of the soil, the fan began to whir.

Ivorson's heart gave a great thump at the unexpected noise. He hastily lifted the battery strap hangar free of the stake, transferred the dowel to his knee, and, steadying it with his left hand, felt along the fan case for the fan switch.

He found it and snapped it off. The fan blade slowed dramatically. At the same moment, the volume of rain diminished abruptly, although the sound of the wind was still very loud.

Before Ivorson could stand again, he heard a squishy noise to his front. His heart gave a galvanic leap. He jerked his head up. All he had time to absorb was the impression of a dark shape flying at him, and then he was bowled over backwards by the force of a flying tackle.

My God, the Viets had discovered him! The realization so paralyzed him that before he could begin to think about defending himself, his assailant had struck him twice.

The force of the assault had knocked him flat on his back. His attacker was astride of him now, groping for his throat. Ivorson looked up into the man's face. The lips were pulled back in a rectus of hatred, and the eyes bulged dramatically. Ivorson instantly recognized him from the team's surveillance photographs. It was Nguyen van Huu!

Huu's mouth was opening. He was going to shout for help! If he did, it was all over. Ivorson flattened his fist to make a sharp instrument of it rather than a blunt one and slammed it, as hard as he could, against Huu's exposed throat.

Huu's head snapped back. Ivorson faintly heard the sucking pop of the windpipe's collapse. He slammed his left hand—a full fist now—into the side of Huu's jaw, putting every ounce of his fear and hatred into the punch.

Huu grunted. His body sagged down onto Ivorson's chest and head. Grasping the Vietnamese by the hair, Ivorson shoved him out to full arm's length and then, raising his own head up and forward as far as he could, yanked Huu's face back downward onto the top of Ivorson's skull. He heard the nose cartilage snap. Huu went limp and collapsed on top of him.

Ivorson went limp, too. The head-butt had done him almost as much damage as it had Huu. Bright lights danced in his eyes. He tried feebly to heave Huu's body off his own and struggled to his feet. He had to get out of here!

His vision cleared just as he regained his footing. He flicked a quick look around and turned to stone. Not a yard away stood the shadowy shape of another man! There wasn't even time for fear before the shape sprang at him.

Ivorson tried to dodge, but he still hadn't fully recovered from the effects of his head-butt, and as the new assailant fell upon him, swinging wildly, he fell sideways across Huu's inert form.

One of the punches caught him in the side and partially drove the wind from his lungs. This new attacker was as strong as a bull. If he landed a solid punch, Ivorson was in deep trouble.

He covered his face with arms and rolled from side to side, too busy defending himself to strike back. Hard blows rained down on his shoulders and chest. As his new attacker drew back his fist for a roundhouse punch, Ivorson recognized him. It was Hoang bac Cam. For Christ's sake! He was becoming the victim of the man he'd tried to recruit. The irony was overwhelming.

And so was Cam's strength. Ivorson's situation was rapidly becoming desperate. The cumulative effect of the rain of heavy blows, even if only to the body, was beginning to tell on him. He hadn't been able to land a single punch himself. Why the hell didn't Orville come to help him? Couldn't he see what was happening?

Ivorson brought his right hand down behind his back, groping for the PPK. He was going to have to use it to save himself, even though the shot was certain to bring a dozen more Viets, probably before he could even reach the wall.

A thunderous fist landed on the side of his head, and his eyes went dangerously dim. Jesus! Another one like that, and he would be finished. Damn it, Orville, where are you?

Through his tear-blinded eyes, he saw Cam draw back his fist for another blow.

Born of desperation, out of nowhere, the idea came to him. "Sengdara is waiting for you," he panted in Vietnamese. "She sent me to get you."

The drawn-back fist froze. Cam's eyes bulged wide. "Sengdara?" he gasped.

Ivorson's hand closed on the butt of the PPK. He rolled left enough to pull it from its holster. If he could just keep Cam talking for one more second, he could slam it against the driver's skull, kill him silently.

"Yes," he gasped. "Sengdara. The girl you love. Her brother is here too, on the wall."

Cam's incredulous face turned toward the wall. Ivorson tensed to strike, but before he could, Cam looked back at him and said, "But Huu told me that Mango killed the policeman."

The chauffeur was staring down at him in stunned bewilderment, his fists unclenched. He was wide open. Ivorson's muscles bunched to deliver the silencing blow, but, at the last possible instant, Cam's question restrained him.

No one started a conversation in the middle of a fight with an intruder who had just killed his boss, for God's sake!

Unless he was more interested in the subject of the conversation than he was in the dead man.

Had Ivorson just said the magic word?

If Cam was only momentarily confused and returned to the attack or shouted for help, Ivorson's last chance for escape was gone.

But suppose there was still a chance to recruit Cam? Then the entire operation might be salvaged after all.

Ivorson's mind worked like lightning, trying to weigh the issue. In the end, he went with sheer instinct. "That's true," he whispered. "This is another brother." Cam blinked and peered in to the darkness toward the wall again.

"Orville!" Ivorson hissed. "Come quickly. I've found Cam." He tugged at Cam's sleeve. "She loves you, Cam. She was heart-broken when you rejected her offer of marriage, but she still loves you and wants you. She is waiting for us now. Come with us. We'll take you to her."

"She's waiting out there?" Cam's face was a rip-tide of hope and disbelief. There was a thump and a scurrying sound behind them, and Orville loomed out of the darkness. Cam recoiled and put up his fists again. Orville burst into a torrent of whispered Black Thai. Ivorson understood nothing other than the word, "Sengdara." Ivorson slowly drew back the hand holding the PPK and took aim on the side of the chauffeur's head. If Cam so much as frowned, Ivorson would brain him.

But he didn't. Instead, he burst into silent tears. Then he scrambled to his feet and reached down to give Ivorson his hand. "Thank you," he sobbed in Vietnamese. "You have saved me."

He pulled Ivorson to his feet and embraced him. Over Cam's shoulder, Ivorson saw Orville grinning at him like a Cheshire cat. He shot Ivorson a "thumbs up." Ivorson's knees went limp with relief. He struggled to free himself from Cam's embrace. All this was wonderful—lifesaving, in fact—but they had to save the hugging and kissing for later and get the fuck out of here.

He freed himself, surreptitiously re-holstered the PPK, gave Cam a big smile, and pointed to the wall. To emphasize the point he grabbed the chauffeur by the arm and shoved him in that direction. He pointed toward the balloon's payload on the ground beside them and hissed at Orville, "Come on. Help me."

They lifted the rod between them, holding it high to keep the camera from dragging on the ground and carried it, as quickly and as quietly as they could, over to the wall, where Orville squatted and whispered to Cam, "Climb upon my shoulders. A friend is waiting on the other side."

The chauffeur obeyed. Orville strained to his feet, and Cam scrambled up, onto the top of the wall. "Jump down on the other side," Ivorson told him. "We'll follow."

"No," the driver hissed back. "I'll help you. Hand me up the equipment."

This was no time to argue with a volunteer. Ivorson passed up his end of the dowel. Cam grasped it. Orville squatted down again. Ivorson took the other end of the dowel from him, stepped upon his shoulders, and Orville lifted him up the wall.

He looked over it, down at Chan's dumbstruck face. He was so giddy with relief that he could scarcely restrain a laugh. "We found Sengdara's boyfriend," he hissed to Chan. "Take this damn thing."

Chan took the offered end of the dowel. Ivorson took the other end from Cam and lowered the payload by the tether rope into Chan's waiting arms, then looked over his shoulder for Orville.

He was waiting, directly below. Ivorson and Cam, both straddling the wall, reached down, took his outstretched hands, and heaved him up to the top. He slithered across the wall and down into the swamp. Ivorson motioned for Cam to follow Orville.

And then Huu groaned.

Ivorson's head jerked around toward the sound. How could Huu possibly still be alive? Ivorson had felt the wind pipe crunch under his knuckles.

Before his mind could do more than form the question, the lights of the compound came back on.

There was only one shutter open on the back of the dormitory, but there were porch lights on the front of the building, on both the first and second floors, and to Ivorson's frightened eyes, they seemed to be bathed in a dozen floodlights. He grabbed Cam's arm. "Jump," he ordered.

Huu groaned again. If he lived to describe what he had seen, the whole operation would have been for nothing. There was only one solution. Ivorson had to go back down into the garden and kill him.

Could he do it? He had refused to allow Wilbur to kill Tran van Cao, even when it was a matter of life and death for him and his family. Could he himself cold-bloodedly strangle the life out of a helpless man?

He looked at the sprawled form in the garden. This was the man who had targeted Ivorson since the moment of his arrival in Laos. Nga's master, who had engineered Ivorson's humiliation—and almost his death—at her hands. With that thought, he discovered that he was, indeed, capable of killing Nguyen van Huu.

He started to move, and the Fear reared up in front of him out of the garden. "You don't have to do this," it screamed at him. "You've got the film. You've even got Cam. You're a hero. Let Huu go. He won't survive, and even if he does, so what? You'll get the credit for having brought back the code. If they change their system later, no one will know why. Run! Take the film and run!"

It had never been this insidiously tempting before. Every fiber of Ivorson's body yearned to believe the Fear. He could just drop off this illuminated wall into the safety of the black swamp and go home to a hero's reception.

But for how long, if Huu lived?

If the Embassy staff found his body and simultaneously found Cam missing, they would never suspect that their diplomatic code security was involved. They would assume that Huu had caught the chauffeur in the act of defecting and had been killed by him.

Thousands of lives, billions of dollars, and years of war all depended on their believing that. And the key to it all was that Nguyen van Huu must be dead when his body was discovered.

Ivorson had to go back inside and make certain of that.

He turned toward Cam and hissed again, "Jump!"

And Cam jumped—back to the ground inside the Embassy compound! Before Ivorson could even react, Cam dashed to the groaning form of Nguyen van Huu, knelt beside him, and with his powerful hands, before Ivorson's startled and grateful eyes, squeezed the life out of him.

It was over in seconds. Cam sprinted back to the wall and reached his arms upward. Ivorson swung his body around so that his legs hung down toward the swamp and his arms dangled inside the compound. Cam's strong fingers closed on Ivorson's wrists, Orville and Chan grasped his ankles on the other side, and both Ivorson and the chauffeur were unceremoniously dragged over the top of the wall to safety.

Goaded by the prospect of Huu's body being found before they could get away, the four of them slogged feverishly toward the road on the dike. Orville and Chan were in the lead, the four-foot long dowel slung over their shoulders, with its infinitely precious cargo between them. Behind them came Cam. Ivorson brought up the rear, just in case the chauffeur had second thoughts.

He was worried about what was going to happen when Sengdara saw him. He couldn't risk having the chauffeur re-defect because of an adverse reaction on the girl's part. He decided that he would shove Cam into the taxi without giving him a chance to talk to her. Then, Orville could drive back to the safe site with her in the Datsun and brief her on the situation.

Surely she wouldn't refuse to cooperate at this juncture! All she had to do was pretend to be overjoyed for a few minutes; an hour at the most. By then, arrangements could be made to smuggle Cam across the river into the safety of Thailand. His ultimate disillusion could take place there, gradually and without jeopardizing the operation.

In order to get Cam safely across the river in Thailand, however, Ivorson was going to need Station cooperation. He also had to get the precious video tape into safe hands, all of which meant making contact with COS as quickly as he could get to a telephone. He didn't want to expose Riley to either Cam or the team members, so he would have to go home and meet COS there.

His mind dwelt for a moment on Riley's probably reaction to the news of what Ivorson had done. The prospect was delicious.

They reached the dike, out of breath, at a quarter before eleven. Ivorson felt completely exhausted, both from physical exertion and acute adrenalin reaction, but at least their luck seemed to be holding. There had been no outcry from the Embassy during their withdrawal.

Ten minutes later, he heard the clatter of the two blacked-out cars coming down the dike road toward them. As they drew abreast, Orville waded up out of the swamp onto the road, Chan, Cam, and Ivorson close behind.

Ivorson took Cam by the arm and directed him to the taxi, while the others began loading the gear. "Where is Sengdara?" Cam asked him anxiously.

"Waiting for us in a safe place," Ivorson reassured him. "You'll see her in five minutes." Cam nodded and started to enter the taxi when Sengdara called to Orville, loud and clear, from the other vehicle.

Cam's head jerked up. He brushed past Ivorson's attempt to detain him, and rushed back to the following car.

Ivorson started after him. Orville was still at the trunk of the taxi. Ivorson hissed over his shoulder at him, "Come on! Make sure Sengdara doesn't mess up."

The two of them hurried back to the other car. Cam was leaning in the driver's window, talking a mile a minute to Sengdara, whose mouth made an "O" of amazement.

Orville reached out a hand toward Cam's shoulder, but before he could touch it, Sengdara recovered from her shock, flung her shapely arms through the car window, and hugged Cam's neck.

She covered his face with kisses, sobbing Black Thai words of which Ivorson understood only the chauffeur's name. Astounded, he shot a glance at Orville. His mouth was also agape. "What's happening?" Ivorson hissed.

"She says she loves him," Orville whispered back.

Ivorson couldn't believe his ears. After refusing to assist further in the recruitment of Cam and completely screwing up the operation, now she'd decided that she loved the guy! "Women," was all he could think of to say in response.

Until that moment, Ivorson had supposed that Orville spoke no English at all, but the Black Thai surprised him. "No shit," he grunted, then grabbed Cam by the shoulders, dragged him out of Sengdara's arms, and shoved him into the back seat of the car. Pushing Ivorson ahead of him, he ran to the taxi.

They turned left on the main road, away from the Viet Embassy. Ivorson couldn't see any disturbance in that direction. Huu's body and Cam's defection must not have been discovered yet.

The tension began to leak out of him. With every passing second, they were safer. In a quarter of an hour, maybe less, it would all be over. He had conquered the Fear, and Peter Ivorson would be the brightest star in the firmament of the Directorate of Operations. Even his father, had he lived to learn of tonight's work, might finally have been proud of him.

At the Monument to the War Dead, Sengdara's car split off and headed for the safe site. The taxi crossed the empty streets around the monument and, a few minutes later, pulled up in front of Ivorson's gate. He jumped out and groped around elbow-deep in the water-filled drainage ditch for the large rock under which he kept the spare gate key.

He found it, straightened up, turned toward the gate, and then froze. Nga! She was here! He could smell the scent of champa flower that she always wore. His eyes strained to find her in the darkness for an instant, and then his mind caught up with his emotions. Nga was gone. She was in Hanoi. What he smelled was in his yard. The big champa tree in the backyard must have come into bloom, and its sweetness was filling the night air.

A hiss from the taxi brought him back to reality. "Patron! Boss!" came Orville's whisper. "You okay?"

He nodded, still too flooded with emotion to speak. He found the lock and opened the gate. Orville drove into the yard and parked. Before reclosing the gate behind them, Ivorson carefully examined the street. Nothing moved at all. Good. He didn't want to get killed by the last shot fired in the war, not after what he'd been through.

"Stay here a minute," he whispered to Chan and Orville through the taxi window. "I'll make a call and be right back to get the camera. I won't take a minute."

He took the spare house key from its hidey-hole and let himself into the dark house. His night vision had been impaired by the lights of the town during the ride back. He had to feel his way into the bedroom and over to the telephone on the bedside table. Peaceful street or not, he wasn't going to make a light.

He found the phone and sat down on the bed beside it to make his call to COS. With the receiver in his hand, a thought struck him. Maybe he ought to call another Station officer after he talked to Riley and ask him to come over, too. It wouldn't hurt to have an independent witness to their conversation. Only, who would do that for him?

From behind him came the unmistakable sound of a revolver being cocked. He froze, the receiver half way to his mouth.

"Hang up, you son of a whore," chirped a familiar, sing-song voice from behind him.

Chapter Twenty-seven

Ivorson couldn't have moved if he'd wanted to. He was stunned, turned to stone. It was Tran van Cao! Where had he come from? How had he gotten in? Slowly—too slowly—his mind began to function.

His voice sounded squeaky, but it worked. "You can't get away with it, Cao. There's a car full of armed men outside. You may shoot me, but they'll kill you before you can reach the door. You'd better make a deal." He was painfully aware that it was a lie. No one in the taxi had a gun.

"I don't care whether I live or die." Cao's voice, sibilant with hatred, made the statement entirely believable. "Just so I kill you, monsieur." The formal title sounded bizarre, coupled with the death threat.

"Huu wants to be certain that you are dead," Cao chirped venomously. "To assure himself of that fact, he has compelled to risk my life by returning to Vientiane tonight. He will be delighted when I give him the details."

Every syllable was a death sentence. Ivorson knew he had to move, very soon, or die where he was. But Cao was just on the other side of the bed, and his pistol must be trained on the middle of Ivorson's back. He'd be dead before he could get his butt off the bed.

Unless he could divert Cao's attention.

"Huu won't be able to meet you," he said, trying to get his voice under control. "I just killed him."

"You did? Do tell! And how did you manage that?" Cao's voice sounded more amused than taken in by the attempted deception. Still, there was an edge of curiosity in it.

"I crushed his wind pipe," Ivorson replied, setting his feet firmly on the floor. "When my agent, Hoang bac Cam, came over the wall of your Embassy to join me."

"Cam? Your agent!" There was still some amusement in Cao's voice, but noticeably more curiosity. "And when did Cam become your agent?"

"Oh, before I met you," Ivorson answered airily. "I don't guess I ever mentioned that little operation to you, did I?" He tried to fashion a convincing chuckle. "Do you remember all the questions I used to ask you about him? Pure cover.

"If you doubt it," he went on, tensing his thigh muscles, "you can ask him yourself. He's just outside the bedroom door, with a gun pointed at you. KILL HIM, CAM!"

As he shouted the last words, he hurled himself sideways off the bed to the floor. Something enormously heavy hit him in the upper right side. He heard the roar of Cao's revolver, thunderous in the confines of the bedroom. He was shot!

He hit the floor very hard. He couldn't feel any pain, but his right arm wouldn't function. He couldn't pull the PPK.

He was lying on his left side. He rolled to his stomach and began frantically groping with his left hand for the butt of the automatic.

His ears were still ringing from the blast of the shot. He couldn't hear Cao moving, but he knew the little man must be coming around to his side for the coup de grace. He might think Ivorson was lying about Cam and the group of armed men outside, but he couldn't be certain. He must have heard the car drive in. He would need to get rid of Ivorson in a hurry.

Anything that slowed or confused the Vietnamese would help. "Kill him, Cam!" he shouted again. His clawing hand closed on the butt of the automatic through the cloth of his long, black shirt. The butt pointed the wrong way for his left hand. He awkwardly tried to draw it.

He heard the sound of car doors slamming and excited voices outside. That should get a reaction from Cao!

It did. There was another tremendous roar, and a slug thunked into the wall beyond him. It must have cleared his head by no more than a couple of inches.

The bed itself was of typical Asian construction, a solid wooden frame of heavy hardwood that went all the way to the floor. Cao couldn't bend down and see him under the bed.

There was nothing to keep him from shooting through the sides of the bed in the blind, however.

The thought made Ivorson roll into a ball and scrabble with the toes of his shoes toward the foot of the bed.

He finally succeeded in pulling the PPK. He struggled to reverse the handle. His right arm was absolutely useless. Thank God it didn't hurt yet.

There was a shower of splinters across his back, accompanied by the roar of another shot from Cao. He had begun shooting through the bed frame!

Ivorson finally got the PPK positioned in his left hand and fumbled the safety to the FIRE position. Thank God he kept a round in the chamber! He shoved the weapon up over the top of the bed and fired in the general direction of the far wall, once, twice, three times. The gun bucked in his hand, and his nostrils filled with the smell of burnt powder.

Cao answered with an immediate shot of his own. Ivorson yanked his hand back down.

The front door squeaked. Orville's agitated voice called him. "Patron! Where are you? What is happening?" Footsteps pounded on the living room floor.

"Don't come in the bedroom," Ivorson shouted. "It's Tran van Cao. He was waiting for me."

There was an immediate profound hush, as if everyone in the house suddenly held his breath. Then, Orville spoke again. Not anxious now, but coldly venomous, deadly. "Cao is in there? My brother's killer? I thank Lord Buddha for giving me this moment."

Ivorson heard a restive stir on the other side of the bed. He thrust the barrel of the PPK over the top of the mattress and fired in the direction of the sound, twice, in rapid succession.

Cao's answering shot ripped through the bedclothes less than an inch from his gun hand, spraying it with kapok from the mattress. Ivorson yanked his hand down again and wriggled further toward the end of the bed. If the little man was concerned about being penned in by mortal enemies, it hadn't affected his marksmanship.

"Patron" Orville called out. "Cease fire. Don't expose yourself. I am coming."

Ivorson didn't want to answer, for fear of revealing his new position, but he had to. If Orville entered the bedroom, he would be an un-missable target for Cao. His mother would have no sons left at all. "Don't come in here," he shouted back to Orville. His voice sounded faint, the words mushy.

Another shot from Cao thunked into the wall beyond Ivorson. He felt the hot wind of its passage on his ear lobe. Damn! That one had been close.

How many shots had Cao fired? Ivorson tried to remember. Was that one the fourth or the fifth? If it was five, he had only one shot left.

That is, if he was carrying a revolver. Ivorson had only the sound of the weapon being cocked to go by.

A new noise from across the bed interrupted his train of thought. A soft metallic clicking. What could that be?

Of course! Cao did have a revolver, and he was reloading it, right now. Its cylinder was open. He couldn't fire it. Now was Ivorson's chance.

He heaved himself erect, looking for Cao in the darkness across the bed, but he no sooner reached his feet than his knees gave out under him, and he collapsed across the bed. My God! He had no strength at all. He must be bleeding like a stuck pig.

With his gun hand stretched out in front of him, he frantically scanned the darkness for a target. He heard the ominous snap of the cylinder closing. The sound was two feet to the left of the PPK's muzzle. He heaved his hand in that direction. It was a study in slow motion. His arm had lost its strength. He willed the gun barrel to keep moving.

Before he could line it up on the sound, there was a flurry of motion at the bedroom door. The overhead light flashed on, and footsteps pounded across the teak floor. Orville had heard the sound of reloading too and was now charging across the bedroom at the Vietnamese! Unarmed, he was running directly at the barrel of Cao's reloaded pistol!

Ivorson's eyes were dazzled by the sudden bright light. Pray God that Cao's were, too. It was Orville's only hope. Ivorson's eyes searched frantically for movement. Where was Cao?

At the extreme left side of his field of vision, he saw a thin, claw-like hand lift a snub-nose revolver above the bed. Cao had backed into the very corner of the bedroom!

Ivorson jerked his gun hand to the left, but the gun didn't move. His arm had no more strength than a strand of boiled noodle. Neither muscle nor willpower would obey his mind.

Cao's face was visible now, twisted in a grin of gloating hatred, his eyes fixed on the hurtling shape that was Orville. Ivorson saw Cao's index finger begin the trigger pull. He tried to center the PPK's sights, but the barrel moved too slowly. Orville was going to die.

A silent scream of rage and frustration formed in Ivorson's mind. Look at me, you fucker, his brain shouted at Cao. I've got a gun here, not two feet from your head. I'm the danger, not him. Shoot at me!

The scream finally found voice, a harsh croak. Cao's eyes darted toward the sound, saw Ivorson's weapon, hand, and face. His eyes widened with fear.

Ivorson saw the barrel of Cao's revolver swing in his direction and erupt in a cloud of white smoke and sound.

Orville's body plunged across Ivorson's field of vision and landed behind the bed in a welter of violent movement. Ivorson felt the bed shaking, but he could see neither of the adversaries. He tried desperately to move, to intervene somehow on Orville's side, but he was utterly helpless, pinned to the bed by his loss of blood.

Someone seemed to have turned off the bedroom light again. He wanted to call out, to summon Chan, but his scream of helpless rage had been the last sound his body was capable of.

His eyesight grew darker. He felt himself being absorbed by the softness of the kapok mattress. Sound faded from his ears. I must be dying, he thought with amazement. That can't be! I can't die. Not me. Not Ivorson. Not after I beat the Fear.

And it was true. This time, he had truly overcome it. During the past few minutes of gunplay, he had been frightened, of course, but normally frightened, still able to think and move and fight.

The Fear was vanquished, and he'd won the secret war, too, practically single-handedly. There was no limit to how high he might go. He couldn't die now. He mustn't die now.

But he was so weak and cold, and it had gotten so dark.

From a great distance, he heard a familiar voice. Orville's. "Patron! Boss! Hang on! We are taking you to the American doctor."

The doctor? Why are they doing that, Ivorson wondered wearily. He didn't want to see the doctor. He had to call Lisa. He'd promised he would, and he wanted desperately to keep his word, if only to tell her goodbye.

Epilogue

Paris, November 1972

The Chief of Station, Paris, punched in the codes of the cipher lock on the heavy metal door that protected the "bubble"—the audio—secure room within a room in the basement of the Embassy—and let himself in.

The Secretary of State was waiting for him, together with the American Ambassador to the Vietnam Peace Talks and the Secretary's entourage of bright young Foreign Service Officers, their bland, look-alike faces presently at idle. Riley was warily respectful of both the senior officials. He had no use at all for the FSOs, but was careful to conceal the fact. One of them might become an ambassador some day.

He entered the bubble and dogged the plastic door closed behind himself. "Good morning, Mr. Riley," said the Secretary, his German accent clearly audible in the greeting.

"Good morning, sir," Riley answered briskly. "Here is the break-out of their traffic last night."

The Secretary took the envelope Riley offered him, broke the wax seal, and scanned the three sheets of typewritten material it contained.

"So," he grunted, when he had finished reading. "Now I know what Le Duc Tho will have to say to me today." He passed the papers to the Ambassador. "When I return to Washington," he remarked, "I will send a note to the Director of NSA and thank him. It is an immense advantage to have broken their code."

"You can thank me, too, then," Riley told him with pride. "I ordered the operation that got it for us, when I was the chief in Vientiane."

The Secretary's eyes grew round behind his thick spectacles. "So? Then I do also thank you." His pale eyes glinted. "But I think such an order must be harder to carry out than to give, not true? Who carried out this order of yours?"

Riley didn't care for the turn the conversation had taken. "A man named Peter Ivorson," he answered shortly.

The Secretary's raised brows indicated a willingness to hear further details on the subject, but Riley had no intention of providing them. Ivorson could handle his own publicity. The sonofabitch was good enough at it.

The Secretary regarded him with an expression of what might have been concealed amusement. "I would think," he said—the last word came out *sink*—"that a man who could carry out such an order would have to be extraordinarily brave and resourceful, not true?" The FSOs gravely nodded their agreement.

Riley didn't answer.

The Secretary's bushy eyebrows arched. "You don't seem to care for my adjectives, Mr. Riley. Would you like to provide us with some of your own?" The amusement in the Secretary's eyes was no longer concealed. A few of the bolder FSOs dared a sycophantic smirk.

That rankled Riley. This bunch of cookie-pushers wouldn't recognize an intelligence operation if it jumped up and bit them on their striped trousers. "Arrogant and disobedient come to mind," he said tersely.

The FSOs looked mildly scandalized. The Secretary's lips twitched. "So? I gather you don't care for this man. Nonetheless, since we have the code, I think he must also have some redeeming virtues. Not true?"

Riley shrugged. "He's brave," he conceded. "And lucky."

"That is a good combination," the Secretary observed. "Napoleon was always looking for it in his generals."

Riley harrumphed. "Napoleon would have had this bastard shot."

The Secretary's eyes were distinctly amused now. "So? I have the impression you also might like to have him shot, not true?"

Riley felt that he was getting on thin ice. He deflected the question. "The Vietnamese beat me to it."

The Secretary's look of amusement vanished. "Was he killed?" he asked.

Riley almost said, "No such luck," but restrained himself. "No, sir. He was awarded the Intelligence Star and has a Station of his own now."

"Good," said the Secretary, smiling again. "It is always satisfying to see merit rewarded."

The FSOs nodded in unison. Riley bit his lip and kept quiet.

6888756R0

Made in the USA
Charleston, SC
20 December 2010